Praise for Lynn Coady's

mean boy

"Coady explores the sometimes uneasy relationship between art and academia . . . with a polish and razor-sharp wit that takes no prisoners. . . . *Mean Boy* is guaranteed to garner attention at this year's major book awards. If somehow you've missed Coady's earlier work, start right now with this one."
—*Calgary Herald*

"A wonderful portrait of a university town and university life, from the high jinks of students intent on accumulating experience to the pontifical evasions and suggestions of well-meaning professors. . . . Coady's portrayal of the jealous tenuousness of friendship, the in-fighting and fierce competitions of the literary world is daring and brilliant. . . . Coady's skill as a parodist and prose writer far surpasses poetic pretension. *Mean Boy* is a tour de force."
—*The Globe and Mail*

"*Mean Boy* is above all a solid and comical page-turner."
—*NOW Magazine* (Toronto)

"*Mean Boy* is a wonderfully savage rip on the world of academia where professor-poets backstab, students write puerile poetry . . . and tenure is granted or denied by succinctly portrayed stuffed shirts. If you have ever taken a creative writing course, you will alternately laugh, cry and blush. For those of you not conversant with the bad boys of poetry, hang on and simply enjoy."
—*The Sun Times* (Owen Sound)

ALSO BY LYNN COADY

Saints of Big Harbour
Play the Monster Blind
Strange Heaven
Victory Meat (editor)

mean boy

LYNN  COADY

anchor canada

Anchor Canada and colophon are trademarks

LIBRARY AND ARCHIVES CANADA CATALOGUING IN PUBLICATION

Coady, Lynn, 1970–
    Mean boy / Lynn Coady.

ISBN-13: 978-0-385-65976-5
ISBN-10: 0-385-65976-8

I. Title.

PS8555.O23M42 2007   C813'.54   C2006-904624-7

Cover design: Kelly Hill
Printed and bound in Canada

Published in Canada by
Anchor Canada, a division of
Random House of Canada Limited

Visit Random House of Canada Limited's website: www.randomhouse.ca

TRANS   10   9   8   7   6   5   4   3   2   1

for Charles

to be possessed or
abandoned by a god
is not in the language

JOHN THOMPSON

1

if you throw the ball,
it just gets him more excited

I.

HE SAT ON HIS DESK, positioned in front of this enormous window with the sunlight streaming all around his outline. I could barely look at him without going blind. He saw me squinting and shading my eyes and squeezing them shut when they started watering, but he didn't move, or close the curtain. He had a little teapot on the desk beside him and he kept picking it up and listening to it. He told me my poem should have a dead person in it.

"Maybe a murder or something," he said, "to make it more exciting."

I didn't know what to say so I talked about what was in the poem already. I said I thought that maybe it was a little wordy, that I hadn't figured out how to distill my ideas yet. I figured he could speak to this—none of his poems are any more than ten lines long, and half the time each line has no more than three or four words in it. He just sat there listening to his teapot as I rambled away, carefully using words like *distill* and *cumbersome*.

"I think maybe it's a little cumbersome?"

Everything I said went up in a question. I sounded like I was still in high school. I knew I had to learn how to stop talking like that, especially around this guy, but it got worse when I was nervous.

"No, no, it's not cumbersome. It just needs something to *happen*. Nothing *happens* in it. There's nothing wrong with a lot of words—I like words."

"But your poems are so . . ." I wanted a really perfect word for this. *Terse. Brief. Scant. Scant? Scant* was good. But did it have any negative connotations? Would he think I meant insubstantial?

" . . . short," I said, before the silence could thicken.

"Those are *my* poems," he said. "And my poems are great. I'm trying to learn not to insist that other writers write poems like mine. In fact I prefer that they don't. Listen to this for a minute." I thought maybe he was going to recite something, but instead he extended the little teapot so that I was compelled to get up out of my chair and come toward him.

I listened. It was full of tea. I could feel the heat radiating toward my cheek. It was making a buzzing sound, sort of like a horsefly.

"Hm," I said.

"It's *buzzing*," he said. "Why do you suppose it does that?"

"I think maybe air is trapped in there or something."

"Well, it's *weird*," said Jim Arsenault, the greatest living poet of our time.

I sit obsessing on this, fingers poised over my typewriter keys. Every time I blink, the silhouette of Jim outlined against his sun-filled window flashes inside my head, like it's been burned into my corneas. I hear him saying, *Well, it's weird.* I hear him saying everything but what I wanted to hear about my poetry. I hear *more exciting*, which means *not exciting*. It's hard to come up with something new, hearing that. It seems like it might be easier—more fun, more inspiring too, some-how—to tear the page from my typewriter's grip, slowly, without releasing the catch, so that it kind of shrieks as if in drawn-out pain.

I have a poem called "Poem Poem" taped to the window above my typewriter—by Milton Acorn, who is my hero because he is an unschooled genius who, like me, is from Prince Edward Island. The poem is about the good days and the bad days of writing poetry. The first stanza talks about a good day, how *Poems broke from the white dam of my teeth. / I sang truth, the word I was . . . Heart and fist thumped together,* it says, a line I love.

Then the second stanza describes the poem "I write today," how it "grins" at him while *I chop it like a mean boy / And whittles my spine. It is truth,* says Acorn with regard to this poem, *the word I am not.*

That's the poem. I look at it when I'm feeling lonely, and when I feel like a moron—a *not exciting* moron—for sitting in front of my typewriter thinking I'm a poet. Sometimes I love it, though—some days are as different from one another as the two stanzas of the poem. That's why I have it up there. Sometimes, even if I'm not writing, just the feel of being alone in my apartment in front of the typewriter is enough. I take off my shirt. I can see myself, I can see what I look like sitting here wearing nothing but jeans and glasses, me and my pale teenage limbs. I look like a poet. I know that I do. I believe in it, those days.

I, I'll type. And that will be enough.

Then there are the other days, when nothing is enough. The poem grins. It grins because it knows it is a terrible poem. It grins in embarrassment. It grins in pity. It grins in superiority. I may be a terrible poem, it grins, but at least I have one comfort. At least I'm not a terrible *poet.* At least I'm not the guy who sat in front of a typewriter for two hours coming up with the likes of *me.*

A girl named Sherrie is busy reading her work for Jim and the rest of us—mostly for Jim. I am busy being made uncomfortable by it. It's all about desire and sex, but there is nothing arousing going on in the least. I expected to not like it because it would be sentimental, but that isn't the problem. It's just

Sherrie standing up there with her yellow curls going everywhere like a doll or a crazed cheerleader, semi-whispering about "folds in flesh" and "shimmering" this and "shuddering" that—it makes me queasy. It's only our second class, for God's sake. *Meeting,* Jim wants us to call it.

Jim doesn't seem to mind Sherrie's stuff. He stands with the same demeanour he has whenever anybody reads. He leans slightly against his desk, stares at the ground, and folds his arms way back behind his head, so that his elbows stick out on either side of it like huge animal ears, a rabbit-man. He'll stand that way for as long as twenty minutes sometimes, depending on whatever anyone's reading. There is a guy named Claude from Moncton who writes villanelles. These villanelles go on forever sometimes, and Jim will just stand there all contorted until the very last line.

Sherrie gushes the last line of her poem, which is actually about gushing in one way or another. I don't know whether to take it literally or not. Probably I shouldn't. It's a metaphorical orgasm. I will say that if asked to comment—I will remark upon the "metaphorical orgasm" at the end. Will I say that I liked it or not? Maybe neither. Better to be noncommittal. *I was intrigued. I was intrigued by the metaphorical orgasm in the last line. I thought perhaps it was a little too clichéd, however.* No, I can't say clichéd. A little too . . . *apropos.*

Jim sighs and unwinds his arms from his head. Claude says, "Hmm," because that's what he says after everybody's poem. A couple of people echo the noise. It's a good, safe noise to make.

Sherrie looks flushed. Her hands were shaking when she was reading. It's kind of an awful thing to do to people, make them read their poems out loud.

Jim says, "Comments?" and I jump at this, because I have a feeling Claude might have clued in on the metaphorical orgasm as well.

"I liked the orgasm," I say.

Jim smiles at me. Sherrie's mouth falls open, her blue eyes expand.

"Pardon, Larry?"

"The *metaphorical* orgasm, I mean. At the end."

"That's usually where you'd find it," quips Claude. I look to Jim for help.

Jim smiles wider. "You liked that, did you?"

"No," I say quickly. There is a distinct shift in Sherrie's posture at this. "I was *intrigued* by it, is what I meant to say. I found it intriguing."

"Why?" says Jim.

Oh my God. Why. Why.

I shrug.

That's no good, I can't just shrug, I'm not in high school.

I say, "Well, you know, just within the context of the rest of the poem. I thought it was kind of . . . well, on the one hand, I guess it was inevitable . . . ?" There goes my voice again, upward, questioning, looking directly at Jim for validation.

"Was it?" says Jim.

"Well," I grin and spread my hands, armpits like a swamp. "I'm no doctor, but . . ." Somebody cuts me off, and I'm glad, until I realize that it's Claude.

"Isn't that a bit if a . . . masculine viewpoint?"

Oh, I can't believe it. I had hoped to regroup and regain my composure while everyone else weighed in, but there's no way he's getting away with that.

"I would argue that it's merely archetypal?" I hear myself say. A salient, insightful retort, utterly destroyed by the question mark at the end. I'm disgusted with everything that question mark gives away. Approve me, agree with me.

"What about the other hand?" asks Jim, looking at me.

"What?" What in God's name is he talking about?

"You said, on the one hand, it's inevitable . . . ," he prompts, "before Claude interrupted you."

Vindication! I glance over to see if Claude is hanging his head in shame, but he doesn't seem fazed. He never speaks with question marks, not even when he's asking questions. It's because of that Acadian accent of his—he punctuates everything with certainty.

"Larry?" says Jim.

I introduced myself to him as Lawrence. I sign all my poems Lawrence. He has never called me anything but Larry.

"On the one hand, it's inevitable," I say, carefully modulating my speech and trying to remember my original point. *Clichéd*. No. *Apropos*. *Apropos!* I sit up.

"But on the other hand . . ." I deepen my voice. "I think maybe it's a little *too* inevitable, if you catch my meaning . . . This is why I didn't appreciate Claude's 'particularly masculine' comment—I didn't think that was apropos, because he didn't let me finish my point."

Oh goddamnit. I start to sweat again, having jumped the gun and sabotaged my entire argument. "On the other hand," I push on, "it's so inevitable as to be . . . a little too . . . clichéd."

Out of the corner of my eye, I can see Sherrie's posture shift again. I'm afraid to look at her.

"I think that's a little harsh," remarks Claude.

"Hm," says Jim, nodding.

Students have been known to hang themselves at Westcock University. The stairwell in the English Department has been a preferred spot for decades.

Everybody waits in pure, frozen silence while Jim nods away and twists back into his rabbit-ears position, like he's giving himself antennae. We all know it's his thinking posture. It seems like if you stuck a pin in Sherrie, she would pop like a balloon right now.

After this particular eternity he lowers his arms. "I like," he begins. Yes, yes? Everyone seems to grow an inch taller in their seats. The metaphorical orgasm? The non-metaphorical orgasm? My poem's better than Sherrie's? Me better than Claude?

"Alfred Hitchcock movies," says Jim.

And he spends the rest of the meeting telling us all about *North by Northwest.* After ten minutes or so, Sherrie realizes she may as well sit back down.

But I can't hang myself in the stairwell, it's been done. Done to death. Me being derivative again, like with my writing. Everyone in the program knows about the first to do it, the inaugural suicide. A lit major hung herself just outside the department doors—one of the first women students the college had admitted. She'd been expelled, for reading "pornography." John Donne, to be specific. Probably that one about the sun—the "saucy wretch"—coming in through the window and waking up him and his girlfriend. Hot stuff.

I always thought it was so great, so literary, the story of the hanging. There is a plaque in the corridor describing it. I love this about my university, this Gothic little history it has, so European, people killing themselves over poetry.

I'm reading in the lounge—I also love the English Department lounge, big and oaken, with creaking wooden floors—musty with the past. The English Department is on the top floor of the Humanities building, the oldest building on campus. The chairs themselves belong in a museum—you should see them. Plush, balding velvet. Leather-bound books laid on the sturdy oak table. Coffee-cup rings, scratches, graffiti dating from the turn of the century. I could live here. I could die here.

The one nod to the present is a high-tech automatic coffee machine placed discreetly in the corner atop an Edwardian end table. I lounge around reading and smelling the stale coffee for hours, soaking everything up, caffeine stench and history, hoping—let's be honest—Jim might lope by, happen to glance in, smile his recognition—*Ah. Lawrence.*

If it sounds pathetic, it is not. I came here for him, after all. He is practically the only great poet I know of who's alive. In this country, I mean. He's the only one to learn from—and he's here, for God's sake, in the same town, school, department as me. Sometimes I can't believe it. It's like being able to call up Shakespeare on the phone.

I get light-headed thinking about it—with joy, and the conviction of my unbelievable luck, and, let's face it, a real sense of predestination. Because something like this can't be an accident, can it? Poetic genius Jim Arsenault arriving on one side of the Northumberland Strait, poetic aspirant Lawrence Campbell growing up on the other? This is the stars in alignment.

And on this day, the thing I've been waiting for happens—if not quite how I have imagined. I hear noises down the hall. The echoes in this place, it's obscene. You imagine people must have never raised their voices above a whisper around the turn of the century. It's as if the acoustics were deliberately engineered to keep you hushed.

Jim shouts, *Arsenault!* Which doesn't make a lot of sense. Maybe he's writing in his office. But he's never in his office—you're lucky to catch him there even during posted hours.

. . . *goddamn Arsenault!*

I envision him shouting into a mirror, overwrought with his latest effort, suffused with self-loathing, disgusted by the certainty of his own inadequacy to the sacred task of poetry. Oh, Jim, I know. Come talk to me. We're of one heart, you and I.

But there's another voice. He's not in front of a mirror after all.

Jim, rumble rumble. Please rumble you rumble rumble rumble. All right? Rumble?

That voice is Doctor Robert A. Sparrow, department head.

Jim shouts his last name again, only I realize it hasn't been his last name at all.

Echoes, echoes, thundering through the hallway. Footfalls—it's very dramatic. Like a movie. I realize I'm just standing in the middle of the lounge. At some point I've risen from the green ottoman with velvet trim, my favourite place to read. I'm just standing here with my jaw dangling and my book dangling from my fingers when Jim appears in the doorway. The book? Of course it's *Blinding White*. Poems by Jim Arsenault.

The thing about Jim is, he's a man. More than that—a guy. He is the new breed of poet. He doesn't fluff himself up, doesn't wear jewellery or turtlenecks. Not like Claude. Claude is still very much in the turtleneck phase. Jim doesn't even wear sports jackets, let alone a tie. Work shirts and jeans. Often he comes to class "straight from the woods," he tells us. He's big on the woods. Or "straight from working on my roof." Or his porch.

So when Jim's angry, he's angry. His face is almost purple, which makes me think of Donne again, "purpling" his fingernail in the blood of a squished bug. Jim catches sight of me out of the corner of his eye as he's clomping past, and spins around looking just goddamn furious. Like I've been standing here laughing at him or giving him the finger. His face looks like he's about to take two fast, long strides forward, lean in, and swallow my head.

He doesn't move, though—he just stands there.

He yells at me, "No wonder she killed herself!"

Jim is addressing me in the midst of a crisis. I am the one he has turned to. True, I'm the only one here, but clearly he's identified me as a sympathetic presence. He knows that I'm *with* him, I'm on his side, that there's us and them and I am *us*.

"Oh . . . hi," I say, " . . . there, Jim."

"She didn't kill herself," Jim hollers. "This place. This *place* is what killed her."

Jim tornadoes into the room at this point, heading straight for the green ottoman. And he kicks it. He kicks the couch.

"I think it's antique . . . ," I start to say.

"It's not about writing, it's about *lit-ret-chaw.* It's not about teaching, it's about dogma. It's about this fucking Victorian *bullshit.*" He kicks the couch again. "Doctrine!" he says. "Sophistry!" Another kick.

And then what I'm afraid of occurs. The ottoman collapses. One of its dainty carved feet buckles under. The balance thrown off, another carved foot gives out, this time in the opposite direction. The couch slouches over onto its frame.

This furniture, every English undergraduate knows, was a gift from Westcock's founding family. No other department is decked out like ours. The university started out as a humanities institution, but it was *lit-ret-chaw* that always held a special place in the heart of Horace Lee Grayson. So back in 1935 the Graysons gifted us with furniture from Horace Lee's own sitting room—or one of his sitting rooms. In our founding father's mansion—which squats overlooking the duck pond, huge and white like one of the swans that live below it—there are many rooms.

My instinct for some reason is to kneel before the slain ottoman. I repress this instinct in front of Jim.

"Jeez . . ."

Before I can really get caught up in the power of my own eloquence, Jim Arsenault has me by the shoulders. He shakes me hard, once. It's kind of wonderful.

"Lawrence," he says.

Lawrence!

"Let's you and me get drunk."

What a pretty day. Long shadows of October filtering through the crimson leaves as Lawrence Campbell and Jim Arsenault make their way across the quad to raise a pint in poetic solidarity. I suggest going somewhere off campus, but Jim is having none of it. Jim is in a hurry.

I check my watch, mentally girding myself. It's four in the afternoon, and I've last eaten at around one. It was a big meal, because I'd skipped breakfast—one of those enormous submarine sandwiches you can get across the street from Carl's Tearoom for under a buck. It was an all-meater. Turkey, pastrami. What else was in there? I think bologna. The point is, I have food in my stomach. I intend to drink whatever amount Jim Arsenault expects of me. I am in it for the long haul.

Jim's talking, and I should really be listening, but the thing is, I'm an awful drinker—I've got to plan this out if I'm going to keep up. There's no way I can have a glass of water at the table, but maybe whenever I duck to the bathroom I can lean over the sink and just suck up as much as possible from the tap. Aspirin would come in handy, too, and as luck would have it there's a convenience store right across from Franklin's Stein, the dumb-named student pub. I can say I'm buying smokes. I don't smoke. But Jim smokes—he lights up in class sometimes.

I can do this. You and me, Jim.

"Are you married?"

"Of course," answers Jim, flicking his cigarette as if I've asked, "Do you like books?" "She's my obsession," he adds.

He says it absently, though, not really the way you would expect a man to say someone is his obsession.

He takes a sip of beer, I take a sip of beer. My goal is to match him pint for pint.

"Why the fuck do you ask me that?" he demands a moment later. Jim curses a lot. Never in class, but all the time in conversation. In his poetry, too—very controversial in this country. You'd think cummings or Ginsberg never even existed.

"Because," I start to answer, and then I stop. The reason I asked was because Jim has been complaining about women for the past twenty minutes.

"I love women," Jim declares, intuiting what I was thinking. "I love my fucking wife." Jim takes another moody sip; I take one too. He has been talking non-stop ever since we sat down.

"I have nothing against women in the classroom," Jim tells me.

I try to jump in. "Well, of course not, but—"

"But that sack of shit Sparrow thinks we should coddle them. That's what's sexist, if I may partake of the new vernacular."

I'm surprised to hear Jim partaking of the new vernacular.

"I mean, for Christ's sake, Sparrow would have us return to the days of segregated education. By 'segregated' I mean, of course, some for the pampered sons of pampered sons, none for anyone else. But God save us from the English boy's school ethos, those bastions of so-called masculinity." Jim smirks, sips. I smirk, sip.

Then Jim has a thought in mid-sip and sprays much of it onto the table. "There's no turning back the clock!" he exclaims. "It's time for them to stand up for themselves, they can't just go running to Daddy whenever they hear something that isn't nice."

It takes me a minute to figure out that Jim is talking about women again. I was still thinking about pampered sons and English boy's schools. In all the scheming and calculating I did to make sure I could keep up with Jim, the last thing I thought about was the fact that I would, at some point, probably become drunk. All my precautions have been directed at meeting one goal only: to not throw up.

And then—oh, and then. Something good happens. Something very, very good. I spot Claude at the bar.

"Sparrow," Jim is saying. "That paper-pushing cocksucker. Is about as radical and of-his-time as that couch in the lounge."

Normally, the reminder of the collapsed ottoman would be setting off tiny flares of anxiety, but I am too happy about where I am and with whom and with regard to who is standing at the bar about to notice us, that it scarcely causes a twinge.

I say, "Yeah!"

Jim smiles at me, relaxing a little. "You're the next generation, Larry. It's up to you. You've got to clear away all this deadwood."

I'm so flummoxed, the only thing I can think to do is to start rummaging around in my satchel.

"What are you doing?" Jim's eyebrows plunge.

"My notebook," I mutter. I stick my entire face in the bag's fusty opening, waiting for the blush to go away. "Good title for a poem. Deadwood. Dead wood."

Jim watches as I squint and write DEADWOOD in block letters beneath the swaying yellow lights of the bar, beneath the piercing jangle of music and the laughter of people who keep dropping their drinks.

Hey Claude. Hey, cocksucker. Hey you villanelle-writing sack of shit. Look over here.

That Sherrie has joined Claude at the bar has only somewhat taken the wind from my sails. Sherrie is odd, after all, with her extreme cuteness like a rabid, blue-eyed hamster.

As the bar gradually floods with students, I realize it's Friday night. This is the night when people go to bars. Ever since I moved out of residence, weekends have meant little more to me than days when I don't go to class. That is because I am a person who eats and sleeps poetry. I live a sterile, booky existence. I thought university would change that; somehow it didn't occur to me that my life could be even bookier than it already was. I worry that this is not how you become a poet. Jim went to Paris when he was seventeen, for Christ's sake. Like Rimbaud. For fuck's sake. Didn't go to university until he was twenty-five, and then somehow blasted his way through to a master's degree in just four years. But at my age—the most crucial time in a writer's development, I've heard him say in class—he just lived. He just wrote.

"Oh, look," says Jim. "There's young Sherrie."

Jesus, finally. I toss a casual glance over my shoulder as Jim raises his hand. There they are, working their way through the crowd, Sherrie's curls a gold beacon. Claude's black turtleneck makes him a bobbing, disembodied head.

Sherrie sits on the bench beside Jim. Claude sits in a chair beside me. It's getting so you have to yell to be heard in here. Everyone screams hello at each other.

Jim leans in to say something only to Sherrie, so I take the opportunity to further welcome Claude.

"Claude, you old bastard," I greet. "Nice turtleneck."

"What did you call me?" says Claude.

"You old bastard," I enunciate.

"I'm a bastard?" says Claude.

"No! I was being cavalier! I was greeting you in a cavalier fashion."

"Well, I wouldn't say I'm a bastard."

That went well. I sit back in my chair.

Claude looks over at Jim and Sherrie and cocks a thumb at me.

"Called me a bastard," he remarks.

Sherrie's face crinkles—confused, worried maybe. She's seen us go after each other in class. Jim bobs his eyebrows.

"Larry!" he grins. "I'm appalled."

Maybe it is eleven o'clock or so, and I am deep in discussion with Claude about Jim and the way he's been treated by Doctor Sparrow, even though I have only the vaguest of ideas what it's all about. Censorship, I'm saying. Academic freedom. The tension between art and institutionalized education—are these things even compatible, I'm demanding to know.

Claude says something like, if you want to do poetry in this country, you need to be at a university and that's just how it is. I tell him that's bullshit, and call him a bastard again. I've been calling him a bastard all night. It's great.

"Jim didn't start off by going to university!" I argue. "The universities came after him, after he published *Even Less*! Milton Acorn! Anse Surette! They're turning all that shit on its head!"

Claude says—and I can't believe he says this—"Let's face it: one of the obvious limitations of Surette's work is his lack of education. It's rough, colloquial . . ."

Claude would say that. I've learned many a terrifying thing about Claude this night. Claude isn't from Moncton at all, for one thing. His *father* is from Moncton but went to the States when he was nineteen—my age—and travelled all over, just like Jim, eventually dragging Claude's mother, and then young Claude, along with him. It was only five years ago, Claude tells me, that his father became all politicized about Acadia and insisted on dragging the pair of them back here to the Promised Land.

The upshot of this, therefore, is that Claude is not the small-time poseur I'd originally dismissed him as. Claude has been to New York City. He's been to San Francisco. He's been to poetry readings at Lawrence Ferlinghetti's bookstore.

"Oh my God! Oh my God!" I yell, to drown out the jitters this knowledge gives me. "That's the power of Surette's writing! That's exactly what makes him great—he's not creatively hamstrung by a bunch of educational doctrine and literary dogma."

Claude leans back and smiles. I look around for Jim—I'm sounding good, I want him to hear me. He was here a moment ago, entrancing us all with an impromptu recitation of Wallace Stevens aphorisms. He just came out with them all of a sudden, in the middle of a conversation about, I seem to recall, the coffee machine in the student lounge—whether or not it fits in with the old-fashioned Grayson furniture. "There is no wing like meaning," Jim abruptly announced, followed by, "Money is a kind of poetry," followed by, "There must be something of the peasant in every poet." He just sat there with his eyes closed, producing one of these after another as we all glanced at each other, wondering if he was having some kind of holy poetic fit. "Ethics are no more a part of poetry than they are of painting," Jim pronounced, finally opening his eyes and smiling at us. "I'm off to take a leak," he added.

So Jim's not at the table anymore—he's been gone a while, come to think of it. But Sherrie's still here, resting her chin against her fist and watching me yell and wave my arms around.

"You've been listening too much to Jim," Claude tells me.

I've decided I love discussing literature when I'm drunk. Not once has my voice gone up in that questioning girl-way it does in the classroom. I am at the height of my rhetorical powers. I'm not even intimidated by Claude anymore, just because he's been to places I've only dreamed about and refers to William Burroughs as "Bill" and appears to have read everything by everybody who's ever written anything in the world—how can I be intimidated by someone who wears turtlenecks and thinks Anse Surette would've been better off with a PhD? It's like saying, it's like saying . . . the Beatles should've gone to Juilliard.

I glance at Sherrie and say the thing about the Beatles to Claude, prefacing it with a "Listen, you Acadian cocksucker . . . ," which no doubt would make Jim proud. Claude leans back even farther.

"So now I'm a cocksucker?"

"It's just another way of saying bastard," I explain. "You've been letting me call you bastard all night."

And then, just when I'm thinking we should get Sherrie in on the conversation, I realize that I've forgotten to keep going to the bathroom for covert sips of water and at any moment I am going to vomit an ocean of beer across the table into Sherrie's lap. I jerk away, cheeks filling, and lurch my way to the exit. Not the bathroom—Jim's in there, maybe.

2.

Deadwood
_&_
- Lawrence the Great!

Cock
your dead
Wood
at some other
sucker.

Oct. 5 /97

DYLAN THOMAS WAS A DRINKER. Ezra Pound. Eliot. Good old Anse Surette is, from what I hear coming out of Fredericton. Too many of them to count. Acorn. Oh, all of them are—were. All the greats, they were all drunks for some reason. That derangement of the senses thing.

Yet it's funny I can't remember reading one poem about hangovers. I've discovered why. Hangovers are unspeakable, literally. There are no words.

Here's the closest I can come up with. You awake having lost your sense of good. You know there is such a concept as good in the world, but you can't remember what it means anymore. It's like having amnesia when it comes to the idea of good. What did I used to think was good? I used to think waking up was good. Getting out of bed, going into the kitchen for a pot of tea. Tea itself. Daylight. Squirrels and birds outside.

And then I remember—I regain the memory all at once. Lying down on the floor is good. Lying down is good in general. Flat is good. Immobility is good. Hey, what do you know: my ceiling is good. So is my carpet, even smelling of endless semesters of undergrad feet as it does. I lie on my carpet and watch the birds and squirrels on the trees outside my window, feeling slightly less that birds and squirrels aren't good anymore.

It's sunny, bright. A postcard autumn New Brunswick day. You'd think that would be good.

A fat mama squirrel appears at the window and stares at me. I know this squirrel. I used to be quite fond of her, in fact, her and all her brood, but now I think the squirrel can fuck off. I decided this a couple of months after I moved in. She sat at the window my first morning here, twitching her nose just like she's doing now, and I was enchanted when I hauled open the window and she didn't even scuttle away. On Prince Edward Island we don't have squirrels. Not like this, anyway—not big, friendly, Snow White squirrels who take potato-chip fragments from your hand and sit solemnly munching just a couple of inches away, like a buddy who's come to hang out. This squirrel, I thought, was pretty much my only buddy, and then her little family started wandering down from the eave to check out the potato-chip action. We'd all hang out in the windowsill together, munching Humpty Dumpty chips, me and my woodland friends. I got to trust them. When I went home for the long weekend, I decided to leave my window open a crack and lined up a few peanuts on the sill, just so they wouldn't miss me too much.

Well, I got home and the little bastards had ransacked the apartment. They tore open my Humpty Dumpty stash and boxes of cereal, and shat on my kitchen counter.

So that was it for me and nature. I never opened my window to the squirrels again. Every once in a while Fat Mama still shows up and gives me an indignant glare, just as she's doing now, as if to say, "We're squirrels, you know? Vermin."

Ring, ring.

"Larry, I've got a fucking cold."

So it's the proverbial morning after, the cold light of day, and we're back to *Larry*. But he's called me at home, which is something new.

"Hi, Jim. I'm sorry to hear that."

"So, you get home all right?"

I look around myself. "Yes. You?"

"After taking a little dip in the duck pond, yeah."

"In the duck pond?" I repeat, trying to think of a witty rejoinder.

"Yeah, the duck pond."

"You fell in?" I ask, trying to picture it. The duck pond is in the middle of campus, central. Livingston Street, the town's main thoroughfare, shoots right past.

"No, I just needed to dunk my head. Clear it. Didn't want the wife to see me drunk when I got home."

While I'm deciding how to reply, a woman's voice pipes up in the background. I can't make out what she says. About three syllables—sharp, distinct, yet indecipherable.

Jim sort of snickers mirthlessly into my ear. "So, Larry," he says. "You did good. You held up your end all right."

"Thank you, Jim."

"Writing poems in a bar . . . you're well on your way."

"Thank you, Jim." I'm aglow. The concept of good now comes surging back to me in all its rosy clarity.

"Look, I can't make our meeting Monday morning, Larry. This cold's going to get worse before it gets better I can tell."

The woman's voice again, with more to say. This time I can make out the last few syllables which are . . . *in goddamn October.*

"That's okay," I assure him.

"No, no. We need to talk about what you're doing. You come on out to the house."

Come on out to the house.

"Tomorrow, when I'm not in such poor shape. I won't breathe anywhere near ya. Bring any new stuff you got. The wife will make some toddies."

The voice again. Something about *toddies* and *arse.* More mirthless snickering from Jim.

"Hear that, Larry?"

"No," I answer, more or less honestly.

"You don't let that scare you," says Jim, not listening and hanging up.

New stuff. I root around for my notebook. *Deadwood by Lawrence the Great.* It's not bad, really—sparse, obscure. Kind of Carl Sandburg. I have no memory of writing it. I don't even know what it's supposed to mean. But oh, well. I turn the apartment upside down in search of a clean sheet of typewriter paper. The headache seems an independent mass floating around in my brain fluid—every time I stop suddenly or turn around, it crashes against the bone-wall of my skull. Fat Mama watches me shuffling back and forth in front of the window until finally I find a scrap of paper that's more or less unmarked. I settle in at the typewriter and roll it into place. A failed poem is already typed on the back, but there's no way Jim will notice, because it's just one word, one letter, scarcely a fleck of ink across the blank, white expanse. *I,* I had written. And then given up.

———

A cabdriver known around campus as Friendly picks me up an hour later to take me out to Jim's place. The cabbie greets me, characteristically, with a smile so wide his upper plate comes unstuck and clacks onto the bottom one. It's almost like his own personal salute. He gums the denture back into place.

"Havin' a bit of a time d'other night, wha?" he says, beaming at me in the rear-view mirror.

"Wha?" I echo.

"Out on the town, wha?"

"When?"

"Friday night, right?"

"Oh yeah. I don't know how I got home . . ."

"I drove you home, buddy!"

"Oh!"

"Good time, wha?"

This last *wha* sounds like a genuine inquiry. I think about it.

"Yes," I say after a moment. "I guess I did have a pretty good time."

Friendly lets out a whoop on my behalf. "Givin' 'er!" he elaborates.

I guess I was givin' 'er somewhat. I realize it's the first time since I got here I can really say I kind of had fun at Westcock. With other people, that is, doing the kind of thing university students are supposed to do.

Of course, I wouldn't be me if I didn't pick apart everything about the night in order to determine why. I need to know, though. I am terrible at having a good time. It's the self-consciousness thing, it's the pressure. Whenever I'm out with people, the stated purpose being "to have a good time," all I can do is sit there neurotically checking myself every five minutes: "Is this fun? Am I enjoying myself now? I think I'm having fun, but what if I'm not? What if the people I'm with don't think it's fun at all? Are *they* having fun?" And on and on it goes. And eventually I'll start to even resent the people I'm with, thinking, to hell with them if they aren't having fun, they're no fun anyway. It's a crazy, fun-destroying compulsion I can't seem to resist. But I resisted it Friday night. Because I got drunk. I forgot to keep checking myself.

Therefore, when poet Jim Arsenault offers me a rum toddie at 1:18 on Monday afternoon, I accept. I accept with aplomb. I say, "You're goddamn right I do, Jim," and do you know what Jim does in return? Yes. On his way to the cupboard, he rests his palm on my head. Indeed, he ruffles my hair.

Oh, we speak of many things that afternoon, Jim and I. He coughs and horks into a Kleenex and tells me he loves my new poem. He calls it a breakthrough. He doesn't mind that it's terse, brief, scant. He doesn't say it should have a murder in it. Jim tells me my new style is "muscular."

I can't quite let myself believe it. I'm afraid an alarm clock is going to ring somewhere and I'll find myself back in Summerside, in grade 9, maybe—the purgatory of high school stretching before me wide as the Northumberland Strait—Jim and poetry on the other side, far and wee.

"You don't think it needs to be more exciting?" I venture. It feels almost dangerous, this conversation. How precisely it seems to be lining up with my dreams.

"Ah, Larry," Jim ducks his head, wearing an expression that is completely new to me. *Abashed* is the word. "I was having some fun with you that day. I'd been marking student poetry all afternoon."

I tell Jim that I understand. And I do. The rum flows into my cheeks and the afternoon sunlight filters through the changing leaves and turns Jim's dingy farmhouse kitchen a gilded, fairy-tale pink: the searing, summertime colour of good.

I no longer am a student poet. That is what Jim means.

I don't find out about the tenure thing until I get back to campus two hours later, having walked back from Jim's place out near Rock Point. It was way too long a walk, and Jim told me I was crazy, but I had an evening class and had to sober up for it somehow.

"Oh, fuck your class and stay for dinner," Jim told me. The entire afternoon he gave no hint of what was going on in the department. "I'll make pasta," he said. He even went so far as to open the cupboard and brandish a can at me. I was dying to. There was something so homey about sitting at a kitchen table with a man who had a cold, a blanket around his shoulders. Intimate. And I still hadn't met Jim's wife, whom I anticipated to be this protean mass of female sensuality, if *Blinding White* was any indicator. Moira. Jim's muse.

But part of me wanted to leave. It's hard to explain. It was so good I couldn't bear it after a while—I knew it had to get wrecked at some point. I would drink too much and then get nauseous or worse—say something stupid to Jim. Nothing gold can stay, that cheesy, depressing poem dictates, and there's a cheesy, depressing truth to it. The afternoon was nothing if not gold. Golden. The rum and the sunlight.

"He doesn't have a cold," says Sherrie.

"I was just there."

We're hissing at each other in a corner of the lecture hall. Professor Bryant Dekker is up there talking about Macbeth. Shakespeare—every English undergrad has to take it. Dekker isn't much of a commanding presence—nothing like Jim. It's telling how the less interesting professors are thrown into teaching these monster classes while the higher-ups get nifty little seminars. Jim's only been here a few years, but he's got cachet because he is what I've overheard Claude identify as a "rock star." This is the Canadian way of saying people in Toronto know who he is. He could be there right now, Jim's given us to understand, getting drunk with the likes of Greg Levine and Dermot Schofield, were he not so appalled and disillusioned by what he saw during his time there, after *Blinding White* was published and he was the toast of the town. I'm dying to know. What he saw, what it was like. He drops tantalizing little hints in class from time to time about "rampant dilettantism" and "flagrant hucksterism." *Ism ism ism,* like the song says.

"Yeah, but he doesn't have a cold, it's bullshit," says Sherrie.

"He was coughing and sneezing, Sherrie—he has a cold."

Everybody talks during Dekker's lecture. You feel guilty, but you do it anyway. He doesn't ever say much about it. Sometimes engineers or economics students here to get their despised arts credit will put their feet up in the back rows and talk at full volume about how hungover they are or how big a shit they took that morning, and Dekker will stand there going, excuse me, excuse me, excuse me, until they stop out of pity more than anything else. Sherrie and I half-whisper as a courtesy, and because we're both suck-ups, ultimately. We don't want Dekker to look up and see us gabbing, to lump us in with the undergraduate rabble.

"Well, it's mighty convenient," Sherrie hisses after a long pause. She always stops to pretend she's listening to Dekker for a few moments before leaning in to talk some more. "Did you know he had a class last Friday when we were in the Stein?"

"When?"

"Then. Three to five."

"How do you know?"

"Because I know someone who takes it. He didn't even put up a sign or anything, so they all just sat there for an hour. That's why I was kinda surprised to see him at the Stein."

I sit there thinking back to Friday. My breakthrough Friday when I ceased to be a student poet. I had thought Sherrie looked surprised. I had thought she was surprised to see me there, hanging out with Jim.

"He had that fight with Doctor Sparrow," I recall.

Sherrie nods open-mouthed like she's encouraging a simple child to form a word.

"I thought that was about women."

Sherrie closes her mouth. Her whole face seems to close up. "What?"

"He was going on about women for the next three hours."

She turns away and listens for a few seconds to Dekker talk about being unsexed by the thick night. Then she speaks from the corner of her mouth.

"Well, whatever he talked about afterward, he was pissed off because they're not going to grant his tenure."

"That's terrible," I say after a moment. I can't let Sherrie know I don't quite understand what tenure is.

"Well, yeah," says Sherrie, back to her retarded-child expression as she fakes paying attention to Dekker. "What did we come to Westcock for if Jim's not going to be here?" She flicks her hand toward Dekker, being ignored and yawned at below us.

"Jim won't be here?" I say.

"Why would he stay? God, he'll be snapped up by U of T, if not somewhere in the States. They're crazy."

All at once, I smell rum. It's me. Sweating.

3.

IT CAN'T HAPPEN because it's like I'm being pulled back across the strait. It can't happen because one minute I'm on the other side of a great man's kitchen table with my poetry spread out between us and gold and fire painting the kitchen, and the next he's a brilliant, distant, fading light on one shore and I'm a small, insignificant blotch on a small, insignificant island with no one to guide me across.

When I was in high school I stole all the poetry books out of the school library. It didn't occur to me that this was such a bad thing to do because whenever I flipped to the card on the back, I only ever saw my own name written there over and over again. Eventually it seemed I might as well keep them at home, and it wasn't much of a surprise that nobody even launched an investigation rudimentary enough to finger Lawrence Campbell as the number one suspect.

The only fuss I ever remember being raised over poetry in my school—or in my young life, for that matter—was when a book called *Even Less* by Jim Arsenault arrived, having just won a national award. More people took an interest than was usual in such matters because Arsenault was an Atlantic Canadian. The library ordered a copy, and an enterprising reporter in Charlottetown even called Jim up for an interview.

The reporter asked Jim things like, why do you live in Toronto? And, have you a wife, and if so, what does she think of all this?

Jim said he lived in Toronto out of necessity at the moment, and, no, he didn't have a wife.

The reporter said, I've read your book and felt there was some unnecessary language here and there. I thought the poems were very well written in places, but some of the language was shocking. Some people down this way, I think, would be shocked by it.

And Jim said this—the reporter wrote it down:

"I am happy to hear it. Didn't Kafka say that's what good writing should do—should act as an axe to the frozen sea within us? I didn't intend for my writing to waft over your readers like a friendly breeze, I'm afraid. I prefer the axe. Let your readers be shocked awake, or let them be shattered to pieces, it makes no difference to me. Only let something happen other than comfort and reassurance."

But you want people to read your book, don't you? persisted the reporter. A great many people, in this part of the country at least, don't enjoy being shocked and shattered.

"Those people, in that case," responded Jim Arsenault, "can go to hell."

The newspaper printed it "H*ll."

Because the library had made such a big deal about ordering the book, they now had to respond to parents, who kicked up a fuss and demanded to know what the school thought it was doing, stocking such filth in reach of children? That's when I stepped in, slipping it off the shelf and into my schoolbag, solving the problem for everyone. The next week the school assured parents the offending material had been removed.

I read the book over and over again. And then I read the interview, which I had clipped, over and over again.

And then I knew three things.

1. I wanted to be a poet.

2. Anyone who had a problem with my being a poet could go to hell.

3. I had to get the hell out of there.

Of all three revelations, the most important was the second. Numbers 1 and 3 had always been present, but in a shapeless, jellyfish kind of way, jiggling dubiously around in the back of my mind. Because much as I loved poetry, how could I *be* a poet? Nobody was a poet, nobody read poetry. That's what had been holding me back, this idea of *everybody*—the everybody who couldn't care less about poetry. But number 2 shook me awake—the insight I gleaned from Jim's interview. This was the missing piece to the puzzle of my future. Number 2 was the axe to the frozen sea within me. Of course. It was so simple. *Everybody* could go to hell.

I will quit Westcock if I have to. I will follow wherever he goes.

Ring, ring.

Good! Maybe it's Jim. I have been wanting to call Jim all day, but I don't have the courage to just ring him up at home like we're old friends or something. The fact of the matter is, much of today's daydreaming in front of the typewriter has had to do with this question—am I allowed to just call Jim at home like we're old friends or something? Weighing the pros and cons. On the one hand, I spent a golden afternoon at his kitchen table, watching him blow his nose by way of punctuating his remarks on my poetry. He invited me—he wouldn't just invite me to his house if he didn't want me around. On the other hand—

"Yeah," I say into the phone like a guy in a movie. "Hi," I amend.

"Is that how people answer the phone now?" says my mother. Not a trace of sarcasm in evidence—she does not know the meaning of the word.

"Hi, Mom!"

"What in hell are you doing?" says my dad, on the other phone.

"Hi, Dad!"

"It's not too polite, I don't think."

"I was working, I was distracted."

"Oh, good for you," says my mother. "What were you working on?"

"Poetry."

"Oh, good for you," says my mother again.

"Something for class?" demands my father.

"Yes," I say loudly.

"Oh, good," says my mother.

"So, how's it going?" Dad wants to know.

"What, the poetry?"

"The whole damn thing."

"I went to Jim's house and we talked about my poetry yesterday for something like four hours."

"Jim, Jim, Jim," says my dad.

"Is that normal?" asks my mother. "Is that what they do?"

"Who?"

"In university?"

"No!" I tell her. "It's not normal at all, not in the least!"

"Oh," says Mom.

"It means he's singled me out, he thinks I'm special."

"Oh!" says Mom.

"So, he's tutoring you, like?" says Dad.

"No! Jim's my prof, Dad, he doesn't tutor. He's mentoring me—he's mentoring me on the side, in *addition* to being my prof, because he likes my poetry so much."

"Do you get an extra credit for it?" Mom wants to know. Mom has studied all my university calendars, trying to grasp things like credit, first-year and second-year courses, how sometimes you can get credit just for doing directed reading or writing a paper or something. When I was registering last summer it took her forever to understand that I could be in my second year at Westcock and take first- and third-year courses. She says it still doesn't sound right to her. University culture, university rules—it is all a Byzantine mystery to the PEI Campbells. It's not like potato farming, or politicking, or running a motor hotel and mini-putt. It's like nothing else they know.

"Well, now, it's lonely around here without you, Larry," Dad tells me—just like he tells me every time he calls. "No one around to sweep off the greens."

"Nobody calls me Larry here, Dad," I say.

"Well, everybody calls you Larry here," says Dad.

We talk for another hour and I tell them every single thing that happened during my week, which they are always content to hear for some reason. Dad tells me how a bunch of drunk teenagers showed up at the motel at one in the morning wanting to play a game of minigolf and he told them he kept a rifle behind the counter and made as if to reach for it and they ran like hell. (You better run! he hollered after them. This thing took the arse off a bear who was moving a damn sight quicker than you punks!) That was the highlight of his week, Dad says.

We hang up, and I'm in a good mood. I feel like going out in the sunshine and buying groceries or something— being productive, responsible. Then I make a mistake. I glance over at my typewriter, the empty page like bared teeth.

I hug the phone. I weave the cord back and forth between my fingers. The receiver clicks and clacks in its cradle.

Ring, ring.

"What."

"Jim?"

"Who's this."

"It's Lawrence."

"Lawrence who?"

" . . . Larry."

Rustling sounds. Blankets, cushions, chesterfields.

"Oh, Larry." he sniffs. Snorts, really. "How's it going?"

" . . . Good, Jim, good." There's a wailing in my brain like a disaster siren; it sounded the moment he answered the phone. *Bad idea. Bad idea.*

"What can I do for you, Larry?"

What are you bothering me for, Larry?

"Um, Jim. I'm just calling to see how you're doing. See if everything's okay."

Cushions, blankets. "Oh, you are, are you?"

There's something dead in his voice and it's like I'm fighting to keep my Adam's apple from plugging up my throat.

"Yes."

"Now, why wouldn't everything be just ducky, I wonder now?"

"How's your cold?" I say very fast.

"What have you heard," demands Jim.

"What have I heard?"

"What have you heard," demands Jim.

"I—I heard there was some kind of problem with the department."

"Some kind of problem," Jim repeats slowly.

"Yes," I say.

"Yes," says Jim.

Jesus Christ, this is a waking nightmare.

"And so I was just calling," I continue.

"Yes?" says Jim.

" . . . to see . . ."

"Yes, Larry?"

" . . . if there was anything I can do." I hurl this last part out like I'm vomiting—with the same sense of helpless revulsion I had on Friday night outside the Stein. Wanting to get it out. Hating to get it out.

More chesterfield noises. Something being poured. A woman's voice then, angry, faint, and urgent.

Who is it, for Christ's sake?

Shh. It's just a student.

Oh.

"Jim?" I say.

"Still here, Larry."

"Listen, I shouldn't have called. I'm sorry to bother you."

"No, no, I appreciate it, Larry, I really do. Is there anything you can do—well, let me see. I don't know, Larry, is there? What do you have in mind?"

"Jim . . . I don't even understand what's going on, I just wanted . . ."

"No, you don't understand, do you. Well, I guess we can't be much help to each other, because I'm afraid I don't understand either. I don't understand a fucking thing anymore."

No one has spoken to me like this ever, in my life. I can feel my stomach contracting, pickling itself in acid. And then something even more terrifying happens. The chesterfield noises again, phone against fabric. A sound, a male sound like I've never heard before, a Jim sound, but not a word. A sob.

"Jim?" My eyes strain against their sockets. "Jim?"

"Fuck off, why don't you!" The barky voice, not Jim anymore. It's his wife.

"I'm sorry . . ."

"Why don't you cocksuckers all just smarten up!"

And she hangs up.

I need to get away from the telephone. Also, I need to stop talking stream of consciousness to my parents every time they call. I need to keep stuff inside like a normal person. It has to fester inside me, that stuff, and get warped and stewish until it blurps out onto the page like tomato sauce splattering onto the white of a stovetop. That's what poets do, real ones. Real poets are careful. They are circumspect. They don't just call each other up in the middle of the afternoon to see if everything's okay.

But he was crying.

I decide to lie on the floor again, catching my typewriter's eye as I do. Finally something has wiped that smirk off its face.

4.

NOW IT'S WEDNESDAY and we sit in Jim's seminar class staring into the void of the blackboard.

"He's not coming," says Claude.

"Bullshit," I grunt. I am trying to be meaner these days, more brutal.

"I mean," says Sherrie as if she has said something prior to this, "if he's only on probation he could still be reinstated, couldn't he?"

Claude leans forward in a rare display of energy. "If he's been denied tenure, that's it. He won't be coming back after this year, he'll go elsewhere. But it won't look good for him to have been denied. Other universities will take it into consideration. They'll wonder why."

"*I'm* wondering why," I say.

The door to the classroom shrieks open and Bryant Dekker shuffles in, hugging his briefcase across his torso as if it could protect him from bullets or wild dogs.

"Hi, everybody," he coughs.

We stare at him.

"Professor Arsenault asked me to take over for him today—he's not feeling well."

In a wonderful, somehow pointed gesture of indifference, Claude raises his arm and looks down at his watch. He doesn't need to do it, because a huge industrial clock hovers on the wall above Dekker's head like a displaced halo. But thanks to Claude's lead, we all think to gaze up and note that it's forty-five minutes into class. Dekker turns to see as well, and then adopts a look like the raccoons my father used to corner in our shed.

"So," he says. "So, uh. Whose stuff are we looking at today?" He puts his briefcase onto the table in front of him. He doesn't bother to open it. "And would anyone have an extra copy?"

Nobody says anything. My hand goes up. Dekker looks at it.

"Lawrence?"

"We want to know what's going on," I say.

Silence as I fold my hands and Dekker takes a careful breath, deliberately prolonged.

"Yeah!" goes someone else. To my surprise, someone has sounded, "Yeah!" from behind me. And suddenly I feel a powerful boy.

Jim Arsenault has not been a departmental favourite since he was granted the usual four-year probationary appointment at this small but prestigious undergraduate institute. Nobody knows why Jim decided to come here. It is assumed he was being clamoured for after *Blinding White* started getting attention overseas. It is assumed that a Canadian poet with an unheard-of international reputation—who also happens to have picked up a master's degree somewhere along the way—would be the dream of every English department in the country. It is assumed he deigned to settle here because he is a native New Brunswicker himself, and his poetry testifies to his reverence toward the land and its people.

But holy God, if it were me I would've killed to get out of these sticks.

Anyway, settle here he did, to the insane good fortune of us all. I knew where I was going to university by the time I finished grade 11—the year Jim arrived at Westcock. Otherwise I would never have given this place a second thought. It was founded by Methodists—precisely the breed of people Jim had said could go to H*ll. It's in Timperly, a town with a population of scarcely three thousand, surrounded by nothing but tractors and marsh. The nearest metropolis is a twenty-five-minute drive across the border—Wethering, Nova Scotia. "Friendly as can be!" announces the highway sign. Population a teeming 4,052.

Right up until I heard about Jim coming to Westcock, my plan was to hie me off to Toronto, figuring that if someone like Jim Arsenault was living there "out of necessity," this necessitated that Lawrence Campbell should live there too. I terrorized my parents by articulating this intention pretty much every day from the moment I discovered *Even Less*. It was Toronto or nowhere, I said to my parents, who have been off Prince Edward Island overnight maybe six times in their combined lives. There was nowhere else to go, I told them, nowhere else to be, nowhere else to write in this hinterland.

But Jim. So Jim came. He bought the house near Rock Point. He settled in with Moira. He gathered acolytes from all across Canada. He initiated the joint creative-writing honours for English students—the first such degree in the country. The department had no choice but to do it because there were so many students like me arriving, more interested in studying poetry with Jim than anything else. Enrolment skyrocketed. Dekker says it "went up," but that has to be an understatement. It skyrocketed—how could it not? And the most amazing thing—or not so amazing, it turns out, if you know anything about what Dekker calls "departmental politics"—is that from the moment Jim showed up on the department's doorstep, Doctor Sparrow has wanted nothing so dearly as an excuse to throw him off it.

I am extrapolating. Dekker didn't come out and say it like that, but he did say that Jim has been "rubbing the administration the wrong way" since his arrival.

"Why?" we all want to know.

"Well," says Dekker. He leans against the table now, seeming to have shed his armour. Dekker is far more at ease simply having a conversation than I've ever seen him teaching a class. He scratches his five-o'clock shadow, searching for the right words. "Jim," he begins. "Well, Jim is a little eccentric."

"Oh my God," I shout over Claude, who is snickering. "That's because he's a genius!"

"Yeah!" goes the yeah-guy behind me.

Dekker looks us over for a moment. A second later, all his armour has been shrugged on again. He picks up his briefcase.

"People," he says, seeming to apologize with the word, "I can't go into it with you. Jim's been told his tenure won't be granted next year—that's all I can say. I've seen the letter, and personally, I think it's a travesty. I've written to Doctor Sparrow and the dean of Arts, and that's all I'm in a position to do. It's—" Dekker sighs into the crease of his briefcase. "It's a genuine shame."

"What if *we* wrote letters?" asks Sherrie.

Dekker places his briefcase down on the table again. "Um," he says carefully. "It's not like I'm instructing you to do that or anything, but if you feel strongly about this, I'd encourage you to follow your conscience."

Claude speaks. He says one word. That word is this: "Please."

We all look at him. The cheerful futility sloshing around in that one syllable infuriates me. We're silenced by it, and Claude gazes at us, finishing his sentiment with apparent effort.

"A bunch of students write letters," he drawls. "*That* will make a difference."

I'll show him, I decide.

The yeah-guy, it turns out, is Todd. I haven't spoken to him before, but I've read and commented on his poetry, most of which is pretty bad. A lot of it rhymes. He can't seem to wean himself from the idea that poetry has to rhyme, and as a result everything he brings to class—often about sex or industrial accidents—has a grotesque sing-songy quality. *And as the coal fell on his head / he thought of what his mother said / work well: no matter what you do / the mine shall make a man of you.*

But now I find that I like him. Todd is all flailing limbs and pissed-off energy, and it's infectious. We huddle outside the classroom.

"This is a pile of crap," says Todd.

"Fucking bullshit," I say.

"A complete pile of shit," says Todd. "Jim's my only reason for being here, for fuck's sake. I could have gone to Dalhousie."

"Me too," I say.

Todd ceases to flail for a moment. "You got accepted to Dalhousie?"

"No, I mean Jim's my only reason for being here," I clarify. "I would have gone to U of T."

"Toronto, man? Really?" Todd looks dubious.

"Well, yeah," I say, "You know, Where Else in Canada . . ."

"Yeah, but Upper Canada," says Todd, and I blink. The only other person I know who refers to it as Upper Canada is my grandmother Lydia, the head of the Summerside Daughters of Temperance Society.

"Where Else in Canada . . . ," I begin again.

"It's just so full of assholes," says Todd. And then he rhymes off a list of names. Toronto poets—most of whom I've heard of but haven't read, because Jim has identified them as "hucksters" for us. On the first day of our seminar he drew a line down the middle of the blackboard. On one side he wrote "Hucksters." On the other side he wrote "The Real Thing." There were a couple of Toronto poets on the "Real Thing" side—Greg Levine and S.M. Munroe—but mostly it was poets from the east coast, the west coast, the prairies—everywhere and anywhere but. He handed out the work of the Real Thing writers but said that to inflict the Hucksters on us would be contamination. I had been feeling cocky that day—the classroom is the only place it happens—and raised my hand. "What about 'Know thy enemy'?" I said before Jim could even call on me. He smiled, overbite leering. "'*Smite* thine enemy,'" he corrected. And smacked the blackboard for emphasis.

"Levine's not bad," I venture, interrupting Todd's list.

"He's not from there—he's from Montreal originally," says Todd. "Everyone thinks Toronto's the place to go if you want to write. The hucksters have all the power in this country, and so they're the ones who perpetuate it. We just buy into all that crap because we think we have no choice."

"Yeah, but," I say, "that's the way it is."

"It's up to us to change the way it is," Todd explains.

I enjoy how angry Todd seems about everything, how the whole world for him is like a scratchy tag on a sweater. We're at the Stein, drinking and planning. It comes to light that Todd is like me—from the sticks. His home is somewhere nowhere on the south shore of Nova Scotia, but, he says, "I make no apologies." This is new to me—I've been making apologies ever since I got here, if only to myself. Not Todd. Todd says he's proud of his roots, his "cultural" background (Scottish, "a Smiley of the Port Duffrin Smileys"—I get the feeling he's about to whip out a family crest), and what he calls his "working-class background." Then Todd rants for a while at all the people who would tell him to be ashamed of his "working-class background." I keep quiet because I would have been one of them an hour or so ago. I mean, this is university, isn't it? Doctor Sparrow is a graduate of Oxford. He even has a tiny English accent, the gentlest of English accents, making him sound courtly and wise but at the same time inevitably debauched, like a Roman in one of those old movies, those old Bible epics. Even Dekker has some kind of accent—not exactly English, but close. Some kind of cross between German and English. Very faint. Very not-from-here. Our benefactor Horace Lee Grayson was—it's undeniable—Atlantic Canadian gentry. He was a landowner from a long line of landowners, first in England and then in New Brunswick. Todd and I attend classes alongside people who appear to be from other planets—I don't know how to explain it. How they talk, how they think. How they talk about what they think. I wave my arms and say things like *Oh my God, that's crazy!* They come out with, *I'm not sure I agree.* And you know what? They win. They win when they say things like that. What I mean is they sit back and ponder and I wave my arms and proclaim and somehow by uttering the most flaccid words imaginable—*I'm not sure I agree*—simply by uttering them in that *way,* that way they have which depends as much on haircuts and shoes as it does on words and ideas—somehow they win. It's like they've won already.

It wasn't until this year I started to understand the difference. The difference is this. It's *breeding,* is what it is. Like show dogs.

In the middle of talking to Todd Smiley I take out my notebook.

"What are you doing?" Todd wants to know. His eyebrows don't plunge like Jim's.

Showdogs, I write.

"Idea for a poem."

I look up. Todd is nodding, pleased.

After a couple of hours, Sherrie arrives with a letter she has drafted during her Victorian Novel lecture. She reads it to Todd and me, Todd *yeah*-ing and twitching the whole time. We edit and drink for another hour—it goes from three pages, to one, to two, and then finally to one and a half. "To Whom it May Concern," we begin, deciding we'll figure out the people to direct our complaint to later. Doctor Sparrow? The dean of Arts? The university president? Waldine Grayson, Horace Lee Grayson's oldest living descendant, who still lives in his big white house above the marsh? We have no idea what we're doing, really, but at the moment it doesn't matter. We're getting it out. Words fly like sparks. We astound one another with our angry eloquence.

Second year is so much better than first. I couldn't get into a class with Jim last year—I had to take all the intro classes first—and therefore didn't see the point of being here. I followed him around campus a bit, even went to his office and sweatily introduced myself. He was polite. He recommended some books, and said he'd look for me in his group next year, but he didn't ask to see any of my poetry, and I couldn't bring myself to thrust a few pages of it at him, as I'd been dreaming of doing (*he glances down, disinterested at first; suddenly a gemlike turn of phrase catches his eye, dazzling him; he looks back up, slowly, awareness dawning, recognizing himself to be in the presence of . . .*). It felt like I was still on the other side of the strait, waving and drowning. I couldn't make him see me.

Plus I was lonely, to be honest. I thought I would never have any friends. I resigned myself to a life of poetic isolation and tried to feel okay about it because I knew lots of writers were misanthropes. Every once in a while, though, I'd think of the great literary friendships and get depressed. Beckett hanging out at Joyce's house in Paris. Shelley tossing them back with Byron. Hemingway and Fitzgerald. Ginsberg and Burroughs. All the beats hung out together. Artists are supposed to hang out together. Often they have a clash of sensibilities or some kind of a pissy falling-out, but then they write about it and it's immortalized for all time, whether they ever make up with each other or not. It doesn't matter if they ever make up—the purpose of the friendship is to provide artistic fodder and rivalry and inspiration. Because writers are fiery and opinionated. You can't expect them to put up with each other indefinitely.

Anyway, I didn't think I'd ever have a friendship like that after a year of living in residence. To have an artistic friendship, you have to meet other artists, and the only people I met in residence were assholes or psychopaths or both. All the sports guys lived in my dorm, Hadwin House—the football and hockey players—and they were, to a man, enormous and crazy. They treated residence like their clubhouse and perpetuated horrific abuse on first-year guys who had just joined the teams. My roommate was first-year and a football player, and they broke into our room at two in the morning, wrapped him in hockey tape, and dragged him screaming down the hall. Later he told me they had shoved him in the utility closet downstairs, crowded in there with him, and solemnly showed him a broomstick. They said they were going to have to shove the broomstick up his ass if he were to be accepted as a member of the team. They said they were sorry but explained everyone on the team had undergone this experience and it had to be done. That's all my roommate would tell me about it the next day, except to add that they had just been fucking with him and eventually let him go back to bed, ha, ha. It was two hours later, I seem to recall—I'd been lying awake with both our desks shoved against the door. But a week or so later another guy told me the joke ended when my roommate turned to brace himself against the wall, bawling, "Just do it! Just fucking get it over with!" and the football guys had to lean against each other to keep from collapsing onto the floor in one meaty, mirthful heap.

Another time some guy from MacLaren House snuck onto our floor, took a shit in a pot, and put it on the stove in our kitchen, on "low." The next day Chuck Slaughter—a massive football guy who used to pay me to write his English papers—went over to MacLaren wearing a pair of rubber gloves and smeared the cooked shit all over the receiver of their pay phone. Then he returned to Hadwin House and called them.

What I'm trying to get across is, it was like *Lord of the Flies* over there. I told my dad I had to get out of residence or drop out. He'd been disappointed because all summer he'd been telling me how university years were the "best of your life," and he was more excited than I was—about residence most of all. I think it was the idea of my living with all those other guys, the masculine fellowship toughening me up. Or maybe it's just one of those assumptions you make about worlds you know you'll never reach yourself: the thing I'm not supposed to have must be what's most worth having.

5.

THERE IS A PIECE by Jim featured in the fall issue of *Atlantica*. It's a review of Dermot Schofield's new collection of poetry, *Malignant Cove*. I seem to recall that Schofield failed to find a home on either the Huckster or the Real Thing list at the beginning of the year. It looks like he's come down solidly on the side of the hucksters with this book.

Jim—I don't know any other way to put this—he wipes his ass with Schofield.

> Perhaps this is what passes for talent in the perfumed salons of the Toronto literary elite, where running low on cognac is the closest anyone gets to hardship and the professor-poets dally in the faculty-club cloak room with colleagues' wives in the attempt to graft some semblance of passion and genuine human feeling onto their airless, obtuse existence. This is no "garden" of "stay" as Schofield professes, although it is indisputably stagnant and fecund—much like a swamp, or a diseased animal— the perfect breeding ground for pestilence and infestation. God grant Canadian poetry be inoculated against the wasting illness that is Dermot Schofield.

I am in the library, poring over the new journals as I always do—feeling sick and envious and excited by them as I always do—wanting to be able to turn a page and see my own name under something so unspeakably brilliant it irradiates the page. I rip out *Atlantica*'s subscription card and stick it in my notebook. So this is the Canadian literature of my time! No more trees and rocks and oceans and lakes and prairies and farms, but barricades. And battle lines—both

intellectual and aesthetic. Upper Canadian snottitude versus
hard-nosed regionalism. City versus Town, fake versus real.
It's raw and pugilistic. Like a hockey game. Or war. It's so
new. I never imagined poetry could be like this.

Another sunny autumn day. I walk across the quad dis-
rupting waist-high dunes of crisp, fallen leaves. Getting
colder now, students wandering about in thicker coats, in
chunky wool sweaters. But I can differentiate them—the
leather coats versus the nylon parkas with polyester fill. The
expensive store-bought woollen sweaters versus acrylic, or
else the threadbare homemade ones. Like the one I have
on—my father's old curling sweater with the moose and
hunter on the back, so stretched out it almost reaches my
knees.

The point is what I'm seeing: I see the difference. I see
campus like a line drawn down a blackboard now.

"It's good," says Dekker, scanning our letter in his tidy office.
Dekker I can't determine. What kind of sweater would he
wear? He clothes himself in the camouflage of academe.
"Heartfelt," he says.

"It *is* heartfelt," I agree. "Everyone will sign it," I say. "We
don't know the best way to go about getting signatures,
though. I was thinking maybe we should post it in the
lounge."

Dekker purses his lips, scratches his clean-shaven neck as
he often does. He's got one of those beards that just wants to
grow. The bottom of his face is always black by late afternoon, and I don't know why he won't just let it fuzz over
completely.

"Chances are," Dekker considers, "if you posted it, it'd be
gone in an hour. They'd just take it down."

"They'd just take it down? Who?"

"The administration," he says. The word sounds like it should have a capital A, like something in an Orwell novel.

"But it's the *students'* lounge," I say.

"Lawrence, they'd find a reason. They'd say the bulletin board was only for departmental business or some such thing."

I'm aghast. "People sell their bikes on that thing!"

Dekker smiles as though I've told a joke. "It doesn't matter. The department has no obligation to be consistent. What they do is, they do what they want, *then* they make up reasons for it."

So it really is an Orwell novel. The place I go to school.

"Is that what happened with Jim?" I ask after a moment.

Dekker waits a moment too. "What happened with Jim," he says at last, "is complicated."

"Yeah, but you said they wanted to get rid of him from the very beginning."

Dekker holds up his hands. "I didn't say that exactly."

"Yes you did, Professor Dekker."

Dekker pauses to creak backward in his chair, stretching his arms behind his head. For a moment I'm afraid he might flip over.

"Oh boy," he says when he finishes stretching. "If I did, if I did say that, I would ask that you forget it."

"You said it to the whole class."

"Oh boy," Dekker says again. Now he looks like he wishes he would flip over. Me left talking to his mute, exclamation-point legs.

And in walks Jim.

Like a ghost invoked.

"Hi!" I scream before anyone can say anything else. The adrenalin—the Jim-adrenalin—that wild, gleeful, fork-in-an-outlet panic—hits me like freezing water.

"Jim," says Dekker, creaking out of his chair to his feet.

He crosses the room in an eye-blink and they shake hands like crazy. I watch them, vision pulsing. I'm standing too, I realize. After a moment Jim stops shaking but doesn't let go of Dekker's hand. He reaches with his other hand for Dekker's shoulder. He folds Dekker to him—Dekker just kind of letting himself drift in, looking dreamy. They pat backs like crazy. Pufts of dust explode from Jim's hunting jacket, twinkling around in the stream of sunlight coming through Dekker's window.

"How are you?" says Dekker, drawing back, coughing slightly.

"*Illegitimi non carborundum,*" answers Jim. His voice is heavy, full of phlegm and gravel.

Dekker grins but doesn't seem to know how to respond. "It's good to have you back," Dekker says. "It's good to have you back," he repeats when Jim doesn't answer.

Jim allows the dusty silence to hang a moment longer. "I want to thank you," he says finally, deflating as he sighs the words out.

"Oh, Jim," balks Dekker, "for what?"

"I heard about your letter."

"It was nothing."

"No," says Jim. "You stuck your neck out, Bryant."

Dekker looks around, shaking his head, trying to form words.

"You stuck your neck out. For me."

Dekker raises his hands, still speechless.

"I want you to know that I know that. And that I appreciate it."

Dekker, it would seem, is as tongue-tied around Jim as everyone else is. He flails around a bit more before his eyes light on me.

"Lawrence," he says, and Jim turns, nods funereally.

"Hi, Larry."

"Hi, Jim!"

"It's Lawrence you should be thanking," says Dekker.

My jaw drops in preparation to deny it. Jim's forested eyebrows plunge—his most intimidating gesture, because you know it could mean anything. He looks that way when he talks of poems he loves. He looks that way when he talks of poems he hates.

"Is that right?" interrogates Jim.

Dekker beams his relief from the weight of Jim's gratitude, explaining, "He and some other students have initiated a—a sort of campaign."

Jim's eyebrows descend practically to the tip of his nose.

"We're just writing a letter," I say. "Like Professor Dekker."

"He's going to get all the students to sign it."

"All the students?" says Jim. His brows ease up. His mouth opens.

"All the students in the department, at least," Dekker amends.

"No!" I say, and Dekker's lips twitch in surprise. "*All* the students. We'll get the whole student body involved."

Jim takes a step toward me, eyebrows and overbite looming.

"We'll take it to the president's office," I babble. "We'll take it to Waldine Grayson if we have to. We're behind you, Jim. All of us—"

And then I can't talk, I've got a mouthful of wood-smoked jacket.

There's music in my head instead of poetry now. I'm jiving down Bridge Street toward Carl's Tearoom. "Rock & Roll,"

by the Velvet Underground. A guy named Luc from
Montreal blasted it day and night in Hadwin House last year
until inevitably some football player would yell at him to
turn off his fucking faggot music before he shoved his entire
record collection up his ass, *and not sideways either, you
French faggot, I'm not gonna just slip it in like a letter in a
mailbox.* I remember that particular threat so well because it
was Chuck Slaughter who made it and I spent around twenty
minutes trying to figure out what it was supposed to mean.
Chuck's rage was often of the incoherent variety.

But Luc never stopped. He played whatever he wanted
because he knew the football and hockey players wouldn't
touch him or his turntable. He played the Doors and the
New York Dolls and David Bowie. He was the only guy on
the floor with a decent stereo, which meant girls always came
to Hadwin House parties. And on those nights, out would
come the Elton John and the Stevie Wonder and they all
bowed down to Luc's power and genius.

I am so into the song I'm practically singing out loud, lips
moving, spreading my hands wide on *FINE FINE music,* getting threatening looks from passersby. Hello everybody.
Hello town of Timperly. Jim Arsenault loves me. Despite all
the amputations, just like Lou Reed says. Amputated personality. Amputated literary ability. Amputated power of coherent speech in his presence. I'm grooving down the sidewalk
in my curling sweater with the moose and hunter on the
back. Past the Sub Stop, where I get my all-meaters. Past
Razors Sharp, where I get my hair trimmed about once a
year. Past Rory Scarsdale Holdings with its stupid, meaning-
less flag— *"Ask For Rory!" 362–9130*—made all the more infuriating by the arbitrary quotation marks.

It doesn't bother me so much today, of course, but the
flag was like an insult when I first arrived. *It's a university
town! Whom are they quoting? If it's Scarsdale himself, then why*

quote? It's his flag. On and on, I ground my teeth over it countless times on my way to the tearoom. I could have stayed in Summerside for pointless quotation marks. The sign outside the Legion: *"Ham Dinner" Friday!* Is it a ham dinner in theory? A euphemistic ham dinner of some kind? Notes left on the table from my mother: *Larry give Aunt Maudie a "ring." Give lawn a "trim." Don't forget to "pick up" new putters.* Her letters are the same—quotation marks jumping around all over the page like ticks.

Anyway, I don't care. I love Timperly. I love quotation marks. I love my mother.

Ring-a-ding goes the bell above the door at Carl's Tearoom. Sherrie's not here yet. I boogie my way into a booth. I'd like to go and play the jukebox but know from experience it's all country and western, with a little bit of Don Messer and Stompin' Tom thrown in to remind us where we come from, and I'm not in a twangin' mood today. I order tea and french fries with Beef Gravy with a jaunty sort of flourish, looking the waitress straight in her remarkable amber eyes, taking the time to ask how she is today. She has a tag over one breast reading *Brenda L.* I say, *How are you today, Brenda L.?* and it goes over well. She tells me she is just dandy. She looks like she'd like to lean over and ruffle my hair, maybe kiss the top of my head. I watch her shuffle away, energyless, like a lady in a housecoat. I think Brenda is maybe around thirty. Quite old. A body that Jim would call *overripe* in one of his poems. But I find Brenda nice, comforting to look at. I bet the under-neaths of her arms would wobble whenever she reached for things. To me that seems nice. Soft. Soft eyes. Soft soft soft hand—that's from Joyce, I think, the only novelist so good he's practically a poet. Soft and white. Smelling heavy and soft, like grandmother's soap. Maybe she has children. Maybe

I could have an affair with Brenda L., instead of bothering with girls from school. It would be iconoclastic. An older woman, maybe with a neglectful husband. It would be theatrical. No one else has wanted to kiss me since I got here. On the head or anywhere else.

Overripe. How does Jim mean it? Like a banana? An overripe banana isn't bad. I look over and see Brenda L. balancing an entire tray of food on her hip.

I take out my notebook and am writing *overripe can mean sweet* when Sherrie sits down.

"Hi," she says.

"Heyyy," I say.

"What are you so happy about?"

I smile. Sherrie flaps her enormous eyelashes. Tweety Bird, that's who she reminds me of.

"Maybe I'm just a happy kind of guy."

Sherrie smirks elaborately at this. Do I not seem a happy kind of guy? Then Brenda L.'s heavy, overripe presence is hanging above us. She stands with her order pad poised as Sherrie looks down at the placemat where the tearoom menu is writ.

"Tea," says Sherrie. I am concerned that Brenda will think Sherrie is my girlfriend.

"That it?" says Brenda. "No fries?"

"No, thanks," says Sherrie.

Look at me, Brenda L., I am thinking. And she does.

"Yours is coming," she tells me. I nod.

Sherrie starts laughing once Brenda goes away. She puts a pompous look on her face and bobs her head a few times.

"What?" I say.

"You!" she says. "You're Mr. Cool today."

My neck begins to burn when I realize all Sherrie's bobbing was supposed to represent my nod at Brenda. I rub at it and hunch my shoulders. *What's* your *deal anyway, Tweety?* I want to say to Sherrie. *Girl poets don't look like you. They're gaunt and sucked-in and wear hippie clothes. They're ethereal, sexless. The only thing you've got down is the frizzy hair.*

"I'm just kidding," says Sherrie, ducking her head to catch my eye. "You just seem like you're in a good mood."

I remember my good mood and sit up. "I saw Jim."

"Oh! How is he?"

I can't remember the Latin thing Jim said in Dekker's office, so I try to come up with something equally sombre and elegant. "He is bowed . . . but unbroken."

"What?" says Sherrie.

"He's good," I say fast.

"Really?"

"Well," I say, "he says he's coming back to work. And I think he was really, really touched to hear about what we're doing."

"Oh, you told him what we're doing?"

"Yeah. Dekker did."

Sherrie smiles, nestling back into her seat. A pink smudge appears on each cheek. Pink and white—her face is like a valentine. "Oh, good," she says. "Oh, good."

Brenda sets two aluminum pots of tea down in front of us, and then two identical cups and saucers. "Fries're on their way," she says.

"Thank you, Brenda L.!" I call. And she bestows her nurturing, head-kissing look before going away. It fortifies me.

"What did he say?" says Sherrie.

"About what?"

"About us."

All I really remember is a wall of eyebrow coming at me, a faceful of wool and sawdust.

"He just said thank you," I answer, floating on the memory.

"Thank you?"

"Yeah—'thank you, thank you so much.' He was a little choked up."

"Was Todd there?"

"What? No—Todd dropped the letter off, remember?"

"So it was just you?"

"No, it was me and Dekker—" I stop and peer at Sherrie. Vast and blue as her eyes might be, they don't give much away. Still, I get it. I get it because I know what I'd be thinking if I was her.

"Oh," I say. "But—you know—he knows it's not just me, Sherrie."

Sherrie pretends to look around for Brenda, concerned about my french fries.

"No, no," she says, flipping a hand as if to say fiddle-de-dee. "It's fine."

"I mean, he knows I couldn't do this alone."

"You told him . . . ?"

"Dekker told him it was a bunch of us."

I can see Sherrie trying to figure out a way of asking if she was mentioned to Jim by name without sounding like she cares. Trying to shrug herself into a Claude-demeanour. I let her work at it for a couple of seconds—in fact, we're both struggling minutely, fumbling for what to say.

"Dekker will tell him all about it," I grope. "I had to take off and meet you, but I'm sure they're talking about it right now."

Now Sherrie has her chance. "Did you say you were meeting me?"

"Um," I say. "Oh yes. I think I did."

We are both adjusting ourselves in the booth, attempting to get comfortable, when it occurs to me to pass Sherrie the edited version of our letter with Dekker's suggestions. He suggests we keep things "positive." *Never accuse,* he has written in the margins, *never make it sound as if you're blaming them for anything.* Say "we encourage" instead of "we demand." We are "sincerely hopeful," as opposed to "deeply disappointed." Brenda brings my fries. Sherrie sees them and decides she wants some too.

We drink our tea and dip our fries in a rather companionable silence after that. Sherrie wants to talk poetry by way of changing the subject, but because I don't care for her poems it strikes me as awkward terrain. She talks about Margaret Avison a lot, and Margaret Atwood, and I start to wonder if it's all a bunch of Margarets writing orgasm poetry in Canada these days. Maybe Sherrie should change her name to Margaret. She should change it to something, last if not first, because Sherrie owns perhaps the worst name for a poet this side of Adelaide Crapsey. Her last name is Mitten. She signs her poems Sherrie Ann Mitten.

"Why the Ann?" I interrupt Sherrie. She stops talking about *The Journals of Susanna Moodie* and switches conversational gears without even a flap of her lashes.

"I thought it would look more serious," she admits. "Sherrie Mitten. Sherrie Mitten. It just looks like some girl's name on the page. It has no authority."

"So you stuck 'Ann' in there?"

"I felt it needed something to sort of *temper* the kind of . . . yearbook-picture sound of it. 'Ann' has a seriousness."

"Why not just Ann? And drop the Sherrie?"

"I thought of that. I don't like the meter."

"The meter?"

"Ann Mi-tten. Ann Mi-tten," she recites, emphasizing the rhythm for me with a lilt of her hand, like a music teacher. "It's too—" she shakes her head "—staccato. It's harsh, somehow. I don't want to be harsh."

More companionable silence, during which I feel sorry

for Sherrie. The problem, really, is all in the *Mitten*—there's just no getting around it. She could be a Margaret and it wouldn't help—the alliteration would make it all the more ludicrous.

"What does Mitten mean?" I ask. "Is it French-derived or something?" I figure if I can help Sherrie with her name—if we can work together to get it just right—I won't feel quite so awkward about the fact that Jim invited me to his home for dinner before I left Dekker's office this afternoon.

6.

I HAVE THIS COUSIN NAMED JANET. She's here, in Timperly, in her last year at Westcock. She started out in a General Arts program but in second year switched to Political Science, and then to Psychology mid-term. My parents were keen for me to spend time with Janet when I first got here because of course it was the big bad town of Timperly and my first time going to big bad university, and the sophisticated and worldly-wise Janet, who'd been living and studying here an entire two years already, could act as my guide and mentor. Therefore I made it my business to avoid Janet whenever possible. On my first day in town, she and I and my parents all had dinner together at the Crowfeather Inn. Janet went on and on about the library's new catalogue system and how unbelievably complicated it was and how it took her forever to figure out, reassuring my parents she would walk me through it however many times it took to sink into my pulpy high-school brain.

Meanwhile, all I could think about was my weird childhood memory of Janet, who one afternoon plucked G.I. Joe from out of my hands and asked him, using Barbie like a puppet, if he wanted to take her—Barbie's—clothes off.

Except Janet never called her Barbies "Barbie"—she always gave them names like Nancy or Priscilla or Penelope. And, not even consulting me, Janet had my G.I. Joe respond in the affirmative. "Affirmative," she had him say. She was keeping Joe in military character, I suppose, even though she insisted on having Barbie call him "Matthew." I sat there and watched this performance for a while—interested, I grant you, because the fact is, the first thing I did whenever I got hold of Janet's Barbies was to rip their clothes off and tap on their hard plastic breasts. There was not much else to do with naked Barbies—turn them this way and that, fondle the unyielding plastic, and feel strangely thwarted.

So Janet and I never went to check out the library catalogue. She called a few days after my parents hopped the ferry back to PEI, and I told her I had already gone to one of the free orientation seminars the library was offering around the clock that first week. I may have sounded snotty when I said this, but Janet didn't care. She'd officially paid for her meal at the Crowfeather Inn. Now she could call home with a clean conscience. *Did you call Larry about the library?—Yes, Mom and Dad, I did.* Sometimes we'd wave to one another from across the quad.

I've scarcely run into her at all this year. We never called each other after that, never had coffee, lunch, or a beer like our parents expected, and neither of us—I felt I could safely assume—suffered a twinge of guilt leading our independent, Westcock lives.

Anyway, now I feel horrible. The delayed guilt comes rushing and babbling over me like high tide when my parents call to tell me Janet is pregnant.

It's a big deal for the Campbells and Humphrieses of PEI, who, have I mentioned, are Presbyterian. Our grandmother heads up the local Temperance Society. To elucidate: we come from a place with a temperance society, and my grand-mother heads it up. Janet apparently went home early this month for Thanksgiving, and the family pronounced her tubby. Aunt Maud neglected to offer Janet gravy come suppertime. Uncle Stan asked if she'd been getting enough exercise. Cousin Wayne reverted to using her childhood nickname of "Chubs." Janet broke down when dessert was passed around and Grandma Lydia "forgot" to add the expected scoop of ice cream to her pumpkin pie.

"Darn it all!" Janet is reported to have sobbed. "I'm eating for two, ya know!"

Boom, went the table. My parents were there, plus, as I've already noted, my temperate Presbyterian grandma, Lydia Humphries.

"Nonsense," Lydia kept saying. "Nonsense." I know she said this, because this is the thing Lydia says when she is angriest of all. She said it when I was ten and allowed myself to be flung from the tire swing in her yard only to alight on a much doted-on patch of black-eyed Susans. "What is this nonsense?" she wheezed, appearing on the porch without her sun hat. The lack of a sun hat, I remember, terrified me. And honest to God, she looked at the flowers but not at me, didn't even ask if I was hurt—just headed straight for the crabapple tree from which the tire swing was suspended and for some reason yanked off a branch. And even though I'd never been exposed to such a thing in my life, some kind of universal childhood knowledge kicked in when I heard the crack of the bough being ripped from the tree. I understood that crack to be a prologue of sorts, an audio hint of what was to come. She was cutting a switch was what she was doing. I always thought you could do that only with willow branches, but I guess Grandma Lydia was improvising that day. My father yanked me off my ass and through the back door, and together we hid in my grandmother's bathroom—Dad pretending all the while that we were there to clean me up—as my mother talked Lydia down from her tower of rage.

That's the first thing I think when I think of Janet at the Thanksgiving table. I imagine Lydia with her switch. I imagine her reaching over to snap Janet's neck between her pink, paper-skinned fingers with their prim old-lady rings. Lydia would have become very still, almost stupid, like a drugged animal. *Nonsense!* Reach, *snap*. It's the only word she knows in that state.

Another crazily vivid memory I have of Lydia. I broke my nose when I was twelve, playing softball. Lydia doesn't have anything to do with this particular part of the memory— anyone would remember breaking their nose. I remember it because it hurt, and because it was the last time I ever played softball, or any sport. There were these guys on the team. They knew I didn't belong there, that I was the kind of kid who was playing because his father yearned for him to do something male and normal. They knew I didn't enjoy it the way they did. That it didn't drive me absolutely crazy when the other team stole a base or made a really great hit, that I just couldn't bring myself to care as much as I was supposed to about an entire afternoon of throwing and hitting and catching and running and throwing and hitting and catching and running. I was an outfielder, of course. I would loiter on the grass thinking about Leonard Cohen, and there were at least a couple of guys on the team who I swear could actually *see* that this was the sort of thing I was standing around thinking about. Therefore whenever we practised, they threw the ball not *to* me, but *at* me, as hard as they could. It always looked very innocent—a vigorous game of catch among high-spirited boys—but for the most part it was guys like Barnard Leary trying to hit me in the head, and me trying to avoid being hit in the head. It was probably only my fifth practice or so when Leonard Cohen or whomever it was I happened to be thinking about got the better of me. I was remembering this really sexy poem that used the word *breasts*—not the singular, *breast,* in the Shakespeare way where it just means chest, but *breasts.* It was my first poem that mentioned breasts. And it was describing the shapes of them—the breasts. And I was thinking about how if these guys knew how much smut there was in poetry books, they would be lining up at the library and poring over them the way they did in grade 5 looking up words like "titular" in the dictionary. Then I was hit in the face.

How else to say it? There's no poetic way of saying hit in the face. I was hit in the face, then I was on my back, and bleeding bleeding bleeding from a broken nose. I didn't know what to do with all the blood. I still can't remember the thought process that led to it, but I took off my shoe, yanked off a sweat sock, and held it to my face. I must've done this in a split second—people were running toward me, but no one had yet arrived.

Anyway, that's not the important memory. It is awful to break your nose, and I looked like a circus freak for a couple of weeks as my face swelled up with fluid and the flesh around my eyes went black, then blue, then greeny-yellow. It was summer, and summer often meant hanging out at Grandma Lydia's because her house was close to the beach, whereas our motel was by necessity on the highway, and my parents were always frantic during tourist season. So I dragged my bloated head back and forth across Lydia's kitchen all summer long, not wanting to go out because I was grotesque. My grandmother not being much of a beach-goer herself, we hung out together baking bread and drinking lemonade, reading our respective books—Lydia enjoyed the great moralizers like Bunyan and Milton—on the porch.

I mostly avoided the tire swing by this point in our relationship.

So here's the memory: Lydia was cutting out sugar cookies, and I was placing slivers of maraschino cherries in the centre of each one. I, as I have said, was twelve, and trying to talk about literature. Lydia, I had noticed, was the only person in my family who really read the way I did. She read for hours— it was the way she filled her days between meals and pots of tea. She didn't quilt or do any of the crafty gramma stuff. She may have crocheted an afghan or two, but only as a begrudging nod to her gramma status. Mostly she went to her temperance meetings and to church. She had dinners with my family and Janet's. But I always got the feeling that Lydia was like me in that everything she did when she wasn't reading was, in her mind, just that—not-reading. That is to say, everything else in her life was, on some level, an interruption.

I guess I thought Lydia might be a kindred spirit. I knew practically nothing about books, but I knew Milton was old and important. I had snuck a peek at *Paradise Lost* but found it impossible to follow. It was full of footnotes aiming to assist twentieth-century illiterates, but these just distracted and frustrated me all the more, seeming to taunt: *you don't understand, do you?* Of course, I found this intolerable. I thought Lydia could help.

It could be that I had been annoying her for the past half hour with my suggestions that we try putting half of a maraschino cherry on the cookies instead of a mere sliver— or, heaven forbid, why not an entire maraschino cherry. The slivers seemed to me minuscule—almost a cruel joke, considering the blandness of Lydia's cookies in general. They were white and hard and, to be honest, sugar cookies only in name. To the twelve-year-old palate they more closely resembled dense, stale crackers. Lydia had told me once that her cookies were so hard because she made them for dipping in tea. I remember being vaguely outraged by this. If the only confections my grandmother ever bothered to make were for dipping in tea, then whom, exactly, was she making them for? I figured out early on it couldn't be me. If I really wanted to flatter myself, I might've conjectured that the maraschino slivers only came along once I started showing an interest in the cookies—Lydia's idea of a grandmotherly gesture, perhaps. But please. If the slivers were for me, they were an insult. If anything, they were Lydia's nod to aesthetics—mere decoration. Positively baroque in her mind.

But at twelve, I still harboured hope for Lydia's cookies—for me and Lydia in general. We both liked books, we both liked quiet. It seemed to me we had things to say to one another.

Here's where it gets vivid—insanely so. Late-afternoon streams of sunshine coming in through Lydia's lace curtains, casting filigree shadows on the kitchen table. The perfect stillness of a summer afternoon in the middle of nowhere, just far enough away from the beach to not be bothered by the sound of breakers or people having fun. The only noise in the room was the dry rasp of Lydia's ancient refrigerator. It seemed too hot outside for birds—some afternoons are like that, hot and still and birdless. I'd long since given up arguing about the cherries but thought it would be cute and endearing of me to try to sneak a couple of halves onto the occasional cookie anyway. Lydia was having none of it. She'd pluck the cherry from the centre of the cookie and flick it back onto the cutting board for me to dissect into respectable slivers. When I kept at it, she reached out to smack me on the hand.

A low growl: "Stop the nonsense."

I did stop the nonsense after a couple of smacks on the hand—nobody can accuse me otherwise. Maybe I did go a little too far dissecting the cherries after that. My slivers eventually became almost transparent—so insubstantial I could scarcely manoeuvre them from my fingers into the centre of the cookies. It got to be as though each cookie had a teeny-tiny red freckle in the middle of it. Anyway, Lydia did not complain or grunt "nonsense" over the freckles, so I assumed all was sweetness and light between us.

The hardest thing about the age of twelve for me was that twilight state. The state of still being a kid but getting my first inklings of the realities of not being a kid anymore. When you're a kid, people smile at you almost like a reflex. They like you automatically, it seems, and wish you well, not just because you're cute but because you're so *blank*. That is, there is nothing about you to dislike just yet, so everyone is pretty much on your side. I don't mean other kids—no, I figured that out long before it was driven home to me with the ball in the face. But adults. You assume they're on your side, at least. And it's around the age of twelve when these assumptions begin to fall into question. You're too big to be cute, your voice is getting weird, your teeth are sticking out, you start to think it's funny to mess with other people's ideas of how a sugar cookie should be.

"Grandma," I said, furiously puréeing one of Lydia's cherries with my knife. "Do you like *Paradise Lost*?"

"Milton is one of the giants of literature," my grandmother said.

"It's about Adam and Eve, right?"

"It is," said Lydia, rolling out a new batch of yolk-tinted dough. "It is about The Fall."

"Isn't it hard to read?"

"Anything worth doing should challenge one."

This threw me off track a little. "Uh," I said. "Really?"

"That's how you know it's worth doing. The Bible is a challenging book as well."

I felt depressed. You know how that is? Sometimes it just

wafts over you like stale air. I couldn't believe she and I were talking about the same thing, the thing that I had only recently begun to identify as—not to put too fine a point on it—my salvation. But Lydia talked about books like she would a hairshirt or a crown of thorns. It made me tired to hear it. But I pushed on and I shouldn't have.

"Well," I said, casually decimating another cherry, "I tried to read some, but I couldn't get anywhere with it."

I shrugged, thinking I sounded pretty adult. I hadn't whined, "I can't understand it," like a kid would do, even though this was actually the case. Already I was cultivating a handy nonchalance toward work I didn't get, which would eventually serve me well in Jim's seminar. The shrug, however, was the *pièce de resistance,* meant to convey, Oh well, perhaps old Milty and I just aren't meant to get along. Ho-hum. Back to Chaucer I go.

I looked up from my maraschino paste to see if Lydia appreciated any of this. Then I saw red.

Not like anger. Like a bright burst of pain in the centre of my face, blinding me.

"Nonsense!" I heard from somewhere.

When the red lifted, she'd gone back to rolling out the dough. She'd flicked me. She'd flicked me on the nose so quick I didn't even see it.

"Wha—" I said. It was a noise that was a question. It was the closest sound I could make to an actual question mark, because the pain, and what's more, the surprise of the pain, left me incoherent. Tears were streaming down my face.

"You're not to be reading such stuff at your age," Lydia said, flipping the blank canvas of dough over and rolling and flattening it into a yellowed wafer-thinness that matched the set of her Presbyterian lips.

That is my memory of Grandma Lydia. That is the only memory I need.

———

This is all a long-winded way of saying, Poor Janet, at Thanksgiving dinner. Words I doodle into my notebook while talking on the phone with my parents. I'm expected to call her now. And go see her. Bring her food. Rub her feet. Who knows what. I am the only member of the family close by.

"They let her come back to school?" I say, surprised.

"Well, Grammie and Uncle Stan didn't want her to," concedes my mother.

"I'd say the damage is pretty much done," says Dad. "You don't put a girl through school for four years so she can throw it all away."

"Even though that's what she done anyhow," completes my mother.

"Who's the father?" I ask.

"She says nobody."

Nobodaddy. Like with Blake.

"Some arsehole," extrapolates Dad. "One of them hippie professors is my guess."

"Oh, no," I say, wanting to guide my father away from his "hippie professor" theories in general. I should show him Bryant Dekker and his clean-shaven neck some time.

"Well, I wouldn't be surprised," grunts Dad. "All them draft-dodger Yankees coming over here with the free love and what have you."

"Dad," I say, "these people are *scholars.*"

"Well la-de-fuck," says Dad.

The F-word always sends my mother into pained and scandalized titters—the legacy of a repressive Humphries upbringing. "Stop it, Dad," she giggles.

"But is she going to finish?" I say, trying to get the two of them back on track.

"Who?" giggles Mom.

"Janet."

"Yes!" says Mom.

"She'll be ready to drop come final exams," remarks my father.

"How many months is she now?"

"Around three."

I count on my fingers. "She'll just make it, maybe."

Mom says, "I'm sure they'll give her an exemption or something if she can't."

Dad says, "Oh, they will not. Let a girl out of exams to go have a baby!"

"Well, if they're reasonable."

"Reasonable!" Dad yelps in a spasm of hilarity. "Oh, excuse me, I can't write my final exams because I have to go have this here illegitimate baby. Oh, that's fine now, dear, you just go right ahead and give us a call when you're finished up."

"Hey!" I say. "Janet was home working at the museum last summer, wasn't she?"

My parents rumble noises like yes.

"Well, there you go, it didn't happen here at all. It was someone from back home."

The two of them are silenced, so happily assured were they that such a calamity could only take place in the Sodom that exists off-island.

"Hippie professors!" I start to gloat.

"No, no, no," says Dad. "I remember she did go back for a week in early August to set up her apartment, now, so there ya go."

"No, no, no," I sing back at him. "Aunt Maud came with her, it couldn't have happened then."

"She coulda snuck out."

"Oh, for God's sake, Dad, there were just as many opportunities for Janet to get pregnant hanging out on the beach all summer at home."

"Bullshit," mutters Dad.

"Nonsense," echoes my mother.

"Could've been a tourist, I suppose," Dad amends after a moment.

"Anyway," I say, "what am *I* supposed to do for her?"

"Just be around," says my mother. "Make yourself available."

"Keep an eye on her for Stan and Maudie," says Dad.

"Get her things," adds Mom.

"I'm not going to spy on her."

"Nobody's telling you to spy on her," says Dad. "But if that little bastard shows his face, you file a report."

"The little bastard is over there somewhere with you guys," I sigh.

"I'll believe it when I see it," says Dad. "Meanwhile, you keep an eye out."

"I'm very busy with school right now, you know."

At this point I've dragged the phone over to my closet, started pulling out shirts and pants. I wonder how I'm supposed to look for supper at Jim's.

"Larry," calls my mother, like she can sense my attention wandering, "Janet has ruined her life *forever.*"

I freeze in the middle of fingering a hand-knit sweater I got for high-school graduation.

"Do you understand that?" my mother interrogates.

"Mom," I say, "Janet will be okay. She'll have a degree—"

Dad snorts, and via that snort, I suddenly see the future as they do. Janet passing the rest of her life at home with Stan and Maud. Taking tickets—ticket after ticket—just as she's done every summer since junior high at the Hollywood Horrors Wax Museum. Endless hellfire dinners, with Lydia ablaze at the end of the table.

7.

THE WHOLE TIME I was on the phone with my parents, I kept having to stop myself from asking them what to wear and how to behave tonight at Jim's. I can only assume that if they knew, they would have imparted such knowledge to me long ago—it would be an instinct by now. As it stands, I'm on my own.

Remember that this is university, and this is 1975, and this is poetry, first and foremost. It's not like going to Aunt Maud's for Thanksgiving. Jim himself never dresses up. If anything, he dresses down—the more auspicious the occasion, the mustier Jim's attire. Last year at the department Christmas party he showed up caked in ice. I don't think it was deliberate—apparently his car had broken down a little over halfway between Rock Point and the university, and, it being an ice storm, there was no one on the road to give him a lift. So Jim trudged for an hour or so and showed up looking like Jack Frost, right down to the icicle hanging from his nose. I remember how Doctor Sparrow looked. Doctor Sparrow was wearing a blazer and a festive red turtleneck and kept sucking the ice cubes out of his drink and crunching them to bits in his mouth. ("He's keeping them cool in there," I overheard somebody say.) Jim had one of those parkas you can buy at Canadian Tire, with fake fur trimming the hood. The fake fur was completely matted with ice, and he dripped wherever he went—you could map his movements by the splats on the carpet. I remember I had hoped to speak to Jim that night, but he took forever to show up and had a boisterous crowd around him the moment he did, wanting to know what had turned him into the abominable snowman. So I just sat by the food table eating clumps of cheese off of toothpicks until I started to feel disgusting. What did Joyce call cheese? Corpse of milk. That's how the cheese started to taste after a while. The next day, I hopped the ferry home for the holidays, thinking I might as well stay there for all I was getting out of my university years.

Now my patience has paid off. Another thing to remember is that I'll be meeting Jim's wife. I can't dress like a total slob. The fact is, Jim's Jim and I'm not. I can't get away with work pants and a Stanfield's T-shirt, like Jim had on underneath his parka the night of the party. I'll wear the hand-knit graduation sweater and comb my hair. I'll bring my notebook with the new poems just in case. I see the three of us—Jim and me and Moira—sitting around by the fire drinking hot toddies late into the night, Jim and me reading our poetry to one another as Moira sits listening, her face one of pensive contentment. Just as Jim describes her in his poem "Erato."

"Hey, man," greets Todd Smiley. "Like, your hair is parted and everything."

Todd is wearing work pants and a Stanfield's T-shirt. A grubby old man's cardigan completes the ensemble. He looks every inch the poet.

"Hey, Todd," I say, taking a seat in Jim's sitting room. "Hi, Professor Dekker," I add, leaning over to shake Dekker's hand. "Hi, Chuck," I say to my old dorm-mate Charles Slaughter, who is sprawled on the other side of the room in an enormous armchair. "How've you been?" I ask in a loud voice, trying to drown out my surprise.

Chuck waves his beer at me by way of response.

"You look like you're going to communion," cracks Todd.

"Please. I'm Presbyterian," I crack back, very cool. "Out, heathen."

"Ah," smiles Dekker. "Sectarian conflict. How old-world."

Todd flashes a look at Dekker. He takes this stuff seriously.

"You guys talking about religion over there?" Chuck drawls from his throne across the room. "Jesus, Campbell. You sure know how to get a party going."

We all laugh, for some reason. Maybe relief—Todd seems to be throwing sparks tonight. Then again, Slaughter—whatever the hell he's doing here—has a strange way about him. He brings his own kind of electricity to a room. I couldn't figure it out when we lived together in Hadwin and I can't figure it out now—but he's immensely, inexplicably, likeable as well. He is huge and frightening and has called me "fuckwit" since the day I met him. He is not particularly interesting aside from his horrific size and his ability to maim on the football field. Yet Chuck can do no wrong. Guys love him, girls love him, profs love him—he's just one of those guys. That must be how he got himself invited this evening. Even Jim loves him.

"Hey, Chuck," I say, leaning forward. "I didn't know you knew Jim."

Slaughter waves his beer around some more. "Oh yeah, we go way back."

Enter Jim from the kitchen, where he disappeared after leading me here and inserting a bottle of Ten-Penny Ale into my fist. He looks for the most part like he always does—grizzled, slightly grimy. His face has a misty sheen from peering into some bubbling pot.

"How's everybody doing? Drinks okay?"

We all smile and grunt.

"Larry! You didn't meet my wife yet!"

Blink, and Jim disappears back into the kitchen. I hear the barky voice—short, clipped syllables. *Listen, I'm too fuckin' busy.* And, blink, Jim reappears again, his arm around a woman.

Tiny. Like a branch off a crabapple tree. Not overripe at all.

"Moira," says Jim.

I stand up, wondering if I should clamber over Todd, who's crouched on the floor, to shake her hand. Instead I sort of lean toward her slightly. Almost a bow.

"Nice to meet you," I say.

"Yeah," says Moira, scratching her scalp and looking around. "I didn't meet any of these other ones yet neither," she remarks to Jim.

Starting with me, Jim introduces us all by name. No one else stands, and so I sit. Slaughter does the beer-wave again.

"Good, then," says Moira. "I gotta get back and keep an eye on that stew."

Blink. So that's Erato. I can't get over how skinny and—and *gnarly* she is. Her speech is pure backwoods—a bit like Brenda L.'s.

When Jim returns, Todd starts digging around in his satchel and I instinctively clutch my own, thinking that perhaps some poetry will be read after all. But he pulls out a bottle of wine.

"Jim," he says, holding it out. "Before I forget."

Jim takes the wine, scrutinizing the label in appreciation. "Oh, very nice, there, Smiley, very good indeed. You didn't have to do that, now."

Jim told me not to bring anything. Suddenly I grow sultry in my graduation sweater—should I have brought something? Did Chuck Slaughter bring anything? Did Dekker bring anything? Are you supposed to bring something even when people tell you not to? And if so, how did Smiley, with his touted working-class background, happen to school himself in such social graces? Jim places the wine on the table alongside two other bottles. Two. One provided by Jim himself, the other perhaps by Dekker. But Slaughter is with me. He must be. Charles Slaughter wouldn't be caught dead toting a bottle of wine around.

"Anyone want some of this now?" it occurs to Jim to ask, gesturing to the wine.

"I'll stick with my beer," says Slaughter. I peer at him. He's drinking a different brand than everyone else. Kill myself.

Jim keeps blinking in and out of the kitchen, materializing to put on an album and light the fireplace and then ducking back through the swinging door to get more beer and check on Moira. It's nerve-wracking for me, the erratic jolts of Jim-adrenalin hitting my system every few minutes. I can scarcely concentrate on whatever conversation we manage to start while he's in the kitchen.

"How's the letter coming?" asks Dekker.

"It—" I begin.

"It's finished," says Todd. "We're ready to start collecting signatures Monday."

I look at Todd. "We should figure out some kind of strategy for that."

"Should be easy," shrugs Todd.

"Well, no, not easy," Dekker starts to say, but Jim descends on us with a clinking armful of Ten-Pennys.

"Beers all around!"

None of us are finished our original beers yet, but Jim is undeterred. "Just take it now," he says, shoving them at us, "and that way you're all looked after at once. Larry!" He clamps a hand down on my shoulder and I feel myself sink about an inch into his chesterfield. It feels like he's trying to push me between the cushions.

"Yes, Jim?" Thinking of the cushions remind me of the phone call where Jim was crying. It's hard to believe, looking at him now. He is all smiles and swinging gorilla arms.

"How ya doing?" He shakes me by the shoulder. "Ya good?"

"I'm great!" I beam up at him.

"How ya like that record? Ya like that record?"

It's an old-time country-and-western album twirling around on Jim's lopsided turntable. To my ears it sounds like a series of squeaks and whimpers. "I love it," I tell him.

"Goddamn right," says Jim. "That's Hank Snow right there."

"Oh," I say.

"Why don't you play some fuckin' music from this century?" Slaughter shouts from his throne. He's sitting so far away, I don't see how he can keep track of the conversation.

Jim waves one of his fanlike hands in Chuck's direction. "The philistine in our midst will not be acknowledged."

"You call me *Phyllis*?" demands Chuck, jerking forward in mock anger. Jim guffaws; his overbite could eat the world. I've never seen him guffaw. He's very different overall than how he usually seems. For one thing, he's got an accent like Moira's.

"We were just talking about the petition," says Todd, practically jumping up and down in his spot on the floor for Jim's attention.

Jim whirls around in the centre of the room—the circle of us—like we're all playing some kind of kid's birthday game. *Button, button, who's got the button?* I haven't seen him sit since I arrived.

"Oh, the petition," he drawls. "God love you fellas. How's it going?"

"We start collecting signatures Monday," I say.

"Well, God love you. All typed up and everything?"

"Yep," says Todd, before I can utter *Sherrie*.

Jim is looking restless from just standing engaging in conversation. I can see his long limbs starting to twitch with the desire to wander around and poke and arrange things. He makes a move toward the record player.

"Oh, I just gotta play this one. You fellas gotta hear this. I bought this down in the states—Kentucky," he says, thumbing through a series of albums stacked beneath the turntable. Then his accent shifts. "Not that I necessarily approve of American cultural infiltration, in fact I've pretty much had it up to here, everywhere you turn in this country you run up against Yankee garbage, but this kind of stuff, now—this took place long before the nation as a whole sold itself to the highest bidder. This could cauterize the wounds of that particular transaction if anyone gave a shit anymore, which no one does . . ." He finds what he's looking for, shuffles it out of its jacket, and holds the record out to check for scratches and dust. Then, with the delicacy of a surgeon, he places it onto the turntable and lowers the needle.

More whimpers and squeaks. We all sit and listen for a moment, Jim with his eyes closed. Keeping them closed, he says, "I just want to thank you boys again for everything you're doing. Except for you, Slaughter—as usual you've done dick-all." His eyes pop open, twinkling, to see that Slaughter is showing him a listless middle finger. "Anyhow," Jim resumes following a short, toothy guffaw, "I want you all to know how much I appreciate it. But tonight's not the night for worrying about any of that bullshit. Tonight's just a night for friends, all right? Friends and poetry."

He smiles down on us like Jesus in a painting. The next moment, he's tornadoing into the kitchen, shouting merry orders at his wife.

Three hours later and dinner is yet to be served and I am starving and have guzzled three beers and am having a wonderful time. Jim designated the evening a night of friends and poetry, so Todd and I got right to it—the poetry part, at least. We poked around the bookshelves together at Jim's invitation, me feeling overwhelmed by all the stuff I hadn't read and knew I should—*George Herbert! I haven't even gotten to George Herbert yet!*—and Todd throwing out commentary about everything, as if he'd devoured every single volume by junior high. ("Oh, Jacques Prévert—God it's been such a long time . . .") At some point we started discussing Rimbaud, who I think was a prophet and who Todd keeps saying was a fruit. I wave my arms and tell him that's no kind of argument, but Todd says he doesn't care, he thinks Rimbaud stank and was a fruit.

"Campbell," interrupts Charles Slaughter after having sat listening to us with his face in a knot of distaste. "It's bad enough you like poetry, are you telling me you like *fag* poetry?"

"Look!" I huff, aware I'm being baited but enjoying it somewhat. "It's *all* fag poetry. I mean, poetry is faggy in general, I've accepted that long ago—"

"Well, this is pretty much the thrust of my complaint," says Chuck.

"Excuse me," Todd interrupts. "Poetry is *not* 'faggy in general.' I don't know what you guys think you're talking about. Robert Service!"

I groan and hold my head. "It rhymes!" I say before I can recall that Todd's poetry rhymes too.

"So what?" thunders Todd.

Chuck spreads his hands. "Sorry, man," he says. "Rhyming is gay."

Dekker has his fingers entwined across his chest, very much the professor. "The future of literary discourse," he remarks.

"I mean," I say, "I've been told my whole life poetry is not manly. Okay! I accept that! It's not manly—fuck it, I like it anyway."

Todd shakes his whole body like a wet dog. "No, no, no, that's the old way of thinking. Campbell, you're living a hundred years in the past." He holds his fist in front of my face and starts counting off fingers. "It's *not* about rich people, it's *not* about privilege and decadence, it's *not* a bunch of counts and lords walking around in a field of daffodils, wandering lonely as a cloud wearing monocles and cravats. It's about real people living real lives! Working and fucking and hunting and scraping out a living . . . and *community* and *family*."

"Family?" I repeat, horrified.

"Todd," interrupts Dekker, "Rimbaud was no aristocrat."

"Yeah, but my point is," says Todd, turning feverishly to glance at the actual authority in our midst, "it's not about that visionary shit anymore. It's about *real* life and *real* people. The concrete. Blood, sweat, and tears."

"Visionary shit," muses Dekker.

I'm about to tell Todd he is crazy. If poetry is about real life and real people, then I should be writing about Grandma Lydia's sugar cookies and working at the mini-putt all summer. I should be writing about my dad's curling sweater. Poetry—I'm about to quote T.S. Eliot—is an escape from reality, not an embrace of it. Or something like that. I don't quote it because I'll never hear the end of it from Todd if I get it wrong. But *escape* is the operative word. *It's an escape, an escape!* I want to wave my arms and yell. Then Todd shuts me up. He throws down his trump card, as it were.

"Like Jim writes," he says, folding his skinny white arms.

"Like I write," says Jim, emerging sweaty from the kitchen. "I assume you've been discussing *brilliant fucking poetry* up to this point."

"Yeah, we have," drawls Charles Slaughter. "I'm about ready to shit my pants just to change the subject."

"Don't do that," advises Jim. "Dinner's served."

What time is it, ten o'clock? Eleven? I stand up and my brain sort of wobbles in its fluid, reminding me of last month's hangover. I should be careful. I should eat a big dinner. I should ask for some water. I look over at Todd and am gratified to see him stagger minutely and check to see if I'm looking.

Jim leads us to his huge slab of a dining-room table, covered with what appears to be a bedspread. There are rolls and butter and the two bottles of wine and a pile of knives and forks sitting in the centre of it, waiting to be claimed. Moira appears, cigarette dangling from the middle of her mouth, carrying a steaming cauldron that appears to weigh more than she does. She hefts it onto the table with a ponderous *slosh*.

"It took so long," she tells us, "because *this one* wanted dumplings." She points across the table at Jim. Lydia used to threaten to chop off fingers whenever we pointed. Like the farmer's wife, with a carving knife, in "Three Blind Mice."

Jim passes out cutlery, intoning, "You don't have stew without dumplings," like he's quoting Cicero or someone.

"They're just flour and water, and we already have rolls," Moira gripes, taking a seat. "I never made the damn things before in my life."

Dekker reaches to open one of the bottles of wine. "You weren't in there all night slaving over them, I hope," he says to Moira.

"No, no." She leans back in her chair, looking perfectly relaxed to be out among us at last. I had thought perhaps she was shy. "I got a TV in there to keep me occupied."

Dekker pops the wine and pours Moira a glass, which she seizes.

"Go easy on that," Jim tells her, filling bowls for each of us. He passes me one.

"This smells amazing," I say.

"Yes, yes," says Moira—I don't know to which one of us she is responding. "The potatoes wouldn't cook neither."

I poke at my stew. The potatoes are in a near-liquid state, like porridge.

"Larry! You didn't get a dumpling!" scolds Jim, splashing a mound of dough into the centre of my bowl. There are no napkins, so I wipe the splatters from my face with the sleeve of my graduation sweater.

Todd is already eating. "This is great!"

Slaughter is already finished. "I'd like another of them doughy things."

Dekker is intrigued by his dumpling. "What do you call these again, Jim?"

"Dumplings! Just like mother used to make. Some people call them 'doughboys' in these parts. Soak up the juice."

"Hm," says Dekker, chewing.

Jim pours everyone a glass of wine, placing each glassful beside the bottles of beer we all brought to the table. I realize, in my usual overly-self-conscious way, that this is one of the first sit-down dinners I've ever been to where a blessing has not been said. It leaves me with a strange feeling of incompletion—or maybe it's something as banal as a violated sense of my own entrenched Presbyterian propriety.

At that moment Jim raises a glass, as if he's read my mind, felt my itch for ceremony. He hasn't even let himself sit down yet.

"To friends and poetry."

"Oh, Christ," Charles Slaughter sighs, wiping his mouth with the bedspread tablecloth.

"All right," amends Jim, laughing. "Poetry later. To friends. To good friends—the real thing."

We raise our glasses and clink. I stand to make sure my glass connects with Jim's—we're on opposite sides of the table from one another. He looks me in the eye and winks.

Somehow I end up on the couch beside Moira. I am kind of annoyed. When I got up to go to the bathroom I had been having a pretty wonderful conversation with Jim about what Todd said earlier. How poetry's not about visionary shit anymore, or being written by fops and courtiers about their pansified concerns. Jim warmed me with his response to Todd, he warmed me to my centre like a hot gulp from the teapot. He said, in essence, Todd was wrong. He said Todd is excited by the kind of poetry that is being written now, and for good reason—because it speaks to him personally, it speaks to his background. Suddenly the experience of people like us *(us!)* is no longer being dismissed, explained Jim. It counts for something. But that doesn't mean, he said, that we don't have anything to learn from those who have come before us.

"Rimbaud was just some hick from a farm!" I burbled at this point.

"Rimbaud was just some hick from a farm," agreed Jim. *Like us, like us.* "He didn't let that limit him. He didn't let that stifle his imagination."

"That's exactly what I was trying to say!"

I was bursting to talk about a hundred other things with Jim, realizing this was the moment I'd been waiting for since the day I came to Timperly. Intimate friendship with Jim Arsenault, conversing like old pals over beers in his living room. I could hardly contain myself. At that moment, however, the same was true of my bladder—I hadn't used the bathroom since I'd arrived, afraid I might miss an opportunity just like this one. So I excused myself, wincing with pain and reluctance, and made my way to the kitchen. I had to go through the kitchen to get to the bathroom—like in a lot of old houses, it had been installed as close to the wood stove as possible. Grandma Lydia has a similarly unappetizing set-up in her evil, be-doilied hut.

The kitchen looked as though a couple of bags of flour had exploded therein, followed by a minor typhoon. The strangest thing, however, was the dog. There was a dog just sitting there, in the middle of the flour, staring at me as if I was the bizarre apparition instead of it. I didn't remember seeing a dog last time I was at Jim's. As I stared back, it got to its feet, went to the corner of the room to acquire a brownish tennis ball, carried the tennis ball back to where it—the dog—had originally been sitting, and placed it—the ball— on the floor. Then it sat down to resume looking at me. When I smiled, it ducked its head and nudged the ball so that it rolled toward my feet.

I kicked the ball slightly, heading to the toilet, but the dog sprang to its feet and began to spin around in rapid circles, barking its head off. The thing looked to be taking a fit—I was expecting to see foam at any moment. It wouldn't stop barking. I shushed at it and waved my arms, which made it bark louder. Somehow I'd driven Jim's dog insane.

"Don't throw that dog the ball!" Moira shouted from the next room.

"Okay!" I sang back. "Shh!" I said to the dog. The dog shrieked barks back at me, so loud its voice cracked. I thought it was going to be sick.

"If you throw the ball, it just gets him more excited!" Moira yelled.

"Okay!" I ran to the bathroom and shut the door. The barking stopped like a recording had been switched off.

I stood there for a while after I'd used the toilet, looking around. There was no tub, no shower either. I wondered where Jim and Moira bathed. I explored the medicine cabinet. Aspirins and anti-flatulent.

When I came out, the dog was sitting in the same spot, with the filthy ball in its mouth. It placed the ball on the floor the moment I stepped across the threshold, then lifted its beady eyes to meet mine—aglint with psychotic readiness.

———

Of course Jim was gone from the chesterfield by the time I manoeuvred my way out of the kitchen, replaced by Moira, who sat alone viciously biting her nails.

God, stop that, I wanted to say when I sat down beside her. She was chewing away at the cuticle of her thumb with a sick, desperate fervour—the way you imagine wolves in leg traps would gnaw at their own ensnared limbs.

After Moira explained to me one final time that I must never play ball with the dog, as it "only gets him riled up," I sat down and asked, needing to change the subject, so how did you and Jim meet? She hasn't stopped talking since.

At this point I don't even remember what her original answer was. Jim is huddled by the record player arguing with Charles Slaughter about the finer points of bluegrass music. Todd is talking beseechingly of Robert Service to Professor Dekker.

Moira is saying:

"Well, my brother's in jail now, but I'm keeping his things for him whenever he gets out, but we don't know when he's getting out because he got himself in quite a bit of trouble and he never told us what. Like, million-dollar trouble, he said. So he's in jail down in the States and there's nothing we can do about it—don't know why he's there or what he did. But anyway, he sends me all his things, so God knows what all's in there, but I write him and I tell him I'm gonna sell half this crap because we're dead broke and if you're in million-dollar trouble, why don't you send us some? But he's in jail, right, so he can't do nothing one way or the other. And he's just: whatever you do, don't sell my dragon blade. And I would never, ever do that because I know how much that thing means to him. It's like this blade that you throw, he got it from Thailand, like ancient Thailand fighters used it or something and—you should see this thing. I don't know what the hell it's made of but it's perfectly balanced. It just feels, like, powerful in your hand—you can feel the power coming off it. I threw it into an oak tree once, this huge, thousand-year-old oak, and you know what? Tree died. Dead. So this thing, you know, if I were to sell it we'd probably be set for life, but I'd never do that to him, it's all he's got left."

Chew, chew, gnaw, masticate—the whole time her fist is practically in her mouth, she's got some kind of oral fixation—I wish she'd have a smoke. I stare at her and slurp at my wine and try to feel some kind of attraction, but Moira is nothing like I imagined. She doesn't have the welcoming cushiness of Brenda L. to her. She's all edges and angles—pointy shoulders, jutting collarbone—with epic circles under her eyes. Jim describes her in his poems as having a face like the Madonna, a moonface, radiating bliss and wisdom like you see in paintings. Similarly, I seem to recall, he describes her as silent. That's also how the virgin is depicted—smiling, close-mouthed like the Mona Lisa. Soft and round.

The other thing is, Moira's talk is crazy talk. *Tree died. Dragon blade.* Or perhaps there is some kind of secret profundity behind it all that I am too drunk to detect. What did Jim call it? *The muse's antique lying language.*

I'm sitting on the floor trying to tell Jim two things. One, that I read and enjoyed his review of Dermot Schofield's chapbook in *Atlantica*. Two, that I am sorry not to have brought the bottle of wine I purchased specifically for this evening, and I would have to bring it to him at a later date.

"Don't worry about it, Larry, we're not hurting for booze around here."

"—left it sitting on my kitchen table—don't know what I was thinking."

"Ah, you can have it yourself when you get home."

"Can I have a glass of water?" I say, but my question gets lost in the conversation. Jim has brought out a bottle of whisky, handed out glasses, and plunked it into the centre of the room along with the basket of uneaten buns from dinner. I'm finding the whisky strong, but it isn't so bad if I take a bite of bun with every sip. All of us are sitting on the floor except Slaughter and Moira. She's still up on the chesterfield, and Slaughter hasn't left his throne.

"I don't know what I'm gonna do with that cocksucker when he gets here," Jim is saying to Dekker.

"Just go through the motions," Dekker replies. "Let him do his reading, put him up for the night."

"I'll be damned if I'm putting him up here."

"I doubt the department will spring for a hotel room."

"I'll pay out of my own pocket if I have to."

I figure out they're talking about Schofield. When I babbled his name earlier, Jim went off on a bit of a tangent, and now, I realize, he's still on it.

"Schofield's coming here?" I ask.

Jim twists his mouth. "I invited him. Back before I knew what he was capable of."

"What was he capable of?"

Dekker starts to answer with a grin, but Jim gets there first, reaching toward the centre of the room for the whisky bottle. "Bad faith. Bad poetry."

"Come on now, Jim," says Dekker.

"You come on, Bryant."

"Your review of *Malignant Cove* was great," I say, because it seems as if Jim needs cheering all of a sudden. "Did I tell you that already?"

He whirls on me. "My review was *honest*—that was my purpose in writing it. It was a reaction precisely against the mincing, rubber-spined pabulum someone like Schofield is spewing from his professor's chair at York or wherever the hell he is."

Todd, whose chin has been bobbing around on his chest for the past half hour or so, manages to hoist his head upright at this.

"Malignant Cove is in Nova Scotia," he slobbers, the slack of his mouth kind of reminding me of Janet, ten years old and immersed in her Barbie pornography. "Is he from Nova Scotia?"

"It doesn't matter where he's from anymore," instructs Jim. "He's cast his lot with the cynics and whores of Upper Canada."

"He sounds like an asshole!" I enthuse. This wins me a grim nod from Jim.

"Malignant Cove is a real place?" says Dekker, leaning toward Todd.

"Yeah—a place. It's about like it sounds," Todd slurs into his chest.

Dekker shakes his head again. He's been doing that a lot this evening. "This is a fascinating part of the country," he says, leaning back in Jim's rocking chair with a tight, pleased smile on his black-stubbled face. I wonder where the hell he's from anyway.

I'm happy to note that every time Todd or Dekker disappears into the kitchen on his way to the bathroom, a round of frenzied barking ensues. It wasn't something about me personally that maddened Jim's dog. Chuck Slaughter would seem to be lacking a bladder—he hasn't budged all night. Maybe all the piss has been steadily trickling out of him throughout the evening, soaking Jim's armchair. My grandfather Humphries was like that near the end. Maybe that's why Slaughter never stands up.

The dog's name, I've determined from Moira's kitchen-ward shouts of reproach and instruction, is Panda. Jim named it Pan originally, but Moira tells me she thought it was stupid.

Now we are packed in Jim's car heading downtown to steal the flag with the misplaced quotation marks from Rory Scarsdale Holdings—*"Ask For Rory!"* I can't remember how this got decided, but I must have started it. I told them about "Ham Dinner" at the Legion back home, giving the lawn a "trim." We are all convulsed, laughing and making quotation marks in the air with our fingers every time one of us says something. Only Slaughter is oblivious to the hilarity. Slaughter is driving and foaming at the mouth over Scarsdale. From Chuck I have recently learned that Scarsdale also runs the Mariner—a bar at the bottom of town by the railway station, where all the locals go. Slaughter says he got kicked out of it once, by Scarsdale himself and his "goons."

"Buncha fuckin' townie rubes figured they'd kick the shit outta me, Scarsdale doesn't lift a goddamn finger."

Chuck is bubbling away on the topic of Scarsdale like an overcooked stew. We're laughing because he hasn't ceased his litany since we left Jim's place. It's remarkable. After seven hours of warming Jim's armchair, drinking beer and only occasionally complaining about how dull an evening he was having, Slaughter suddenly came alive. He leapt from the chair at the name of Scarsdale, seized up Jim's telephone, and started maniacally dialing numbers with his cigar-sized fingers. He was calling Rory Scarsdale, we eventually deciphered from the stream of obscenities—calling him right then and there—although God only knew how Chuck could have had his number memorized, he might have been calling his parents for all we knew.

Conversation stopped as Slaughter stood panting, dominating the centre of Jim's sitting room. It was no wonder he'd

scarcely stood up all night, I realized, looking up at him from
the floor with a bun hanging out of my mouth—the place
was too small for him. He listened for a moment, waiting for
someone to pick up on the other end of the line. I was wondering what time it was again when I heard Slaughter furiously suck in a breath—*Hup!*—in order to scream into the
phone, *"Fuck you Scarsdale you flabby piece of shit I wouldn't
set foot in your goddamn rat-infested shithouse if somebody set it
on fire and stuck my own mother in there I'd just let her burn
up 'n be caught dead in that fucking little pisshole you with your
goddamn flag don't even know how to use fucking quotation
marks you illiterate ignorant inbred why don't you go screw your
sister some more, asshole? Then who you gonna throw outta your
fag-hole fuckin' bar?"*

Charles slammed down the receiver and threw his fists
into the air, shuffling his feet back and forth like
Muhammad Ali. We applauded out of fear and wonder.
Somehow from this emerged the consensus that we had to go
and get the flag outside Scarsdale Holdings. It was an
obscenity, we determined—a flapping and dangling insult to
literate men everywhere. Moira said she was going to bed.

Jim is in the front seat. I am all cuddled up in the back
between Dekker and Todd, my legs bunched because of the
hump in the centre. Todd should really be sitting here,
because he is the shortest, but he told me he gets sick sitting in the middle, which I assumed to be a load of shit.
But before I could argue, Slaughter told us to get the fuck
in the car.

"Time to stand up against irresponsible punctuation!"
Jim is shouting in the front seat.

"Time to stand up against assholes in general!" yells
Slaughter, bashing his fist against the horn four times in a
row. The road is completely deserted and I think this is a
good thing. "We'll grab that flag and we'll head down to the

Mariner and we'll fucking make him eat it," Slaughter jabbers. I'm staring at the back of Chuck's head, but I can see drops of spittle landing on the windshield in front of him. I look at Dekker, who has his head in his hands, but he's laughing.

"Not the best idea," Jim advises Chuck. It's like they've forgotten about the three of us back here. "You ever been to that place?"

"I told you, man, I got dragged out of it by a bunch of his fat fuckin' cronies."

"This is what I'm saying," says Jim. "Guy's got cronies. Actual goons. He's like the Godfather."

"Slow down," whispers Todd beside me.

"The Godfather of Timperly?" titters Dekker.

"Don't laugh," advises Jim, raising his voice so we all can hear. "You'd be lucky to get out of the Mariner with your nuts on straight, Bryant."

"I'll puke," says Todd.

We're roaring through downtown and there is not a soul to be seen anywhere—there's scarcely even any cars parked nearby. All of Timperly must be tucked in its collective beddy-bye. We own the town, it feels like—we *are* the town at night. And it's snowing, whirly white flakes, the first I've seen all year. The streetlights turn the black sky a dim orange and the white flakes yellow, like bright, airborne flames. Scarsdale's flag waves at our approach, quoting some cheery, unknown personage who exhorts us to "Ask For Rory!" We hear it snap in the strengthening wind once we've all piled out of the car. Slaughter whoops a whoop of ownership, a kind of Viking whoop of claim-laying which bounces off the stone buildings and the streets. Smiley whoops a whoop of vomiting by the car's back tire. Jim skips like a schoolgirl across the street and leaps like a dancer to try and reach the flag, gorilla arms extended to their full simian length. He snags it, dangles for a moment above the sidewalk, then lets go, shoes slamming against concrete. I walk toward him, raising my face to the glowing sky, leaving fresh-snow footsteps like I did in the flour on Jim's kitchen floor. It's so quiet and empty and the snow is so new it's like everything's just sitting here waiting for us to take over. Big flakes brush against my face, melting as they go.

it's not healthy to be dwelling
on that sort of thing

8.

A POT OF TEA can usually sustain me through an entire poem—two or three if they're short. It has to be a big pot, though, enough for four or five cups. My parents furnished me with a small Brown Betty to see me through my first year at school, but the thing infuriated me. I wouldn't even be through the first draft and I'd have to get up and boil more hot water, having run out after only one mugful. It shattered my concentration, so I gave the Brown Betty away to Luc, who used it to steep magic mushrooms, and headed to the Co-op seeking something with a little more heft.

I overdid it. I came home with this enormous blue thing that could hold about a gallon and a half. I'd been over-whelmed by the size and the sky-blueness of it, its clean util-itarian lines. It was not like any pot I'd ever seen. Every teapot my mother and grandmother own—and between them they could go into business—is filigreed with foliage and flowers and women in bonnets and the like. The kind of thing I never would have gotten away with in residence—Chuck Slaughter would probably have taken a shit in it. So at first I considered swiping one of the tiny tin pots from Carl's Tearoom, since they were the only remotely masculine versions I'd yet encountered, like something you could bring with you camping. The problem again was with size. Those held about the same amount of liquid as the Brown Betty I'd started out with.

This might sound like a lot of fuss and consternation over a pot, but poets have their sacraments, and a bottomless pot of tea is mine. Last year I went on a bit of a Gary Snyder kick, which got me interested in Japanese culture, and I remember reading something about Japanese tea rituals.

That makes sense to me—tea as a kind of sacrament, like the Catholics with their bread and wine. You boil the water, you inhale the warm steam, letting it open your pores, you pour it from kettle to pot, pot to cup. Milk, sugar. And then you sip the hours away, letting them come, letting time unfurl. That's where I need the reassurance, that's the reason I have to fortify myself with a ritual of warmth. You are sitting at your desk facing possibility—the possibility of failure—in the shape of an empty white page. A window into nothing, the universe of blank. The question: Am I here or not?

But then the tea's ready, and you get down to work.

So here I am, sitting in Carl's, carefully emptying out some of the water into my saucer so I can add the milk and sugar to the pot in advance—that's my particular ritual. It keeps me from having to interrupt my thoughts by adding milk and sugar with every cup. A lady sitting in the booth beside me in the opposite seat watches with polite interest, almost as if she assumes I'm performing for her benefit. The thing about Carl's is, the booths are attached to one another, but there's no wall or anything separating them. When strangers sit down at the next booth, it almost feels like you're on a blind date.

She's what you would call a little old lady. Blue hair, hat pinned into it. Gloves, even—not because it's cold out, although it is, but because she's the kind of old lady who wears gloves when she goes out on the town. Blinking and smiling at me, until I have no choice but to look up and smile back, nice Maritime boy that I am.

"I've never seen *that* before," she remarks, nodding at my teapot. "Is that a new way?"

It reminds me of something that would happen at home, in PEI. What I want to know is this: is there anywhere in North America I could go right now where I'd be out in public and people would fail to give a shit how I take my tea? Is

there anywhere old ladies neglect to look you up and down
before taking it upon themselves to pronounce on your
behaviour? Where it doesn't behoove cab drivers to stick their
heads out their windows as they drive by to tell you that your
shirt's untucked? (Friendly did this, passing me in his cab as
I was shuffling my hungover way to Carl's. *Honk! Clack!
Forgot yer shirttail, there, buddy!*) Admittedly, this lady probably thinks herself very indulgent and forward-thinking, tol-
erating such heresy as she is. Such anarchistic tea-handling.

"It's just the way I like it," I explain. "It's what I always do."

"Well, good for you," encourages the lady. "You should
have it however you like."

Carl's is a hotbed of radicalism today. They'll send troops
like in Québec if we're not careful.

"Are you a student at the university?" she inquires. I look
around me, weary. Any part of my table that is not supporting tea-related paraphernalia is covered with books and
looseleaf. Final papers were due last week, and soon exams,
and then Christmas. But before Christmas, just before the
break, Dermot Schofield is coming to town to give a reading.
It strikes me as a strange time of year to be doing such a
thing. Jim assures me he's doing it now "just to make our
lives difficult." I find that it's working. Jim has appointed me
to help with Schofield when he's here.

Todd arrives and takes over where the old lady is concerned. Todd is happy to speak with her, because of his
working-class background. Old ladies are "authentic" as far as
Todd is concerned, representing "living history." They begin
chatting, for some reason, about the harvest excursion in the
twenties. Todd hasn't been here for five minutes and this is
what he's talking about—in his element discussing illiterate
Maritimers riding the rails westward-ho in the twenties to
find work. To me the prairies sound like PEI dropped in the
middle of a field and steamrolled flat. Todd tells the lady both

his grandparents went west on the train, and many of their relatives. Excitement! Perhaps the old lady knew them! What were their names? Smiley this, MacDougall that. She is sorry to say she can't remember coming across any Smileys, but she did meet several lovely Nova Scotians from the Annapolis Valley. Todd swallows a pucker of distaste. I've heard him disdain the Valley as a breeding ground for Baptists.

Unfortunately, the lady is now in a Valley reverie, remembering her rosy, apple-blossom youth and the trips she made to visit her friends in King's Landing—once they all came to their senses and returned east, that is, dust-covered and traumatized by the endless miles of flat. I imagine it would be the farmhand's equivalent of staring into a blank page. Empty sky. Non-stop horizon. *Am I here or not?* There wouldn't be enough tea in the world.

I doodle these ideas into my notebook, waiting for Todd to dispense with his friend now that she's betrayed her affinity for the Baptists. *Empty sky. Non-stop horizon.* Would it ever occur to Todd to write a poem about the harvest excursion? What would he say if I brought one to class? Tough tit if he doesn't like it. Jim requires a manuscript of no fewer than ten new poems before the break. I've written very little since "Deadwood," and even though I usually have at least that many in reserve, my reserves are drying up. Besides, my sensibilities have transformed themselves these past few months. My usual five-page opuses strike me as rambling, self-involved wankfests. I need to be meaner, more sparse. Muscular. Two-word stanzas. Fuck it—no stanzas whatsoever. Stanzas are for the likes of Claude, with his villanelles. Smiley, with his hymns to industrial mishap.

At last, the lady pulls on her gloves and bids us good day. Todd nods, baronial. I wave.

"Thought she'd never leave," Todd confides.

I raise my eyebrows at him.

"How's your head today?" he inquires, all business.

"Sore," I say.

"Me too," says Todd. "Tea."

"And french fries," I recommend. "Grease helps for some reason." We're here to study, but I can already see it will take us forever to get down to it. Todd is bouncing around in his seat, his small blue eyes flashing this way and that. I am thinking he must have gotten laid last night.

"Where did you disappear to, anyway?"

"What?" he squints, focusing on me with reluctance.

"You left the party early."

"Oh fuck, man, I was sick." Todd says this fast, eager to dispense with the topic. So that's not it, he must have really been sick. It was a Christmas party at one of the girls' residences—they somehow wangled special permission to hold an open house. Sherrie invited us. We got to weave in and out of fragrant female bedchambers all night long, being handed a different shot of booze in each room, lounging on their quilted beds and fondling their stuffed animals on our laps. It was sort of maddening. The smells reminded me of Janet's bedroom, when we were kids. Many things have been reminding me of Janet lately. Paramount among them, the occasion when I saw Janet a couple of days ago, walking down the other side of the street with a friend. She waved to me, I waved to her—just as we always do. I haven't called yet to ask her how she is and what she needs. Safe on the opposite side of the street, however, I at least took an interest. I peered at her gut. It was bigger, but so was all of Janet from what I could see.

"Well, you're looking pretty lively today," I say to Todd.

"I checked my mailbox this morning," Todd tells me.

"Exciting."

"I forgot to check it Friday, so I went down to check it today."

Todd has thick lips. You notice these details with a hangover. They are thick, and they glisten slightly. As I watch, he licks them as if to add polish. *Don't have those french fries after all, please, Todd.* But I wonder how to deter him, as mine will be coming soon.

"So?" I prod. I want him to finish talking so I can look away from his lips.

He places a letter in front of me. Westcock University stationery. I get an envelope like that every once in a while, informing me of grades or the status of my scholarship.

"Doctor Robert A. Sparrow, department head," says Todd.

"Crap!" I say.

"Yeah," says Todd.

We heard nothing after collecting the signatures. It took us a week of setting up tables, arguing with engineering and economics students who refused to believe the university administration was capable of doing wrong, and reassuring hockey players who accused us of being communists and threatened to kick our heads in. The football players fell into line thanks to the efforts of Charles Slaughter. Every once in a while he would drop by our table between classes to make sure no one was "taking liberties with you fuckwits," because at one point he arrived just in time to stop a guy who had ripped the bottom half of the petition from the clipboard and wiped his ass with it before crumpling it up and making for the door. Chuck practically picked the guy up with one hand, turned him around to face me, and recommended an apology. Then the guy had to smooth out the crumpled half of the petition and go find some Scotch tape to put it back together again. I watched Slaughter closely the whole time, taking in the cliché of him. The ludicrous coincidence of the guy's last name. How second-nature it was for him to grab a total stranger by the scruff of the neck and tell him precisely what to do next. He did it with a bored and absent-minded smile, like a cashier making change.

And yet, after all that work, we heard nothing. Even Jim had sort of lost interest. He was back in class, standing around with his arms twisted behind his head—as brilliant and animated as ever—but now that the official complaint was underway, he stopped asking about it and returned his attention to merciless critiques of our poetry. One day in class he used the word "banal" in reference to one of Todd's ballads. I couldn't bring myself to look at Todd for the remainder of class.

But that, of course, is Jim. He doesn't play favourites when it comes to poetry, and I shouldn't have expected him to. Clearly, he was saying with that "banal," there would be no coddling or kid gloves in the classroom and it didn't matter what anyone might have done on his behalf. I would have it no other way, and would expect nothing less from a great poet and teacher.

Once the signatures were all collected—and I swear to God we got practically everyone except for the occasional weirdo who claimed to "never sign anything"—we sent them, along with our endlessly revised and impeccably typed letter, off to the dean of Arts, the president of Westcock, and Doctor Sparrow. Then the three of us, intoxicated by our own bravado—drunk on fear—went out to get even drunker downtown. We took ourselves out for pizza at the Italian restaurant and talked and screamed laughter at each other's wisecracks and found that none of us could eat.

"I've never done anything like this before," whispered Sherrie into her plate.

I knew what she was saying—I knew exactly what she was saying. *I've always been so good.* And this is what I'm thinking as I look down at the letter teetering on top of my pile of English books.

"What does it say?" I ask Todd.

"He wants me to come see him."

"Just you?" I demand.

"That's what it says," says Todd.

"Why doesn't he want to see me? Or Sherrie?"

"I don't know," says Todd. "When was the last time you checked your mail?"

"Oh," I say.

December 2, 1975

Dear Mr. Campbell,

I am in receipt of your letter and the petition you have circulated regarding Professor Jim Arsenault and the Department of English. The concern of yourself and your fellow students has been noted, and your efforts are appreciated. Please make an appointment to speak with me at your earliest convenience.

Sincerely,

Robert A. Sparrow, PhD
Chair, Department of English Literature

Oh, but I have *exams*. I have a literary reading to organize—doesn't anyone understand this? And I have to talk to Janet before Christmas, because when I go home everyone will expect us to have fostered a close and nurturing affinity. What's more, they'll be wanting their "report." And what about Christmas presents? I don't have any money, I never know what to buy. Should I get a present for Jim? Can't I put the meeting with Doctor Sparrow off until the new year?

No, I can't, because I'll see him at the Christmas party. I'll see him in the department. I'll see him everywhere. In my dreams, when I go to sleep.

I call Sherrie. Her letter is identical except for the name in the salutation.

The next person I call is the departmental secretary, Mrs. Marjorie Gaudet. The trick to handling fear is to get it over with as soon as possible. It's like jumping into a freezing cold stream which may or may not contain piranhas. You don't know until you take the plunge. The important thing is, it's over and you don't have to stand on the shore shivering in your trunks, peering into the depths anymore. Dermot Schofield arrives early next week. My first exam is on the Thursday after that—Dekker's Shakespeare, which shouldn't be too bad. I just need to get this out of my head in order to function. It's like being called to the principal's office. Except I have never been called to the principal's office.

On top of it all, I'm supposed to write ten new poems, and how exactly am I supposed to pull off such a thing under this kind of pressure? I read something by someone—I think it was Wordsworth—something like, poetry is intensity recalled in times of tranquility. Not intensity recalled in times of even *more* intensity, no, that's not how the great man put it. So where's my tranquility? This could be a good argument against the study of creative writing in a university setting, come to think of it. But that's not an argument I would ever make.

Ring, ring.

"Hello, this is Doctor Sparrow's office."

"I'd like to make an appointment to see Doctor Sparrow, please?"

"Mm hmm?" says Marjorie Gaudet. "Your name, please?"

"Lawrence Campbell."

Scribble, scribble, she is writing my name into a book.

"And to what does this pertain, Mr. Campbell?"

Doctor Sparrow's secretary uses impeccable grammar. I don't know if I can do this.

"It pertains to . . ." I say, deepening into my classroom-speaking voice. "Uh, it pertains to . . . Professor Arsenault?"—and up it goes, right on cue, spiralling into its old, reliable question mark.

There is another quick scribble-sound. And then, "Oh!" says Mrs. Gaudet. To my surprise, her tone has faltered as well—I detect the exclamation point in her voice.

"Is this about the *petition?*" she wants to know, voice hushed with a conspicuously unprofessional *interest.* In me. The guy on the phone.

And now I know we've really done something.

Ring, ring.

It's my phone. Someone is calling me. Therefore, it must be my parents. Certainly it wouldn't be Marjorie Gaudet, calling me back, to let me know Doctor Sparrow doesn't need to see me after all, that he's decided on summary expulsion.

"Hello?"

"Larry!"

It's Jim. Balm. I molest the receiver.

"Hi, Jim!"

"Howya doing, kiddo?"

"Well—actually I'm a bit crazed."

"Oh, Christ, Larry, you're not worried about exams, are you?"

"Among other things . . ."

"Listen, Larry," he says before I can beg for reassurance about Doctor Sparrow. "I've just been going over this grant application stuff for Schofield's reading—"

Who? What?

"—I just realized we're supposed to be promoting the fucking thing all week long."

"Promoting?"

"Schofield gets an evaluation sheet after the reading, where he basically gets to report on us."

"That's outrageous!" I declare, rallying.

"So if he doesn't think we did a good enough job, the cocksucker could get our funding cut off for next time."

I am comprehending approximately none of this.

"He'd do that?"

"Yes, he'd do that. He'll just be looking for an excuse to screw us over, particularly after my review. That's exactly the kind of asshole Schofield is."

"Jim," I say, "I'm sorry, I'm feeling kind of scattered today. *How* could Schofield get our funding cut off . . . ?"

I hear a staticky sigh on the other end of the line. "All right, Larry, listen carefully this time. Basically, we have to kiss Schofield's ass the whole time he's here. We gotta put posters up all over town so that he sees we made an effort, and we gotta get people out to the reading."

I'm stupefied. I had assumed it was understood by all concerned that the only people coming to Schofield's reading at Christmas-exam time would be the students in Jim's poetry seminar. All eight of us.

"How many?" I say. "How many people?"

"We should try and shoot for twenty."

"Twenty?" There won't be twenty people left on campus.

"So I need you," concludes Jim, "to get to work on that."

"Okay," I answer faintly. I drag the phone to the cupboard and, balancing receiver under chin, use my free hand to reach for my colossal blue teapot. "Listen," I say, struggling with the logistics of this. "Jim?"

"Yeah, kid?" I can hear him putting down his papers and smacking his lips.

"I got a letter from Doctor Sparrow—"

Jim tells me he knows. Todd has told him about the letter from Doctor Sparrow. Todd is certainly fast-acting. Like a laxative. I eventually found out that the reason he was invited to the dinner at Jim's house last month was because, indeed, Todd had called him up and explained to him in intricate detail his role in getting the petition started.

Jim is talking a mile a minute. Loudly. He is calling Doctor Sparrow the same sort of names he has just used with regard to Dermot Schofield. Only with greater volume and relish. He says not to let that bastard intimidate us. He advises that we refuse to see him individually, that we "stick to our guns" and "not take any shit." He suggests we threaten to "hold a fucking sit-in" like the students at Berkeley, barricade ourselves in his office, rifle through his files. Get blankets and pillows and sleep there throughout the holidays. Get the entire campus up in arms, alert the media, march through town, wave placards, break windows.

"You gotta show these shitheads you won't be pushed around," Jim is saying. "That their time has come and gone, the wheels are in motion and the goddamn revolution is at hand!"

I return to the couch with Big Blue on my lap, listening. In the kitchen is the comfortable sound of my kettle gasping with heat. In my ear, the less comfortable sound of Jim. I'm thinking about the Christmas ferry to PEI all of a sudden. Cape Tormentine to Borden. Ferrying across the Christmastime sea, homeward bound.

9.

IT SMELLS LIKE BOOKS and antiques. Oak and dust. Velvet and leather and panicking students. The ghosts of undergraduates past.

I am alarmed by my reaction to Marjorie Gaudet today. She's a type like Brenda L., only older, even older than Brenda L. Jim has another word for women like this: *blowsy. Overripe* is forgivable if slightly lamentable in his poems, but *blowsy* is pushing the limits of acceptable female physicality. I looked it up, after reading it in *Blinding White,* and found that the basic meaning appears to be *bloated.*

I know it doesn't mean the same thing, but I always imagine *blowsy* has something to do with women's blouses.

The problem is her breasts. They're big, because Mrs. Gaudet is a big woman overall. She has children, I assume. Maybe dozens of them—she looks like the type who could handle it. But today in particular, her breasts strike me as big. Too big, uncomfortably big, exploding from beneath her unbuttoned brown cardigan, shoving it rudely aside. So blowsy is Mrs. Gaudet, so overripe her breasts, I keep imagining that every once in a while she has to lean forward, when no one is around to see, and rest them on her desk.

It's this image that gives me the hard-on. Plus she's so nice. She smiles at me when I arrive, calls me Mr. Campbell, and confides that she was much impressed by our *initiative* in getting the petition together. She asks if I'd like a cup of coffee while I wait for Doctor Sparrow to "finish up." I try to imagine what he could be finishing up. I picture him wiping blood from his fingertips—the corners of his mouth—with a silken handkerchief. Humming to himself. "Greensleeves," maybe.

I ask for water. Mrs. Gaudet heaves to her feet to get it for me. She thuds off down the hall, creaking in a pair of solid

high heels—as sensible a pair as high-heeled shoes can be. I
wonder where she's going to get the water. Will she just fill it
up from the tap in the women's washroom? I picture it and,
moronically, get harder.

Doctor Sparrow's door opens. I shuttle to my feet. He
looks around, frowns in my direction, then slumps against the
doorframe, taking in the fact of Mrs. Gaudet's empty desk.

"Oh dear," says Doctor Sparrow. "Now where has
Marjorie gone?" I don't answer, because I don't get the sense
that he's addressing me. But after a click or two of silence, he
looks directly into my eyes, with the blank aspect of a robot
needing input. Or else the single-minded yet somehow
mindless expression of Jim's dog Panda, willing me to throw
the ball.

"She just went down the hall for a moment," I smile,
folding my hands in front of my pants.

"I'm right here!" Marjorie calls, emerging from the washroom somewhere down the hall. The echoes in this place—
she can hear our conversation like we're beside her. The
thudity-thud of her sturdy secretarial heels can be heard gain-
ing urgency. "I'll be right there!" she yells. "Do you need anything?"

"I can't recall what I'm doing next!" calls Sparrow, even
though he could mutter it and she'd probably hear.

"You're seeing Lawrence Campbell next!"

"Who?"

I smile harder, making my lips tight and thin and blood-
less. But he's not looking at me. He has that off-in-the-
distance look people get when addressing the unseen.

"Lawrence Campbell!" Marjorie yells, and I can feel my
name bouncing off every single surface in the department.
"He's right there in front of you."

Doctor Sparrow straightens in the doorframe, swivels his
head around. I imagine I hear a creak.

"Ah," he says, adjusting his glasses.

"The *petition*," elucidates Marjorie.

My hands drop to my sides.

Doctor Sparrow is a put-upon sort. The first five minutes of our conversation entail him sighing vague endearments and non-blasphemous oaths.

"Oh my," he murmurs windily, shifting a stack of papers from the centre of his desk to a nearby table. "Oh dear," cleaning his glasses. "Oh goodness me. Lawrence Campbell. Just allow me to get my bearings. It's a busy time of year, wouldn't you say?"

"Yes."

After a few more sighs and whispered groans, he settles into his chair. It doesn't creak like Dekker's. He's a trim, grey-haired man. The only non-neat thing about him is a scraggly salt-and-pepper beard. It's wispy, made up out of patches. The pink of his chin peeks through here and there. It bothers me.

Finally Sparrow heaves a bigger, more cleansing sigh than the previous one and places his hands on his desk. We face each other.

"So *how* are you?" he beams.

"I'm fine, sir."

"Well done," he replies. "You were all most upset over Professor Arsenault, I suppose."

I'm impressed at how quickly he has gotten down to it. "Yes—"

"Of course. He's an inspiring teacher, no doubt."

"Absolutely."

"We get such wonderful reports of him."

"You do?" I don't mean to say this pointedly, but, because of my surprise, it comes out that way. Sparrow nods and leans back as if I have made some kind of pithy, sagacious retort that he now must pause to consider.

"Well, this," he remarks following the pause, "is the difficulty with dynamic personalities such as Professor Arsenault, wouldn't you say? At their best, they are unsurpassed—extraordinary, uncompromising in both art and craft."

"Yes," I say.

"It's an admirable trait in an artist."

"It is," I say.

"Yet the craft of teaching, Lawrence. Is something else entirely."

"He's an *inspiring* teacher," I remind.

Sparrow nods furiously, apologetically, waving his hands a little as if to clear away smoke. "You're an aspiring poet yourself, yes? I understand you've won several competitions back in Newfoundland."

"Prince Edward Island."

"Oh, I'm so sorry. That's not the same place at all, is it?" He rests a hand on his chest, abashed.

"No," I laugh, to put him at ease.

"Well, bravo, Lawrence. And a scholarship no less. You're a superlative student."

I sit and smile.

"Have you thought of graduate work?"

"Um," I say, getting ready to deepen my voice. I've gotten to the point in my self-training where, whenever I hear myself say *um,* my voice deepens instinctively. But the question mark. Watch the question mark. Do not succumb to the question mark.

"Well, I'd like to try my hand at getting published," I state, voice level with conviction.

Sparrow's salty eyebrows almost fly off his head. "Of *course!*" he exclaims, startling me. "But that goes without saying! You're already well on your way!"

"Well," I say, treading carefully to keep from sounding ridiculous, "I hope to have a—maybe a chapbook ready by the time I graduate." And still no question mark. Sparrow is bobbing his beard at me again, eyes wide with affirmation. *And I want it edited by Jim. I want it supervised by Jim. I came here for the Jim Arsenault Midas touch and I won't let you take it away from me.* It's a perfect opportunity to say all and any of these things, but I don't. I'm too busy blushing at having articulated my fondest wish to this English guy.

"That's wonderful, Lawrence," says Sparrow with strength and conviction. I gaze out the window. Sparrow's office overlooks the entire marsh and the fields of salt hay beyond. I can see a weather system approaching in the distance—wild, blowsy, multi-hued clouds piled up on the horizon as if some crazed god has bulldozed a snow-covered mountain range and is slouching with his load toward Timperly.

"But Lawrence," calls Sparrow, "looking at your transcripts, I see your course load has been somewhat eclectic for an English student."

"Well, the requirements are a bit different for the creative writing option," I remind Doctor Sparrow.

He wilts a little. "Yes, the creative writing option. I confess, I keep forgetting about it, which is an appalling thing for a department head to admit, I suppose, but there you go. It's been underway for such a short time. But Lawrence," he adds, perkening, "I hope you were planning to take my Elizabethan poets course next year?"

Because Doctor Sparrow appears to hope this very much, I don't contradict him.

"It's just that," I explain, "I'm very interested in, and—you know—very excited by—modern poetry—"

More furious, commiserating nodding from Sparrow.

"—and what's being done in this country. I find it very . . . exciting."

"Of course you do!"

"In fact, I was very much looking forward to taking Jim—Professor Arsenault's—Canadian poetry seminar next year. I was very excited to see it offered in the calendar."

Stop saying *very excited.* Stop saying *very exciting.* Stop saying *very.* Stop it.

"Lawrence," Sparrow interrupts. "Yes. Absolutely. A young man—a Canadian boy like yourself would of course be interested in the poetry of his time and place. It's laudable. But, I wonder, have you ever heard the expression, one must know the rules before one can break them?"

"It's not that I, that I, um, *disdain* literary history!" I explain in a high-voiced panic set off by the awfulness of the words *Canadian boy.*

Sparrow looks away, clears more smoke, embarrassed for us both. "No, no, no, no, of course not."

"It's just that I've already read—like—*everything.*"

And this wins me my first look of reproach from Doctor Sparrow.

"Now, Lawrence," he admonishes, mouth disappearing behind his beard. "Everything?"

At this juncture, I opt to sit back and shut up.

"Marvell? Spenser? My goodness, but there's so much, Lawrence. Aside from the poets themselves, so many great thinkers who've informed the tradition. Virgilius Ferm?"

Virgilius Ferm?

"Coleridge? Johnson? Milton?"

"I've read some Milton."

"I'm glad to hear it. But English literature, Lawrence, is a vast canopy, stretching back over centuries. To aspire to contribute to it without attempting even a rudimentary grasp of what's come before you is to—well, is to insult that tradition, I'm afraid."

There is something about the British manner of phrasing

that fascinates me. The effect seems to be to terrify and soothe you all at once.

"Doctor Sparrow," I speak, deeply, "I *love* English literature. Probably more than anyone in this department. I would be the last person in the world to insult it, let me assure you."

I think it is the first time I've ever used the expression *let me assure you,* and I'm pleased with the way it turns out, like one of my mother's Duncan Hines cakes, gold and quivering with perfection. Didn't stick to the pan, as it were. The fact is, I'm falling into the rhythms of Sparrow's own rarified speech as I sit here. Sparrow is looking at me. He is looking at me with approval, I would venture to say. If I were feeling bold, I might even identify his gaze as one of admiration.

"I," says Doctor Sparrow, once we've passed a couple of cozy, appraising moments, "could tell that just from looking at you, my boy." He smiles, places his hands on his desk, and stands as if about to hug me.

Which he doesn't do, even though in a sort of daze I've half risen to meet him. He goes to the window instead, framing himself in the approaching, darkening stormfront. He spends the next thirty minutes telling me about Oxford, his alma mater. *Ancient Oxford,* he calls it, and he rhymes off names. Name after name of the great scholars and poets who have roamed its halls through the ages. More. Erasmus. Sir Walter Raleigh. I had no idea. Doctor Johnson. Donne. It's as if he's unfurling the history of English literature before me like an endless, gilded carpet. So many great writers came from Oxford. Over actual centuries. We don't even really have centuries in Canada.

Great scholars like you, Lawrence. Such as you've already shown yourself to be. Great poets like the poet you no doubt have within you. Young men like yourself are the inheritors of that tradition.

The sun is starting to set, and the clouds have taken on

untamed hues of pain orange, broken-nosed red and black-eyed purple. Fiery and otherwise indescribable. Doctor Sparrow crosses back to his desk at one point, and a long white hand disappears into its oaken depths. He has pamphlets, brochures in there.

10.

THE STORM HITS smack in the middle of Jim's seminar on the last day of classes. We're reviewing another poem by Todd, a brand-new poem, and you know how it goes? It goes like this:

```
west
        we wind
        on
                the
                endless        trek

        a
         way
        in hopes of

harvest
```

The title being, "The Harvest Excursion." He beat me to it. I think it's the worst thing he's written yet. Where's the rhyming couplet? Where are the maimed steel workers, the exploding blast furnaces?

"Okay, come on now, if you write it all out as a sentence it's completely—banal," I blurt. I know. I shouldn't use "banal" yet a second time when it comes to Todd's poetry. I felt what it did to him last time. But Jesus Christ.

"I'm not sure I agree," remarks Claude. I look at him. He smiles at me.

"Like," I say, "if you just scatter the words around on the page, is this supposed to imbue them with some kind of supplementary *depth?* Does just sprinkling them around like that make a sentence *poetry?*"

"I think that's a very traditionalist approach," says Claude. I hear Todd gulp somewhere behind me. We're supposed to do our best not to speak when our poems are being discussed. No doubt he was gulping back an infuriated "Yeah!"

"Oh, come on!" I yell, because Claude does not believe a word of what he's saying and everyone in the room knows it.

"Larry," interrupts Jim, "make your case, if you have a case to make."

"West we wind on the endless trek away in hopes of harvest," I say, rapid-fire. "I'm sorry, but I just don't think it's a poem. It's a—it's an offhand remark at best."

"I'm surprised at you, Larry," says Jim. A branch slams against the window, yanked from a tree. We all jump and look outside. It's a blank white page out there.

"Looks like Christmas is coming," Jim remarks. He's mighty jocular today, considering his nemesis Schofield arrives in two hours. After complimenting Todd on his "adventuresome" new approach, Jim extols us all to remember the Schofield reading at seven and lets us go early. He tosses me his car keys and tells me to be careful on my way to the bus stop to pick up the man himself.

"You want Todd to go with you?" he asks before I can leave. But Todd can't come with me, because Todd was the first out the door.

How would I feel if I were Todd? I'd be ecstatic to have Jim's approval. I wouldn't care what a fuckwit like me had to say about his adventuresome new style, but he's clearly pissed. I'm pissed myself. I clutch Jim's keys, pressing the metal into the pads of my fingers, wondering why I should be feeling as pissed off as I am. It's Jim. And Todd. Jim called Todd's poem "muscular," is the problem, which I thought was what my poems were. "Deadwood," for example. *Cock your dead wood at some other sucker.* Okay, perhaps it was as much an offhand remark as Todd's. Perhaps I did write it when I was blind drunk. Perhaps I haven't been able to come up with anything as "muscular" since.

The question that's really bothering me: Are both Todd's and my poems good or are they bad? I think Todd's was bad, Jim thought it was good. And Jim thought mine were good, too.

How do you ever know for sure? And how does Jim decide, anyway? What criteria does he use? Does he have some kind of chart?

Another problem. I have read and enjoyed the work of Dermot Schofield. I wanted to be able to have something to talk about with him when I picked him up and brought him to check in at the Crowfeather, and so, confident I would find much to disdain within its pages, I checked out a copy of *Malignant Cove* from the library. Much to my chagrin, I thought it was great. A little bit like Al Purdy, but more lonely and slowed-down, without as much storytelling. I got lost in it. Maybe not every single poem—not like *Blinding White,* but then, what is? There were some incredible lines.

One poem was just this list of words, and Schofield stating whether or not he felt they were "man" words or "woman" words. Not feminine or masculine, he emphasized, like in the French, but man and woman. But it was clear the poem was about something more than that—not about man and woman in general but about a certain man and a specific woman, together and separate. He made it feel intimate somehow, this list of words. Like a peek into someone's bed-room. *Basket* was a woman word, he said—although that seems obvious enough. *Stone* was also a woman word, but *rock,* he said, was a man word. *Sleet* was a man word, he said, and *deaf. Road* was a woman word, "counter to expectation," the poem said, and *frame.* And then it ended with words that couldn't be categorized, according to Schofield. *Rib,* he said, and *water* couldn't be categorized. They were all so weirdly arbitrary that it was beautiful, the poem. And it all lined up somehow—it made sense. I want to ask him how he did that.

And then she turns, the poem ended in a strange, two-line stanza. *And when she turns, it falls to dream.*

Of course, I had to keep reminding myself that *Malignant Cove* is, as Jim says in his review, "a mucus-like sheen of mendacity, glossing over the fundamental bad faith at the centre of the poet's existence." Lies, okay, but lies well told—I'll give Schofield that. Beautiful lies, in some instances.

In any event, Jim has cautioned me to steel myself for an encounter with a complete and total asshole, and that I have.

Driving downtown, I'm depressed to see that all the posters it took me an entire day to staple to every telephone pole in Timperly are in the process of being ripped to shreds by the wind. The snow is too dry and falling too fast to melt them off, but if it turns to freezing rain, as the weathermen warn it might, they'll all degrade into pulp. They've been up a week, but the problem is they contain directions to the Social Sciences building, where the reading is being held. Anyone coming from outside of town won't have any idea where to go.

All week I've been carrying posters in my satchel, shoving handfuls of them at every warm body I came across, even those who protested I'd already given them a bunch. At one point, Slaughter threatened to shove them all down my throat and up my ass simultaneously if I brought another poster anywhere near him. Sherrie nicely offered to help, so I gave her half to post in the girls' residences and bathrooms. Todd, however, never offered to help at all—it could be because he was miffed that Jim had bestowed upon me sole responsibility for promoting the Schofield reading.

Anyway, as big a pain in the ass as it was, the posters were useful in a couple of ways. It gave me an excuse to talk to Brenda L. (I gave her two posters, one to put up at Carl's and one to take home and consider "a personal invitation"), and it gave me an excuse, at long last, to get in touch with cousin Janet.

The much-avoided encounter went thus: Ring, ring. Hi, Janet! It's your long-lost cousin Lawrence here. Larry! How's your year going? I was going to call to see if you wanted to head home on the ferry together. Why, that sounds great, Janet, what a coincidence. I was just calling to find out when you were planning on leaving, as a matter of fact. Since you'll be here, I'd like to invite you to the literary reading of the century . . . and so forth. The upshot of our little talk was that Janet invited me over for tea. On the same day I had to put up posters. It would be, I thought, a good way to take a break from putting up the posters. And having to put up the posters would be a good excuse not to have to stay at Janet's too long.

Janet answered the door, filling the frame. Plump, pink, and aglow with impending motherhood. I hadn't expected it to be so manifest, her situation. She hugged me, to my horror. The Campbells and Humphrieses are not known for public displays of affection. Her breasts pillowed against me. Her stomach too.

"Here's some posters," I said, shoving them at her.

"It has been way too long," said Janet. "This is stupid, with the two of us living in a town of this size."

"I know," I said.

"I have beets for you that have been sitting here since September!"

"Beets?"

"Yes, beets. Mom and Dad brought me over a shitload of beets from the garden and told me to give you a bunch . . . I'm so sorry, they're out in the porch."

"Don't worry about it, Janet," I called, but she'd disappeared out the back with the handful of posters. Janet has what must be the greatest student apartment in town. I've always hoped to inherit it once she graduates. It's the main floor of a small house with a front and a back yard. Her little old landlady lives in a bigger house next door and charges Janet next to nothing. They are dear friends, reportedly. The little old landlady bakes for Janet every week.

"Here you go." Janet emerged, now posterless but with a plastic Co-op bag of beets from three months ago.

"Thanks," I said, taking it.

"I guess your folks are worried you're not eating your vegetables."

"Like I'm going to start with beets," I said.

Janet furrowed her brow, near-insulted. "You can always pickle them."

"Oh, right," I replied in all sincerity. I dutifully imagined myself standing in my bachelor's kitchen stirring a cauldron of purple, bubbling gore, pickling jars lined up across the counter. Shades of my mother and Grandma Lydia in their ruffly white aprons at summer's end.

It wasn't too bad a time overall. Janet made tea and served me butter tarts, oat cakes, and raisin pie, all courtesy of her landlady. I sucked it all up the way underfed college boys will. Janet did too. She got up and ran to get ice cream to put on everything at one point. Afterward, I'm buzzing on sugar, and the posters seemed to fly up onto the telephone poles all by themselves.

While it never occurred to me that I might have anything in common with Janet, it did occur to me that afternoon that I probably had more in common with her than with anyone else in my family. We made giddy fun of Grandma Lydia for a while—which is kind of a conversational autopilot we fall into whenever we get thrown together—and then mocked Cousin Wayne, who has been managing the Hollywood Horrors since last year and apparently fancies himself a real businessman these days. Nothing was said about the contents of Janet's uterus, but I did convince her to come to the reading and bring as many people with her as she could. We made a plan to hop a bus and catch the noon ferry from Cape Tormentine a week from tomorrow. I called my parents that night to let them know how diligent I had been, looking in on my cousin at such a busy time of year.

The fact is, I have not studied for Dekker's exam at all. But I've read all the plays, for God's sake, written my A papers about Lear's madness, Hamlet's tragic flaw, Iago's inscrutable motives. I'm good on Shakespeare. I've got Shakespeare down. I've got a couple more days to cram for the rest. Plus there is my science credit to think about. Diligently—for I am nothing if not diligent—I mentally dissect the human immune system as I weave my way through the white sheets to the bus station to pick up Schofield. The wind wobbles Jim's car like a boat every time I come to a stop sign. It happens that the bus stops at a massively inconvenient location—a decrepit '50s diner halfway between Wethering and

Timperly. Just sitting there on the border between the two provinces with its spacy '50s architecture and non-existent paint job. The consensus is that Spanky's is not necessarily a theme restaurant, but merely a restaurant built in the '50s which didn't have the money or inclination to update its aesthetic as the decades rolled by. So now it's attained "retro" status, simply by waiting out the years. There is absolutely nothing retro or interesting about the food. You can get hamburgers, soggy french fries that any self-respecting Carl's patron would turn their noses up at, and egg salad sandwiches. Milkshakes—but you can get those anywhere. There isn't even a jukebox playing Elvis or Buddy Holly.

So anyway, this is all to lead up to the image of Dermot Schofield balancing his considerable bulk on a stool at the counter, sucking up a strawberry milkshake as if having wandered into a particularly dismal edition of Archie comics. There is no mistaking Schofield. He is the only person in the restaurant, aside from the cook and the cashier. The cook clatters invisibly in the kitchen as the cashier natters into the phone. I am able to glean that she is talking to her boss. She wants to close the place and go home before we all get snowed in together.

"No—there's no one," I hear her snap before I can approach Schofield. "Just me and some asshole off the bus."

"Dermot Schofield?" I say, squaring my shoulders, extending my arm in preparation for a firm and uncompromising handclasp.

The guy on the stool adjusts his glasses, peers through them at me. Here's what he's like: as if a shaved grizzly bear put on a tie, parka, and thick pair of Henry Kissinger glasses and decided one horrible winter's day to come out of hibernation just for a Spanky's shake. You'd think his ass would swallow the tiny stool supporting it. Then he stands and I am about three inches tall.

"Hello." He engulfs my hand in what feels like a catcher's mitt. I'm flummoxed.

"I'm Larry," I say, forgetting how I'm Lawrence off-island.

"Hello, Larry," says Schofield in a surprisingly reedy voice.

"I hope you haven't been waiting long."

"Not at all."

"The bus got here an hour and a half ago," says the waitress, who has come over—after hanging up on the boss—to see what all the excitement is at this end of the counter.

"Oh my God," I say.

"Maybe you got last year's schedule or something," offers the waitress. Schofield is already shaking his head and smiling.

"It's fine, it's fine," he reeds at me.

"I'm so sorry, I had three-thirty written down!" I stammer, quick not to say *Jim told me three-thirty.* Because Jim is speaking loud and clear in my mind, at this moment. *He'll just be looking for something, Larry. Any little chink in the armour—anything at all—he'll just be waiting for me to fuck up.*

"It's all my fault," I tell Schofield in a firm, forbidding tone. I almost am glowering up at the man, daring him to doubt my incompetence.

Schofield smiles down, a thin crease between bulbous cheeks, beneath inscrutably thick glasses.

"Absolutely no problem whatsoever, Larry, please," he murmurs.

We drive about ten feet before coming to a whiteout.

"My gosh," remarks Schofield, looking around him, out at the impenetrable white. I wonder if he is fighting back the same subdued panic I happen to be struggling with. It's like being lost in the dark—only it's light. You tell yourself the same sort of things. There's nothing to be afraid of, everything's fine, the world hasn't actually dropped away even if that's how it looks and feels, even if that's precisely the evidence of your eyes.

"It's no big deal," I say. "We'll creep. We'll just creep."

Of course, those things you tell yourself in the dark— *there's nothing to be afraid of, everything's fine*—they don't actually work in this case, do they? Because we are on a major highway between the two provinces. There are eighteen-wheelers barrelling along this corridor on a regular basis.

"Perhaps we should pull over for a while," suggests Schofield.

"We'll *creep,*" I insist, figuring the eighteen-wheelers will be just as apt to hit us if we're parked on the side of the road. The yellow line has disappeared, and they'll be all drugged up—"crazy on the speed, and the acid and *tokes* and what have you," like my father used to assure me the potato truckers who came across on the ferry always were. So the eighteen-wheelers—their drivers out of their minds on drugs and lacking even a yellow line to orient them—won't know where they are on the road. They'll hit us if we're moving, they'll hit us if we're standing still. They'd probably hit us if we were sitting out in the middle of a field. Right now it feels as though we could be upside down and flying ten feet off the ground and I'd have no way of knowing it. For all I know we're plowing through a snowbank—actually *under* ten feet or so of snow. There's no way to tell. It's white. *How was your drive? It was white.* So why not creep? At least we'll be moving when they smash into us. Nobody will be able to say we were sitting around wasting time when we got smucked. *They were creeping, by God, creeping right along there in the snow like regular troopers. There was no stopping them.* Plucky young poet Lawrence Campbell and his precious three hundred pounds of Canlit cargo.

"Perhaps you'd like me to drive," suggests Schofield, his reedy voice subdued.

"Oh, no," I say. "I'm fine."

"It's disorienting, isn't it?"

"It's a little bit disorienting," I agree.

"Claustrophobic," remarks Schofield.

Headlights in our face. A roar filling our ears.

"*Jesus cocksucking Christ!*" I ululate.

"—just the snowplow," says Schofield. I pull over to what I imagine and hope to be the side of the road. I yank the emergency break and stare straight ahead. I don't put my head in my hands.

"I'm happy to drive," says Schofield after a moment.

"Maybe we should just wait it out a little bit."

He looks at his watch. I can't believe the guy is looking at his watch with us sitting here surrounded by the bleached void. It's like tumbling through space and wondering what the temperature is outside your spacesuit.

"Lots of time to the reading," he pronounces, leaning back as if into an armchair in front of a fireplace. It's a thing with burly men—they look cozy, no matter where they are. The only time they appear to be uncomfortable is standing up, having to sustain all that mass on their own.

I lean back as well, gazing out the window, which is dumb, because there's nothing to gaze at. I'm play-acting for Schofield, like, *dum-de-dum, why, look at all the stuff that's going on out there.* He must think I'm a fool. I lurch forward to turn on the radio.

It's imperative to stay off the roads this evening, scolds the announcer in a Lorne Green baritone.

And then tinkling piano. *Eine Kleine Nachtmusik.* I swallow, sigh. Another snowplow rumbles past like some kind of leftover ice-age leviathan.

"Are the headlights on?" asks Schofield.

"Um," I check. "No."

"Maybe we should keep them on. High beams."

I have this conviction that I should contradict Schofield. That it's important he understands who is in charge here. Not to let him see me sweat, as it were. No chinks in said armour. Thinking this, I nod and flick on the high beams.

Then my right leg is heavier than my left. The catcher's mitt is resting on it. Oh no. Oh no. This man equals five of me.

"Larry," says Schofield.

I stare straight ahead. I make a nose like *eeyore*.

Schofield pats me. On the leg. Once. "Listen," he says. "Don't worry about it. All right?"

I look down at my leg. Nothing but worn-in Woolworth's jeans adorning it now. I deflate, and make myself look Schofield in the glasses. Smile. "All right."

"Okay," says Schofield smiling back in a grandfatherly sort of way. "We still have quite a bit of time."

"You must be hungry," I say. This occurs to me because in fact I am hungry myself.

"The milkshake will hold me."

I wish I smoked or something. We'd have something friendly to do to pass the time.

"Do you smoke?" I ask the poet.

Schofield shakes his head. "Afraid not. You?"

"No."

"Hm," says Schofield.

We stare out the window. The white is darkening, turning bluish. Getting late. Seconds roar past.

"The thing is," I say without really knowing it's coming, "I'm not a very experienced driver."

Schofield purses his lips and nods.

"I got my licence a couple of years ago, but, you know. All I ever did was drive around the back roads. I never even went into Charlottetown."

"I see," says Schofield. "You're from PEI?"

"Yes!" I'm happy about this turn in the conversation. It feels like this is going somewhere.

"I love PEI," the poet tells me. "We spent some summers there when I was a boy."

"I'm from near Summerside," I say. "Have you ever been to Summerside?"

"I love Summerside," Schofield rejoins. "It's beautiful."

"It *is* beautiful," I enthuse. I think about Summerside. The very name of the place. You can scarcely imagine it buried in a snowstorm. I wish I were there right now.

I glance over at Schofield. There's silence again. It seems we have both fallen into melancholy thinking of Summerside.

"So anyway," I continue—and realize as I do that Schofield had interrupted as a means of excusing me from continuing. "I guess this kind of driving is pretty new to me."

Schofield's pursing and nodding again.

"And—ah—" I add, "I'm sorry."

Jim would smack me if he were here. Or, no. He doesn't do that. He doesn't have to. He looks at you. He folds his arms. He manoeuvres his eyebrows in just such a way as to make you feel impaled. *You are showing weakness, Larry. You are letting him see you sweat. You're nothing but a big chink-riddled suit of armour.*

"I've got an idea," says Schofield. His voice is reedy again. Jocular.

I look at him. "You do?"

The catcher's mitt dabs at my leg a second time. "Why don't I try driving for a bit?" He smiles. "You can tell me where to go."

I look away from him, mirroring Schofield's signature gesture—the nodding, the pursing. It's a good gesture, I realize as I perform it. Respectful, while not giving anything away. A face-saving gesture, which I have need of right now.

Unspoken: We'll just pretend like he didn't make the same suggestion five minutes ago. I open my door. The wind wrenches it out of my hand.

"But we'll just *creep*," I hear Schofield call from some-where behind me. "We'll creep like you said before."

I stagger to the other side of the car, blasted by ice-white and freezing nothing.

The Crowfeather Inn has no record of a reservation for a Dermot Schofield.

"Really?" I keep saying, over and over again. "*Really?*"

"I'm so sorry," says the man behind the desk.

"Surely you have a room available?" prods Schofield.

Let me handle this, Dermot, I want to say. I've grown up in the motel business. I know how to deal with these people. But actually I'm intimidated, because the Crowfeather is nothing like my parents' place, called the Highwayman. ("We rob ya blind!" my father will joke counterintuitively to tourists.)

The Crowfeather does that turn-of-the-century thing with its decor, like the English Department but without all the dust and burnt coffee smell. Plush chairs, velvet drapes, gilded wall-paper, sumptuous tones, whereas the Highwayman has buoys and driftwood hanging on the walls of the lobby. Nobody I know likes the Crowfeather in particular. Apparently a couple of American hippies emerged from the woods one day where they had been living in a commune since the mid-sixties. Most of the hippies left after a couple of years, rumour has it, because they were developing scurvy during the winters. The current proprietors of the Crowfeather stuck it out, however, hitchhiking back and forth into town for vitamin supplements and other sundries—back and forth, back and forth—until finally they realized they were spending more time in town than at the commune. So then they sold the commune and bought an ostentatious yet shambling Victorian home on the edge of town whose ancient owner—a Grayson, no surprise— had freshly died. It was revealed at that point that the two American hippies were rich—had more money than they knew what to do with. The commune had been like a hobby to them, and now starting up the Crowfeather was their hobby. This annoyed locals, who were further annoyed to see how well the inn did. People made fun of it initially, just as they had made fun of the commune. But the hippies took out ads in *Harper's* magazine and *The New Yorker*. They made Timperly, New Brunswick, a summer holiday destination— something no home-grown entrepreneur had ever accomplished. Still, locals disdain the place, say that it is "big-feeling." They feel obliquely ripped off by the Crowfeather Inn somehow. It's the Westcock crowd that keeps the place going—sucking up the antiques, the opulence. It's the only fancy place to eat in town. The dining room is every student's first choice whenever their parents come to take them out. It's constantly booked for graduation dinners and small, tasteful wedding parties, and to entertain visiting dignitaries like Dermot Schofield.

I'm wondering if I should call Jim, admit defeat, when the man behind the desk says, "Oh, absolutely, sir. Absolutely we have rooms," and I release my breath. Schofield's enormous shoulders shift beneath his parka. He seizes a pen in his catcher's mitt and begins to fill in the paperwork.

"How long will you be staying, sir?"

"Just the one night."

"On your way somewhere for Christmas?"

"To Nova Scotia, yes."

I peer at the desk guy to see if he's an American hippie. But he's leaning on his counter, getting comfortable, prepared in that Maritime way to talk all night long about geography and weather systems.

"Where in Nova Scotia, now?" His accent grows folksy now that he knows he's not dealing with an Upper Canadian or someone from the States. "I've got a sister up in Yarmouth," he proffers.

"Down Antigonish way," Schofield obliges.

"The Highland Heart of Nova Scotia," recites the desk guy, quoting some tourist brochure from days gone by.

"That's right," smiles Schofield, passing the pen and paper back across the counter. The man scrutinizes it.

"Now, Schofield's not a Scottish name, is it?" he inquires, nearly scolding. "I thought it was all Scotsmen up that way."

I could curl up on the floor with ennui. Give me a hippie any day over this. It's like Todd after a couple of beers: What's your mother's name? Nope, Protestant, don't approve. What's your father's name? Catholic, good, check. What part of Scotland, *exactly?* Hm, nope, a shame. If it were a mile farther south, I'd be buying your drinks.

"Just your basic English name," admits Schofield, "with Dermot tacked on for my mother's side of the family."

The desk guy squints. "Irish?"

"That's right."

North Irish or South Irish? Black Irish or Purple Irish? Up Irish or Down Irish? I can just see the guy gearing up for a cross-examination. But the paperwork stops him. He remembers we're here to do business.

"Of course we'll be needing a deposit," he tells us with a gesture of embarrassment.

"What?" I say. "What?"

"A deposit?" repeats Schofield. He's as surprised as me.

"It's policy," explains the desk guy.

Schofield is nodding. I peek to see if he's pursing too. Yes. He's pursing.

"Excuse me," I say. "But I—I've worked in the hotel industry and I've never heard of having to give a deposit."

The desk guy stares as if he's just noticed me and wonders why I haven't been thrown out yet. "It's pretty common these days," he says.

"Well, it seems a little mercenary."

He raises his eyebrows at me. "This *is* a business."

I realize, with that bob of the eyebrows, that the desk guy is not going to give in. I feel hot and desperate like I'm having a poem scrutinized in class. He doesn't see anything at all wrong with asking for a deposit.

"Well, I'd just like to know what the world is coming to," I hear myself barking.

"You would, would you?"

"Yes," I bark. "I would."

"Mr. Schofield," says the man behind the counter. "Is this your *son?*"

It's the only time I've ever really wanted to punch someone, aside from my grandmother.

"How much?" say Schofield.

"That will be thirty dollars, please."

"Gah!" I say.

"That's fine," soothes Schofield, reaching into his back pocket.

My mind is flopping around like a dying trout. How much can the room be if the deposit is thirty dollars? Did Jim know how much the room would cost when he booked it? But of course Jim never booked it. He must have forgotten in all the pre-Christmas bustle. I look down and see that I am tugging on Schofield's arm like a child, which is pretty much what I feel like, standing beside him.

"Mr. Schofield," I say. "Jim will cover this. I mean, the university will pay you back for everything."

"That's fine, Larry, really."

"I'm so sorry," I bleat, aware I have lost all credibility now. So much for keeping my cool. So much for showing him who's in charge. "I wasn't expecting any of this."

"Larry," says Schofield, avoiding my gaze as he hands a fistful of tens and fives over to the desk guy, who stands like he's hearing none of this. "It's not your fault. These things happen." Relieved of his cash—probably all the cash he has on him—Schofield looks down at me and smiles. "Okay?" he inquires. He is waiting, patiently, for me to tell him it's okay. It strikes me as a weirdly maternal thing to do. I wonder if he's going to touch my leg again.

And now the man is buying me dinner at the inn.

I fought it. I demurred. And then I veered into outright reluctance when Schofield persisted. So the reluctance became balking. Still Schofield was adamant. The balks were then upped to a series of objections—I lingered there for a while—Schofield must be tired, he must be sick of me, he must want time to prepare for his reading. Soon I found myself writhing and shouting and gnashing my teeth in the Crowfeather lobby. No! It was insane! We were supposed to be his hosts! And here he was having to pay for his own hotel room! I couldn't ask him to buy me dinner on top of all that! I almost got him killed by a snowplow!

The whole time Schofield rocked back and forth on his heels—uncomfortable standing up, uncomfortable with my discomfort. He explained to me that in fact he *was* tired, but that didn't mean he couldn't use some company. He would be reading pieces tonight he'd read dozens of times in the past. He required no time to prepare.

"I only get nervous about the reading," Schofield told me, "when I'm left to myself. What I need is distraction. Conversation."

But I'm a *cretin,* I wanted to protest. For the past hour all I'd been able to think about was getting the hell away from Schofield on the assumption that he wanted nothing more than for me to get the hell away from him. I couldn't just let go of this conviction all at once.

"Think about it," I pleaded. "You don't want to sit around talking to me before your reading. My God, you've done that for the last hour on the drive over here."

"This is different, Larry. Now we can relax. Have a bite to eat and some wine and relive our triumph over the elements."

Agonized, I looked around the lobby for a pay phone. "I could call Jim for you."

Why can't I be rich, I was whining internally. Why must I be poor. I don't even have money for Christmas presents. Why can't I be a hippie from the States with nothing to do but buy up patches of New Brunswick. Why can't I be the one lavishing money on the visiting poet instead of the other way around.

Schofield started laughing then. I could tell it was from a kind of frustration. "Larry," he said. "*You're* here. For the love of God, man, just come and have a bite to eat with me. Are you going to make me beg?"

Schofield asks if I like white wine or red and, because I don't like either, I toss a mental coin and say red. It comes and we sip. All of a sudden I am tired. I am thoroughly tired, having driven myself on fumes and nerves for the past few hours. A basket of bread arrives. Schofield takes one bun, cuts it in half with his knife. Butters it, eats it in small bites. Meanwhile I have polished off the rest of the basket.

"Sorry," I say, idly shaking the basket.

"Growing boy," remarks Schofield.

That word again.

The nice thing about being this tired is, I don't have the energy to be nervous anymore. After a few more sips of wine, the nervousness drains away. I don't even feel bad about eating all the bread. The wine tastes like nothing to me—dusty nothing. It tastes like the English Department. I seem to be experiencing it somewhere inside of my nose instead of my palate.

"So you're a student of Arsenault's," says my host. With that word, with that *Arsenault,* my defence system attempts to creak back into gear. Am I dining with the enemy here? Was this some kind of plan—wear a guy down, invite him to dinner, pour wine down his throat, and then—

"Yeah. Yes. I'm in Jim's poetry seminar."

"How are you liking it?"

"It's *absolutely wonderful,*" I enunciate.

"I'm sure," says Schofield.

"Absolutely. Wonderful," I repeat, looking him in the eye, trying to penetrate my gaze through the thick lenses of his glasses. I wonder if they're the kind of glasses that make your eyes look bigger. If so, Schofield's eyes must be pinpricks. Beady little pinpricks.

Suddenly the word *pinprick* appeals to me so much I have to dig out my journal, making apologies to Schofield as I do. I realize, as I envision it on the page, my preference seems to be for words that are meant to be two but that become more interesting merged into one. Deadwood. Showdogs. Pinpricks. It seems to intensify yet open up the meaning all at once.

Schofield watches me write, for lack of anything else to do. He doesn't say anything, just waits.

"I get these words in my head," I explain, feeling that it's my job to break the silence. "It's not like I ever get ideas for entire concepts or phrases. It's just these single words that I like. And I don't even know why I like them. My journal is full of words, all by themselves."

"That's valid," says Schofield. I don't know what to make of his response. Is he being condescending? I peer at him. His glasses flicker in the candlelight.

"Anyway," I shrug, stuffing my journal away, "I go with it."

"Some poets are word-oriented," says Schofield, dipping his head like a sage, "and some are image-oriented. I'm word-oriented, like you. I see the words on the page before I write them."

"Yes!" I say, leaning forward.

"Arsenault is image-oriented," adds Schofield.

I sit back again at the mention of Arsenault.

"Well, I don't think there's anything wrong with that," I say.

"Certainly not," agrees Schofield.

"I mean, have you read any of Jim's work?"

"I've read a great deal of Arsenault's work," is Schofield's reply. "I'm his biggest fan."

This confuses me. It confuses me because Jim clearly hates Schofield, and I assumed there had to be a good reason why. But after reading Schofield's poetry and meeting him, the only logical reason left for Jim's dislike is that Schofield must dislike Jim every bit as much—or at least his poetry, which, let's face it, amounts to the same thing.

"Well—" I say after a moment of sitting with my mouth open. And then it just comes out. "Jim's mad at you, you know."

A mirthful little crease appears between Schofield's big cheeks. "Arsenault," he says, "has never been shy about letting people know when his feelings are hurt."

I fold my arms. So here they are at last—Schofield's fangs. Admitting to have hurt Jim's feelings, and having the audacity to snicker at it on top of that.

"What did you do to him?" I demand.

Schofield's bulky mass sort of jumps minutely up and down in its chair. Laughing. The man is laughing.

"It was entirely my fault, I have to admit. I committed the cardinal sin, Larry. I reviewed a friend's work."

"You reviewed *Blinding White*? Where?"

And what kind of soulless thug would Schofield have to be to give a bad review to *Blinding White*?

"*Atlantica*, a year or so ago. If anything," he says, dabbing behind his glasses with a napkin, "it was biased in Arsenault's favour. I was afraid I'd be accused of pulling my punches. Because of our friendship." Schofield puts the napkin down and blinks a few times. He seems to start when my face comes into focus.

"Don't worry, Larry," he assures me, arranging his features into ersatz seriousness, as if in mockery of mine. "Arsenault has already put me soundly in my place."

I think about Jim swinging his arms around in fury the night we all had dinner at his house.

That the man would sit here *laughing*.

Our food comes, and I look at it. I've ordered what was described on the menu as a Rustic Chicken Stew. It's tomatoey. I've never heard of tomatoey chicken stew. Is "rustic" supposed to serve as a code? For tomatoey? Don't the hippies realize this is New Brunswick? Everything is rustic here.

We're eating now. I haven't responded to Schofield's last remark, and probably am coming across as snotty.

"I read *Malignant Cove*," I tell him, eating around the tomatoes.

"Did you?" says Schofield. He sounds surprised.

"I liked it," I admit. "I liked it a lot."

"Thank you very much, Larry," he says in one breath. I look up, and he's staring intently at his plate, chewing a mouthful of food. He must have expelled the words in such a manner so as not to slow down his fork's progression toward his mouth.

"The poem about the man words and woman words . . . It was really amazing," I say.

Schofield looks up at me, his expression boyish. "Oh," he says, smiling quite a bit. "I like that one too."

I can't help but smile back. Delight, that's what Schofield is feeling. A grown man and a published poet experiencing delight when some nineteen-year-old compliments him on a piece of writing he's particularly proud of. I want to be him so bad all of a sudden.

"It must be great being a poet," I say before I can stop myself.

Schofield starts bouncing in his chair again, pinprick eyes squeezed shut.

"Well," he says, "you're a poet, aren't you, Larry? You tell me."

"I mean a *real* poet," I say, giving him something of a warning look. Don't patronize me, Dermot. We both know the difference.

He stops bouncing as a result. "You mean published."

"I mean published," I agree. "Reviewed, acknowledged. *Known.* Celebrated."

"I don't know if I'd call myself *celebrated,*" Schofield demurs.

"You've won awards," I insist.

He nods. "I have."

"So?" I say. "This is what I'm talking about."

"It's gratifying," Schofield acknowledges after a moment.

Gratifying? I open my mouth in exasperation.

"Of course, there are always reviews like Arsenault's to be endured," Schofield smiles.

My face goes hot, I don't know why. Jim was the one who wrote *mucus-like sheen of mendacity,* not me. On some level, I guess I must have had myself convinced that Schofield could never have read it. How could he have accepted Jim's invitation to come here after seeing himself compared to a smelly, stagnant swamp, a wasting sickness in the body of Canadian poetry?

Schofield sees me blushing and holds up his hand to make it stop. "It's all part of the game," he tells me.

"Game?" I say. "Poetry?"

"Not poetry," he says. "What you're talking about. Being reviewed, acknowledged, *known.* Not writing poetry, but being a poet."

"There's no difference," I insist. "If you're an artist, you're born an artist . . ."

"But that's something else altogether. I'm talking about being a poet—in your terms. Known, reviewed, acknowledged."

"But it's indistinguishable," I say.

"It's very distinguishable," contends Schofield.

"You don't write for an audience?" I challenge. "You write just for yourself? Into the void? With no hope of acknowledgment or, or public appreciation?"

Schofield kind of sighs into his rib-eye.

"No, no," he replies.

So I sit and wait. The poet takes a contemplative moment to smooth out a clump of mashed potatoes with the back of his fork.

"When you're published," he finally begins, looking up, " . . . it's wonderful. The first jolt is one of validation: I've done it. Somebody else out there—perhaps someone who's already published poets I admire—has published me. Suddenly I'm not the only one calling myself a poet anymore."

Nod, nod, nod, goes my salivating head.

"It's a wonderful feeling of *legitimacy,*" Schofield continues. "You've proven yourself a member of a pantheon you've idolized your entire life. That's important. It's important to achieve that feeling of legitimacy—that external validation. I am by no means telling you not to aspire to that. I'm not telling you to write to the void, that wanting to be published makes you some kind of sellout. That's nonsense."

"Okay," I say, sitting back, the wind of belligerence somewhat taken from my sails.

Schofield sips his wine, glancing away. Watching him, it strikes me that he finds this subject torturous. He continues to gaze for a good minute and a half at anything in the restaurant that isn't me.

"Is there a 'but' in there somewhere?" I prompt.

"It's just—" he begins, wriggling around in his chair as much as a three-hundred-pound man is able. "You think the *embarrassment* is going to go away at some point. But it doesn't. It's public, so it's intensified. And then your peers come along and they—" (a careful glance at me, he knows we're both thinking *Jim* at this point) "—intensify it even more."

I stare at him.

Schofield meets my look with a small wince. "I'm not explaining it very well—"

"No, no," I lie.

"It's just—when you've idealized something for so long as this pure, true, untainted thing—when you've wanted to belong to that world for so long, it's *painful* to discover—once you're there—that it's . . . ," Schofield flails. "It's just . . . ," he waves his hands around. "It's *high school*," he finally expels.

Schofield follows this up with a full-bodied sigh, before—torture victim in repose—going limp in his chair.

I've folded my arms again. Very tight. Practically giving myself fucking breasts.

II.

IN THE PARKING LOT of the Crowfeather, Jim's car is buried up to the grille in snow—we don't even bother getting in. Schofield pulls up his hood, I stick my hands in my pockets, and we trek the three blocks to campus, heads down. Sometimes a small town can be a blessing.

And sometimes a snowstorm can be a blessing. Like when you are annoyed and worn out from talking to a person and need an excuse to keep quiet for three blocks. I am angry at myself for letting him buy me dinner, drinking wine on his dollar, letting myself be lulled, sucked in. You talk to Jim about poetry, you feel electrified—he rhymes off names, cites brilliant passages, strings them all together like pearls in any random conversation, makes you feel like the world is a place that brims with beauty and genius at all times, no matter where you are—Timperly, Summerside, Malignant Cove, or anywhere. Jim reminds you that the poetry is always there, illuminating the otherwise dim-bulb world, and the poetry, once you've got hold of it, is all that matters—is what brings the good back to life.

You talk to Schofield about poetry and he squirms in his chair and tells you it's *high school*. The whole point has always been that poetry was and is the opposite of high school. And elementary school. And Summerside, and the Highwayman Motor Hotel and Mini-Putt. Cousin Wayne turning his eyelids inside out, administering Indian burns. Lydia with her nose-flicks and *nonsense*. It's an *escape*. It's the literal *deus ex machina*. The thing that lifts you up and out.

Here's a moment of clarity. I don't like Schofield because I'm afraid I am him. I'm afraid I will be the kind of poet that he is, instead of the kind of poet that Jim is. Schofield reminds me of myself. He is nervous and squishy on the subject of poetry. It makes him embarrassed. On some level, he thinks what he does is stupid, unworthy. All I've ever wanted to believe since I started filling Hilroy notebooks was that at some point, life would grant me the acclaim—the *validation,* as Schofield put it—to allow me to shake this omnipresent conviction that *I am an idiot for doing this.* Now I've just come face to big fat face with the possibility that it might never go away, the idiot-conviction.

In high school, grade 8 to be exact, a bunch of girls got hold of my orange Hilroy. Orange was for formal, old-fashioned stuff, stuff that rhymed—imitations of Donne and Byron and the like; blue was free-verse beatniky crap (I actually had a teenager's eight-page howl against PEI scrawled in there, called "A Phony Island of the Mind"), and green was for prose. So these girls, they cornered me in the parking lot, the head cheerleader among them clutching it rolled up like a magazine in both hands. We didn't actually have cheerleaders at my high school because the Lydia-types running the PTA pronounced such things indecent. But if we had, this group would have dominated the squad.

The girls said they had read the entire orange Hilroy and were afraid I was going to kill myself. It was agonizing, because they were nice girls, I suppose—they seemed genuinely concerned at least—even popular girls, but they were stupid girls. Therefore, stupid, popular girls had been the first on earth to read my poetry. The leader-type gazed at me with her dull, earnest eyes and said, "We're really worried about you, Larry." She'd never spoken to me before in my life.

"You see," I tried to explain, "the Romantic poets were always making these overblown statements, like, Oh, I'm gonna kill myself if Lady Gwendolyn fails to return my love, and I was just . . . trying to . . ."

"Yes, but, Larry," interrupted Stepford cheerleader #1, "we don't think it's *healthy.*"

They all nodded, marble-eyed, golden hair billowing. They were kind of like penguins in their uniformity.

"It's not *healthy* to be dwelling on that sort of thing, writing it down in a *book* over and *over*."

"It's perfectly healthy," I argued. "You know, I'm learning to be a poet, so . . . this is the kind of thing I have to *do*. I'm practising. It's just like if you girls wanted to be, like, dancers or something . . ."

"I want to be a *nurse*," #1 told me, drawing herself up in all her blonde authority, "and you don't see me trying to take people's pulses or giving them sponge baths in the hallway." She kept gazing into my eyes, didn't even allow herself a smile of superiority.

"Poetry is different," I writhed.

"Well, we're really concerned, that's all we're saying." #1's chin wobbled tinily and for a second I thought she was going to take my hand. "We thought of bringing it to Mr. McKinnon," she added. Who was the guidance counsellor.

"Oh, Jesus Christ!" I said.

"But we won't," #1 assured me, "if you promise never to do it again. Not to think about this kind of stuff. Ever. Again, Larry."

I opened my mouth. It stayed open for a second. "Okay," I said.

"Okay," smiled the nurse-in-training, with a nurse's comforting, patronizing, fascistic pat on the arm.

So they whirled away, a carnival of skirts and ponytails, leaving me in a state of such nut-crunching mortification that for a while I genuinely believed I hadn't lied to #1 when I told her I'd never write again. Never. Again. *Jawohl, Fräulein*. Just don't let me experience anything remotely akin to this feeling at any given point in the future. Burn the Hilroys—hell, I'd been planning on burning the green one all along anyway. Report to Dad as caretaker-for-life at the

Highwayman Motor Hotel. Don coveralls, maybe a straw hat. Communicate in friendly grunts that bespeak a brain injury of some sort. Be picturesque, rustic. Quaintly inscrutable for the tourists when directing them—through a series of spasmodic gestures to accompany the grunts—to Lucy Maud Montgomery's house.

And the girls didn't tell Mr. McKinnon—they just told the rest of the school. Hilroys were ripped from my arms everywhere I went for the next few months, gleefully opened and pored over while I stood pinned against various walls, poles, and lockers. All the scribblers revealed, to everyone's disappointment, were history notes, long division, and the like. I'd caught on fast, you see. So maybe I owed the Stepfords a debt of gratitude.

Hide. Divert. That's what I learned about being a poet in high school. Deny it like you would a contagion, a betrayal.

Outside the room where Dermot Schofield is supposed to give his reading, Sherrie, Todd, and everyone else from Jim's class—plus, to my gratification, a couple of strangers—stand huddled in the hallway, coats folded over arms.

"What's wrong?" I say as Schofield and I advance, patting snow from ourselves.

"It's the wrong room," says Todd, leaning thuggishly against a wall.

I look at the door. A sign—a piece of looseleaf scribbled on with pen—reads, *Dermot Schofield Reading Here Today 7 p.m.* The writing has a ghostly, half-there quality to it, as though the pen was nearly dry of ink. I have to step close and peer to read it. The sign is written in the same sprawling scrawl that prettifies my returned poetry assignments.

Beyond the sign, through the window, I can see a class taking place. It's a big class, and looks to be right in the middle of its business. The students have that slouched, resigned aspect of being halfway through, as opposed to the alert, anticipatory demeanour of being about to go home. The prof has a dogged, dug-in sort of look.

I glance over at Schofield, as if for an explanation. He stands slightly apart from the group of us and actually gives an apologetic shrug.

"Well, I mean the *sign* is up," I say, looking around for help, for Jim.

"But there's a class in there," says Todd.

"Well . . . did anyone say anything to them?"

I keep looking around, hoping my eyes will hit upon someone who will step forward, roll up their sleeves, and decisively take charge. They all just stare at me.

"No," says Todd at last, in what I must say is something of an insolent tone. His eyes drift over my shoulder to where Schofield is standing, and he takes a few steps forward. "Hi," he says, holding out his hand. "I'm Todd Smiley."

"Dermot," says Schofield.

"I really liked your last book."

"Thank you very much, Todd."

So now I turn to Sherrie for help.

"Maybe they're going long," she suggests, gesturing to the closed door. "Sometimes the profs get carried away."

I peer through the window again. Some of the students within are starting to notice me.

"Should we—should we ask?"

"Maybe," answers Sherrie, bringing her teeth together in a gesture of delicacy.

"Maybe," I repeat, in such a way as to let her know how distinctly useless is her response.

Everyone in the hallway kind of shuffles around, parkas and corduroys rustling, minute signals of impatience directed at me.

I knock, quietly, and then open the door.

"I'm sorry," I tell the class. The students take me in with relief and gratitude. The prof turns to me with a glazed sort of look.

"Yes?" he says.

"We're supposed to hold a poetry reading in this room tonight," I tell him. "I was wondering—are you going late?"

The prof blinks a few times. "No," he tells me. "We're not going late, we're here another hour. We're here every Friday."

"I thought classes were over," I say, half-hoping to convince everyone in the room they've made some kind of a mistake.

"Today's the last day," blinks the prof, frowning at me.

Oh, yes. I had a class today, didn't I. My mouth moves as I try to think of a sentence to get these people gathering up their coats and bookbags. Your cars are being towed. There's a storm out there, you know. I could pull the fire alarm.

"If you don't mind," interrupts the prof, "we have a great deal to get through."

I nod and quietly pull the door shut.

Failure, but not for long. As I turn back to the huddle with contrition, I can see Jim coming toward us, trucking down the hall with his long, loping strides. Slaughter is with him, perpetually large and bored.

"Jim," I say.

And am ignored. A big grin is cracking his face as Jim lopes past me toward Dermot Schofield. A strange noise is coming from somewhere behind the grin, an animal-istic, drawn-out kind of moan which sounds like, *Ehhhhhhhhhhhhhhhhhhhhh?* Like a long question. Jim doesn't stop, doesn't take a new breath until he is face to face with Schofield. All heads swivel as if magnetized.

"*Ehaaaand* there he is," finishes Jim. "The fat bastard himself."

Another shrug from Schofield. Apologetic, yet again. Sorry to be a fat bastard.

"How are you, Jim?"

"Fuck that," says Jim, grabbing hold of Schofield's mitt. Then, with his free hand, Jim throws an arm around the fridge-like shoulders, tries to pull Schofield toward him like he did Dekker in the department that day. But Schofield neglects to float into Jim's embrace in the same easy, half-dreaming way that Dekker did. Taken by surprise, he loses his balance and stumbles. Jim catches him in an exaggerated gesture, calling, "Whoa, there!" as if Schofield is some kind of disoriented steer, too dumb to register the damage it's capable of.

It strikes me that Jim is performing for everyone.

Schofield gains his footing, lets himself lean into Jim for a moment and get his back patted. He rests one of his swollen hands between Jim's shoulder blades for a quick moment.

"It's good to see you," says Jim, now holding Schofield by the shoulders as if to keep him steady.

"It's good to hear that," mutters Schofield, reaching up to remove and clean his glasses. The gesture means Jim has to let him go.

Then the inevitable awkward silence, during which Jim takes the time to look around, focus in on me, and ask what everybody's standing around in the hall for.

Maybe poetic friendships are the only true friendships, where each friend feels entitled to be as ruthlessly—even viciously—honest as necessary when it comes to discussion of the other's work. After all, the work is what matters, the work must always come first. And poets know this implicitly, which is why they bear no grudges when they meet face to face, even after all the blood sport that has taken place on the page.

I wonder if Todd will grasp this when I tell him what I think of his Harvest Excursion poem.

Lately I've been thinking a lot about Keats—Keats, who was said to have been killed by a bad review. I tend to trade off a lot on the Romantic poets. For a while, Byron was my man, and when I heard Byron was friends with Shelley, I got interested in Shelley, but Shelley never managed to grab me by the guts in the same sort of way. Then I read somewhere about how Byron was always making fun of Keats—whom Shelley considered the bee's knees—so I turned to Keats, ready to mock him in kind, taking my cue from my man George Gordon. But I found I didn't mind Keats. In fact, I liked Keats. He was sort of quiet and sly. And pretty soon I liked Keats better than Byron and Shelley put together. I began to be annoyed by the very romance that first attracted me to Byron, his courtly affairs, his flouncing, self-important sojourns to calculatedly exotic locales. After a while I even found his club foot an irritant—it struck me as a ploy for attention, a physical flaw contrived to give himself some kind of air of tragic predestination, like a mark of Cain. Around this time, *Childe Harold's Pilgrimage*—to which I was on the verge of building a shrine the year the Stepfords cornered me—started to get on my nerves. Oh boo hoo hoo, poor Childe Harold—this struck me as the overarching theme of the poem. Boo hoo hoo, look at me with my sullen tears.

And here is the line that outraged the Presbyterian island boy in me the most:

with pleasure drugg'd, he almost longed for woe

He almost longed for woe. Why? Because of all that pleasure. What with being a lord and sleeping with noble-women and drinking wine out of a skull and such.

So this was what got me looking at Keats, checking out

the enemy camp. I found out that Keats was a commoner, and this was why Byron made fun of him all the time. After Keats's death, Byron relented somewhat, said maybe Keats didn't stink quite so bad after all. All that snottiness because Keats hadn't been a lord, like Gord. Byron, for all his iconoclastic posturing, was a snob. He was an upper-class twit.

I'm thinking so hard, hoofing it across the quad through the storm, that by the time I get inside the building, I realize I didn't even notice the snow and wind lashing against me. This happens to me sometimes. I start thinking about writers who make me excited or angry, begin ranting inwardly, then zone out. I heave myself up the two flights of stairs, trying not to be creeped by how dark and empty the stairwell is—the suddenness of the silence after being outside in the howl. Trying not to think about the girl who hung herself for Donne from the very railing my hand is on. I've been tasked to see if Mrs. Gaudet is still lingering about the department—a futile task, in my opinion, as it's after seven o'clock on a stormy Friday night. But Jim seems to think she might still be working and, if so, can open another classroom for us. The squeak of my wet boots against the floor is amplified into ear-puncturing shrieks by the stairwell acoustics. I stick Jim's key in the lock, groaning as I yank open the department door, and my groan echoes too.

Did she *shriek?* my morbid imagination pipes up. *Did* she *groan? Dangling away in here? Waiting to be found?*

The department is dark except for a light in the student lounge and one that pours into the hallway from beyond Mrs. Gaudet's open office door. I squeak rapidly down the hall, relieved as much by the fact that there's another living being in here as I am by the knowledge that Jim has guessed right, that the dogged Marjorie is working late. Solid, resolute Marjorie will save the day. It must be going on 7:30 by now.

Standing in Mrs. Gaudet's dimly lit office, no Mrs. Gaudet in sight, no coat on the rack, her ashtray emptied, her typewriter covered and files put away, I am going to confess that I was relieved by a third thing a moment ago. I was relieved that I wouldn't have to do what Jim instructed me to do if Mrs. Gaudet had gone home. Which is to go through her top drawer and fish out a key to the conference room downstairs. Her keys are in the top drawer, Jim said.

I find that I don't want to. I thought I could. I nodded rapidly when he told me to, nerves jazzed on what I could see was Jim's rising annoyance. When he heard what the interloper prof had told me, Jim flung open the classroom door himself and demanded to know what the hell was going on. The students all sat up straight and the prof did his blink-thing a few hundred times before reiterating that this was a *class* and he was *teaching* it. Jim claimed to have booked the classroom weeks in advance and the prof told him that simply wasn't possible, he was there with his group every Friday night and in fact he had been teaching that same class in that same room for the past three years. Jim then demanded, for some reason, to know what the class was, and the prof told him—blink after perplexed blink—that it was a second-year Sociology seminar. Jim curled his lip as if to say that he had expected as much, snorted, and slammed the door.

"Well, fuck!" he spat at the bunch of us in the hallway. (Apologetic shrug again from Schofield—another signature gesture, along with the nodding and pursing.) Practically in the same heartbeat, spittle from the *fuck!* still glistening on his lips, Jim had his arm around me and pulled me aside. It sort of hurt, Jim's hand on my shoulder. Then with a red, somewhat pulsing face he told me what to do. And I was ready to do it.

But now I don't want to. Go digging through Mrs. Gaudet's top drawer. It doesn't seem right. It seems dirty, almost, and I feel my bowels constrict in the same way they did when I was eight in Janet's bedroom, witnessing the compromise of Barbie and Joe. The same mix of doom and excitement elbowing its way around my intestines.

Because it would be kind of interesting to go through Mrs. Gaudet's drawer, when you think of it. A woman's top drawer is a private thing, you would expect. There, Mrs. Gaudet would place the items she requires most, personal items, items she needs quick, effortless access to. Women's things. Lipstick. A mirror, maybe. Earrings. An extra pair of pantyhose. And what about panties themselves? Women need backup, they can't just leave the house in the hope that a single pair of panties is going to get them through the day. Women are organized like that, they're obsessive about this kind of stuff. My mother practically packs a suitcase every time she goes out to buy mushroom manure.

Therefore, the overripe Mrs. Gaudet's top drawer is trembling to burst with creamy silk underthings. Voluminous see-through bras, equatorial garter belts, maybe a whip somewhere near the bottom. And it's up to the intrepid young Campbell to pry open her treasure box, stand for a brief, unsteady moment drinking in the sight of those lurid pinks and blushing peaches, before Lawrence—reckless, now, panting slightly—thrusts his sweaty-palmed hand down into the inviting, satiny folds within. To emerge with—the treasure. The grail. The key.

Our hero!

"Lawrence."

For the second time this month I'm facing the head of the department of English with a bone in my pants.

"Hi!" I say.

Doctor Sparrow squints at me and smiles just a little through the wisps of his beard. "You spooked me," he says after a moment. "I thought you were our ghost."

"Oh, I'm sorry," I scream.

"Not at all," says Doctor Sparrow. I stare at him. On some level, I understand the expression *not at all* to mean *that's all right,* or *don't worry about it.* But at this particular high-strung moment, it strikes me as the strangest thing to say in the world. *I'm sorry. Not at all.* It's like an attempt to negate the last thing I said. It feels almost belligerent.

"Is everything all right?" Doctor Sparrow wants to know. *Not at all! Not at all!*

"Oh yes!" I assure him, my hand still poised on the handle of Mrs. Gaudet's open top drawer. I'm reminded of this fact when Sparrow allows his gaze to flicker downward. It takes in the open drawer and then bounces right back up to meet my eye.

"Are you," he asks, still smiling behind the wisps, "in need of something here?"

"In fact . . . ," I say, gulpingly.

Sparrow arches his eyebrows. "Yes?"

"We're having a bit of a problem."

"We?"

"The reading tonight."

"Reading?"

"Dermot Schofield."

Sparrow remains blank. I clear my throat.

"The reading Professor Arsenault organized for tonight?"

"Ah." Sparrow tilts his chin and shifts position slightly to indicate that now he remembers. But also, barely perceptible, the same slight wilt I witnessed when we spoke in his office. When I reminded him of the creative writing option.

"It's a poetry reading?" questions Sparrow.

"Yes," I say. "Dermot Schofield. We put up signs?"

"Ah, yes, I remember now, Lawrence, yes."

"Well, it's supposed to be going on right now," I explain. "The reading."

Sparrow frowns. Behind the wisps. "This is a strange time of year for a reading," he says.

I can't believe he didn't see any of the signs. I put them everywhere.

"I know!" I exclaim. "It *is,* and with the *storm* and every-thing . . . But anyway, the problem is, we don't have a room."

"You don't have a room for the reading?"

I shake my head. "It's been double-booked."

Sparrow keeps frowning. He blinks a few times as well, seeming to have trouble with the information. It seems to me that poets and writers and academics as a whole are not a breed of people meant to be faced with logistical problems. We all seem to go intellectually limp.

"What can I do to help?" asks Sparrow after a moment of this.

"Well, that's why I'm here," I explain, recovering, regain-ing the powers of explanation and coherent speech, "digging around in, in the drawer. Jim said Mrs. Gaudet had a key to the conference room in here . . . So I—" I end the sentence at that point, gesturing twitchily at the desk.

Sparrow comes over and starts poking around in the drawer himself. "Yes, yes," he mutters, rifling through Marjorie's pens and paper clips—not a garter belt in sight. "I believe she does . . . somewhere."

"Um, maybe it's one of these," I say, holding out the key ring I've already uncovered. Sparrow peers at it.

"But Lawrence," he says, "the conference room is no place for a poetry reading. Why not just have everybody come up here?"

"Up here?"

"To the lounge. There's plenty of room—how many peo-ple do you suppose are in attendance?"

"Maybe around ten or fifteen?"

"Plenty of room," repeats Sparrow. "You're welcome to

bring up some extra chairs from the conference room, if necessary."

It's a perfect idea. The lounge, with all its Grayson antiques and the coffee machine and the fireplace. Classy. I envision Schofield resting one of his massive arms on the mantelpiece.

"Maybe we could light a fire!" I say.

"No, no," smiles Sparrow, "that fireplace hasn't been lit in decades—the place would go up like a pile of twigs."

"Oh," I say. "But still. It's perfect!"

"Oh, good," nods Sparrow, clasping his hands together. "Problem solved!"

"We really appreciate this, Doctor Sparrow," I babble, not quite knowing on behalf of whom I'm speaking when I say *we*.

"Not at all," Doctor Sparrow murmurs, pleased with himself behind his beard. "Happy to be of assistance." He crinkles his eyes at me, sparkling like jolly old Saint Nick's.

Next, I nearly kill myself. My boots are still wet. In response to my hurry and exhilaration, they let out a particularly anguished shriek halfway down the stairwell before somehow managing to manoeuvre themselves out from underneath my body, thrusting their way upward to look me momentarily in the face before all three of us come crashing down with a reverberating thud. No *smack*, or *crack*—my skull hasn't bounced against the floor. But, ow. It's the kind of shock to the body that makes you need to be still for a moment. Lie there getting yourself together. Listen to the walls and metal handrails continue to resonate with the thud and the loud *ooof!* you involuntarily made when your lungs hit the tile. Wonder if you would even know if you were injured right now—bleeding internally, a hairline fracture. What if you can't get up? What if you're here all night, just lying here, gazing up at the top-floor railing, from which the Donne-girl hung herself? What if she eventually materializes above you—at midnight, maybe, blue face mooning down? And what if she fell? What if you had to watch her decomposed body hurtling straight at you as you lay powerless to move, here on the landing?

I'm down only for a second, but I imagine all these things. It's like those stories you hear about dream research—how dream time works differently. People can dream entire operas in the space of a minute, apparently. I read about this one guy who had an endlessly elaborate dream about the French Revolution. He was an aristocrat, captured by the revolution-aries, imprisoned in the Bastille, tried by Robespierre, and finally brought to the guillotine. He awoke the moment the blade dropped, only to discover that the headboard of his bed had fallen onto his neck. It was surmised that the entire dream must have taken place in the split second the moment the headboard detached itself and fell.

So here's me, dreaming on the floor, contemplating my upcoming tussle with the corpse, my as-yet-undiscovered hairline fracture, my future as the nation's premier paraplegic poet. And dreaming of that, I also dream something else way back in my head—something suffused, I'll admit, with a weird, masochistic euphoria. It's a brief thought, like a dirty, forbidden impulse—a Freud kind of thought, like sleeping with your mother—there but almost not. For just a second, one luxurious split second, I convince myself my neck is bro-ken. I dream it into being.

I dream these words, murmured by students and lovers of literature throughout the century to come. Pored over by diligent readers of literary biography. Keats died of a bad review. Byron drank wine from a skull.

. . . *and Lawrence Campbell broke his neck—for Jim Arsenault.*

12.

IN BRYANT DEKKER's living room, we sit fondling steaming mugfuls of mulled wine—it's like we're drinking hot blood. None of the cups in the Dekker household have handles for some reason, so people balance them on or between their knees, trying not to burn their palms. I have worked out an ingenious method of pulling down the cuffs of my shirt and manoeuvring the cup between my protected wrists. Sherrie is watching me as I take a precarious sip. She's smiling. She has both hands wrapped fearlessly around her own mug.

"It's really not that hot, Lawrence."

I hate the mulled wine. I hate the mugs. I hate Dekker's place, which is the opposite of Jim's creaky, unpretentious farmhouse. It's because of Dekker's wife. She is six feet tall, blonde, and mean, with an unlikely hippie sensibility that dominates every corner of the house. Woven rugs of vaguely oriental design, plush bloblike furniture meant to be sunk into so that it's impossible to lean forward and have a conversation with Jim or anyone else. It's the kind of furniture you're supposed to loll around on preoccupied by your handleless mug as you sniff at the surrounding incense and soak up *chi* or whatever. And just when you've managed to choke down your last gulp of mulled wine, Ruth Dekker comes along and yanks the mug away.

"I'll get more," she says in her terse, maddening accent. Ruth's accent is Dekker's times ten, like Princess Anne with elocution lessons from Zsa Zsa Gabor. I've given up trying to place it. When I got my first look at her at Schofield's reading, settling into one of the Edwardian loveseats with Dekker and lighting up the room with her canary hair, I'd instantly thought, *Sweden.* And also I'd thought, *Wow, she's gorgeous.* But after stealing a couple of more glances as Schofield coughed and hemmed up by the mantelpiece, I realized Ruth wasn't actually gorgeous at all. She just possessed the kind of traits you instantly assume make a woman gorgeous when you first register them. Blonde. Amazonian in height—at least as tall as Jim. But a closer look at Ruth shows you that her hair is stringy, her complexion ruddy, her jawline expansive and uber-Slavic. It's a man's jawline, and her hands are man-hands. Big-knuckled like my Grandpa Humphries. I looked away from Ruth with a shudder, thinking that. A grandpa-handed woman.

"Lawrence," Dekker said to me after the reading. "Please meet my wife, Ruth." At which point I had to shake one of those things. Her skin was so dry it left scratches on mine.

"I didn't know Professor Dekker was married," I said, tired from everything and running out of cogent small talk.

Ruth smirked, then, the smirk that hasn't left her face all evening.

"I am this town's best-kept secret," she said.

Whatever that was supposed to mean.

Ruth Dekker, it turns out, is a painter, and her paintings are all over the house. Each canvas takes up approximately one wall. For the most part, her work consists of a lot of different-coloured blobs—blobby like her furniture—although on the wall directly across from me is a rendition of a big orange toilet against a grey background.

"I like your toilet," hollers Todd across the room to Ruth at one point. Todd has showed no aversion whatsoever to the mulled wine this evening.

Ruth turns her radiant smirk on Todd. "That toilet," she calls back, "was in my apartment in Cape Town. It was the only thing in there that ever worked. It became kind of a god to me, eventually."

No one knows what to say. All night Ruth has been making utterances that have the context and rhythm of jokes but are completely unfunny.

Jim and Schofield are curled up on their respective blobs of furniture in the far corner of the room—the farthest possible point they could be from me, it would seem. They lean toward each other, immersed in conversation. Jim is gesturing, explaining. Schofield is pursing and nodding. Todd sits on the floor about a foot away from them, craning and yearning and generally being pathetic.

Meanwhile, Claude, of all people, has somehow ended up sharing my blob. After several moments of sitting side by side in silence, he is the one to give in and toss out a conversational gambit. I've been content to loll and sip and languish thus far. "So how did you like the reading?" he wants to know.

"I thought it was okay," I answer carefully. "How did you like it?"

"Schofield's brilliant," says Claude, sighing as though he hates to admit it.

I had assumed Claude would be too cool to just come out with it like that. Don't care. Be bored. I look at him with my mouth open.

"You didn't think so?" he asks, frowning.

"Of course," I say. "It was the best reading I've ever heard. I just didn't think it was your kind of thing."

"Because it was good," states Claude, lips forming a straight line.

The reading, in fact, was like nothing I'd ever seen. By the time we got everyone chairs, and ran back and forth between buildings a few times to make sure there were no confused souls lingering outside the Sociology seminar, the hour was closing in on eight. Janet showed up accompanied by the very same sweet-faced old woman who was so indulgent of my tea-drinking at Carl's. This turned out to be her landlady, Mrs. Dacey. I shook Mrs. Dacey's gloved hand and took a moment to compliment her on her raisin pie, because it has occurred to me again that Janet's house is going to be available after she graduates this year. Then I led them to a couple of good seats close to the mantelpiece.

That was our crowd. The eight of us from Jim's seminar, a couple of strangers, Janet, Mrs. Dacey, Bryant and Ruth Dekker, and Charles the-sore-thumb Slaughter. I kept waiting to see Doctor Sparrow come slinking around a corner to take in the show. But he never did.

Schofield just sat down in a chair by himself until Jim went up to him and told him he could start.

When Schofield stood and turned to face us, I thought he was sick. His eyes were squeezed shut behind his glasses, and his head was down. In his right mitt, he held an untidy clutch of paper that must have been shoved in his jacket or pants the whole time I was with him this evening.

"I would like to thank . . . ," he said.

Schofield's face blossomed red the instant he started speaking. I had never seen anything like it except in grade 6 when Joey Cahill got so pissed off at the math teacher that he blurted she could kiss his ass. An instantaneous faceful of red, just like Schofield now. I nearly stood up and walked over to help him to a chair.

"I'd like to thank my good friend Jim Arsenault," Schofield managed to finish, "for inviting me to be here today and for exerting such a profound and felicitous influence on myself and, I would have to say, Canadian poetry as a whole. We are all of us the better, for the likes of Jim Arsenault—I say that with all sincerity. He makes me proud to be a fellow practitioner. I would also like to thank the department of English, one Larry Campbell, who was kind enough to keep me company this stormy evening, and, as ever, the Heritage Arts Coalition, which made this and so many other wonderful events like it a reality. I am deeply grateful for the opportunity to read to you today. I thank you all for being here."

Schofield did not raise his head, shift his position, or open his eyes once during this entire speech.

He's having a heart attack, I thought to myself, watching his face pulsate as he chewed out every syllable like a series of minuscule light bulbs.

And then Schofield raised his head, eyes open, looked directly out at us, and recited his poetry for twenty minutes. It was like he was possessed by gods. Or demons. It was wonderful. It was riveting. He started with the man-word/woman-word poem. He did not consult the twisted sheaf of paper in his right hand at any time during the recitation, although he did pause to shuffle the pages, for some reason, between each poem. He *performed* the poems, giving them exactly the right cadence, emphasizing precisely the words and phrases he wanted us to most notice. His reading voice was nothing like his speaking voice. It was an actor's voice, and not the least bit reedy. He was a muted, less stagy Gregory Peck.

And yet, it wasn't as if he was acting—there was no sense of remove, like how in a play everyone pretends the actors aren't standing there in front of you but are somewhere else, oblivious to your presence. Schofield was by no means oblivious to our presence. He leaned toward us as he recited, he looked us in the eye, he harangued, he appealed, he explained. That was especially how the man/woman poem struck me—as a patient, meticulous explanation of something ineffable. It's the same kind of feeling I sometimes have listening to classical music, or even staring at the lines in the palm of my hand, sometimes. The sense that there's a language there, that something is being expressed, communicated. Something infinite, beyond words.

But Schofield did use words.

My cousin's landlady raised her hand the moment Schofield finished his recitation, having dropped his head again and thanked us. She sat there with her entire arm in the air like a septuagenarian schoolgirl, while everybody else clapped hard and long.

"Hello," said Schofield when he finally peeped through his scrunched eyes and noticed what Mrs. Dacey was doing.

"Hello," she said back.

"Did you have a question?"

"Yes, I do," said Mrs. Dacey in a clear and rather youthful voice. "I would like to know," she continued, "why is it people feel they have to concern themselves with matters of the bedroom so much lately."

Schofield looked around as if not quite sure where he was.

"Do you mean people . . . in general?" he asked after a moment.

"I suppose I do," said Mrs. Dacey. "I suppose it's something you see quite a bit nowadays. But I thought you might be the man to ask, considering the nature of some of those poems you were reading."

Schofield blinked a few times behind his glasses. "They were *my* poems."

"Yes, I assumed that," Mrs. Dacey snapped, sensing condescension. "You're the man of the hour, so to speak."

Jim interrupted at this point.

"I think," he said, rearranging his limbs in his chair in a pertinent sort of way, "with the storm and people needing to get home and everything, we may have to keep the questions to a minimum this evening."

Mrs. Dacey responded to Jim, but kept staring at Schofield. "Storms don't bother me," she told him. "I walked here from my house and I'll walk back. I'm not bothered by any storm, never have been. I grew up on the Bay of Fundy with the wind coming straight off the Atlantic Ocean every winter. You'd never see me bat an eyelash in a storm."

Schofield pursed his lips and nodded at this.

"All the same," said Jim, and didn't finish the sentence—as at a loss as I've ever seen him. No one came to his rescue.

"So let's hear it," said Mrs. Dacey to Schofield.

"*Bedroom matters,*" repeated Schofield.

"Yes," said Mrs. Dacey. "You tell me: What's the story on that, now?"

"Well, I can't speak for others," Schofield began.

"I understand that," Mrs. Dacey assured him.

"But I can say that love . . . and poetry, historically, have always gone hand and hand. Um. Shakespeare, for example—"

Mrs. Dacey was having none of it.

"Love is one thing," she interrupted. "But I'm talking about things that go on, or should only go on, in the privacy of the bedroom. *Bedroom . . . matters.* Love is fine, and I think it's just wonderful if a poet wants to write something about love, I have no problem with that at all. But here's my question—"

We waited. Nobody could look at anything in the room except their own twiddling fingers in their laps.

"Why is it that people think there's this need these days to discuss private and intimate things for entertainment? For the amusement of others? You see," said Mrs. Dacey, shifting her weight forward, "what people don't seem to understand is that *that* is basically the definition of pornography.

Entertaining others, in the public arena, with private and intimate things. And I'm just afraid that people get so caught up in their art or selling their books or whatever that they don't realize when they are crossing certain pornographic boundaries."

Mrs. Dacey sat back and folded her hands, keeping her bright little eyes pinned on Schofield. Dermot's own huge mitt was resting against his heart as if to quiet it down.

As the seconds passed and we all sat waiting for Dermot's defence, the entire English Department began to vibrate with the noise of what can only be described as a guffaw—a guffaw in the truest sense of the word. In fact it onomatopoeically came close to sounding like the word *guffaw*.

"*Hawg!*" it went. "*Hawg, hawg, hawg, hawg!*"

It was the loudest, rudest laugh I've ever heard. It was coming, I noted, craning my neck along with everyone else, from Charles Slaughter, seated sprawl-legged in the back.

"*Hawg, hawg, hawg, hawg, hawg, hawg, hawg!*"

The furniture shook with it.

Mrs. Dacey straightened her delicate shoulders once Slaughter was finished. It took him a moment or two.

"I beg your pardon if I've said something funny," she said, not fazed, not taking her hamster eyes off Schofield. By this time I was somewhat in awe of Mrs. Dacey.

Schofield, meanwhile, had used the eternity of Slaughter's mirth to get himself together. He gazed straight back at Mrs. Dacey and assured her she had said nothing funny at all. Then he even managed to apologize for the laughter without being accusatory toward Slaughter—as if Schofield himself was somehow responsible. Then he answered her question.

He didn't turn red. He seemed to be still, slightly, in the world of his reading. Not an awkward, blushing fat man who hadn't taken a shower in the past twelve hours, but a humble sage, infinitely gracious and wise. I sat with my fists clenched, rooting for him.

"For many people," spoke Schofield, "love and the act of love are inexorably entwined."

"I know that," huffed Mrs. Dacey, apparently ready to meet his argument point for point. Schofield held up a hand.

"If I may," he said, and Mrs. Dacey sat back.

"Absolutely, the two can exist in exclusivity to one another. Filial love, fraternal love . . ."

"The love of a pet," offered Mrs. Dacey, and I was afraid Slaughter might start up again.

"Of course," agreed Schofield in haste. "And some of the most celebrated literary and historical examples of romantic love have been platonic, so to speak. Dante and Beatrice, to cite just one example."

"Love that is *pure,*" Mrs. Dacey insisted.

"Absolutely," said Schofield. "But surely you'll agree, there are far more examples of romantic love that are . . . erotic." This time Schofield actually stopped and waited for Mrs. Dacey to interrupt. She just sat there for a moment.

"Well—I'm not so sure about that," she said at last.

Schofield nodded. "Well, I'm afraid I have to insist on this point. Tristan and Isolde. Héloïse and Abelard. Romeo and Juliet."

At this point Mrs. Dacey regained her vigour. "Excuse me," she said, "but I believe you're talking about Shakespeare again. But Shakespeare doesn't talk about breasts and thighs and . . . *sweat* and what have you."

Up went Schofield's big mitt again. "You'll forgive me, but he speaks of all that and more."

There was a short pause.

"Well, I'm not a big fan of Shakespeare, frankly," said Mrs. Dacey.

Schofield deflated a little at this.

"Well," he mumbled, seeming to back down just when I felt he had scored some points off old lady Dacey, "what other writers do is beside the point, I suppose."

"Exactly!" pounced Mrs. Dacey. "That's exactly my point."

"What you're really asking is about me, about what I write, what I've read this evening."

"Well, yes," admitted Mrs. Dacey with a bit less certainty. "You as a representative, I suppose. Of all you types. You art people. Your generation."

It occurred to me at this point to stare a few daggers across the room at Cousin Janet for hauling this battle-axe to the reading, the reading I had nearly killed myself over. But Janet had been in thumb-twiddling mode since the inquisition began.

Schofield took a breath, nodding and pursing at *you types.*

"You can't answer, can you," demanded Mrs. Dacey, sniffing blood, sensing victory.

"No, I can," argued Schofield, "but surely you understand this is a difficult topic. It's immensely—" (he looked around at the group of us as if in appeal) "—*personal,* of course."

I nodded when Schofield's gaze passed over. To help—to let him know he wasn't alone. Mrs. Dacey folded her arms. "Once again, you're just adding to my point. That's what I'm saying: it's personal, what you're talking about. It's *too* personal."

"But the very act of writing poetry is personal," said Schofield.

"Well, maybe you shouldn't be writing it, then," rejoined Dacey.

Holy crap, I thought. Is this what it's like? When you're a poet? Old dames who've spent the past sixty years reading nothing but *Ladies Home Journal* and *The Farmers' Almanac* come forward and put you on the rack?

"All right," said Jim, unfurling his limbs abruptly and standing to his full six-foot-something height. "It *is* getting very late, people have to drive home—"

"Jim," said Schofield. Jim glanced over, opened then closed his mouth, and finally sat down again.

"I have been in love," said Schofield.

Outside, the wind screamed, cracking the iced-over windowpanes. Everyone in the lounge seemed to gulp in unison.

"I am still in love," added Schofield after surveying the room for a moment. "It was, and is, the most transcendent thing that could happen to a man like myself. I am a person who thought such an experience would always be beyond my reach."

Schofield took a breath and glanced, briefly, down at himself in a gesture of disbelief, as if flowers had sprouted from his chest. *Oh no,* the gesture seemed to say, *what's happening now?*

"What I've just said is a very bald statement—it has little art or poetry to it, but, I think you will agree, it has weight. It has strength. It's a powerful thing to say: 'I have love. I who thought I would never have love.'"

It was a powerful thing to say, all right. Behind me, I could hear Sherrie's breath catch in her throat. My own tightened.

Schofield continued, pinkening only a bit. "Surely everyone has had occasion to doubt, has found themselves alone, asking of the universe: Will there be love for me? Ever? Anywhere? If no one here has had occasion to ask this question, I'd ask that you speak up, just so I know I'm not on the wrong track here. It's the kind of thing you always assume about other people but rarely ask, isn't it? It's not the sort of thing we usually speak about."

Not only did no one speak up, no one so much as breathed. It was awful but fascinating—Schofield up there, forced to say what no one ever said, like someone being made to dance at gunpoint.

He took another breath as if on our behalves, nodding without the pursing. "Okay," he said, "I was pretty sure that would be the response. So you'll notice some of you are very young, and already it would seem you've asked yourself this question. It goes to show, I think, how universal this experience is. It's not a comfortable moment, is it, the moment that question arises? Your body feels like this huge, hollow cavern with your soul bouncing around inside, bashing against your ribs, trying to get out. Just trying to make contact with someone, any other living, thinking, commiserating being. Most of you, I'm sure, will recall this feeling, this misery of isolation, and I am hoping that for most of you, that feeling has passed. Even if it has, however, its memory resides within you somewhere—and it's a cold spot, isn't it? It can't be warmed up. It's a fear that can never be completely expelled. Yes?"

Schofield paused to look around the room. As the glint of his glasses shifted toward me, I felt my mouth close, my tongue gluing itself to the roof of my mouth. My jaw had been hanging open for who knew how long.

"All right," sighed Schofield, now very much showing signs of fatigue from his hours on the bus, his battle with the elements, his time with me. The colour and consistency of his face reminded me of swollen bread dough, listing on the counter after the first deflating punch from my mother's fist. Only then did it occur to me the poor guy didn't even have a lectern to hide behind. That's what was missing, why he came across as so vulnerable and alone up there. We should have found him a lectern from downstairs, he shouldn't have had to stand here before us, naked but for a sheaf of paper he didn't even look at.

"All I want you to know is," he continued, "I have lived with this feeling I've been describing for approximately thirty or so years. I had almost given up hope of being loved. Please just imagine that for a moment, the desolation, the hollowness of it—day in and day out."

Sniffles from somewhere behind me.

"But, ladies and gentlemen, I'm now in love, as I said earlier. Now imagine the, um, *beauty* of that, after so many years. How it would be like emerging from life underground. It *is,* and it may be private, but I want to express it. I'd like you to know. When you wonder about love, about your own worthiness, maybe you'll read a poem I've written about it. Maybe you'll recognize yourself in there. I want to evoke my feelings, my ragged faith, my desolation, and my subsequent salvation so completely, so perfectly, that for you there will be no mistaking what we have in common. At least—that's part of what I'm trying to do. And sometimes, when I'm doing this," and here he nodded toward Mrs. Dacey, "I have to be explicit. Because I know that my experience is human, and the more palpable I can make it, through the writing, the more you will know, as a reader, that I am telling you a kind of truth. A truth we don't talk about, and maybe even can't. That, I hope, is the value of what I'm doing—assuming we can speak of poetry in such a way. I mean, assuming we even *should*—"

That line from the Acorn poem above my typewriter. *It is truth, the word I am not.* Schofield's face contorted and he groped with one hand, as if the words were revolving around his head faster than he was able to organize them into speech.

"I am trying to," groped Schofield, "communicate as best I can. I want to *help.* I want you to know." He looked around. "I'm sorry. I just don't know how else to say it."

And then he shrugged like a wince, smiled like pain, and moved slightly away from the mantelpiece, looking to Jim. The Schofield reading was over.

13.

"WHAT A PILE OF CRAP that was," says Todd, slouched against yet another wall, waiting for me when I emerge from the Dekkers' upstairs bathroom. The bathroom is full of art as well, but not Ruth's. Pictures of paintings and of photographs—cut out from magazines—are taped all over the walls, and tiny African sculptures have been placed on every available surface alongside of the cans of shaving cream and bottles of toilet water.

"What?" I say.

"The crap Schofield was talking before."

"After the reading?"

"Yeah. Poetry is about love and—and *communication,* oh my fucking God."

Todd is making it sound stupid, what Schofield said, and it incenses me. I feel protective after seeing him blush and stutter all alone up there.

"You gotta like the way he shut the old lady up, though," I say, being offhand and, in order to emphasize my offhandedness, slouching against the wall along with Todd.

Todd smirks, eyebrows bouncing. "Yeah, but you can tell he believes that crap."

"Well, okay, maybe it's a simplification," I allow. Because, let's be honest, what Schofield said was embarrassing. It's not the kind of thing you're supposed to say if you're a guy, and a poet, and standing in front of an assemblage of people. I can't be caught defending it outright.

"Is it *ever,*" agrees Todd.

"But, then," I say, attempting to switch tracks, "what *is* poetry about, anyway? I don't know. Who can say?"

"It's not about fuckin' beauty," says Todd. "If anything, it's about dredging up all the shit."

"Dredging up all the shit," I repeat. "All what shit? From where?"

"From wherever it comes from."

"It comes from your colon," I say.

"What I mean is," says Todd, "buddy is up there saying that poetry has to be beautiful, and I think that's fucking dangerous. Sometimes it's gotta be ugly, or even, even *banal* or obtuse. Maybe, sometimes, it doesn't even have to be about anything. But it's not about 'the human soul,' for Christ's sake. Sometimes it isn't going to be pretty. People aren't going to *like* it necessarily. That's what I would have told that old bag if it was me standing up there."

"But you're still talking about communication, just like Schofield was saying," I argue.

"*I have been in love,*" quotes Todd, ignoring my point, tucking in his face to give himself a Schofield-esque double chin. "Jesus. Poetry is about pain—suffering it and inflicting it, not telling the world you finally got laid at the age of thirty-five or whatever. That's just sad. It's about breaking bones—breaking and then re-setting them so they grow in a completely different way."

What, I marvel to myself, has Todd been reading? "Where did you get that?" I demand, assuming it's a stolen quotation.

Todd shrugs. "It's just something I came up with." He looks around, as if to check for spies. "I've been doing a lot of experimentation lately."

"Oh yeah?" I say. "No more cave-ins and pit ponies?"

Todd's blue eyes flicker up at me. "It's not that I'm not interested in those stories anymore, it's just that I'm becoming more and more taken up with *form* itself. There are people in this country who would laugh their asses off at the kind of shit Schofield was spouting tonight. There are people for whom poetry is an end in itself, it's not about *meaning.*" Todd utters the word *meaning* as if he was saying "little girls' dresses." "It's about getting underneath meaning, it's about bypassing meaning."

"Bypassing meaning?" I say. "So what does that leave you with? Gobble-de-gook?"

"Yes," answers Todd, folding his arms, "in some instances, it leaves you with gobble-de-gook."

"Who?" I want to know. "Who's doing this sort of stuff? And where?"

"Claude is," answers Todd. "And Vancouver."

Claude? Vancouver? I don't know where to begin.

"Claude writes villanelles!"

"That's only part of what he does. He experiments with form in general, so you know, he tries out villanelles. He's tried sestinas, sonnets, haikus."

Haikus? Is it supposed to be *haikus,* with an *s?* I rack my brain for the plural of *haiku.* I thought it was just *haiku.* How I long to make Todd look like an idiot by pointing out such a fundamental mistake, but I can't remember which it is. I'm not sure. Frustration churns behind my eyes and I switch tracks yet again.

"What does Claude know about Vancouver?" I do my best to imbue the word *Vancouver* with the girly-dresses quality Todd evoked before.

"Claude's been all over," Todd reminds me. "He's been to Paris, like Jim. He saw the Black Mountain poets read in New York City. He knows about all the different movements."

Movements. It reminds me of the way Gramma Campbell used to discuss her bowels after every meal. I don't want there to be *movements* when it comes to poetry. It's hard enough trying to figure out Hucksterism versus the Real Thing, just trying to write a line that's any good.

"Since when are you interested in the kind of stuff Claude does, anyway?"

Todd shrugs some more. "We both experiment with form." At some point in the past few months, it would seem

Todd has traded in his pissed-off energy for an obnoxious faux-apathy.

Please! I want to spit at Todd. Your poems all rhymed because you never read one that didn't before you got here. But we're interrupted by a groaning noise from somewhere beneath us. It's the staircase, suffering under some massive weight, followed by the heavy thunk of footsteps. I clench guiltily, thinking it must be Schofield, until I see Chuck Slaughter's bristled, bulletlike head appear, accompanied by the dual hams of his shoulders. I'm not exactly relieved.

"There you two fuckwits are," Slaughter greets, pretending to punch Smiley in the gut. When Todd instinctively caves in at the gesture, Slaughter takes the opportunity to seize him around the neck in a headlock.

"How do you like that?" he inquires of Todd, who flails. "Not much with the reflexes, are we, Smiley?"

"How you doing, Chuck?" I say, backing up a little.

He releases Todd and shoves him lightly away. "I'm going to nail that Mitten one," Slaughter imparts. "I'm going to pound the mittens right off her."

He looks glazedly cheerful at this admission. I am terrified for Sherrie.

"Oh yeah?" croaks Todd, holding his neck.

"Just coming up here to make my intentions known to Campbell."

"To me?" I repeat.

"Well, I seen you two hanging out sometimes."

"Not really," I say, jackrabbit fast. "We talk about— books, poetry. You know . . . Susanna Moodie."

Slaughter nods, "You're after one of her friends?"

Todd snorts.

"No," I say stupidly. "Susanna . . . Moodie." Stop talking, stop talking. Because I can feel myself gearing up to explain to Chuck how Susanna Moodie is a Canadian literary figure, but *The Journals of Susanna Moodie* isn't actually the journals of Susanna Moodie but is a book of poetry written by one of the Margarets *purporting* to be . . . I will be drop-kicked down the stairs before I can utter the second *Susanna.*

Fortunately, Slaughter cuts to the chase. "So you don't wanna do her?"

I recognize the question to be a snare. If I say I don't want Sherrie, I'm a fruit. If I say I do, I'm potentially a blotch on Ruth Dekker's upstairs rug. I have to think fast. I don't think fast enough.

"You know," I say, trying for casual, slouching hard against Todd's wall, "it's never even occurred to me, really."

Chuck opens his mouth and Todd cocks his head, both sets of hands settling on both sets of hips. They are big and little versions of each other.

Slaughter drawls, "It's never even *occurred* to you?"

"Of course it's occurred to me," I correct. "I just—she's not my type."

"Oh yeah? Blonde, and a fox? So what would be your type, Campbell?"

I give up talking and thrust both hands in the air. Slaughter is smiling, non-violently, and I am surprised to realize he knows exactly what he's been putting me through.

"Be my guest, that's all I'm saying," I tell him. In the next instant, I'm seized, immobilized, and hoisted into the air. Slaughter suspends me above his head like a barbell, holding me against the ceiling, pinned and fluttering like a moth. But before the terror and vertigo can register, he swings me back onto my feet, pulling me into a pig-iron embrace.

"Ooh, I just love you, Campbell," Slaughter murmurs into my hair. "You're just the *duckiest.*" And then I'm shoved into Todd, who shoves me away.

"Christ," I say, pulling my sweater down.

"*Hawg, hawg, hawg,*" guffaws Chuck. "Oh, my good men, my fuckwitted friends, I am so high right now."

Todd and I gape. Me because the blood hasn't rushed from my head yet, and Todd because he's from Sheet Harbour and thinks only hippies and Satanists get high.

"The first dose kicked in right in the middle of that old lady's diatribe. All of a sudden her voice just sounded fucking insane to me. She sounded like a spring peeper. I don't even know what that is, but her voice, it sounded like *peep peep peep* to me and I thought, she sounds like a spring peeper. But *mean.* And then I thought, she's a big, mean spring peeper. And then I got this picture of a bird like fucking Big Bird or something but *mean,* right, like an evil Big Bird. And then I just fucking lost it."

I'm smiling through my confusion and rapid heart rate. This is the most I've heard Slaughter say since the night of Rory's flag.

Todd laughs a little mechanically. "What are you on, man?"

"Mushrooms," Chuck replies. "We're standing in the mushroom capital of the world, here, you fuckwits didn't know that?"

"Wow," says Todd, sounding impressed, trying to be cool. Todd, of course, has never taken a mind-altering substance in his life. Drugs are for Beatnik poets, whom he deplores for their depravity and self-mythologizing—for their popularity, basically.

"Here," says Slaughter, digging around in his pockets. "Eat some."

"Oh," says Todd, doing some fast thinking of his own. "No thanks, man. Not tonight."

"Why not?" I goad. "Tonight's as good a night as any."

"Listen to Campbell," advises Chuck. "He's not as big a pussy as he comes across." Slaughter seizes my hand, turns it over, and sprinkles what looks like a few shrivelled bird turds into my palm.

I am a poet experimenting with drugs! I think, bounding down the stairs. *Blake! Rimbaud! Ginsberg! Derangement of the senses!*

We decide to head over to the Mariner. It's that kind of night. I picture us all traipsing down to the Mariner together, maybe stopping at Scarsdale Holdings to yank down another flag—we already have three stashed in Slaughter's dorm—and the bunch of us getting mystically, majestically fucked up like merry pranksters on electric Kool-Aid, far into the morning hours.

But as we arrive downstairs I see Schofield on the landing shaking hands with Ruth and Dekker. This is not how it's supposed to go.

"You're going?" I interrupt.

He turns to me. Fatigue seems to emanate from the man like heat, or a smell. "Larry," he says. "I wanted to thank you again for everything."

"But we're all heading downtown for a beer," I protest. "You've got to come."

"There, now!" says Jim, appearing from the living room. "I told him it was too early!"

"It *is* too early," I complain, and Jim flings an arm around me.

"Listen to this lad," he tells Schofield, pulling me close, heat radiating into my shoulder from his armpit. "Wise beyond his years. We're all expecting great things from Larry—aren't we, Bryant."

I had forgotten about Dekker and Ruth standing there waiting to conclude their evening. Dekker is smiling like a genial host, but Ruth is sucking in her cheeks in an intentional sort of way, as if to make her expression unreadable.

"You should come too, Professor Dekker."

Dekker grins and glances at his wife. "Ah, Lawrence, it's a bit late for us old guys, I'm afraid."

"Oh, listen to him!" yelps Jim. "You'll give us all a bad name, Bryant."

Dekker shakes his head. "We've got a lot of cleaning up to do."

Since I'm not quite as interested in prolonging my evening with Dekker as I am with Schofield, I lean over to continue working on the latter.

"How are you going to get back to the inn?" I ask over the noise of Dekker's excuses. "Come out for one beer and I can walk you back."

"I have a cab coming, Larry, but thank you."

"A cab! That's crazy, it's only a five-minute walk!" I declare. "We'll just duck into the Mariner for a quick beer and duck back out again and you'll be home."

Hearing myself wheedle, I realize that this is a technique I've learned from Jim. To just keep denying what the other person says until you get the answer you want. Make your alternative sound like the most natural one, whereas the other person's alternative should be depicted as mild lunacy.

But Schofield is smiling and shaking his head.

"I'm exhausted, Larry." His face changes as something occurs to him. "By the way—is it Larry or Lawrence?"

"Um," I say, not sure what I want it to be for Schofield. "Larry's fine."

"Larry. I thought I heard people calling you Lawrence earlier."

"They do, sometimes," I say, moronic.

"Well, then," says Schofield, reverting his features back into the pained, apologetic smile of a second ago. "As I was saying, Larry. It was good to meet you, and I'd love it if you'd write to me sometime—send me some poems. I edit the student journal at Ralston and we're always looking for new work. And now, I'm sorry, but it's been an exhausting day."

Although thrilling, I don't let the invitation to send him my poems throw me off course, as it was clearly intended to do. "Beer'll perk you right up!" I insist, having heard Jim use this line to great effect on countless occasions.

I'm feeling confident and aggressive with Schofield, which is certainly not my usual demeanour, and I can't help but wonder if maybe this is the effect of the mushrooms kicking in. Will I start *hawg-hawg*-ing soon? Before I'm able to squelch Schofield's resolve?

There's a honk outside, startling me, as it's like a more nasal version of Slaughter's *hawg*—and not much louder. No doubt it's Friendly ready to grin and clack his dentures at Schofield, ferrying him through the snowdrifts across town to the Crowfeather. Dermot reaches to accept his parka from Ruth, who's just stood there with it for the last five minutes as Jim and I, entwined as we are, applied the pressure to Schofield and her hubby. Now, handing over the coat, she's glancing at Dekker and replying to a question it would seem he just asked. She's saying, "It doesn't matter, Bryant."

"Are you sure?" says Dekker. "I won't be more than an hour."

"It doesn't matter," repeats Ruth.

"It doesn't matter!" says Jim, trying to reform the words so that they sound a touch more lighthearted than they did coming out of Ruth. Shit! Jim should have been working on Schofield and me on Dekker this entire time—Jim is the expert, I the apprentice. Schofield is leaning into the living room, now, waving and saying his goodbyes to everyone, and I duck out from underneath Jim's armpit to follow.

"Dermot," I call as Schofield moves to the door. I realize my hand is extended only when Schofield grabs it.

"Thank you again, Larry," he says. I can feel the warmth and dampness of his big mitt seeping into my skin. He's going, I realize. There's no calling him back. The fact of it is as solid and certain as his hand in mine.

"I didn't even get to tell you how much I enjoyed your reading," I say. "And all the stuff you said."

Schofield nods rapidly in that way that tells me he doesn't really want to hear it. He's probably endured all the hedging, uneasy compliments he can stand.

"No *really*," I emphasize, trying to gain traction on the slippery, too-large mass in my grip. I feel like I can't let him go until I've gotten something across. "You inspired me," I add, suffering the insufficiency of the words the moment they're out.

"Thank you Lar—" He's looking away from me.

"*No,*" I insist, yelling a little in my frustration. "I can't explain it. I want to explain it but I can't."

Schofield meets my eye and moves a little closer. He puts his other hand on top of mine and leans forward. "Larry," he says above the din of other guests now saying their goodbyes and rummaging around at our feet for their boots. "It's impossible. It will *always* be impossible."

He gives my hand a squeeze before pulling away. Friendly honks again from the street and I feel a blast of cold air. Schofield hollers a couple more quick goodbyes before seeming to slip through the merest crack in the door.

Somehow he made the words sound reassuring.

14.

"THAT ASSHOLE," Jim keeps repeating as he blazes a trail ahead of us through the drifts. "That lousy prick."

The snow has let up, leaving these vast, wind-formed dunes for us to manoeuvre our way through. But the flakes are dry and powdery, like dandruff. The dunes collapse the moment Jim sets foot in them.

"He was very tired," I assure him for the eighth time. Jim thinks Dermot Schofield went out of his way not to say goodbye to him. A deliberate snub. "He was so tired he couldn't see straight, Jim."

"Didn't even say *goodbye* to me," marvels Jim for the ninth time.

"Jim," says Dekker, closing in on his tenth time. "He did. I heard him. It just got lost in the hubbub. Everybody was hollering goodbye to everybody else."

"That *prick,*" repeats Jim, staring into an approaching dune. It's annihilated under his boots as we continue on.

"He said goodbye," insists Dekker.

"Everyone said goodbye," complains Jim. "It's easy to just fucking wave around the room and say goodbye. I thought we were friends. We sat in a corner talking Pound and Li Po all night. I go to all the trouble to bring him out here . . ." Jim puffs out a harsh sigh of disbelief and betrayal. Then shakes himself, tightening. "Well, to hell with him," he says with finality. "I mean, I've had it with this guy."

"Yeah, to hell with him!" calls Slaughter from a couple of paces behind us. "Let it go, man."

Jim shakes his head, the air of desolation settling around him again. "It's just one thing after another," he says in a tone that alarms me. It's a tone I've heard only once before. Over the phone. Cushions. Kleenex. "I don't know why I put up with it. I just keep going back for more."

It's bizarre and unnerving to realize how easy it is to hurt Jim's feelings—I can only assume this is part of being a genius, one of the downsides. But it's frustrating too—a pall has been cast over the evening, and it won't get better unless I can snap him out of it. It feels as if it's my responsibility somehow. I spent the last eight hours with

Schofield, after all. I heard him say myself how much he admires Jim.

"He was singing your praises to me all afternoon, Jim."

"Oh horseshit, Larry, don't you know when you're being snowed?" Jim snorts this at me. "He was trying to get you on his side, trying to make me look irrational."

"Maybe he'll call you tomorrow before he gets on the bus," I suggest, deciding to back off. For all I know, Jim's right—I never read the review, after all, Schofield's review of *Blinding White*. For all I know it will confirm everything Jim's said about the man. Maybe Schofield is like Iago, Janus-faced—pointlessly evil.

"Who gives a shit," says Jim, quickening his pace as we approach the corner of Scarsdale Holdings. Rory's latest flag, a brand-spankity new replacement of the last one we pil-fered, dangles there in the depleted wind.

"Flaaag!" screams Slaughter, taking a run at it. It separates from the pole with ease, as if Rory isn't even bothering to secure them anymore. Slaughter makes a show of trying to rip it in half, but the nylon is too strong. He goes at it with his teeth for a minute or so, and then finally settles on balling it up and wiping his ass.

"Hey, Jim," I pant, trotting to keep up, and he grabs me around the shoulders again.

"Larry," he says. "You're my main man."

"That's me," I agree.

"What would I do without you, kid?"

"I don't know," I say. "Die, probably!"

"That's right," Jim agrees with an utter lack of humour. "I'd keel right the fuck over, my friend." We walk in stride for long enough to make me feel self-conscious, but I would never dream of breaking Jim's embrace. He speaks again only as we turn onto Station Street. A block away, we can see the lights of the Mariner flashing, cars pulling in and pulling away, people standing around the front entrance, laughing and seeming to breathe fire, the way their breath plumes out in the cold. It's the first time I've been here, and I can't believe it. It looks to me like the biggest, most popular bar in town—a bar like you'd find in the city. You'd think the university crowd would be out here every weekend. I'm about to remark on this to Jim, but he speaks again, every bit as serious, every bit as grim.

"There are people in the world, Larry," he tells me, "who know what it means to be a friend. And you're one of them."

I do my best to stare straight ahead at the oncoming bar, squelching my instinct to beam up at Jim like a child on Santy's knee.

"Thank you, Jim," I say, attempting to match his grim tone.

"And I am lucky enough to have you as a friend," Jim adds. He gives me a squeeze and then bashes me twice on the chest with his opposite hand, as though trying to start my heart. "I am lucky enough," he emphasizes, raising his voice so that Dekker and Todd and Slaughter can hear, "to count this fine young man amongst my friends."

The night, I think, the night can do what it wants now. The night can take me anywhere it wants to go.

Inside the bar, everything speeds up in a disjointed kind of way. Is this because I'm high? I decide that when I stop asking myself if I'm high, that's when I'll be high, and abruptly resolve to forget about it. Inside the bar are bodies and smoke, a blue, apocalyptic fog looming over everyone's heads. I push my way through assorted human limbs: arms and shoulders, backs and asses. It's an apocalyptic scene in general, reminding me of those paintings by Hieronymus Bosch, the suffering sinners on Judgment Day—what my grandmother's daydreams probably look like. But nobody appears to be suffering much here. This, I think, is what the scene would look like pre-Bosch's vision—before the divine shoe drops, as it were; before everyone finds themselves naked, writhing, and suffering. It stands to reason they'd be naked, writhing, and having fun.

Music blares. Jim is on a mission to find us a table—mission impossible, you might call it, as there is scarcely any floor space to be had from what I can see. He stations us by the bar and plunges through the wall of arms and asses.

"How you doing?" Todd screams in my ear.

The truth is, I'm dizzy from the sudden change in temperature, the bodies, and the smoke.

"Great!" I yell. "This place is pretty cool!"

"Yeah!" agrees Todd, spinning away to face the bar. I watch him, wondering what he's up to. Something strange and over-eager in the *Yeah!*—the way he's just negated it by turning his back. He's not ordering a drink from the bartender—the bartender is completely overrun down at the other end. Todd is just standing there, looking down at the brass rail.

"Smiley's tripping!" screams Chuck. Todd turns around halfway, eyes darting.

"What?" he says.

"You're gone, man!"

Todd drums his fingers on the bar. "No, I'm not," he says after a moment or two, facing away again. Slaughter grins at me, wiggling his fingers around his head to indicate the extent of Todd's high. Doubtful, I look back at Todd, notice his shoulder blades jutting beneath his yellowed T-shirt. As I watch, he places his hands quite deliberately upon the brass rail. Grips it.

"Yeah, that's right," blasts Slaughter over the blaring horns. "Brace yourself, buddy. You're in for a wild ride."

At this point Dekker leans in to get our attention, not even bothering to try and be heard above the music. He simply waves a hand toward the crowd, from where it turns out Jim is beckoning with the vast gesticulations of his monkey arms.

"He's got a table," I marvel out loud, smacking Todd between the shoulder blades. "Smiley! Jim's got a table."

We're about five steps away when I glance back to notice Smiley hasn't moved. His yellow T-shirt glows under the lights, creating something of an aura. A strange compassion fills me at the sight of Todd's glowing, motionless back. It's odd to realize how unaware people are about the backs of themselves. An entire side of your body with which you are completely unfamiliar but which everyone else gets to see.

"Todd," I say, sidling up to him, trying to catch his eye. "Jim's found a table."

Todd doesn't look up. "I'm not sure," he says.

"Pardon?"

Todd stretches his fingers slowly before resettling them into their grip on the rail. His fingers are stubby, like the rest of him, but he fans them like a concert pianist warming up.

"I don't know," he articulates, speaking louder for my benefit. "I'm just not sure, exactly."

"No," I yell. "He's found one for us, it's okay."

No answer.

"Are you *high,* Todd?"

Todd winces a little at the word.

"I'm just saying," he tells me, in a tone that's either peevish or pleading, "I'm not *sure.* I'm a little bit apprehensive, here."

The temptation to mock and mess around with Todd is, to my surprise, completely cancelled out by the helpless look he suddenly shoots me from beneath his brows.

"What are you apprehensive about?" I ask, leaning in so I won't have to yell.

Todd licks his thick lips and wiggles his fingers some more against the rail. "I'm just a little bit concerned," he explains, speaking more slowly than I think I've ever heard him, "about turning around."

"Turning around?"

Todd nods, three times. It takes an eternity.

I don't know what to say, so I turn around myself to see if I can gauge where Jim and the others have settled themselves. There's no sign of them amongst the masses. The bartender finally appears and asks if either of us want a drink. Todd won't meet his eye.

"Have a beer, Todd," I encourage.

"No," says Todd. "I'm too concerned."

I hold two fingers up to the wired, wiry bartender, who nods and darts off toward the fridge. That's all my money for the night. A night on the town with Jim and his impoverished acolytes is usually predicated upon an unspoken agreement that the profs will pay for drinks. I wonder if he would ever think to reimburse me. Christmas is coming. I have no money for gifts.

"Todd," I try again. "It's okay. You can turn around."

Todd sighs as if he's listening to an idiot. "I'm not *sure*," he repeats.

"I know," I say. "I know you're not sure, but, really. Look at me." I lean my back against the bar, resting my elbows on it like a gunslinger. When Todd glances up, I make a point of surveying the room, a look of supreme contentment smearing my face. Then I try to meet eyes reassuringly but he jerks his gaze back down at the railing.

I feel a tap on my shoulder. It's the bartender, whom I pay. I place Todd's beer in front of him like a nurse doling out medicine.

"Just have a sip," I say. "Beer'll perk you right up."

Todd squints at it. Yet another eternity passes. It must be one in the morning at least.

"I'm not *sure,*" he emits finally.

"Oh, Jesus, Smiley, have a sip of beer!"

He removes one hand from the railing as if afraid he'll lose his balance, then wraps it around the stubby brown bottle.

"Ah," says Todd, as if refreshed by the mere feel of it.

"There," I say. "Now sip."

As I watch, Todd takes the weirdest sip possible. He keeps his head bowed, juts out his lower lip and upends the bottle at a ludicrous angle. When, involuntarily, he finds he has to raise his chin somewhat to keep from slobbering beer all over himself, Todd shields his eyes with his opposite hand. That's when I figure it out. There is a mirror behind the bar.

"Todd," I say. "Is it the mirror?"

Todd places his beer on the bar and now wraps both hands around it, swallowing.

"This is what I'm trying to figure out," he explains.

"What are you seeing in the mirror? Is it the evil Big Bird?"

Finally a more recognizable expression passes over Todd's features. Good old contempt. He even turns his head to make sure I take it into account.

"For fuck's sake, I'm not *hallucinating,* Campbell."

Losing sympathy, I fold my arms. "Then what's the problem, Smiley? I'm not the one who's acting like a freak here."

Todd winces again. "I'm acting like a freak?"

"Yes," I say. "You're acting like a bit like a freak, I'm sorry to say. That's why you have to pick up your nice beer that I was generous enough to buy you—"

"I'll pay you back," he interrupts.

"Okay, good," I say, "because I'm pretty broke to be honest. Anyway, as I was saying, that's why you have to pick up your beer now, and come and sit down at the table."

The music changes, goes disco. The men growl and yell things, but some of the women yelp for joy and wave their bums around, which causes the men to settle down. I content myself with watching the bums as Todd deliberates, but this is getting boring, and every second that ticks past is a second shaved off the potentially wild night I could be having with Jim.

"*Todd,*" I say. His shoulders jump.

"Okay, maybe just leave me here for a while," speaks Todd rapidly, renewing his grip on the beer.

"Are you serious?"

"Maybe I'll just stand here for a bit. People just stand at the bar, sometimes, it's not weird."

I rub my forehead, watching Todd's knuckles whiten. Todd, I realize, is paralyzed with self-consciousness about how high he is. This strikes me as an appalling repudiation of everything I've ever heard regarding drug use. I immediately regret having swallowed the bird turds. The last thing I need is to be more self-conscious than I am now. Maybe, I think, I can get myself drunk enough to vomit up the bird turds before they take hold and have me staring at the railing alongside of Todd. Maybe, from here on out, as a poet whose responsibility it is to explore the depths of personality, to peer beyond the doors of perception, mushrooms won't be my drug of choice. Maybe psychotropic isn't the way to go. Maybe pot—*the tokes,* as my dad would say—would suit me better. My father harbours a great disdain for "the tokes." *Wacky tabaccy,* he also calls it, which strikes me as strangely affectionate.

Meanwhile, Todd won't budge.

"So you want me to leave you here then?" I say at last.

Silence from Todd.

"Yes?" I prompt.

"I *guess,*" says Todd.

And now I know Todd doesn't really want me to leave him here alone. I drink some of my beer, several swallows in a row. I'm hoping I can dampen my conscience by doing so. Drink myself into not giving a shit whether or not Todd wants me to stay. This is the last thing I want to be doing on a Friday night at the Mariner with Jim. I want to talk about French surrealism, I want to dance with older women in halters with upper arms like Brenda L. Maybe even with Brenda L. herself—surely Brenda must go out on the weekends, and I've never seen her at Quackers or the Stein. In Timperly, that only leaves one place—this place. I peer into the crowd.

"Hey, Todd," I say brightly. "What if I were to go and get Jim? Would that help?"

Todd does some more maddening drumming with his fingers—thumping lightly away on the beer bottle. At some point, he seems to have swallowed quite a bit of it, and his drumming has a hollow, musical quality. *Tunka-tunka-tunk.* "I *guess,*" he says at length.

So it's clear he doesn't want me to go get Jim either, but to hell with it—I resolve to play dumb on that front. I push myself away from the bar and stretch a little, just to give Todd some time to get used to the fact of my going. I can see his shoulder blades twitch.

"I'll just be a second," I yell, leaning toward him.

Todd nods tightly.

"Todd," I hear myself saying, "do you just wanna go home?"

Todd swallows.

"I really, really do," he says.

When I look around the bar, it's meant as a gesture of despair and resignation. There is no utilitarian aspect to it—I'm not seeking anyone this time. Mostly I am just stretching my neck and coming to terms with the fact that my evening is ruined, my second wind wasted. I'll have to escort poor, stoned Todd back to his dorm, and by then I'll be too tired and disgusted at Smiley's neurotic half-assed high and my complete lack of one to do anything except trudge my anti-climactic way home through the snowbanks.

But, in the midst of this dejection, potential salvation appears. It's Sherrie, of all people. Accompanied by Claude, of all people. Sherrie and Claude at the Mariner, waving at me with an ecstatic grin of relief at having lit upon a famil-iar face—Sherrie, that is, not Claude. Claude is not the sort to grin. Whereas Sherrie's whole *being* is like a grin. It's a cliché, I realize, as I watch her blonde head sailing toward me through the crowd, but she lights up a room. It's not just her hair, it's everything. Her stride, her pink Valentine face. And then there's Claude—dampening, darkening her wake. Doing everything he can with his sullen presence to dull Sherrie's vivacity. Maybe Sherrie likes to be seen with Claude for precisely that effect. She knows it is untoward to be so bright, especially if you're a poet.

"Lawrence!" She hugs me for some reason, perhaps ner-vous about being here. It is the first non-mother-aunt-or-cousin female hug I think I've ever received. It's fantastic. She smells like Ivory soap.

"I didn't know you guys were coming," I say. I hardly talked to Sherrie all night, I now recall, except to grouse about the mulled wine.

"Charles said I should come," she says, looking around, taking in the townie bacchanals.

"Charles?" I repeat.

She wrinkles her nose at me. "Charles Slaughter. You know Charles."

"Oh, Slaughter, yeah," I say, maybe a little too loud. *I'm going to pound the mittens right off her.* "Charles," I say again. "He's a nice guy, Charles."

Sherrie bobs her head, half in reply, half to the music.

"Yeah," she says. "He's funny. You wouldn't think he liked poetry by the look of him."

"No, you wouldn't," I agree.

Claude has moved around us to talk to Todd, who hasn't flinched or looked up at their arrival.

"Lawrence!" Sherrie turns to me as if something has just occurred to her. The blue of her eyes could blind a person. "You did a super job with the reading tonight."

I feel something happening in my chest. It's stupid—another cliché. Swelling.

"Thanks," I say. Except for Schofield's, this is the only acknowledgment I've received all night.

"The lounge was the perfect place to hold it!" Sherrie enthuses. "They should hold all the readings there from now on."

"I know," I nod.

"Todd is completely messed up," Claude calls to us.

"No, I'm not," Todd says into the bar.

"And I was thinking," continues Sherrie. "We should hold *student* readings sometime. Wouldn't that be great? Maybe in the new year."

For pretty much the first time since I got here, I stop scanning the crowd for Jim. Imagine being like Schofield was tonight. Imagine putting it all out there, on display. I turn to face Sherrie. "Do you think anyone would come?"

"Even if they didn't, we all could read for each other," says Sherrie. "But we could advertise in the student newspaper and stuff. Put up signs."

"I don't want to be the one to put up signs." It seems wise to insist on this right off the bat.

"I'd put up the signs if you want," says Sherrie.

"We'd have to ask Doctor Sparrow, if we wanted to hold them in the lounge," I say, thinking out loud. Sherrie, abruptly, turns her body away and resumes gazing into the crowd. She nods hard in time with the music. I've said the wrong thing, invoked the wrong name. None of us seem to have gotten around to telling each other about our independent meetings with Doctor Sparrow. With exams coming up, and the reading and everything. But now, seeing Sherrie in a posture of blatant evasion, I find myself suffused with curiosity. Of course, if she tells me hers, I'll have to tell her mine.

And then a body extricates itself from the writhing mass, a bigger body than that of anyone in the room, and Charles Slaughter descends, plucking the awkward, tweedy spectre of Doctor Sparrow out from between us. He slings a casual arm around Sherrie, who shines up at him in gratitude. If I were to lose a leg, it occurs to me, looking at him, like if I lost it in a war or something like one of the Vietnam vets, they could very well rip one of Charles Slaughter's arms off and replace my leg with it. It would be a perfect fit, if a little more muscular, a little more ruddy in skin tone than the rest of my body.

"What is in your bum?" Sherrie wants to know, poking at the spot in the back of Chuck's pants where one of the "Ask For Rory" flags bulges out.

"Ah," says Charles, nodding wisely like Confucius. "What *isn't* in my bum?"

Sherrie laughs; Slaughter smirks, pleased with himself. I should be laughing too, and am about to, when something in the words give me pause. They sort of echo for a moment, circling around before quite catching up with my brain. The question is, I think, slowly coming to grips with it: *what isn't*. That's what Slaughter is saying. The question is *what isn't*. Not the other way around.

Then all at once, the meaning rushes at me, striking me as fantastically poetic—charged with depth. Does Slaughter even comprehend what he just said? I close my mouth—which I had opened to laugh—and scrutinize his meaty face.

He stares back at me. There is an expression Slaughter wears sometimes—a contrived sort of expression of worry mixed with distaste. You'll see it when you tell him you don't want another beer just yet, or you've got too much studying to do to go out on the weekend. An expression that lets you know you've given the wrong answer—that there is something lacking in your character which Slaughter, for one, finds deeply disconcerting. I'm seeing that expression now, and it heightens my alarm—my sense that something is gathering in the air around us, coming to a head.

Slaughter *sees* me, I realize. His look is a reflection of everything I lack. The unsavoury puzzle of me exists in the crease between his eyebrows, the displeased pucker of his lips.

Lawrence Campbell? he's saying. And I can hear the words. The question. The unbearable *doubt.* I can hear it coming out of his eyes. And as I hear it, he raises his arm—the arm that could be my leg. He raises his muscled, ruddy, football player's limb, extends it like a telescope. Unfurls his index finger to practically the tip of my nose, then circumnavigates the finger around it, slowly. He's getting ready, is what he's doing. He's preparing us both with this ritual. He's about to pronounce. He's going to say it. He's really going to say it.

15.

ULTIMATELY, WHEN I PIECE TOGETHER Friday night, I can't help but conclude that it would have been the most fun I've had this year if not for the mushrooms. For the rest of the evening, every time Slaughter looked at me with his bottomless Saint Bernard's eyes, I would shudder, thinking my soul was being penetrated. Slaughter would repeat the swirly, point-at-my-nose thing which he knew had freaked me out thoroughly the first time he did it, goggle his eyes just to push me even closer to the edge, and then *hawg-hawg* his ass off as I sat clutching myself, trying to keep my anxious limbs from flying off my torso.

That was the thing that stuck in my mind and metastasized—the notion of Chuck's arm replacing my leg. It caused me to obsess upon arms and legs. It was all I could see of the crowd for the rest of the night, just a jumble of flesh-coloured snakes intertwined like the mating ball my father and I discovered one summer at the bottom of a dry well on Grandma Lydia's property. The entire floor of the well was nothing but a clenched, writhing sphere.

After that, it's all impressions. Vignettes. Glimpses of the night I could have had if not for the turds:

Sitting across the table from Jim—no one else present—or perhaps my attention is just so focused on Jim, it's like the others have blinked out of existence. That seems likely, because it feels as if I've never concentrated so hard on anything as much as I am concentrating on the fact that I cannot understand a single word Jim is saying. Or not that exactly. I understand the words themselves, just not what they mean when strung together. I hear *Rimbaud,* I hear *Blake.* I know to whom and what they refer—the fact that the words refer not just to people, but ideas—that the words are now embodiments of something huge and near-divine. It's why Blake went crazy—why Rimbaud just stopped writing after a while. That brush with heaven, or something like it. Schofield called it the universal, but he made it sound like a good thing. Is it a good thing? Was it a good thing? With some poets, some of the best poets, you think: moth against light bulb, zapped junebug twitching on the summer porch.

The madmen like Blake, the exiles like Rimbaud, the squadron of those who drank to death. Insect Icaruses. Why? Because of that notion—that unnameable thing, concept, idea—now embodied in the names of the poets who've been singed by it. In some cases, burnt up.

I hear *bastard* and I hear *Sparrow* and I hear *Schofield* and I hear *ungrateful.* Nod, nod, nod. I hear the word *try* and *trying* three or four times. I hear *uphill battle* and *why.*

But only one complete sentence manages to wade its way across the moat of my addled perceptions. Mostly I've been divining the conversation by keeping track of the feeling-tone of what Jim is saying. I can tell from his face and the timbre of his voice that what's required is a series of sympathetic nods accompanied by the occasional outraged scrunching of the brow. But this sentence, it smashes its way through.

I feel like I'm disappearing from the ground up, kiddo.

The tone is all appeal. The feeling all despair.

And yet it seems to me he kind of cheered up an hour or so later. At one point there were women at our table, leaning over to converse, and whatever Jim was saying, it was clear he had them mesmerized. And then there were some men around, too. Laughing with Jim and Slaughter about something, shouting things to make everyone laugh even harder, sloshing their drinks around.

And then just two more things. Two other burps of memory from that evening, after my head started to clear a little.

————

One, Slaughter. A flat hand slams into the table, rattling people's beers. A python suddenly drops from the ceiling onto my neck, its weight pulling me to one side. Into Slaughter. His face against mine. Slaughter's arm. It could be my leg.

He hisses. He's the snake in that cartoon. What is that Disney cartoon, with the boy who gets lost in the jungle? There's a snake and a tiger. But there's also a singing, dancing bear who looks out for him. That cartoon, what's it called, where the animals all talk like jazz musicians?

"Look!" Slaughter hisses, or manages to hiss. How is he able to hiss a word like "look"?

"What?" I say, still grappling with his arm. Slaughter clenches it tighter for good measure.

"Scarsdale," hisses Slaughter. "Right the fuck there."

He points. I look. There is a man standing at the bar, both hands on his hips. To my discomfort, he is staring directly back at us. Scarsdale. Scarsdale takes no shit from those who would stare and point, it would seem.

"Here's what I'm going to do," half-whispers Slaughter, his mouth practically up against my ear. "I go up to him, right? I say, Hey, fuckwad, this belong to you? I whip out the fucking flag, man! I whip it out from my ass!" Slaughter's muscles twitch and flex in his excitement and I feel he is on the verge of cutting off my windpipe.

"Or, no! How about this, I go up to him, like, la, la . . . Hm, oh I'm kinda uncomfortable here, I don't know why . . . Seems to be something jammed up my asshole, hm, wonder what it could be. And then like, dum-de-dum. I start pulling the flag out of my ass!"

"Lawrence is turning red," Sherrie's voice speaks from somewhere.

Slaughter gives me one last, affectionate clench.

"I'm gonna do it, man!"

And then he's gone. For the rest of the night.

———

Thing two:

I don't think it's much later. Sherrie is still around—
Slaughter's abandonment must not yet have registered. I
don't know why I remember this moment in particular,
why it should stand out, because nothing actually happens.
My paranoia has abated enough to let me take in my surroundings somewhat. To my relief, I am able to raise my
eyes without the scenario translating immediately into a
reptilian Last Judgment scene. For short periods, I can
watch people dancing and be fascinated by their movements, the light dappling their bodies. But every now and
then things will go a bit snaky—there's a moment when a
group of women are all waving their arms in the air in unison—and I have to look away.

When I turn to see who's left at the table, it's Sherrie,
looking down into her Coke. And Jim, looking at Sherrie,
with folded arms.

I get the feeling I have stumbled into something. Like
when you're switching around the channels on TV and come
across a scene which is clearly a significant part of some narrative, a moment that's heavy with meaning. The two characters face off in silence, but you can feel something weighty
in the air—something that's gone on well before you arrived,
something with a lot of no-doubt-fascinating twists and
turns. *This looks like it might be good,* you think to yourself,
settling down to watch.

But then the credits roll. You realize the show is over.
You've come in too late.

16.

```
the ass of the head
and what is in it,
or is not—
The question
of which should take
its rightful place up top—
Is the axis
the ass-kiss
the pinhead
on which this angel

squats

December 7, 1975
```

MY FIRST DRUG-INSPIRED EFFORT. It may not be "Kubla Khan," but into my midterm portfolio—due on Jim's desk Monday morning—it goes. I woke up from dreams of snakes and limbs and wrote it at once, Big Blue steaming at my side.

It started with a nagging feeling. Something is nagging at me, I thought. It felt like the mental equivalent of having to piss. So I dug out my notebook—not ready to unleash the merciless clackity-clack of my typewriter keys this early— and out came "The Ass of the Head." Smooth and easy. It reminded me of the time I was six and saw a cow give birth at a neighbour's farm. It's not a memory I cherish, in partic- ular, but I do recall with a sort of poetic relish the *glide* of the experience—the smooth and perfect glide of the final moments. Once the difficult stuff was out of the way, the rest of the creature's wet body just slid right on out, easy as pie. After an infinity of struggle and suffering, and only a little bit of throwing up on my part, the thing abruptly pooped itself into the world like it was no big deal. To me this will always be the best and only metaphor for writing poetry, although I will probably never say so out loud.

Then I just kind of fawned over it for a while, "The Ass of the Head." I imagined Jim extricating it from my portfolio, his sudden, surprised smile at the title (the smile fading as he becomes engrossed). It was a bit sing-songy, and I didn't quite understand exactly what I meant by "this angel," which was worrying, because the whole poem seemed to kind of hinge on the image. But maybe that was okay. Maybe it was supposed to be enigmatic, the angel. This was poetry, after all. And why "this" angel, I wondered, why didn't I go with "an" angel or "the" angel? Who is the angel? I wasn't sure it mattered. I decided to leave it. Leave it to the portfolio. Leave it to Jim.

So now the poem is neatly typed and snugly ensconced in my midterm portfolio alongside "Deadwood" and a few other new ones ("Showdogs," "Stormfront," and "Thanksgive"—a tribute to poor knocked-up Cousin Janet). The rest of the portfolio I've padded with old stuff. But it's finished, and so you'd think my conscience would be clear. Still, something is nagging at me. Something from the night before. Another unwritten poem, perhaps? I flip the pawed, soiled pages of my notebook for clues. And there it is.

pinpricks

————

Ring, ring.

"Hello, this is the Crowfeather Inn, Peter speaking."

"Yes, may I speak to Dermot Schofield, please?"

"Mmmmm. Just a sec."

The flipping of pages. The tapping of a pen. It sounds like it could be one of the hippie proprietors, with his casual *mmmm* and soft way of talking. My parents told me this was the thing they most noticed about hippies, once they started showing up to hitchhike around the island and mustering the toked-up audacity to ask my father, not for a room, but for permission to camp out behind the motel. "For free!" Dad always marvelled. "Lousy armpit sniffers think they'll set up a squat on my land for *free!* Well, I showed *them* where the gun was." Dad is always saying he showed people where the gun was. But he's never showed anyone where the gun is. Dad is a softie. I remember quite clearly the canvas lean-tos pitched out back. He even let the hippies light fires.

Regardless, the tents and the fires—that wasn't what really got up my father's nose. It was their voices, the way they talked. That deliberately gentle, deliberately inoffensive mode of speech. "Made you want to punch 'em in the face," Dad always said.

"I'mmm sorry," says Peter the hippie. "Mr. Schofield checked out bright and early this morning."

"Bright and early?" I repeat.

"That's right," Peter practically whispers in my ear.

"Um," I say. "Did he go to the bus station?"

"I believe he did," affirms Peter.

"How were the roads this morning?"

"Oh, fine," Peter tells me, happily. "They had the plows out all night."

"That's good," I say, twiddling the phone cord, twiddling away my guilt. "Did he get a cab or something?"

"Mmmm, no," slurs Peter. "I believe he got a lift out to Spanky's with one of the other guests."

"A lift?" I repeat.

"Mmm-hmm," murmurs Peter, as if in seduction. It really does make you want to punch them in the face.

"Did he," I say, "did he, like . . . Did he have any trouble with the bill, or anything?"

There is a pause. "I beg your pardon?" says Peter.

"I just want to make sure he got away okay," I apologize. "I was . . . I was his host."

"You were his host," repeats Peter in a slow, soft, and measured cadence. Dulcet tones, as they say. What is a dulcet? At the moment, I'm assuming it is a big machete-shaped thing one uses to hack a person into strips. Or else something like Moira's dragon blade. Who would have thought such tones could be so cutting?

———

```
Dear Mr. Schofield,


It is the day after your reading, and I am
feeling guilty. I should have thought to drive
you to the bus station this morning, but Jim


Dear Dermot,


Dear Dermot Schofield,


Hi there, Dermot!


Dermot, hello.


Dermot:


Dermot;


Attention: Dermot Schofield
ATTN: De
```

Dear Mr. Schofield,

It is the day after your reading, and I just
wanted to let you know once again how much I
enjoyed it. I also really enjoyed meeting you
and would like to apologize if I made you
uncomfortable at all with all my nervousness and
rudimentary winter driving skills. Too bad about
the storm, I'm sure we would have had lots more
people out to the reading had the weather been
more ~~accommodating accommodating element~~ co-
operative

~~What you said about love, it almost killed me.~~

Dear Mr. Schofield,

Thank you so much for coming to town and giving
such a wonderful and impressive reading.
Everybody was talking about what you said afterward. I just wanted to let you know how much I
enjoyed meeting and spending time with you. I
can't thank you enough for taking me to dinner
at the Crowfeather. It was a privilege just to
speak with ~~a poet of your stature and abilities~~
you. I'm afraid I did a poor job of expressing
this as we were saying goodbye, so I thought I
would write and try again.

~~You were really patient and kind to put up with
all my idiotic~~

~~Mostly I wanted to let you know that our
discussion~~

Please find enclosed a cheque for one hundred
dollars, to cover the amount you paid for your
stay at the Crowfeather Inn. As I have been
helping Jim with the administrative side of the
reading, he asked that I get the money to you;
however, I thought it best not to send cash in
the mail. So I hope you don't mind if I send a
personal cheque. Once again, I apologize for the
mixup with the deposit, and the room where the
reading was being held, and not being on time
to meet your bus. It was all totally my fault.

I'm also enclosing three poems for your journal,
one of which I just wrote this morning!

I very much look forward to the opportunity to
speak with you again one day. Thank you again
for ~~gracing~~ visiting our campus. It meant a lot
~~to me~~.

Yours truly,

~~Lawrence~~ Larry Campbell

I will fix it later.

3

rustlingleaves

17

I'M TOO SICK to do anything. Every time I look down at a page—be it my notebook or the library copy of *Poets of Contemporary Canada* I brought along—my guts heave. Janet's not sick. I'm so sick, I begrudge her this fact. I thought pregnant women were supposed to be puking constantly, but she actually looks pretty content for a girl with no future—all curled up in her seat across from me, wool coat draped over her knees, immersed in George Eliot. Janet is never to be seen without some hefty old novel under her arm. As long as it's not of this century and is over six hundred pages, she'll read it. Must be the Lydia in her. Janet says she doesn't like "modern" literature. She once told me she finds Hemingway "bland," and because everyone is so influenced by Hemingway, it's all bland now. I think she just likes reading about corsets and *pince-nez* and the like.

Every once in a while she'll look up at me, not so much out of concern but, I imagine, because it's unsettling to have me sitting across from her just staring into space. And I'll admit—I'm not just staring into space. Sometimes I'll forget myself in all my nausea and sit staring at her. To get my mind off the nausea, I'll wonder about Janet. The girl with no future. She's got four months worth of baby in her now.

"Oh, Larry," says Janet when she looks up at me. Her face pinches. "You're so green!"

I force a verdant smile before turning my face to the window. The sky is grey and the sea is greyer, choppy. "The chop," I've heard seagoing types call it. Gotta look out for that chop, they'll say. Chop's bad today. Would make a good title for a poem come to think of it, "The Chop." But I don't write it down.

The rainbow of awfulness I'm experiencing this morning comes in a varied spectrum. Green is for my hangover—because there's no way I'll accept that, after all these years, I've lost my sea legs and have turned into one of those mainland types who need to take a Gravol before even setting foot on the pier. So the green is a hangover green, not, I emphasize, a seasickness green. Any seasickness I may be experiencing is a direct result of the hangover, is what's causing the slightly yellowish tinge to the green.

Then there's the red. Red is for fear, and Christmas. Yellow doesn't work for fear as far as I'm concerned, it's too sunny a colour—daffodils, Van Gogh sunflowers. Yellow is not of my spectrum today, except in the sickly tinge it brings to the green. Red is what's fear. It's alarming, gory. Red is the colour that warns you to stop. Blood, Santa Claus. He opens his jolly old bag and out comes—nothing. Because I still have no money for Christmas presents. Especially now.

Then the red merges with blue. It doesn't form a cheery purple as you might expect, because this blue is too dark. The blue of guilt and apprehension. When the red bleeds into it, the tone goes muddy. Just one big, brownish Rorschach blotch of worry over Jim, and whether or not I have let him down. Assuredly I have. Assuredly he will never talk to me again.

It is my own fault for not having grasped how sad a man Jim is. There is a basic melancholy at his core, the same universal sadness at the centre of every creative genius—all those suicides and self-destruction artists who came before. Let's see, who killed themselves? Berryman, off a bridge, not three years ago. Celan, in the Seine. Sylvia Plath—the old head-in-the-oven trick. She left lunch out for her kids before lowering the door, kneeling down, leaning forward as if in prayer.

Then there are the more social types, like Dylan Thomas, who did it the convivial way. The kind of suicide where you can still pretend to everyone you're having a good time, you can still attend the shindigs. You could be in the middle of a swinging hotel room, shouting *chin-chin!* and wearing a lampshade on your head. No one but you would know. Maybe not even you. Armies of them, the sad ones, in bars, at parties. Gregarious to the end.

See, the fact that I am thinking of Jim with respect to these types, the fact that I am thinking *Jim* and *suicide* as I sit here riding out the chop. This tells me I should never have left. This tells me I made the wrong decision. Who'da thunk it? Lawrence Campbell, fucking things up. Getting things wrong.

And why?

Because I wanted to go home for Christmas. I wanted to go home. I wanted presents. I wanted to be fed. I wanted to see my mom and dad.

Why else?

I wanted to get away from him.

What I've learned: Jim gets excited first, he gets manic. Like one of those birthday-party sparklers, popping and crackling crazily away before sputtering out. When I arrived at his office the Monday after the Schofield reading, he was on his feet. His posture struck me—how straight he stood—like a man experiencing upright electric shock, all the bones and muscles stretched to capacity. He was in front of his bookshelf reading. *Blinding White.* It seemed as if his hair should have been standing on end.

I knocked on the door frame to get his attention. His head shot up, expression remote, like a face on a totem pole.

But when he saw it was me, he smiled. Blinding white.

"Larry!"

"Jim!" I laughed.

"Just the man I wanna see!"

"At your service!" I rejoined.

There is something about being greeted in such a manner—the dazzling smile, the joyful moment of recognition. It takes your breath away. It takes your doubts away. I felt confident and happy at once. I flopped into the ripped leather chair Jim keeps in the corner of his office for students. The seat sags so deeply, has been flopped into by so many varieties of butts, it's almost like sitting on an overlarge open toilet.

Simultaneously, I frisbeed my portfolio onto his desk. "There it is," I announced as it skidded to a landing.

"What's that?" said Jim.

"My portfolio."

"Oh! Nice going, kid." Jim moved around to the other side of his desk. He flipped open a folder and made a quick checkmark somewhere before smiling back up at me. I stretched a leg over the arm of his chair and slouched deeper into its bum-hole.

"So?" said Jim. "That it for the semester?"

"One more paper," I sighed. "No more exams. But I'm finished. I just have to type it."

"What's the paper?" Jim asked, stuffing my portfolio into a drawer without a glance.

"Classical literature. *Antigone.*"

Jim shook his head in seeming repudiation. "*Oedipus Rex,*" he said. "Ya done that one yet?"

"No." I made an instantaneous mental note, as I always do when Jim mentions work he approves of.

"*That's* the play," he said, coming back around to the front of his desk in order to sit on it. "That's the only one you need to know. That's the one that's set us down the path we're currently on."

"The guy pokes his eyes out, right?" I ventured.

"Freud," replied Jim, confusing me. "Shakespeare. Fathers and sons, that's the kernel of it, Larry. That's the whole thing. It all comes from *Oedipus Rex.*"

"I'll read it," I said.

"You're goddamn right you'll read it. Then you come over to the house and we'll talk about it over a shot or two of rum."

"Sounds good," I said, before closing my lips over an otherwise foolish grin.

"Larry," said Jim, jolting forward. "I have to tell ya. Friday night got me all fired up."

I blinked. "The reading?"

"Goddamnit, we have to be doing more of that sort of thing around here. It's exactly what's needed, don't you think? We forget in this place, it's a forgetting-factory, we get so buried in things like grades and texts and committees and meetings and then one day you wake up and say, Wait a minute. This is about writing. This is about art. What in hell are we doing?"

I adjusted my ass in the gully of Jim's chair in order to lean forward. "Jim," I said, nodding. "That's so true, you know down at the Mariner Friday night Sherrie and I were talking about this very thing, holding readings on a regular basis—"

"And listen, kid," interrupted Jim. "I never had a chance to say this, but you did a *great* job on Friday."

My words were abruptly cut off, not because of Jim interrupting, but because I found myself having to cover up yet another stupid grin.

"A *great* job," re-emphasized Jim.

"Jim," I said after a moment, drinking in his look of significance and appreciation. "Thanks so much. It really means a lot that you—"

"So here's the plan," said Jim, clenching his hands

together in front of his chest and then shaking the knot of them at me. "Let's do it again. Right now. We'll do a Christmas reading."

I stared, my mouth went slack. I was thinking of the date, calculating. It was Monday, December 15, the year of our lord nineteen hundred and seventy-five. I had just completed writing my final paper, had only to type it. I wanted to go home for Christmas.

"A Christmas reading?" I repeated. "You mean . . . on Christmas?"

"No, no, no, not on Christmas Day, of course not," snorted Jim.

"Oh!" I laughed, carefully.

"Nobody's gonna wanna go to a poetry reading on Christmas Day!" Jim bellowed, practically holding his sides.

"Of course not!" I said, laughing louder, more carefully.

"We'll do it this weekend," said Jim.

I pressed my lips together again, no longer to hide a grin, but sucking them in slightly. I could feel the delicate crunch of the veined flesh between my teeth—pulpy, like a wedge of orange.

"Well, Jim," I said after a moment. "Friday would be . . . the nineteenth."

"Still be a few people around," Jim shrugged. "When were you planning on taking off?"

"Friday the nineteenth," I admitted. I had it all set up with Janet and my parents.

"Well, you can put it off 'til after the weekend, can't you? Get some drinking done with me before heading over on the boat?"

"Um," I said.

"How long the ferries running?"

"I think right up until the twenty-fourth," I admitted.

"There ya go!" said Jim.

I coughed, fixing a deliberate look of mulling-over on my face. "My only concern," I said, noticing my leg was no longer flung over the arm of the chair. My comfort and confidence seemed to have abandoned me, going off hand in hand like the dish running away with the spoon. "My only concern, I guess, is that probably every one *else* would be gone home."

Jim waved a hand, miming a backhanded slap. "Ah, there's always a few stragglers around."

"Sure, sure," I nodded. "But, you know, the kind of people on campus who would go to a poetry reading . . . I mean," I flailed for a couple of heartbeats, wondering if Jim was aware that normal people, as a rule, don't even like poetry. And if not, did I want to be the one to break it to him. "Well, for example, the bulk of Schofield's crowd were people from our seminar. It might be best left until the new year, don't you think, Jim?"

Jim's face darkened. His eyebrows plunged, causing something in my throat to ascend. He lowered his head and scratched it with both hands.

"I gotta tell ya, Larry," he said, looking up at me when he was finished. "I'm just jazzed. I'm ready to do this *now*. I haven't read from my work in so long and I realized this weekend that one of the things that's been blocking me is clearly just a lack of—of feedback. The ongoing isolation of this fucking place, the lack of peers. I'm just living out there on the point with a woman and a dog and then I come into town and meet students and mark papers and try not to feel under fucking siege by Sparrow and his cronies . . ."

Jim lowered his head again, scratching minutely. Oh, I thought, understanding. He wants a reading for *himself.* Somehow it made more sense to me then. It seemed that if Jim Arsenault wanted to do a reading, we should call off exams, alert the media, and book Grayson Hall for the event.

But at the same time, I knew it could never work. To try and hold a reading in less than a week would never do Jim's poetry justice. It would inevitably be half-assed, even more half-assed than Schofield's, and the only people present would be me and Dekker. I had to convince him of that.

"I wanna do this," Jim said, looking up at me.

"Then we'll do it," I replied.

18.

APPARENTLY DAD'S PLAN is to cross-examine me about my diet all the way to Stan and Maud's, where he'll be able to dump the pregnant niece without having to utter a word to her. Normally, I wouldn't mind this sort of thing so much, understanding that the food obsession is parental instinct, and after months of tea and canned ham I'm about ready for my fatted calf. But the green of my hangover, tinged yellow with seasickness as it is—the mud of my guilt about Jim—it all kind of gets sloshed together, stirred up by Dad's deliberate ignoring of Janet. The colour goes a deep, brick red, finally taking on an irascible, copperish glare.

"So don't they feed you at university, or what?" he wants to know.

"No," I say. "They don't."

"What?" My mom turns around in her seat. If she weren't buckled in she would climb up onto her knees like a kid. "How can they not feed the students?"

"That was last year, Mom, when I lived in residence and had a meal plan. I'm off campus now." Why is it they can never keep track of this? Why must I reiterate and re-confirm every exotic aspect of university life every time I see them? It's like children who insist you read from the same storybook over and over again.

"Can't you still get a meal plan?" Mom wants to know.

"Why would I do that, when I have my own kitchen? I'd have to walk to campus three times a day."

"Well, you're not using your kitchen," barks my dad over his shoulder. "That's clear enough."

"How do you eat?" my mother wants to know.

"I go to the store. I buy bread. I buy tea. I buy peanut butter. I take the food back to my apartment, I put it in the cupboard—"

"You're not getting any hot meals, that's the problem right there," says Dad.

"I buy soup."

"Your mother will give you a roasting pan to take back," says Dad.

"I don't have an extra roasting pan," demurs Mom.

"We'll pick you up a roasting pan at the Co-op," amends Dad, who pronounces it *cwap.* "You take that. You buy yourself a chicken, or one of them little pot roasts. You stick it in the oven an hour or so. Throw in some onions, potatoes, and there you go."

I look over to Janet not so much to confirm that she's laughing at me, but to gauge precisely how hard. I assume she'd have both fists stuffed in her mouth at this point. But Janet's moonface is as serene as the one Jim describes in "Erato"—the face that is nothing like Moira's. She's gazing outside at the rolling white.

I envy her outsider status. I want very much to involve Janet in the conversation at this point, if only to discomfit Dad.

"Janet eats well," I state. She turns and stares at me. That was the wrong thing to say, I suppose.

"Do you, dear?" Mom inquires, lowering her pitch.

"I guess," says Janet, still staring.

"I mean, her landlady cooks for her. She's really lucky." I try to shoot Janet a comradely smile, but it gets filtered through my bad mood and hangover and feels greasy, insincere.

"Well, she bakes," admits Janet.

"Oh, does she bake for you?"

"Yeah—she's really great."

"Isn't that nice," says my mother. Dad is driving in silence. It's my turn to add to the conversation, but I know that the moment I do, he'll jump right in again, assured that no one will make the mistake of thinking he's talking to Janet. So I let there be silence.

Therefore, my mother starts rambling away. It's always Mom who bears the burden of keeping things upbeat, and one way she does it is by forcing her voice into its highest octaves. The higher she goes, the more despairing she is of the overall mood, you can tell. At the moment, dog's ears are pricking up across all Prince Edward Island.

Bryant Dekker was my salvation, having negotiated a pretty cagey compromise with Jim. Dekker told me he'd been planning a Christmas party on the weekend—he and Ruth. Nothing to do with the university, per se, just a quiet get-together with folks from the neighbourhood. The Dekkers only moved to Timperly five years ago, apparently—Dekker says "only," but to me five years seems like a long time. Ruth, he said, was having trouble getting settled, and they've been trying to "forge bonds" in the community ever since. There would be punch, more mulled wine, fondue, and the like. Jim could give his reading at the party. It would be casual, Dekker stressed to Jim. A casual, convivial atmosphere. Unpretentious, he emphasized.

Jim didn't know. He wasn't sure, at first. To read untested material in front of strangers?

Your audience would be mostly strangers no matter

where you were, Dekker reasoned. Imagine if you were reading in Toronto or somewhere.

But would they be respectful, wondered Jim. Would they understand that this was a literary reading? Would they stand around talking about shovelling their driveways and property taxes and what all while Jim was trying to read?

Dekker assured him they would not. Everyone in town had heard of Jim, was aware of his reputation. They would recognize the occasion for the honour it was.

But, balked Jim, a more formal environment might be—

Jim, said Dekker. You *hate* formality. Remember?

And so it was agreed. I told Dekker I'd help in any way I could. I was so grateful to him for taking over. I would have gotten down on all fours and been the coffee table if Dekker had asked me to.

Slaughter would not be around, which was probably just as well. Slaughter had already returned to wherever he was from in Ontario. One of the innumerable, indistinguishable communities that circle Toronto like the gaseous rings of Saturn. Markham or Scarborough or Barrie or somewhere. Slaughter once told me he came to Westcock to study only because his dad had, and his dad's dad before him. They had all played football. They were that sort of family, the kind you see in movies. Man-families, with cabinets crammed full of trophies, actual cabinets—a mere mantelpiece would never hold. Edging out the mother's crystal and china.

I only knew Slaughter was gone from talking to Sherrie. He hadn't bothered to say goodbye to anyone else.

Then came the phone call to inform my parents of the changes to my travel plans, the inevitable reproach in the form of my mother's emotional devastation that the trip would be delayed a mere day, the hustling to get off the phone before my father could pick up and commence outraged cross-examination, and finally the phone call to Janet to let her know of the change as well.

"So if you want to grab Friday's ferry without me, no problem," I told her.

Janet said that was fine, but a few minutes later called me back.

"I was just talking to Mom and Dad," she said. "They say I might as well just wait the extra day and come back with you and your folks. No point in making two trips."

"No," I said, "I guess not." I was in a hurry and didn't know what else to say. I hung up without inviting her to the reading.

Then I settled in at the typewriter and tapped out my last paper of the semester with extra care, re-doing entire pages as opposed to my usual method of X'ing out the more minor typos. I am forever short of correction tape due to my impractical habit of composing poems on the typewriter. The profs don't seem to mind the occasional X. Most of them are just impressed I can do my own typing.

I handed the paper in on Tuesday, and the rest of the week was set aside for luxuriating in free time and solitude. It pleased me to think I had reached a point in my life where free time and solitude were luxuries instead of the primary conditions of my existence. It had been a busy semester, I reflected. It had been a good semester, for all my outrage and anguish over what the department was doing to Jim. I went from having no friends and no life outside of school and poetry to having something that actually resembled a social circle—even if I don't actually like Todd and Claude that much, and live in vacillating mortal fear of Charles Slaughter. Still, they were people I knew and saw and talked to every day, and together we had accomplished something. I had a community, what's more, a community of more or less like-minded souls. Something I used to dream about back in Summerside reading about Gertrude Stein's salons in Paris, the Bloomsbury group, and so forth.

And not to put too fine a point on it, but in the space of four months, I had established myself as drinking buddy and confidant of the one person who mattered most.

So: it had been a good semester. I was glad it was over. I needed a break. I needed a few days of Big Blue and leisure reading in Timperly, and then I needed someone to roast a turkey for me while I drowsed in front of my parents' fire-place in PEI with a candy cane half-hanging out of my mouth.

Ring, ring. Wednesday morning. Eleven A.M. You know who it was?

"Hi," she said, when I answered the phone.

"Hi," I said back, waiting.

"It's me," she said impatiently.

"Is it?" I replied, stalling for time. A crazy part of my imagination was thinking it could only be Brenda L. from Carl's. We had talked from time to time, she had the poster from Schofield's reading, she could have asked around, looked me up in the student directory. The voice definitely had Brenda's dodgy New Brunswick twang to it—a kind of terse-syllabled edge.

But she just sat there breathing on the phone, waiting some more, like it would be an insult to have to identify herself.

"I'm sorry," I said, giving in, "I don't—"

"Jim Arsenault's wife!"

She could have said Yoko Ono. Liza Minelli. I wouldn't have been more surprised.

"Moira?"

"Yes!"

"Hi," I said.

She replied with a puff of static breath, as if blowing dust out of the receiver. Some baffled silence from me. Then: "So whaterya up to?"

"What am I up to?"

"Whaterya doing today?"

"What am I doing today?"

"Yeah. Whaterya up to?"

"I'm just, uh—" Panic thought: What if Moira wanted to have an affair with me? I couldn't think of any other possible reason for the call. You heard about such things with artists. Jack Kerouac and Neal Cassidy. The pre-Raphaelites—Rossetti and those guys. They were supposed to have swapped girl-friends like hockey cards. And what if Jim approved, had even proposed it? You heard about that sort of thing too. "I'm just, uh," I said.

"I'm just uh I'm just uh," Moira repeated in dunce-tones, reminding me of a few select assholes from high school.

I cleared my throat. "I'm just getting some reading done," I told her. This, I've found, is a powerful thing to say when you're a university student. People immediately respond with deference, imagining you in your cold-water garret thumb-ing through mountainous tomes, squinting by candlelight.

It didn't work with Moira. She blew into the phone some more. She was sighing—she punctuated everything she said with sighs, I recalled now. I remembered our discussion on the couch in October. *Tree died, sigh. Dragon blade, sigh.* It was a kind of oral signpost, meant to assist the listener in gauging the depth of Moira's hardship, the torment of her existence out there on Rock Point.

Sigh. "Sitting on your arse, areya?" said Moira.

"Well," I said. "Technically, I guess."

"*Technically,*" repeated Moira. Again with the dunce-voice. Then I remembered a trick of my father's. A thing that he does when on the phone with someone he doesn't want to be. He straightens. He kind of tucks the phone beneath his double chin so he can fold his arms. Then he looks at my mother (for some reason) with impatience. He says, "So what can I do for you today?"

"So, Moira," I said, placing a hand on my hip instead of folding my arms—lacking my Dad's excess chin to hold the receiver in place—"what can I do for you today?"

Another hard-done-by burst of static. "Jesus, you sound like an accountant or something."

I waited.

"Well," she said in her abrupt accent. It sounded like *welp.* "The old fella's wondering why you don't come up to visit."

From our evening in October, I knew "the old fella" was her pet name for Jim. The only other thing I'd heard her call him all evening was "that one," or else, "that one there." And then she'd point across the room with her cigarette.

I let my hand fall off my hip and carried the phone over to the couch.

"Really? He wants me to come up there?"

"Welp, he said you two were supposed to talk about a play or some such thing."

"*Oedipus Rex?*" I said after a moment.

"What?"

"*Oedipus Rex,* was that the play?"

"I don't know what in hell play it was. He just said you were supposed to come up. So I said, well, why in Christ's name don't you call him and tell him to come up, but now he's all in a sulk."

"He's in a sulk?" I repeated.

"Yes, he's in a big goddamn sulk and won't call you, so I said to hell with it, I'll call him myself."

I thought about this. "Is he angry?"

Another blast of breath in my ear.

"I don't know," sang Moira, making her voice extra aggrieved and long-suffering, just in case the series of sighs weren't doing the trick. "He just gets like this," she said. "He just needs someone to talk to—he can't talk to me."

"He can't?" I repeated, curious enough about their relationship to inquire further, to be willing to prolong this otherwise maddening conversation. "Why can't he talk to you?" I wanted to know.

"Because I am so fed up with this bullshit, I'll fuckin' drive him through the wall, that's why," explained Moira.

19.

I ASKED FRIENDLY to stop at the liquor store on the way out to Rock Point because it seemed wise to bring an offering of some kind. But the ride out there took so long, I twice almost popped the cap and started passing the pint back and forth across the seat between Friendly and myself. What the hell, I thought—exams were over and it was practically Christmas. Plus, I was now a far more experienced drinker than I had been at the beginning of the semester. I hardly ever threw up anymore.

"Nah, nah, nah," exclaimed Friendly when I suggested it to him. "The wife's rippin' at me as it is, I come home stinkin' of rum and that'll be the end of 'er."

"Wouldn't go over so well, eh?"

"Nope, but I'll tell you my magic formula," said Friendly, lowering his voice as he turned off onto the dirt road leading in to Jim's. "I'll be making a stop myself at the liquor store on the way home today. I get a six pack for me, a bottle a' goof for the old gal, and everything's right as rain for the rest a' the night."

"She likes the goof, does she?" I smiled, wondering what goof was, peering down the road at the farmhouse. Something had possessed Jim to paint the place black after he bought it—although it's since faded into a darkish, bilious green—with satanic red trim. I could just make him out, standing open-jacketed in front of the chopping block, Panda running in circles at his feet.

"Well, it makes her romantic," said Friendly, craning around in his seat to favour me with a confidential wink and a ribald clack of his dentures. But Friendly's tone grew subdued as we rumbled along the plowed road, drawing closer to the house. Jim stopped whatever he was doing to watch the car approach, the way people who live in the middle of nowhere will. Panda's mad barks penetrated the closed car windows. The dog leapt around Jim like an oversized jackrabbit or a capering demon.

Jim was holding a thing in each hand. Both things were black.

"What in Christ's name has this one been up to?" Friendly murmured, re-adjusting his plate.

One of the things was a gun, a rifle. The other thing I couldn't make out. Its shape was indefinable, merely a mark, some kind of violent black blotch, like a jagged hole torn into the bright winter reality, exhibiting the nothing that lay beyond. And leaving blood. Leaving blood. There was blood on the snow in front of him.

I paid Friendly for the cab ride slowly. I thanked him slowly. I got out of the car slowly.

Jim has a complicated relationship with the crows, it turned out. He had just finished shooting one out of the sky, on behalf of his dog. They "teased" Panda, he told me. Because crows, he said, are smart. They are cruel and cunning and they know dogs are stupid, so they tease them. Crows, he told me, have a particularly malicious sense of humour. Dogs don't have a sense of humour, Jim went on to explain, that's what makes them vulnerable. Dogs are like young children—open and trusting. Crows are like slightly older children—jaded, knowing, a bit drunk on the power of this.

"Now don't get me wrong," said Jim. "I like crows, for the most part. I admire them."

"You admire them?" I said, watching him wind twine around the mangled bird's reptilian feet.

"Well, they're tough," said Jim. "They're sneaky. They're no aristocrats, mind you—there's nothing majestic about them, but they've got their own sort of splendour, their own code. They're the Artful Dodgers of the avian world."

Jim hung the mess of crow from a tree, giving it a jaunty poke in order to make it swing. Blood sprinkled itself around. He told me the other crows would take this for a warning and keep their distance. It seemed to me he was talking out of fairy tales. Panda was going insane at our feet. The dog seemed to have been convinced that Jim would at some point hand over the crow for Panda to devour. Seeing it suspended out of reach—swinging and sprinkling away— added insult to injury.

"Shut up," Jim said to Panda. Seeing he had Jim's attention, Panda barked louder, crazier. "Shut up!" Jim yelled. Panda gurgled in frustration and staggered around in a couple of desperate circles. It was clear he would start up again at any moment.

"Go get the ball," suggested Jim, and the dog took off.

We stood outside throwing the ball to Panda for about an hour. I was not really dressed for it and kept having to wipe my nose on the sleeve of my jacket for lack of anything else. I felt dazed, numb. It was a lot of things—the cold, the way Jim's black house loomed behind us, the dangling crow, the red slashes in the snow like a crime scene. But also it was Jim. There was something about Jim's mood that infected me, made my thoughts feel dull and muted, hypnotized by the dog rushing back and forth; the endless imperative to keep hucking the tennis ball. Panda did not get tired of it. Neither did Jim. It was something to do with Jim's mood—indifference. Resigned to the hellish boundlessness of Panda's single demand.

I couldn't stand it after a while. My feet were in sneakers, and therefore numb. So were my hands—red, bare, and caked with half-frozen dog slobber. I remembered the rum.

"Jim," I said, pulling the pint from my jacket. Before he could even respond, I had the cap off and was downing a shot.

"Well, look at him go," remarked Jim with a smile. The kind of smile you might give across a casket, at someone's wake.

See, this is what I hate. The minute we're in the door, Mom puts on the tea. The first thing my nose and ears detect is a pork roast crackling away in the oven, producing a smell of such comfort and joy my eyes almost roll back inside my head. But here's what's astounding: at no time in my life can I remember my parents ever leaving the house when there was something in the oven. Dad is what you might call a reverse firebug. He's obsessive on the subject of fire prevention, perhaps owing to an incident with Jack Daniel's and lighter fluid during a summer's camping trip we took when I was a kid. One minute he was kicking the barbecue into the lake and the next the cuffs of his polyester pants were alight—they went up with a synthetic gasp and melted against his calves.

So Dad, to put it mildly, is vigilant these days when it comes to fires. The idea that he risked home and business to make sure the number one son got pork for supper takes the edge off my appetite somewhat.

My mother bustles back and forth, banging the biscuit tin against the cookie tin, taking down plates, making a big deal of me, home, in the kitchen. Dad heads to the living room to wrangle with the fireplace. None of that is what I hate exactly, although it kind of is in a way. But mostly it's the noise coming out of my mother. This weird sing-song she keeps chanting, a sort of mantra, as the Eastern-religion types call it.

"Tea for Larry, Larry loves his tea, God only knows—don't you, Larry? You'll have some biscuits with that, won't you? Larry can eat biscuits, that's for sure. A bit of cheese maybe, or—oh, I have some nice raspberry preserves from the bushes out back, Larry loves raspberry—don't you Larry?"

What is she doing? She's asking me questions and talking to herself at the same time. It's the strangest thing—she isn't even looking at me as she digs around, mumbling as though senile into the cupboards. We go through this every time I come home, and this, I realize—this thing that's happening right here and now, this ritual of ours—is precisely what I hate. Because I've finally figured out what she's doing. My mother is reassuring herself that I'm here, and—most importantly—that nothing has changed.

It never used to bother me before, in fact it felt natural and good. Me plunking my malnourished ass into the vinyl chair, my mother swirling around, clattering plates down in front of me, extolling me to let the tea "have a good steep" before reaching to pour myself a mug, Dad messing around in the next room with the fire, getting things nice and toasty in there for whenever I'm ready to come in and "have a good sit."

It annoys the hell out of me all of a sudden.

"Mom," I say, "sit down."

"Just let me cut you a couple of slices of bread. Nice fresh bread today."

"I've got a ton of biscuits here, Mom, it's almost supper-time."

"But you love the fresh bread," insists my mother, sawing away at a new loaf. "Just one or two slices."

"I know where it is if I want it." I make my voice firm. I don't think I've done it with her before. My deeper, question-mark-free, in-class voice.

My mother stops and looks up at me.

"Are you sure?" she says. As if I've just told her her bread tastes like shit. As if I've sprouted wings and am flitting around the light fixture above us.

"Yes," I almost yell.

"Well you don't need to yell, Larry."

"I'm not yelling, Mom. I'm being emphatic."

"Well, I don't know why you need to be so emphatic about a couple of slices of bread."

"*You're* the one who's being emphatic about a couple of slices of bread," I explain. "I'm responding in kind."

Mom puts down the bread knife. "Dad," she calls. "Will you have a piece of bread? I cut some for Larry, but he doesn't want it now."

In trundles my father, wiping slivers of wood from his pants.

"What's he got against bread?" Dad wonders aloud to the cosmos.

I jerk forward and seize two handfuls of biscuits.

"Look! Biscuits are bread! Look at all this bread I'm hav-ing! Clearly I have nothing against bread!"

"Other people might wanna eat those you know," Dad remarks as he pulls up a chair.

"He's being emphatic," emphasizes my mother.

"So that's what he's doing," says Dad.

"Supper's in an hour, Larry, you shouldn't have all those biscuits." My mother is turned away from me now, facing the stove.

I place the biscuits back on the plate, as opposed to throwing them at something. I take a moment to arrange them, being a bit prissy about it in order to annoy my Dad.

He looks at me in disgusted silence until I give in and meet his eyes. "Don't go putting those back on the plate," he says slowly. "Jesus Christ, is that what they're teaching you up there in university?"

"Yes," I reply. "They don't feed me in university. They teach me to grab biscuits. Second-year Biscuit-Grabbing."

I never realized how much they resent it. How nervous it makes them.

At Jim's, the kitchen mostly smelled like dog. The whole house smelled like dog and wood smoke, so pungent it fogged out even Moira's cigarettes.

Moira herself was at the table, smoking and watching a small black and white television with terrible reception.

"Hi, Moira," I said.

"I'm not cooking," said Moira without turning around. She jabbed her smoke in my direction.

Jim told her she didn't have to. "Me 'n Larry are more than capable," he said. "Just take that thing upstairs."

I didn't know what he was talking about until Moira, expelling a brutalized sigh, leaned forward and turned off the TV. She yanked the plug out of the wall, wrapped the cord around the set and hoisted it under her arm like you see some women carrying their toddlers. In the other hand she balanced her ashtray and smokes.

"You make sure you keep that fire going then," she yelled on her way down the hall.

Jim went to the stove and threw in a couple of chunks of wood. Jim's wood stove was just like the one at Grandma Lydia's, before she had electricity installed. As a kid, I got to mess around with the stove a lot because it was my job to dispose of Grandpa Humphries's used Kleenex. It's remarkable the crap adults are able to convince kids to do in the guise of having an important duty bestowed upon them. It probably wouldn't have been so attractive a prospect to me if it hadn't meant I got to burn stuff up. It was fun, manoeuvring the handle into the slot, then heaving the cast-iron burner aside to peer into the mini-inferno beneath.

I looked around for an electric stove or microwave, but it seemed the Arsenault kitchen was equipped with neither. Something occurred to me. My Grandpa Campbell's house was old as well, but a two-storey, unlike the Humphries's cottage. There were vents in the ceilings so the heat could travel to the upstairs bedrooms. As kids, me and Janet and Wayne would lie on the floor after we had been sent to bed, listening at the vents, hearing every word the grown-ups uttered. Mostly we couldn't believe how much they cursed when we weren't around. The vents were not complicated— they were basically holes in the floor with a decorative grille to keep us from sticking our hands or feet down into the kitchen.

So I craned my neck. Upward. Jim and Moira's kitchen had the same kind of vents—maybe Moira was even crouched up there listening. It dawned on me then just how old Jim's place was, as old as Grandma and Grandpa Campbell's, as old as Lydia's. I hadn't recognized this before—that is, I knew his house was old, but, on PEI anyway, every house I've been in that was built before electricity is—how do I put this?—kept up, as they say. Jim's place is cozy, but it hasn't exactly been kept up. Which seems like a bad idea, with an old house. My father hates them, he says they're firetraps. Before I was born, and before they took over the Highwayman, my parents had been thinking of buying a big Georgian home on the outskirts of Charlottetown and turning it into an inn, a poor-man's Crowfeather. But Dad said the thing was a money pit. The cost of rewiring alone would have devoured any possibility of an education savings for me. That's a strange thing to think. My parents could have had an inn with electricity, or a son with a future. The idea that one equals the other; one cancels the other out.

"Jim," I said, "you guys only have the wood stove here?"

Jim removed a couple of plastic tumblers drying in the dish rack and plunked them on the table. He was moving slowly, answering even slower. Water circles formed.

"If it'd been up to me," he finally rumbled, "there would-n't even be electricity. But that one upstairs," he tilted his chin heavenward, Moiraward, "she had to be able to get her stories on TV, otherwise it was no deal."

I glanced down at the wainscotting. More vents. "But you guys have a furnace, right?"

Jim waved a hand as he sat down, and I heard something pop in his back—so loud in the quiet kitchen it made me twitch. "Never use it," he said.

"Really?" My voice went high with effort. Even with half a pint of rum into us, the conversation was unspooling with about the same ease experienced by that pregnant cow of my youth, straining to expel head and hooves. "Why not?"

"Ah," Jim poured what remained of the rum into the tumblers. "It's ancient, for one thing. Who knows when the vents were last cleaned. Safer to just leave it be."

"Yeah, but it must get freezing in here."

Jim wrapped both long hands around his glass for a moment before cocking an eyebrow at me.

"You cold, Larry?"

Actually, I was sweltering. The wood stove had probably been going since dawn. That's the thing about heating a two-storey house with one stove. The only way you can get warmth into every room is to let your kitchen be a sauna.

"Not at all," I said.

"Well, there you go."

Just to show him I was sincere, I shuffled off my jacket and hung it on the back of the chair. Jim watched, dully, before squinting back into his drink. These heavy silences kept occurring, which still the booze was doing nothing to dispel. At one point when we were outside, I realized we had been chucking the ball for Panda at least twenty minutes without saying a word to each other.

But that makes it sound like I was participating in it, the silence. And I don't feel I was, exactly. That is, the silences were all Jim's—they were a Jim thing. I was suffering them, as opposed to participating in them. Jim was the author of the silences; I was his audience. They seemed to spread from his mood, like a dark liquid creeping over a surface, seeping into the ground. I guess I was the surface—I was the ground.

Panda's toenails needed cutting. The only noise for a few moments was the sound of the dog clattering and snuffling around somewhere under the table before flopping on top of my feet and starting to snore.

"You cut all the wood yourself?" I inquired at last. God help me, I thought. We could be talking about metaphysical poetry right now. This was a conversational gambit I might use with Uncle Stan.

Jim leaned back and, for some reason, unbuttoned the cuffs of his shirt. Slowly, he started rolling them up. The deliberation of this gesture was unnerving. My defence system kicked in, shot some adrenalin into my bloodstream.

He's going to beat you up now, it told me. I touched my nose—a thing I do whenever I feel threatened. Instinctively, I covered my nose. Thank you Lydia Humphries for that particular quirk.

The rational part of my brain instructed me to sit tight—Jim would not just haul off and punch me for asking about wood. But his mood, it was so weird. I didn't know what to expect.

Jim rolled his sleeves as high as they would possibly go—practically to the shoulder. Then he looked at me, raised his arms, and flexed. His biceps popped out.

"See?" said Jim.

"Wow." His arms were so long and ropey.

"That's what keeps me fit. Used to work out at a boxing club in Wethering for a while, but who needs it? You try chopping a cord of wood every day, see who messes with ya."

I imagined Jim in his yard, heaving the axe—sweat flying from his black hair—bringing it down on a slab of wood with a satisfying, splintery *chunk* that echoes through the surrounding woods as if to warn it what's to come. There was something so primal about the image, so Canadian, so Jim.

"Let me know if I can ever give you a hand with it sometime," I offered.

Jim nodded, upending his tumbler of rum. "Maybe we'll go out a little later, chop some to bring in."

Panda lay heavy on my feet. He groaned and shifted, warming my ankles against his chest. One of my feet began to tingle for lack of circulation, so I moved it, causing Panda to gurgle indignation before jumping up and clattering to the corner of the kitchen where a tartan blanket was laid out for him. He flopped down onto it with an aggrieved huff he may well have learned from Moira.

Jim had his head cradled in both hands, suspending it above his empty glass. It was a desolate position—childish, too, somehow. Like a kid told to sit there until the broccoli has disappeared from his plate. I could see tiny flecks of dandruff standing out brightly against Jim's hair, seeming to have landed there like snow.

After forever, he raised his head to look at me. His eyes, although bloodshot, were precisely as black as his hair. He was like Dracula—Dracula with dandruff. His lips pulled themselves back from his teeth.

"Larry," he whispered. I met his eyes and wanted to cover my nose again.

"A piece of advice. If you're going to bring booze over here, next time bring more than a pint."

Jim looked back down at the pointless glass on the table, long fingers raking his cheeks.

Minutes of nothing went by. Panda snored. The little hell inside the wood stove crackled away.

20.

CHRISTMAS EVE, the yearly trudge out to the car to plow through the snow to Stan and Maud's for dinner. I wasn't in the best of moods all day, anticipating it. I can't understand the point of us going over there every year. Not to mention that all week I've been inwardly griping at the necessity of having to buy a present for every last member of the Humphries family. This is a Christmas Eve tradition—we all get together at Stan and Maud's, stuff ourselves, watch Maud pour my mother one glass of wine too many so she starts giggling in a semi-hysterical way at everything coming out of Lydia's mouth, and then open our presents to and from one another and marvel inwardly at each other's bad taste. Truth be told, I have the feeling this whole ritual was initiated on my behalf, to give me the feeling of a big family Christmas seeing as I'm an only child. I'm *old* now, though, I wanted to tell my parents, I'm almost twenty, I don't give a shit. I don't need someone to play dinkies and army men with after dinner. But parents get weird about their traditions, just like they get weird about a couple of pieces of bread, should you turn them down at the wrong time.

I pled poverty. Ever since September I've been explaining to anyone with a potential interest that I have no money for Christmas presents outside the immediate family.

"Just write everybody one of your nice poems, Larry," said my mother. "They'd love it. Grammie loves to read, you know—she's always reading."

About that time Dad slipped me his usual silent twenty-dollar bill, but it was December 24 and what exactly was I supposed to buy? I wracked my brain for the purchases of Christmas past. It was ridiculous. I had a short time off school to relax and recharge and here I was in downtown Summerside wracking my brain over what to get my grandmother and personal nemesis for Christmas. Why did we go through this every year with the Humphrieses? Maud and Janet are okay, but Lydia is evil, and Wayne and Uncle Stan are more or less blatant in their estimation of me as a homo.

I would, I decided, participate in the charade no longer. I went to the bank, broke the twenty into fives, and stuck each one into a Christmas card when I got home.

So now I'm sitting in front of the fireplace in my good sweater and pants, waiting for it to be time to drive out to Stan and Maud's. I've been diverting myself with two books since I got here, one of which is my decrepit copy of *Blinding White.* Ever since I got home, I've been going over and over the poems, trying to puzzle things out. Fit the stanzas together in such a way that Jim's personality will suddenly reveal itself to me in all its complex, dazzling clarity. How to decode the mystery of the past few weeks, the way Jim has been? It feels like it's my duty to figure this out—as the guy who loves Jim's work the most.

The other is a year-old issue of *Atlantica* which I smuggled out of the library because I didn't have time to go through it before the holidays. Reviewed in this particular issue? Jim Arsenault's *Blinding White,* by Dermot Schofield.

I have spent the entire day doing everything but reading Schofield's review backward and upside down, and this, as near as I can tell, is the line that exploded the friendship, spurring Jim to retaliate with the foaming rabidity of *wasting sickness* and *mucus-like sheen of mendacity:*

Arsenault strives—occasionally struggles—to achieve just the right balance of humour and pathos.

It's not even one line. It's two words.

Dad walks in, sighs to himself and wipes something invisible from the crotch of his pants. He sits down and watches me reading for a moment, which I am meant to be aware of. He may as well be smacking his lips and rolling up his sleeves. It starts with one word.

"Studying?"

I move the book to the side of my face so I can see him. "No," I reply—maybe being a bit short, because Dad has seen me with this book lots of times and I've already told him what it is. "Reading Jim."

"Didn't bring anything else to read?"

"Yeah," I say, picking up *Atlantica* with my free hand and

waving it at him before positioning *Blinding White* in front of my face again. "I'm just reading Jim right now."

"Haven't been reading much else since you got here."

"Yes, I have. I've just been carrying this one around with me for times like these."

"What times?" interrogates Dad.

I move the book aside again.

"You know, like when we're waiting to go somewhere. Is Mom ready yet?"

"What about having a conversation with your parents?"

"We can do that too," I say—although, judging from his mood, I'm thinking a conversation with Dad is about the last thing I want to pursue right now. Dad, I know, has never been big on Christmas Eve at the Humphrieses' either. But heaven forbid anyone suggest doing otherwise. It's like church—you're not supposed to enjoy it, but you're not supposed to go around acting like you don't enjoy it either. And so we repress in the grand familial tradition, letting the rage and frustration emerge at more appropriate times—such as now.

So Dad goes off. There's no other way to describe it.

All year long, my father complains to the cosmos, all he's been hearing about is this Jim guy. Jim this, Jim that. Doing a reading with Jim. Having dinner over at Jim's. Heading out to a bar with Jim. A bar, if you please. Not a word about studying.

Jim *is* what I'm studying, I try and remind him.

Balls! rejoins Dad. You know things are about to get serious when Dad starts hollering *Balls!* He uses it as a kind of conversational guillotine, to lop your sentence in half so the first part of your argument plops uselessly to the floor while the rest of it dies in your mouth. *Balls* lets you know this discussion is not about give and take, there's no free exchange of ideas about to be enacted. *Balls* reminds you who, exactly, is in charge.

I put the book aside, cross my arms, and dig in.

"Don't give me that sullen look," warns Dad.

"I'm not giving you a sullen look, Dad. I'm just sitting here."

"I just want to know what you've been doing since September. You show up off the boat half-dead with the hangover, you put off coming home so you can stay and get drunk with 'Jim'"—Dad always says "Jim" in quotation marks—he manages to convey them by rearing back his head, widening his eyes and otherwise looking incredulous—"Does the school know about this? That 'Jim's' getting his students drunk and God knows what else?"

"I didn't stay to get drunk, Dad. I stayed to help with the reading."

"And what's with all these goddamn 'readings,' anyway?"

"That's what poets do. They give readings."

"Well, here's what I'm hearing, Larry." Dad leans forward, therapist-like, for a moment. "I know you like poetry and readings and what all, but on the rare occasions we get you on the phone these days, I'm not hearing about that stuff. I'm hearing you're off to pick up some bastard at the bus stop, or you're running around putting posters up across town."

"I—"

"Now maybe I'm just some idiot who didn't get past grade 9, but it seems to me the whole point of sending a kid to university was so he wouldn't have to be running around doing chores for some prick. That's what I was doing when I was your age, for Christ's sake, and I didn't have any reason to hope I'd amount to much more. I was sweeping up at the rink and working stints on people's farms and anyone would have called me a fool to think I could do better. Now here's you with all your scholarships and awards doing the same goddamn thing."

"I am going to *school* to learn to be a *poet*," I say. "That's *all* I care about."

I choose to emphasize this because I know it's the one thing that really drives my father crazy. He is convinced that any day now I'll come to my senses and switch all my courses to law.

"That's being a 'poet,' then, is it?" he demands. "Running around like a chicken with a wick up its arse? Putting up posters, chauffeuring people around?"

"It's being part of a community, Dad," I explain.

"First," says Dad, jerking forward again, this time with such violence his butt pulls the couch along with him, "don't give me that oh-don't-I-just-have-the-patience-of-Job attitude, all right? Second, that man is a professor at Westcock University—why doesn't he have some uneducated dickhead like me to pick people up at the bus stop? Why couldn't he have called a cab? We're not sending you to school so you can clean up someone else's shit."

"I don't get it!" I yell, losing my patience of Job. "Half the time I'm here you tell me I'm too big for my britches, I've got it easy, when you were my age you were working in the woods, you almost lost a hand in the sawmill, you had to piss on your toes in winter to keep from getting frostbite on the way to school. Now—what? You're telling me I'm too delicate, I'm too good to move chairs around and put up posters?"

Dad is looking at me. His mouth moves.

"Which is it? What do you want me to be? You want me to be the guy who organizes poetry readings, or you want me to be the guy who sweeps up at the rink?"

Dad keeps staring at me. His face contorts like a sudden, infuriating stink has filled the room.

"Well, for Christ's sake!" he erupts. "There's gotta be another option in there *somewhere!*"

————

My grandmother's Christmas frock is the bilious, black-faded green of Jim's house in the woods. The sleeves go all the way down to her wrists, and white eyelet trim pokes girlishly out from beneath them. More eyelet pokes out from the neck. It's as though the dress is full of eyelet instead of my grandmother. Slung about her bed-knob shoulders is a festive rain-grey sweater. A grotesque Christmas corsage of glitter and plastic berries completes the ensemble; she has suffered Aunt Maudie to pin it to her breast at some point in the evening.

As I watch from my Santa-spot beside the tree, Lydia somehow manages to slit the end of the envelope open with one of her stubby fingernails. Lydia is the soul of fastidiousness on these occasions. She doesn't tear into her presents like the rest of us, but carefully removes each piece of tape, balls it between her fingers, and places the ball on the end table beside her. Then she proceeds to unfold the paper from the gift before refolding it back into a utilitarian square, to be re-used in seasons to come.

"Perfectly beautiful paper," she will glower at the rest of us, sitting there in our respective piles of shredded waste. "There was a time we took nothing for granted in this country. Such days are behind us now, it would seem."

If I thought that Grandma Lydia was constitutionally capable of experiencing pleasure, I would say she takes more pleasure in amassing her neat pile of wrapping-paper squares than in any other aspect of the holidays.

I watch her slide the greeting card from its envelope. The envelope she puts aside—it can of course be Scotch-taped for future use. I know how this is going to go down. Stan and Janet have already opened their own cards, each identical to the other. A big poinsettia on the front, with *Holiday Greetings* written in gold. So I know how this is going to down. Lydia said nothing as Janet and Uncle Stan (on behalf of himself and Aunt Maud, to whom a single card was addressed) unsheathed their own fresh-from-the-bank five-dollar bills. She said nothing as they muttered their bemused and insincere thanks, as my mother loudly proffered eggnog and my father hunched over the elaborately photographed tie-flying manual he'd unwrapped from Maud and Stan only minutes ago. Back then, things were holly-jolly. There was still some comfort and joy left wafting around the room.

I see now the cards and bills were a mistake. But I still can't accept how big a mistake they are. I'm still feeling a little indignant about the whole thing. Because how could what seemed like such simple genius only a few hours ago be such a mistake? To the extent that the blood in my face is boiling like acid? To the extent that I want to crawl in behind the Christmas tree and start sucking on the plugged-in icicles—electrocute myself among its needled fronds?

But before that can happen, Grandma Lydia has to open her present from her grandson. And am I imaging this, or is the old bat making a production of it? Maybe she's old and shaky, but does it really take this long to extract a card from its envelope? Does she really need to be turning it this way and that? Examining it from all sides?

Lydia coughs—*ahem*. She holds the thing up to the light. Squints. Get this—the monster adjusts her glasses.

"Holiday," reads Lydia. "Greetings."

The only one who looks at me is Janet, wrapped in an afghan in a corner of the couch. She's got her lips pressed together in an expression of sympathetic mirth.

Lydia takes her crotchety hand from her glasses and opens the card. She holds it at a nice distance from her body so everyone can experience the effect of the flaccid five-dollar bill wafting into her lap. She affects not to notice, entranced by the ten-cent charms of *Holiday Greetings*.

"*To Grandmother Humphries,*" reads Grandma. She's not letting merest detail escape that milky old eye of hers. She even reads the lousy poem printed on the inside.

"*Wishing you and all your guests / A Christmas that's the very best!* Well!" says Lydia. "I see. *Love your grandson Lawrence.* Indeed. Lawrence, now, is it?" The milky old eye rolls up to meet mine.

"Larry likes to be called Lawrence now that he's in college," my mother explains.

On the radio, the faithful are being summoned by a heavenly choir, joyful and triumphant.

"And in college," inquires Grandma Lydia, "do they teach one that *guests* rhymes with *best*?"

"It's what's been printed in the card," I mutter.

"Oh!" Lydia's batlike shoulders jump, and she examines the card again. "Yes. I see now. And a fine card it is, boy."

She's never called me anything but that.

"*Guests, best,*" she repeats.

"I told him he should write you one of his *own* poems," near-shrieks my mother. "You know how he loves to write poetry."

Cousin Wayne belches and gets to his feet simultaneously. "I'm gonna get a beer," he announces.

"Get me one," say Stan and Dad in stereo.

Lydia doesn't even glance at Wayne as he lumbers past. Not so much as a milky-eyed glower for old Cousin Wayne.

I'm just about to turn to the tree and haul out a present for Maud when my mother's voice pierces the air again.

"There's some money for you there, Mummy." She points into Lydia's crotch.

The monster's shoulders jump again. "My!" she exclaims, retrieving the five. This too, she holds up to the light. "Well, this will come in handy, no doubt. I can always use a bit of pin money. My, my, my. Thank you, boy."

She places the five back between the folds of the card before setting it atop her pile of salvaged wrapping paper. I lurch, a second time, at the gift for Aunt Maud.

"What times we live in!" my grandmother pronounces, leaning back and folding her hands. "Brave new world! So pragmatic—here is a bit of money, please buy something for yourself. And yet even during the war, in times of such profound deprivation, we always scrambled during the holidays. Scraping together whatever we had. A plum pudding. A simple homemade scarf. Anything, you know, simply as a gesture, a token of appreciation. And to think, all that bother could have so easily been dispensed with. Things are so streamlined these days. Unfettered by sentiment."

Wayne appears in the doorway with a can of beer, which he cracks and tips toward me in a wordless toast. Maud passes the box of Turtles up toward him, and Wayne manages to grab three in one manly hand.

Come, let us adore him, the radio recommends.

My father sighs, too defeated by the atmosphere to repeat his request for beer. A man should not have to ask twice.

"Hey," says Janet, swinging her feet down from the couch and leaning forward. "Hey, everybody." We turn to look, grateful yet surprised. Janet's been keeping the expected low profile most of the evening—as Lydia glowered and Dad looked in every direction but hers, and Uncle Stan, for some reason, doted excessively, loading her plate with second and third helpings and dumping a slice of pie onto it before she had even finished sopping up her gravy. Stan, it was apparent, had at some point graduated from horror to happiness with respect to Janet's situation. He was pleased about it. Aunt Maud, on the other hand, maintained a rosy, almost drunken, flush of embarrassment—but I think it had more to do with Stan's behaviour than with Janet herself.

Of course, it goes without saying that all of this went without saying. There was talk, but it was talk about hunting (Wayne), fishing (Dad, Stan), how good the dinner was (Mom, me), and how Stan and Maud had received a very fine set of linen napkins for their anniversary but perhaps they had been lost or misplaced and that would explain their wasting good money on the paper snowman napkins we were currently using, which would only be tossed in the garbage by evening's end (Grandma Lydia).

That is to say, the talk wasn't real. It was soundtrack, mood music, like that jangly, nerve-scraping piano that plays over silent films. But the movie itself was all about Janet, we knew, and talked louder. Janet kept her head down all the while. That was her role. That was her place.

"Listen, everybody."

Now she removes the afghan from her meaty lap, puts it aside. None of us like the gesture, the deliberation of it, the way it seems to call us to attention like a curtain being pulled into the wings.

Because what's she going to do, recite? Tell us a story? "The Night Before Christmas"?

21.

THE BUNCH OF US sat and stood facing Jim—a petrified forest of holiday revellers in the Dekkers' mistletoed living room. He crammed a hand into the back pocket of his jeans and extracted a crumpled piece of notepaper, eyes crawling over us the whole time like rats across a garbage heap. He uncrumpled the paper, cheeks sucked in and lips puckered as if trying to hold back bile. My own mouth had long gone dry. Jim was like a gunfighter facing an enemy. Waiting for the bad guy to make his next move.

"I would like to begin with a quote from William Blake," he barked. The party had gone dead a moment before. It had taken Jim into account—absorbing the black of his presence—and keeled over into open-mouthed silence. I stood and watched the way, I imagine, I'd stand and watch an airplane spiral smokingly toward the earth. I stared along with everybody else.

What had we done? To make him hate us so much?

"But YOU ought to KNOW," Jim shouted, sending a sudden hum through the crystal port glasses Ruth Dekker had set out, sending a mini tsunami of ripples through the punch bowl.

"What is GRAND is necessarily OBSCURE to *WEAK. MEN.*"

He nearly screamed the words: *WEAK. MEN.* Spit flew, and landed. The Dekkers' living room was really pretty small when you jammed twenty or so people into it for a literary reading. Spread throughout the house—as we had been for most of the evening before Jim arrived, sweaty and hate-eyed—you didn't notice it so much. But—yes—crushed into one room together, an unwashed poet bathing everybody in spittle and contempt—quarters felt a bit close.

"I just wanna get this the fuck over with," Jim told Dekker and me when he arrived at quarter to eleven. The reading had been scheduled to begin at nine. He had shoved his parka at me, and it smelled like his breath, which was sweetly rotting oranges.

"Jim—what's wrong?" Dekker asked of Jim's back. Jim was plowing his way to the punch bowl.

He scooped punch to the brim of his handleless cup and sloshed his way over to the Dekkers' Christmas tree, which had received many compliments that night. It was enormous, for one thing, the angel jammed almost horizontally up against the ceiling. Every single ornament was handmade—many of them by Ruth, I'd overheard earlier. There were elaborate woven snowflakes and wreaths, turtledoves with real feathers, and carved wooden Santas and elves. There was no tinsel or plastic bulbs hung with elastic bands or pipe cleaners—pretty much an aesthetic holiday staple at the Campbell household. It was the nicest tree I'd ever seen. Jim stood beside it with one hand dribbling punch and the other on his hip, as if competing. He glowered, like he resented the competition.

I suppose, his demeanour spoke, *you people are more impressed by this gaudy empty symbol of a gaudy, empty holiday than you are by me.*

If we were, we weren't for long. The crowd soon grew very impressed by Jim indeed. He stood there, glowering with his oil-slick eyes and, like some kind of telepathic alien, steadily began sucking the good cheer from the room.

I was standing in the doorway to the hall, hugging Jim's coat, remembering the bleak, inexorable way his mood had washed over me a few days before. Later I flattered myself with the conviction that I'd succeeded, at least a little, in cheering Jim up. We'd spent well over an hour splitting wood in his yard, Jim giving me pointers on my flaccid, drunken technique as the two of us took turns holding our hands beneath our armpits to keep them warm while the other heaved the axe. Afterward, he'd been more animated over supper, praising my strength and endurance at the chopping block, telling me I could really be something if I'd just pull my nose out of a book from time to time and build myself up a little. We ate an entire loaf of Moira's potato bread between the two of us, and killed three tins of beans. Since there was no booze left in the house, I went home that night feeling sober and restored, if gassy. This explained the anti-flatulent in the medicine cabinet. The next day I couldn't raise my arms to type—even reading, holding a book up in front of my face, was a whole new avenue of suffering. But I didn't care. I'd gone to Jim. I'd been with him in his time of need. I'd helped him, I thought.

But I hadn't. Jim's purple-black mood hadn't dissipated. On the contrary, it had taken on strength since Wednesday—it had deepened in hue. Jim's mood was like the Blob: it ate every mood in its path. He was currently coating the room in it.

I felt deceived.

"*WEAK. MEN,*" yelled Jim. At some point, Sherrie had sidled noiselessly up to me. I don't know how she managed it without me noticing, considering the stale silence that had overwhelmed the room. She dug her fingers into my arm—fortunately cushioned by Jim's parka. We stood that way.

"Jim!" yelped Dekker, hustling over to the tree. "I haven't even given you a proper introduction . . ." He turned to the room, nose and forehead glistening with either perspiration or Jim's airborne spittle of a moment ago. He bared his teeth in a lock-jawed smile. "Everybody—if I could—"

"*Fuck* that, Bryant," said Jim. "I'm here to read *poetry,* everybody, do we all understand?" His eyes crawled around the room, faux-indulgent. "I'm not here to give a holiday toast," he enunciated. "I'm not here to wish you comfort and joy. This isn't Dickens, are we clear? Scrooge isn't showing up with a turkey any time soon. Scrooge is in his fucking counting house, where people like him will always be. The misers don't reform. The philistines don't grow miraculously enlightened, the hucksters never see the light and walk the straight and true path. *What is Grand is necessarily obscure to WEAK MEN.* The weak stay weak, they don't change, you know why? Wanna hear the paradox? Because their *weakness* is their *strength.* Their ignorance is their bliss. Their wilful obliviousness is their power. Is everybody paying attention? Their *power*. And they're sure as hell not going to be giving up their power any time soon. Not at Christmas, not at any time of year. It's a *joke*," Jim spat. "It's a *fairy tale*."

Dekker turned his back on the crowd at that point. He stepped in close to Jim, head down, speaking.

"I will," Jim said. "Of course, Bryant. That's what I'm here to do after all."

Dekker said something else.

"I *will*," repeated Jim, downing his punch and bending forward to place his handleless cup on the coffee table. The empty mug wobbled for an instant before toppling to its side. A thin rivulet of punch trickled onto the table, made a minuscule river before colliding with a linen napkin, where it blossomed into a startling red stain, a sudden poppy. Jim wiped his mouth with his wrist.

"So let's get this show on the road. The first poem," said Jim, with no poems on hand that I could see—the piece of paper on which the quote from Blake had been scrawled had been recrumpled and tossed at the tree—"is called 'I, said the Sparrow.'"

Beside me, Sherrie kind of squeaked.

Whereas I winced. Mainly I was dismayed at the shoddy aesthetics of it. You don't write poetry about real people and identify them by name—even I knew that. You change the names, like in *The Rape of the Lock*. You do it even if everyone knows whom you're talking about—and in this case, was not half the room made up of junior professors? Dekker had said the evening would be informal, that it would just be people from the neighbourhood, but this, after all, was the university town of Timperly. The people from the neighbourhood of a young professor and his wife are by necessity going to be other young professors and their wives. And so I winced again—a delayed reaction—at the politics of it. The aesthetics were bad, and that killed me, but the politics, I realized, were worse. I registered this at the sight of Dekker with both hands covering his proto-beard, the way they were pulling his eye sockets floorward. The bottom-insides of his eyes shone red in the candlelight. He became instantaneously haggard.

Jim was reciting. I tried to listen out of loyalty, but the work was incoherent. I was glad it was incoherent—that was probably fortunate. First there was something about someone called "Cock Robin," who was shot by the Sparrow, "with his bow and arrow." Then Cock Robin turned into Sisyphus. And the Sparrow became Zeus, "the swan-god," and then a bull. And then there was this big part about Zeus being in heat, wandering around mounting everything that moves, "the dumb thrust" of his "Disneyland-loins" and his "Mickey Mouse cock."

The politics were very bad.

Zeus, as sketched in the poem, was a complete banality and a pointlessly powerful buffoon. Zeus was a thug, we were meant to understand. A dangerous imbecile. So Zeus is lumbering around, happily raping nymphs and whatnot, and the noble but robin-sized Sisyphus endeavours to save a nymph or two. Zeus, "enraged child," is having none of it and flicks Sisyphus down into Hades "like a fresh-picked snot."

"Rolling rock, rock and roll," recited Jim. *"Welcome to America."*

The fact that Jim was making the poem up as he went along was growing steadily inescapable. It was nothing like what was in *Blinding White,* with its simple, resonant two-word lines, its three-line stanzas. This hurt to realize.

"Abandon all hope, in the home of the free."

It was so terrible. He was doing a kind of beatnik thing in his recitation, drawing out his vowels, speaking in rhythms as though a bongo and bass were playing in the background.

"*Just roll that* rock, *and rock that rolllll.*"

Nearby, I could hear hissing. I looked over and saw it was Dekker, speaking under his breath.

Finish, he was saying. *Finish.* He was hissing the word without moving his teeth.

Dekker noticed me looking, returned my gaze and shook his head in a tight, futile sort of gesture. Beneath the scruff on his neck I could see his Adam's apple bobbing away as if it was trying to escape.

"*Rollllllll,*" Jim was saying, pinwheeling his hands. He was adding hand gestures now.

One time in class, someone brought in a poem in the shape of a tree. It consisted of nothing but the words *rustlingleaves rustlingleaves rustlingleaves.* We didn't know who wrote it, because Jim blacked out the name before passing out copies, which was unusual. Also unusual was that he didn't give us our standard opportunity to discuss it among ourselves before weighing in with his own opinion.

Everybody? he said, after reading out loud every single instance of *rustlingleaves* written on the page. It took about two minutes.

I'd like you all to pay very close attention to what I'm going to say with regard to what I just read. All right? It isn't a poem. It doesn't count. It is insulting.

But actually, began Claude, the instinctive contrarian.

No, Jim held up a stop-sign hand. *We're not discussing this, folks. I just want to be very clear, so it doesn't happen in my class again. If you pass this sort of thing in to me in the future, it's like not having passed in anything at all. Do we all understand?*

He smiled, scanning the room, face by face. We nodded. Even Claude.

It's serious, *what we're doing here, folks,* said Jim. *If you don't think so, study business or engineering. Get a job. Get married. Be a productive member of society. Don't read. Don't dream. The only trick will be to keep as busy as you can until you die.*

Then Jim ran out of words. He had sort of petered out after repeating *rolllll* a few times—embellishing it with a variety of circular hand gestures—and now he paused to take stock of the audience. You could see him sort of coming back to himself as he looked around the room. A nasty awareness returned to his eyes and he straightened up and took a deep, restorative breath. This could only mean one thing: that he was going to continue.

Dekker was beside him as Jim expelled the first word of the next of who-knew-how-many-more stanzas to come. The word was "sucking." He exhaled it.

"Sucking—!"

Dekker's hand descended on Jim's shoulder. "Let's all thank Jim—"

"*Sucking* dirt-marrow from fossilized—"

"For the honour of this evening's—"

"I am by no means finished."

"—reading . . . I'm sure we're all thrilled to have sampled—"

"I am by no means finished, ladies and gentlemen."

"—this excerpt from Jim Arsenault's new work—"

"And I do mean *gentle* men. For indeed I've never seen so many *gentle* men gathered in one place."

It was like watching a couple of old vaudevillians comically vying to drown the other performer out—spreading their arms

in order to shove the other guy into the background. Dekker
would take a step in front of Jim and Jim would duck underneath Dekker's arm to get in his two cents and then Dekker
would have to manoeuvre himself a second time to obliterate
the crowd's view of Jim and Jim would come poking out from
over Dekker's opposite shoulder. The crowd, fortunately, was
entirely on Dekker's side. They clapped with unfeigned enthusiasm the moment Dekker stood before them.

"Everybody please enjoy the rest of the evening,"
appealed Dekker.

"Oh, Jesus, yes, enjoy yourselves if nothing else," Jim
taunted, resigned now, and leaning against Dekker's back as
though it was a bar. "Eat, drink, and be merry, as the saying
goes."

The partygoers were backing away like animals toward
the kitchen and into the hallway.

"Car wreck," someone muttered, brushing past me.

I still had the parka. I still had Sherrie's fingers embedded
in my arm. I was fantastically hot. "I've got to put this stupid parka somewhere," I said to Sherrie.

Over by the tree, Jim was waving and calling things to
people as they retreated. Dekker had turned to him again
and was speaking low. He had his hand clamped onto one of
Jim's arms just as Sherrie had clamped onto mine.

Sherrie didn't answer me. Just as I turned to look at her,
she moved closer, her head down like Dekker's, so that I
couldn't see her face. I was about to say something else—I
don't know what, exactly—*What do we do now?* or *Thank
God that's over.* But Sherrie was doing something that
stopped me from talking. She was pressing her forehead into
my shoulder. She had choked up on my arm and now her
fingers were digging into my bicep, no longer cushioned by
the parka. The muscle wobbled under her grip. It was still
stiff from chopping wood.

This is a rather intimate gesture, a bland, remote sector of my brain observed. It was the part of my brain that understood girls. The knowledge it stored was scarce. Therefore, it operated slowly, mechanistically. Gears grinding with disuse. *Perhaps you should say something,* it ventured. *Perhaps you should say something like, Sherrie, are you all right?*

Meanwhile, stupider parts of my brain were roused by Sherrie's gesture and clamouring for their say. They sounded a bit like the guys from my high school, or like Chuck Slaughter. These parts of my brain weren't creaky or cautious at all—they would never let a little thing like a lack of hard data get in the way of their self-expression. They had been yelling at me about stuff since I was twelve years old. They were all mindless enthusiasm and boundless imagination.

SHE WANTS YOU, MAN.

She doesn't "want" you. Girls don't grab your arm and shove their foreheads into your shoulder when they "want" you. They do something else, I think. Not that.

But that part of my brain had nowhere near the certainty of the dog-dumb, clamouring parts. It's exasperating to realize the inside of my head is so similar to the outside world in this respect. That is, the stupid ones make all the noise, get all the attention. The smarter ones are never as sure of themselves, would never presume to make such blanket assertions as SHE WANTS YOU AND NOW IS THE TIME TO MAKE YOUR MOVE; to make such audacious demands as PUT YOUR ARM AROUND HER PUT YOUR ARM AROUND HER PUT YOUR ARM AROUND HER NOW, YOU PUSSY.

But I couldn't put my arm around her, because Sherrie had it in a kung fu grip.

SO PUT YOUR OTHER ARM AROUND HER, PUSSY.

But if I put my other arm around her—well, that would be pretty bold, wouldn't it? I'd basically be enveloping Sherrie with my body if I did that. We'd be pressed against one another. Her head would be underneath my chin. Her curly hairs would go up my nose. I might sneeze into her head.

Sherrie's grip was loosening. Against my shoulder, she sniffed. It was a huge, wet sniff.

DO IT DO IT DO IT NOW.

I inclined my head toward Sherrie's. My neck cracked as I did. I raised my other arm, brought it around, placed it on Sherrie's shoulder, which was warm beneath the scratchy green sweater she had probably put on to be Christmasy.

THAT'S NOT PUTTING YOUR ARM AROUND HER.

I patted Sherrie's shoulder a few times like I was trying to knock a burp out of her. Instead, she sniffed again.

"Sherrie?" I said. And she backed away, pressed her hands against her eyes and went upstairs.

GO AFTER HER! the dogs barked, but my head asserted itself. My head said to leave her alone. Sherrie had been crying—she hadn't been pawing at me in lust. She was crying. For some reason, she was crying.

I should ask her what is wrong.

There was something missing from the thought, however. It lacked conviction.

When she comes downstairs, I'll ask her what is wrong.

But no. I was lying—the desire wasn't there. It was inescapable: I didn't want to know. I didn't want to talk about it any more than Sherrie did.

Because?

Because there is something going on between Sherrie and Jim.

No.

Yep.

No.

———

It was about then that Jim began to throttle the Dekkers' tree. Trimmings flew. Elves and Santas clattered to the floor. Breakables tinkled—the sound was almost merry. The noise filled my head, crowding out everything else, and for that I was almost grateful. Jim wore a Grinch's tiny-hearted smile and two eyes made out of coal.

"What about that?" he was inquiring of Dekker over the din. "Whaddabout that, now, Bryant? Holly jolly! Holly jolly!"

It was quick, like earthquakes are. A riotous handful of seconds and the world comes crumbling down. Dekker hadn't moved, but I had. In fact, I moved so fast I stopped Jim. I stopped him by pressing the parka into his arms, heard myself saying, *Here y'go. Here y'go, Jim.* Like we were still standing genially around the foyer with Schofield, handing out coats and saying our goodbyes. And Jim's autopilot kicked in. It noticed something being offered and instructed Jim's hands to unwind themselves from the trunk of the Dekkers' tree and accept the offering.

"Thanks, kid." Jim swept the parka across his shoulders like a cape. He turned to Dekker as if expecting praise.

"Jim," said Dekker, in the faint voice of someone punched. "You *cunt.*"

Jim and I looked at Dekker in amazement. He looked back at us in amazement. We stood like that—in the amazed and wordless void of the moment. It felt like a kind of temporal hinge, the limbo between spinning a wheel of fortune and watching it tick-tick-tick to a halt.

But the moment was punctured by laughter. Ruth stood in the doorway to the dining room, laughing the ugliest laugh I've ever heard come out of a woman. Horsey and jagged. Mannish, like her hands. At least Chuck Slaughter's grating laughter the night of Schofield's reading had been genuine. At least it had the virtue of actual mirth. All we could do was cringe at Ruth's and wait for it to stop. She didn't laugh long. Ruth's was a utilitarian variety of laughter, and not meant to be sustained for a great length of time. It was meant to be used like a whip—in sharp, corrective bursts.

Jim had taken a couple of steps forward and was standing with his chest puffed like a threatened rooster. Ruth didn't even look at him. She looked to her husband—grinned with every tooth in that colossal Slavic jaw.

"So, Bryant?" she called like one child teasing another across a playground. "*This* is your genius?"

She flicked her eyes at Jim before returning to the guests in the dining room. Most of the professors and their wives were no doubt from Britain or the States, but they behaved like good Canadian guests, politely averting their gazes.

"You can clean it up, *Obed*," Ruth added as she turned.

I looked to Dekker instinctively. What was *Obed*?

Whatever it was, it turned him red. Dekker whipped his head around, as if looking for something to break. For a second I thought he might go after the tree himself. The last thing I expected him to do was collapse onto the couch, which is what he eventually did. He stretched his arms across the back of it as if relaxing, and looked at the ceiling. I watched his Adam's apple struggling away.

"Please take him home, Lawrence."

Jim sniffed. "Fuck that," he rumbled, lurching toward me.

And once again I found myself lodged in the inferno of Jim's armpit, being propelled toward the door by the burning force of his weight, and will.

————

Then Janet informs us she's not pregnant, that she's never been pregnant at all, by point of fact. And so a cheery little Yuletide hell breaks loose, my second of the season.

22.

AT FIRST I HAD BEEN MILDLY THRILLED with the situation. Dubious, considering Jim's behaviour, but still pretty pleased with myself. Todd wasn't around, Claude wasn't around. Like Slaughter, neither of them had been willing or able to scuttle their Christmas plans to hang around Timperly for Jim's reading, and I figured this made me, by default, Loyal Buddy #1 in Jim's eyes. To whom, after all, had he turned for comfort immediately after his fallout with Dekker? Who else *was* there but steadfast young Lawrence?

Jim basically said as much on our walk to the bootleggers to buy more rum.

"You're always there, kid. That's one thing I really love about you. I turn around, and there you are."

What I hadn't bargained for was Jim's second wind, which hit as soon as we left the bootleggers'. I'd been considering calling a cab, because for the past hour Jim had been staggering and slurring and I was starting to worry he wouldn't be equal to the walk around the corner to my apartment. But the moment we stepped out into the snow he straightened up, inhaled a dose of winter air, and commenced an immediate rant against Bryant Dekker as if we'd only just left the party. The arm I'd helped him sling around my shoulders just moments ago went from the dead weight of an anaesthetized snake to a muscular, crazily swinging appendage on a wakeful and perversely lucid man.

"This guy, this guy," Jim ranted. "True enough, he may be the only man at Westcock worth sitting down and having a drink with. But Jesus Christ, he's a constant disappointment to me. A *constant* disappointment, Larry! Claiming to care about poetry. Avowing his desire to forge a new aesthetic, to set the present structure on its ear. It's horseshit. When push to comes to shove, it's a pile of shit! Bryant's a good guy, yes, but if the best you can say of a man is he's a 'good guy,' then, I'm sorry, but that's no man at all, Larry."

I was left with nothing to respond, since the protest I'd been about to make, that Dekker was "not that bad a guy," now struck me as a bit flaccid. Plus, I was struck dumb at Jim's vigour. He wasn't even slurring anymore.

"Here is a man who has betrayed himself, his country, his background—who has left it all behind, and for what? *Tenure?*" Jim practically threw up the word. "At *Westcock?* A dull, unremarkable, medium-sized fish in an insignificant swamp of a pond like this? Little house on Duffrin Street? A pretentious cold fish of a wife? *This* is what has the guy paralyzed? *These* are the sumptuous rewards that keep him in his place, that muzzle him in the face of authority, of bourgeois morality? *Christmas trees?* Christmas trees? Oh yes, a man must have his Christmas trees. Above all else. Before art, before truth, before anything pure. For the love of God, don't take away my Christmas tree. Don't dare topple one of those expertly hung adornments. Don't dare disrupt the facile joke of perfection you see before you . . ."

Weirdly, I could see Jim's side of it. Even in the face of his irrational rage and the fact that I knew he had done Dekker wrong. Christmas trees *were* pretty insipid—Christmas itself was like that. And Dekker *was* kind of a wimp, he *did* have that air of fear and paralysis about him. And even though I understood and sympathized with it—and knew it existed in me as well—it seemed to me that the fact that I was young made it more excusable. I still had time to excavate it, to make myself more like Jim—more fearless, more willing to sacrifice for what Jim called art, truth, anything pure. But Dekker was middle-aged. He was tenured, he was married, he probably wrote the kind of poetry no one ever knew about. Dekker was locked in. He had locked himself in— that's what Jim found so contemptible.

I found I didn't disagree with him.

Yet I defended Dekker to a point. I reminded Jim how Dekker had gotten behind him during the tenure dispute, written letters. *You stuck your neck out, Bryant.* As far as I knew, he was the only faculty member who did.

"Ah, Larry," Jim sighed, flopping on my couch. We were in my apartment now, and Jim hadn't even paused to look around, to comment on the surroundings, in which I took a kind of monastic pride. I'd shoved my typewriter aside and was using the desk for a bar—had set up a glass with ice for Jim and was opening the forty-ouncer we'd procured from the bootleggers. I had been kind of hoping Jim might comment on the typewriter. Its obvious centrality, its place of privilege in the window. But Jim was still going on about Dekker.

"Yes, he wrote letters, and that's a huge deal for someone like Bryant, admittedly—going on the record. Which is why I appreciate it so much. But goddamnit, Larry, you can't have it both ways. You can't be on both sides of the fence at once, and that's what Bryant's always striving for, that's his goal— the middle, the lukewarm, unremarkable, morally ambiguous middle—and that's what I can't help but disrespect. You cannot have it both ways. Pick a side, for fuck's sake. Pick a side and fight for it."

I handed Jim his drink and ducked my head to glance at the kitchen clock. "So," I said. "You want the couch or the bed? You're welcome to either."

Jim became still and scrutinized me. It was as if he had abruptly sucked in all the rage he'd been flinging around the room a moment before and focused it on me in a single unnerving beam of intensity.

"Where's your drink?" he wanted to know.

Feeling a sudden need to busy myself, I pulled my desk chair over and sat myself across from him. Maybe Jim would be inclined to stretch out if I gave him the couch to himself.

"I gotta catch the ferry early tomorrow," I explained. "Christmas," I rolled my eyes and shrugged so Jim would understand I had as much contempt for the holiday as he. "But you're welcome to hang around here tomorrow as long as you like. As long as you don't mind locking up."

Jim stared at me a moment longer before slumping forward. My couch was low to the ground and sagged, so his entire upper body was practically between his knees. He dangled his head like someone fighting off nausea.

"Christmas," he said into the floor. "S'posed to bring people together. Instead I watch my friends leave me, one by one."

"Hey, Jim," I said, alarmed. "I'll only be gone a few days, you know? I put it off as long as I could . . . You know how parents are about Christmas."

Jim looked up at me, body still dangling.

"I find it oppressive," he confided, blinking his black, wet eyes. "I find it a particularly oppressive holiday for some reason."

"Oh yeah, me too," I assured him.

"Get yourself a drink, Larry," he told me, talking to the floor again.

"I better not, Jim, I have to get up at seven."

"I said, get yourself a fucking drink!"

There were tears in his voice. I reached spasmodically for the rum from off my desk. When Jim raised his head to look at me, I uncapped it and showed it to him. He kept looking, so I took a swig. He didn't stop looking until I took three more. Once I did, he allowed himself to blink.

"Ah, kid." He knuckled the corners of his eyes like a weepy child. "I'm falling apart, I think."

I leaned closer. "Jim, you're not. You've had a few too many. We all get a little mopey."

"I don't know . . ." Jim shook his head. His voice had broken again, choking off any other words. In fact, he looked very much as if he *was* falling apart. Falling apart right in front of me.

"Jim," I said again, after a moment or two. Giving myself just enough time to register my own awe and fear at the situation—*Jim Arsenault on my couch. Jim Arsenault crying on my couch.* The weirdness of it prickling my skin like salt water beginning to dry.

"Jim," I repeated, not knowing what I could possibly say to make things better. "Don't drink," is what I said. "Don't have any more to drink, okay?"

In response, Jim reached between his legs for the drink he had placed on the floor and took a loud, slurpy sip.

"I'm all right, Larry," he assured me, putting it down again.

"No, but Jim, I really think it makes things worse. I think it makes things seem a lot worse than they are."

Jim peered up at me. "I don't see how that's possible, frankly."

"I think you'll feel better after you get some sleep."

"And so you're telling me," said Jim, "it's all in my head."

"No, no."

"You're saying I'm imagining all this. That I'm under constant siege from the powers that be. That my friends are so busy covering their own asses they don't dare get behind me all the way. One moment they're there, the next—poof. Off lickin' Bob Sparrow's behind lest he question their loyalty."

This struck me as horrifically unfair and horrifically true all at once. I remembered myself sweating and smiling on the other side of Sparrow's desk.

"Jim—you know—we're all in the same boat," I floundered. "Everyone's position is—is tenuous . . ."

Jim straightened, seeming to grow bigger. "That's right, we're all in the same boat and nobody wants to be seen to be rocking it, do they?"

"It's not that, it's just—"

"Ah, Jesus Christ, look at you, Larry. Look at you flailing around trying to justify plain human cowardice."

I made a conscious effort to reign myself in at that point—to cease any involuntary flailing I might have been doing.

"I'm just trying to explain. You have to see it from—from someone like Dekker's point of view."

"I do goddamn see it from Dekker's point of view, I see it from everybody's point of view. I'm the one that's under attack, I'm the one bearing the full brunt of university censure, and everyone around me is terrified they'll be next. Terrified of getting too close and being contaminated. And yet at the same time—"

Then Jim moved closer to me, sidling across the couch on his butt, and suddenly smiling with a grotesque lack of humour.

"At the same time, though, you wanna be close-close-close, dontcha, Larry? 'Cause that raising-shit quality of mine, that's part of the magic, isn't it? And you all wanna get close to the magic, you're all hoping just a little bit of that magic is gonna rub off. But oh, Jesus, not too much though. Jesus Christ, no. Too much and it might start carrying over into our mundane, day-to-day lives, right? Might unsettle things. Too much and the idols might start wobbling on their altars, yeah? And we can't have that, now, can we, Larry?"

I swallowed. "I don't think that's fair."

Jim settled back into the couch, watching me, still smiling.

"I getcha angry, Larry? Little pissed off now?"

"I just don't think you're being fair to me." My face, I could feel, was burning, and so to distract us both from this I took a swig of rum, which caused it to burn even brighter.

"You don't think I'm being fair," considered Jim. "Let's see, now—fair. What would it be fair to say about young Larry?"

Something in my stomach clenched as Jim inclined his head, pretending to consider.

"Jim," I pleaded, feeling myself begin to babble in the panic to keep him from saying the next thing. "I've been, I've been nothing but loyal. I've supported you from day one, I—"

"And so where are you going?" Jim demanded, jerking forward.

I blinked. "What?"

"Where are you going, my dearest and truest of friends? Tomorrow," said Jim. "Tomorrow A.M."

We stared at each other.

"Home," I said after a moment.

"Home," he spat back. "Home for the holidays."

"Like," I said, "tomorrow is the twentieth. It's practically Christmas."

"Christmas," repeated Jim as though the word were coated in slime. "Eat some turkey. See your folks. And meanwhile, I'm alone. Always left alone, when it really counts. So that's your idea of loyalty, is it, Larry? As long as it doesn't spoil your *Christmas*."

Jim dangled forward again, turning all his attention to the drink between his feet. I sat there, blinking and processing. Perplexity wrestling with a kind of perverse thrill. That Jim should want me to stay. That he should need me that much. That my friendship was so important to him, it made him angry I would go away, even for a handful of days. It made him kind of nasty even. And here's where the perversity really kicked in: this joy that Jim should care so much about me as to prove it with abuse—with outright hostility.

And yet of course it was ridiculous.

"Jim, for God's sake. It's like a week. I'll be gone a week."

"I understand, Larry," Jim said around his drink. "Gotta get that Christmas turkey. Gotta getcher presents from Mom and Dad, wha?"

"It's not that Jim, it's just—it's a break. I just need a break."

I felt the truth of it very strongly at this particular point in time. I needed a break—from everything—badly. Fatigue washed over me. I stood and stretched. Jim didn't look up.

"Off to bed, are we, Larry? Gotta catch that ferry, eh?"

"I think we should both get some sleep."

I stood there, looking down at Jim, waiting for a movement, an appeasing flicker of the eye. If I hadn't been so tired, I might have kept waiting for it. I would have sat again and tried to reason with him, I assured myself. I would have stayed up all night if I could. But the booze was dragging at my blood, and the tension of our exchange made me feel like I had swum the Northumberland.

Plus—I was feeling *it*. For the first time ever. The need to self-preserve. The need to get away from Jim and his mood. It was stronger than anything else—any guilt, any imperative to prove myself—and I knew I would find myself making all and any excuses to indulge it.

"You can have the bed," I offered brightly. "You're welcome to the bed."

Jim shook his head and waved me off.

I let myself be waved.

23.

D. Schofield
Department of English
University of Ralston
Peterborough, Ontario

January 4, 1976

Dear Larry,

It was very nice to hear from you, and many thanks for your letter. I was in touch with Westcock administration after Christmas and got the details of my payment worked out, so I return your cheque herewith. But I want you to know how much I appreciate your concern and attentiveness. I enjoyed our talk as well and can assure you there is nothing to apologize for.

You are too kind on the subject of my Westcock reading. It wasn't exactly my finest hour, but neither was it my worst (I'll save that story for another time). As often happens after tying myself in knots trying to express some profound, seemingly inexpressible point, I'll open a book and discover some worthier writer has managed to get it across in a few lines, usually with breathtaking clarity and concision. This time it was Keats:

I am certain of nothing but the holiness
of the Heart's affections and the truth
of Imagination—

To think I could have saved myself (and Mrs.
Dacey!) all that time, all those words. From now
on, Keats goes wherever I do. I'll underline the pertinent passages and have them ready to read out
when I get stuck. I often get stuck.

Best wishes,

Dermot Schofield

So Keats was obsessed with it too, that word. It seems to
crop up a lot lately. The word I am not.

24.

AT THE HUMPHRIESES, as Lydia repeatedly wheezed
Nonsense! and Maud shrieked and yelled and Uncle Stan
made himself a forlorn lump shaking his head back and forth
while the radio pleaded for a silent, holy night, Janet had at
some point interjected the words, "I am going to New York!
I will eat as much dessert as I want!"

Nobody had responded in all the madness except for
me—I snapped to attention like a cat near a can opener. At
this point, however, Janet was not being given a chance to
elucidate. It had been decided after the not-pregnant-after-all
announcement that everything coming out of Janet's mouth
was de facto lunacy.

"Oh, Jannie," Stan kept saying as he shook his big pink
head back and forth. "We would have taken care of you. It
would have been all right."

"You are crazy!" Maud was yelling. "Those university
people have made you crazy!"

" . . . scholarship . . ." I heard Janet say. I held up my hand for silence then, but my mother grabbed it in both of hers and held all three hands against her chest.

"This foolishness *must stop now*," insisted Lydia, quaking in her chair.

" . . . thesis . . ." said Janet. "Columbia, in New York *City*."

My arm twitched against my mother. "Hey," I said. "What?"

"Oh my God," said Maud. "I knew the mainland would ruin her." She stood in the middle of the room and looked around, eyes finally settling on my mother. "I'm so *upset*," she told my mother. "I'm so *upset* right now, Chrissie, I don't know what to *do*."

My mother released my hand and stood to go to Maud.

"I know, dear," she said. Maud quieted as my mother took her by the elbow and steered her toward the kitchen.

"This is just *foolish*," huffed Lydia. You could see her fingers twitching, yearning to wrap themselves around a good, solid piece of hickory. A branch from a crabapple tree would do.

My father sighed in his chair. No one had yet gotten him a beer. Wayne was polishing off his own with the nearly-empty box of Turtles balanced on his lap. He looked like a kid at the movies.

"I've been offered a full scholarship," said Janet.

"Janet," I called, leaning forward. "What?" But Uncle Stan's moaning drowned me out.

"Jannie, Jannie," he keened. "Anything. We would have done anything we could to help you. You'd never even have to lift a finger. I swear. I swear you wouldn't."

Back and forth went Uncle Stan's big pink head, a man's disgraceful tears on his infant cheeks, which silenced us all after a while.

———

When Janet and I got drunk on Boxing Day at a roadhouse called Little Billy's much-favoured by Wayne, she told me the pregnancy thing began as a joke. She and some friends in the Psych department, she said, had initiated what Janet called a "kind of half-assed consciousness-raising group," which I gathered was basically a clutch of girls getting together to drink margaritas and complain about their lives. I'd heard around campus that the Psych department was a hotbed of radicalism and women's libbers because they have two women professors on the faculty—the most of any department at Westcock. And both of them are Americans.

Janet's biggest gripe to this group of hers was that she had packed on twenty or so pounds since arriving at Westcock and the collective Humphries response was, as she put it, "as if I had shot somebody in the face."

Here I stopped her.

"Come on, Janet," I said. "Not really."

"You weren't there, Larry," yelled Janet—who, now that her secret was out, seemed like an entirely different person to me. She yelled over the music at Little Billy's—even between songs, when the music wasn't playing. She took huge gulps of draft between sentences, waved her fleshy arms around in outrage and slammed her mug on the table, sloshing draft all over everything.

"So one night I was ranting away about this," continued Janet, "and my professor, Catherine, kind of joked—you should tell them you're sick or something, like you have a disease, you can't help it."

"Your professor was part of your group?" I interrupted.

"Catherine, yeah," said Janet. "Catherine started the group actually. So anyway, we're all laughing, but then someone else says it won't work, because if you're sick, you usually don't get fat, right? So Catherine hits upon it: You should tell them you're pregnant. How would that go over? And all night long, we talked about the ramifications of you guys thinking I was pregnant, and, Larry it was *fascinating* to critique the family on that level."

I shifted position in my chair. "What do you mean, critique? What was so fascinating about it?"

Janet widened her eyes at me. "You saw yourself the way they acted! Don't you think it was fascinating? I mean, Jesus Christ, your father! He was a case study in and of himself!"

I nodded, although it hadn't occurred to me Dad's behaviour was particularly fascinating. I'd just thought he was being old-fashioned, and kind of a jerk.

"So wait a minute," I said. "You guys *predicted* that everybody was going to behave that way?"

Janet shook her head. "No, no, no, I didn't plan any of this, Larry. We were just kidding around—I never thought I'd actually come out and do it. But they made me so mad at Thanksgiving, all these naughty-naughty grins every time I reached for the potatoes. What's the big deal? Why is it any of their business anyway? Dad's fat! Wayne's fat! Why is it a national tragedy if Janet's fat?"

"You're right," I said, nodding some more.

Mostly my part of the conversation was an exercise in trying to hide my annoyance at being made to feel a dupe. Janet had a point—it's not nice to persecute someone for being fat. But it's also not nice to lie to family. I was the only family member speaking to Janet at the moment and, although my parents thought I was doing it out of an altruistic impulse to act as the familial go-between, what I was really doing was waiting to hear how Janet had managed to get herself into Columbia University on scholarship. This was the only element of the saga I found remotely fascinating.

———

So Janet returned to her girl-group after Thanksgiving and told them what she had done. They were in awe of her, she said. And she was in awe of herself, that she had climbed aboard the ferry back to Cape Tormentine letting everyone in her family go on believing this cruel and fantastic lie.

"Suddenly nobody gave a shit whether or not I was having ice cream on my pie anymore."

"I bet," I said.

"But you should have heard the way they started talking afterward, Larry. Once the shock had worn off, talking like I wasn't there anymore. Well, she's going to have to come home, that's all there is to it. She can't go back to school like this. We'll get her room ready. Maybe Mike Sutherland will give her a job at the *cwap*, Mike owes us a favour. Or Wayne—you could use a hand at the museum, couldn't you, Wayne?

"And Mom's like, Oh, she shouldn't work, she can't work in her condition.

"And Dad's like, No, I mean afterward. She's going to have to do something with her life.

"And finally I say, Everybody? I've only got five months to go before I graduate. And do you know what my mother says, Larry?"

In fact I do. I can guess exactly what Maud would have said.

"She looks at me and she goes, 'But dear. What would be the point of all that now?'"

Janet stares as if she's expecting I'll throw up my arms in outrage.

"Wow," I remark.

It's enough for Janet. "I know!" She hoists the pitcher of draft to top off both our mugs. "My group just couldn't believe it. But Catherine was fascinated."

A lot of fascination going on.

"Catherine—you know, she's not from here," explained Janet, "so she finds all this of great interest from a sociological perspective. She's from New York, from a family of intellectuals."

"I don't see what's so interesting about it," I interrupted. I was getting tired of Catherine. I imagined her perched up among the clouds, goggling down at us through some kind of huge celestial microscope. "It's just parents being parents."

"No, it isn't, though," said Janet. "It's class. That's the difference between where Catherine's from and where we're from. That's what's so fascinating."

"*What's* fascinating?" Our beer had begun to shimmer in its mugs because I was tapping my fingers so hard against the table. Maybe Catherine was a Vulcan, like Mr. Spock.

"*We have no class,*" said Janet. "I mean, there's no middle or upper class. There's just one class."

"Who?" I said.

"Us," said Janet, gesturing back and forth with her hand, at herself and me. Then, to my discomfort, she expanded the gesture to take in the whole of Little Billy's. A few feet to her left was a drunk in a too-small Snoopy T-shirt. His fly gaped open beneath a white halfmoon of belly, and one eye was closed and he weaved back and forth in front of the jukebox playing air guitar to the flute part of "Kung Fu Fighting."

My chair was digging into my back. My body seemed to be rearing itself farther and farther away from Janet the more she talked.

"You keep talking about this whole thing like it's a case study," I told her.

Janet looked down at her beer for a moment. "Well—it kind of was a case study, really. You all were. Catherine suggested I write a paper on it."

I reared even farther back in my chair, so that its feet shrieked against the floor. "What do you mean, we all were?

So you had the devastated mother, the evil father, and then—what—the asshole cousin?"

Janet laughed. When I didn't, she composed herself. "I don't think you're an asshole. My father is not evil. My father—" Janet looked away from me suddenly, toward where the Kung Fu Fighter was now steadying himself against the jukebox. She blinked a bunch of times before turning back. "My father is a very sweet man. But he's not the most progressive guy in the world, Larry, you'll agree with me on that one, right?"

I shrugged, even though I agreed. I wasn't in the mood to agree out loud.

"I mean, he's a product of his culture and time and place, just like the rest of us are."

"Why are you always lumping me in with everything?" I moaned.

Janet cocked her head and gave me a blank, innocent look, like a curious dog. "Because you're a part of things, Larry—you don't stand outside the system you inhabit any more than I do."

"But you do," I argued. "If you're writing about it and critiquing it like you said, you're—you have to make yourself an outsider."

"That's by necessity. How am I supposed to analyze—"

"That's just what I'm saying," I said, leaning forward and feeling my neck heat up. "If you're going to analyze it objectively, you've got to stand outside of things, you've removed yourself."

"Well," said Janet. "For the purposes of writing the paper, I guess. But I don't claim to—"

"I do that too, though," I shouted at my cousin, for we were on our second pitcher of beer at that point. "I do that too. Because I'm a poet. I do that too."

I sat back. Janet regarded me. It was the first time I had

ever announced myself in such a way to any member of my family. I *do* poetry. I'm *studying* poetry. Sometimes even, I *write* poetry. But never: *because I am a poet. I lay claim to this, because I am a poet.*

Janet's the one to appeal to now, after all—the guru to go to—she whose good graces must be sought and won. I like almost nothing about how she did it, and yet the fact that she did it—with no scholarship, with undistinguished high-school transcripts, with no familial support or expectation—is inescapable.

And how did Janet do it? The process, it seems to me, was two-fold.

One: she got herself an ally. Someone powerful. Someone with contacts. Write this paper, Professor Catherine told Janet, and I will oversee it. I will give you the name of journals where you might get it published (and who would have thought there were journals out there for psychology and sociology the same way there is for poetry?). I will send it along to my friends at Columbia, promised Catherine. I will set you on the path.

Two. Two is more complicated. Two involves the internal Janet. Two was Janet taking a giant step backward, like in a counterintuitive game of Simon Says. Remember that game? I hated it, because I hated most games as a kid—anything involving strength or speed or stealth. Mostly I hated the pointless suspense of Simon Says, the kid at the front barking orders—giant steps, baby steps, half-steps, and bunny hops, sending you back if you made the fatal mistake of executing a bunny hop that hadn't been legitimized with the preface "Simon Says." All those games were essentially the same dynamic: inuring yourself to someone else's arbitrary whims.

So Janet executed a big psychic backward step away from her family on PEI. Was it on Catherine's say-so, or by this time was Janet following the dictums of her own tow-headed Simon within, an eight-year-old tyrant telling her where next to place her feet?

Either way, the step is executed, the distance created, the microscope wedged into the gap. So *Mom* and *Dad* become *The Mother* and *The Father*, the house becomes *Their Environment*, the island becomes *Their Society*. Home becomes *Their Culture*.

Ours, in short, becomes *theirs*, and Janet cools, a planet turning from the sun. She leaves them to their oblivious heat. She leaves them to their stifling warmth. The cloistered, body-hot, stultifying safety of their hearth—she leaves it with one giant backward step. She leaves them.

That's what was Two. That's what Simon said to do.

25.

LOOKS ARE EXCHANGED. The clock above the blackboard clicks once, twice. Will it be Dekker? Will it be no one? Everyone has heard about what happened over Christmas. People seem to have soaked up the knowledge the moment they stepped back onto campus, as if by some kind of psychic osmosis. The minutes click by.

A few more clicks in the silence, the occasional responding cough and then—Jim. He comes bustling in a mere six minutes late, and the tension eases from the room as though someone has adjusted a gauge. Shaved, combed, composed, his work shirt buttoned up to the neck. He welcomes us all back with a few perfunctory words and then gets down to the business of handing back our midterm portfolios.

Then the sound of paper slapping against wood as he

meanders past our desks, flinging out manuscripts as though he's dealing from an oversized deck of cards.

"Not bad work, folks, some real innovation going on this past semester. A lot of progress . . ."

Mine lands in front of me. It has a B on it. A fat bulbous B like a set of tits scrawled across my title page by some high-school graffiti artist. I turn it face down on my desk and look up at Jim, but his back is to me as he makes his way down the aisle. His back seems particularly straight, perhaps an effect of the fact that his shirt, I can see, has been ironed this morning.

Jim informs us that he has chosen one poem from each of our portfolios to critique in class this month. "The Ass of the Head" turns out to be the first we are going to discuss. He hands out copies of it next.

I have to stop myself from raising a hand in protest. Things seem to be moving fast. There's none of the expected first-class-of-the-semester lassitude in the air, the feeling we have to work up to things, ease our way back. There's been no catching up, no *How was your holiday?* Or, *What's everyone been reading?*—always a preferred time-waster of Jim's.

I stare down at the page emblazoned with my name and my work, wanting to stall. The characters I had typed in such a self-satisfied hurry glare up at me in mimeographed purple. The purple print adds to things. I'd forgotten about the purple. In purple, the poem seems to have taken on a completely different personality. Sillier, more disposable. Fresh-typed poems in black and white always feel so clean, so austere. Unassailable. But mimeographed copies fuzz the characters, make them look ill-defined, uncertain. And *purple*—the colour defies you to take the writing seriously.

This is student work, the purple announces. Ill-formed, half-baked. Feel free to mark it up, colour in the *o*'s if you get bored, draw faces in the margins. Throw it away when you're done.

There is nothing I can do. The critique commences as I sit staring at my sheet, willing the characters back to black. If everyone could just see how "Ass of the Head" looks de-purpled.

Claude doesn't like the sing-songy quality the poem has to it. The clunky, awkward rhyme scheme. He uses the word "facile" a couple of times.

Sherrie deems herself intrigued by the *this* in the line "on which this angel." Good old Sherrie. "Who is the angel?" she wants to know. A short but lively discussion ensues.

Todd objects to my use of the word *ass*. He finds it deliberately vulgar—"vulgar for vulgarity's sake," he says, "adding nothing of substantial value to the piece." A couple of people near the back argue with him, but, to be fair, they are vulgarity advocates in general, always peppering their own poems with *fuck* and *shit* for shock value.

When everyone is finished taking their kick at the can, Jim speaks. He slides his eyes in my direction for the first time since arriving in class.

"Larry?" His black eyes are ringed with red—the way mine feel. "Nothing to say? You've been uncharacteristically quiet on the subject of your own work today."

A thin smile. I thin one back at him, shaking my head as everyone chuckles at Jim's joke like the miserable suck-ups they are.

"Well, then," Jim says, once they are good and finished. "I guess I'll weigh in." He coughs explosively, then, startling us all. I can't believe that much phlegm has been sitting in his lungs this entire time. Jim has not so much as cleared his throat since class began.

"The poem encapsulates an idea, the idea of a duality, and this in itself is intriguing," he says. "Our poet articulates this duality with the metaphors *head* and *ass*. The question is, are these metaphors legitimate? It depends on what we believe is the nature of the duality the poet is attempting to elucidate. So what is it? Anyone?"

"Ass and head," answers Todd. "Brains versus shit."

"This seems the most reasonable interpretation," nods Jim.

"But is it brains *versus* shit?" Sherrie pipes up. "Because he seems to sort of be saying they're one in the same, the ass *of* the head."

"Shit for brains," chortles Todd, snorting like a sow at the trough.

Jim smiles more widely than I feel the joke really merits.

"That's a good point. And yet the poet reinforces the idea of a duality, doesn't he, with the lines, *the question / of which should take / its rightful place up top*? So this gives us the idea that, yes, it is an either/or situation, it is a struggle between the two."

"But the title," argues Todd, "and the first line contradict that."

"Yes, they do," says Jim.

"Maybe," ventures Claude, "the contradiction is intentional."

I don't kid myself that Claude is rushing to my defence. He's adopting his usual contrarian stance.

"That would be nice to think," admits Jim. "But the poet confuses us further with the ensuing concept of a unity when he evokes the idea of 'the axis, the pinhead.'"

"I thought *ass-kiss* was cheap, coming after *axis*," offers Todd at this point. "I thought it was a pretty cheap pun, really. I just read it and, like, winced. At the cheapness."

Jim nods. Todd is earning a lot of nods this day.

"Also," continues Jim, "the repetition of the word *ass* in this secondary context, 'the ass-kiss,' didn't really work. I'd say it muddied the waters somewhat."

"I took that as intentional as well, actually," counters Claude. "Followed by the *squats* at the end, evoking the idea of shit again. I thought that was actually pretty good, pretty consistent."

From where I am sitting, I only have a side profile of Claude, but I notice the way the light in his eyes flickers as they shift, very quickly, in my direction. Sympathy is the name of that flicker. I can't believe it.

"And," Sherrie jumps in, "the idea of an angel, um, having a . . . taking a . . . *dump* . . . is really consistent with the whole ass-of-the-head idea, isn't it? I mean the whole dichotomy thing—divine human intelligence versus the more base aspect of human nature? I mean, isn't that a really archetypal idea?" Poor Sherrie, her voice, her thoughts—always questioning.

"It is a classic duality, sure," agrees Jim.

"Hackneyed, though," smiles Todd with his eyebrows. It's all he can do not to actually break out in a grin, but Todd's eyebrows are practically floating above his head.

There is silence, during which a couple of faces turn my way. Everyone is waiting for the eruption of arm waving and sputtered objections I would normally uncork at this point in the discussion. I keep my head down, however. I keep my eyes on Jim.

"Hm," he says after a moment, wrapping his arms behind his head, making his characteristic deep-thinking rabbit ears. Oh yes, I think, seeping relief at the sight of those ears. Please. Let us now speak of Alfred Hitchcock films. Now would be the perfect time. They're so rich, after all, and there are so many of them—so much material to discuss. Some shitty little undergraduate poem certainly doesn't merit all this attention. So let's go, let's talk about something that matters. *Vertigo. Rear Window. The Birds.*

"Hackneyed, maybe," answers Jim at length, slowly bobbing his head. "And I do appreciate Sherrie's and Claude's interpretation, but I think they may be reading more into things than the work actually merits."

North by Northwest. Strangers on a Train.

"I suspect they may be giving the poet a bit too much credit in this instance."

Psycho.

"Ultimately, it's a vague piece, I think. It hints at profundity in the hope that intelligent readers will pick up on these hints—as indeed Sherrie and Claude have—and run with them."

Frenzy. Torn Curtain.

"But it relies too heavily on the reader for that—it toys with more grandiose ideas than the author is actually able to get his head around."

Stage Fright. Notorious.

"It's ambitious," allows Jim, "and it's not without its charm. I, for one, rather enjoyed the musical aspect Claude was disparaging."

Sabotage.

"However, that same nursery-rhyming quality should also tip us off that this work is not to be taken all that seriously. It's lightweight."

Lifeboat.

"It's a confection, ultimately."

Rope.

26.

Jan. 17, 1976

Dear Larry Campbell,

Thanks for your submission to *Re:Strain*, but we didn't see anything we'd like to use for our upcoming issue. I didn't really get the short poems, didn't

see what the connection between them was beyond
the similarity of the titles. Seemed deliberately
vague. The longer one was a bit more interesting
but not up my alley, ultimately. Best of luck with
your work.

Joanne

I call up Charles Slaughter, and Charles Slaughter and I get
drunk. Charles Slaughter, I quickly decide, will be my best
friend from here on in. Slaughter was the perfect person to
call—an instinctive part of me knew this. First I went to the
liquor store and bought a giant bottle of rum. Then I called
Charles Slaughter and told him I had a giant bottle of rum.
Slaughter told me he loved me, which was nice, and that he
would be right over.

Slaughter does almost all the talking for the first hour
or so. He tells me about his holiday and how it was just
him and his dad, and his dad was a pain in the ass.
Everything's got to be a project with his dad, complained
Slaughter, even Christmas. There was no sitting around
drinking eggnog by the fire. It was all about going to get
the goddamn tree and putting up the goddamn tree and
decorating the goddamn tree and then taking down the
goddamn tree practically first thing in the morning on
Boxing Day. Then there were the goddamn lights to be put
up and promptly taken down.

"I mean, what is the fucking point of all that? Do you
know what they make you do in the army, Campbell? To
punish you?"

"No," I say. "What?"

"They make you dig a hole. A big fuckin' hole. Then you
know what they make you do?"

"No," I say. "What?"

"They make you fill it up again. That's my dad. That's my dad's idea of a holiday."

Hey, it's Sisyphus again. He seems to pop up everywhere.

I snort. "So what's your dad's idea of a punishment in that case?"

Chuck takes a pull from the forty we've been passing back and forth all afternoon.

"A punch in the fuckin' head—that's his idea of a punishment," grunts Slaughter.

"You?" I laugh. "He punches you? How big is your dad?"

"He wouldn't try it these days," Slaughter assures me. "Much as I'd like him to."

Slaughter hands me the bottle. I swig.

"I'm gonna quit Westcock," I tell him, having just decided. The swig seems to have clinched it somehow. "I'll go to Oxford. I'm gonna be a—an Oxfordian."

"Buncha fags in England," Slaughter opines, unfazed.

"I know," I say. "But everybody's always telling me how faggy I am. I'll fit right in."

Slaughter leans forward to fix me with an earnest gaze.

"You're not faggy, Campbell. You're just kind of a pussy. You can be fixed."

It sounds veterinarial. "Yeah, yeah." I gesture blandly with the bottle. "I just need to work out."

"That and maybe take an interest in something besides books for a change. You didn't come to one of my games last semester."

"I don't understand football."

"You don't have to understand it, Campbell," says Slaughter, looking pained. "You think the only reason to do something is so you can understand it. You gotta stop reading all the time, and get out more. Take an interest in the world around you."

It strikes me as an apt idea, particularly at this point in

time. Forget about understanding. Forget about poetry. That's what Sparrow seems to think I should do. Jim too. Not to mention my good buddy Joanne Not Up My Alley, whoever the crap she is. The universe conspiring against poetry—against poetry combined with the likes of Larry Campbell, that is. Who am I kidding? Who gets to be a poet in this world? The rich and the crazy. Byron and Blake. Because if you aren't rich, it drives you crazy. That's the path on which I've plunked myself.

We decide to stop at the sub shop for a couple of all-meaters to fortify ourselves for the evening. This is where I confess to Slaughter my conviction that Jim is mad at me.

"Who gives a shit?" demands Chuck. "Arsenault is a big fuckin' baby anyway. He's always mad at somebody about something."

The truth of this hits me between the eyes. "You're right. He is, isn't he?" Schofield. Dekker.

"He'll get over it, man."

"The problem is," I add, "he's my prof. You know, he grades my papers." And then I bury my face in my sandwich because this actually isn't the problem at all. It's part of the problem, but it's not the big-picture problem. The big-picture problem is what makes me want to hide my face from Slaughter, my suddenly swimming eyes.

"Just go see him," says Slaughter around a mouthful of pastrami. "Bring him a bottle of booze or something, he'll forget all about it. Jim's always gotta be pissed off at some-one—it's just your turn in the rotation. He got pissed off at me this one time I told his wife to fuck off."

"You told his wife to fuck off?"

Slaughter puts his sandwich down on the table between us. "You ever meet his wife? Oh yeah, you met her out at their place that time with the dumplings. She's a complete bitch, right?"

"Well," I balk. I want to explain to Slaughter that Moria is not actually a complete bitch. Slaughter is from suburban Ontario and so he wouldn't understand. Moira is a New Brunswick woman, I want to explain—but that doesn't work because I've met women like Moira in PEI as well. Moira is a rural person, is the best way I can think to describe it. She doesn't put on airs. Moira would never have been exposed to airs in her life, is the thing—and if she ever was, she would dismiss them immediately. As airs.

"She's just—she's *harsh,*" is what I end up saying. "She's blunt."

"She's a douchebag," Slaughter contends. "So one night last year I'm over there, right, and I'm playing with the dog and the dog's going apeshit the way it does the moment you give it any attention, and she's going, Stop teasing that dog, stop teasing that dog, and I'm like, I'm not teasing the dog, we're playing. And the dog barks some more and she goes, I'm telling you for the last time to stop teasing that dog before I kick your goddamn head in."

This makes me laugh, because I can hear it. I can hear Moira's voice forming the words. Also because Chuck is demonstrating for me the face he wore when Moira threatened to kick his head in.

"So I'm like, Yeah, all right, whatever, fuck it. I mean, that's what I meant to say, but I think it came out sounding more like, *Aw fuck you.* So Arsenault—who was drinking so much I thought he must be asleep this whole time—he fucking leaps out of his chair. Just . . . *leaps,* right? And his eyes are coming out of his head. Whad you say? Whad you say? And I'm like, Nothing, man. And Jim, you wouldn't believe it, I've never seen anything like it, the guy is right up in my face going, No! I heard you say something to my wife and I want you to repeat it to me right goddamn now, Charles. So he's calling me Charles. So it's *that* way, right? And, you know, I could have killed him. Jim's tall, but he weighs something like a hundred sixty, I could have put him through the wall."

Slaughter looks relaxed and happy telling this part of the story. The absolute assurance that Jim could never have hurt him but Slaughter could easily have crushed Jim. Watching him I think, This is what carries Chuck through life. This is what makes him so scarily likeable. This is where all that confidence comes from. The simplest of formulas.

"So what did you do?"

"I stayed calm. You gotta stay calm. I had a coach in high school who taught me that. He taught me that when you find yourself getting pissed off, you gotta look at the person in front of you and ask yourself if you genuinely want to hurt this person. Like, you have to be able to take a step back, because, at that particular moment, you may really think you do. Fuck, I've had that feeling more than once, you know? Like with my dad for starters. But this coach, he taught me to count to ten and really think about it. He used to say that was my main responsibility in life, 'cause I'm so big. He was the guy who drilled it into me I could really kill someone, you know? 'Cause it's not something you really believe when you're a kid, that you have that kind of power."

Slaughter nods his head in an attempt to appear solemn, but actually he still looks pretty cheerful. Imagine having such a confrontation with Jim. Eyes bulging. Red face pulsating down into mine.

"So I just left," concludes Slaughter, thrusting his hands into the air by way of demonstration. "I just backed up. Whatever you say, Jim—I'm gonna split. And Jim—fuck, he really is lucky I didn't drive him, come to think of it—he's like, Yeah, that's right, you better get the hell out of here you goddamn Neanderthal, this isn't a zoo, we don't have enough bananas to feed a full-grown gorilla, all this sort of bullshit. *Personal* stuff, you know? All the crap you think about a person but never say. The kind of crap you can't take back, and you're really goddamn lucky if the guy decides to forgive you afterward, you know? That kind of shit can end a friendship pretty effectively."

Slaughter furrows his brow, belching meditatively. He shoves himself to his feet to find a pay phone and call Sherrie.

All the crap you think about a person but never say. I remember. I remember coming very close.

27.

I WAKE UP THE NEXT DAY feeling slow, but not sick. Vague, as opposed to queasy. Remote. Detached. The tea is extra invigorating, and I seem to be lacking my usual frantic impulse to do something intellectually improving—like bash out a half-assed poem just so I can tell myself I produced something, or go poring though back issues of *Atlantica* to try and figure out what it is all these published poets seem to be doing right in the face of my multiple unpublished wrongs.

I try to find a word for the edge I'm lacking. It's important to figure out, because this is the first time I can ever remember waking up without it—and it's good to wake up without it. If I can name the quality, perhaps I can continue to keep it at bay. So what is it? What is that desperate, metallic flavour of energy that drives me through my days? In its unhurried, detached state, my mind circles, taking its time while I slurp tea from Big Blue, watching snowflakes pile up on my window ledge outside. After a lazy while, it alights, my mind does.

The word is *dread*.

I take another long, noisy slurp.

So. I wake up every morning feeling dread. I sit down at my typewriter feeling dread. I shrug into my jacket and wind my scarf around my neck, I shoulder my satchel and trudge my way to school, I sit down in a lecture hall, I get up to go to the next class, I do it all, every day, in a state of dread.

Yet today, a reprieve. From the dread—the dread I didn't even know was there until now. All thanks to drinking gallons of rum with Charles Slaughter. I am no scientist. Who knows why saturating my bloodstream with alcohol would have such a salutary effect? People always tell you drinking kills your brain cells. Whole slews of brain cells, the educational reels warbled at us back in high school, completely annihilated—the spark sucked out of them. The film would show us plump cartoon brain cells, their rosy cranial environment gradually deteriorating into a sodden alcoholic swamp. Wading through the muck, the cells would soon degenerate into grey, sad-faced raisin creatures before keeling over with a murky splash. One raisin would be labelled, Memory of First Kiss. Another would be Hand-to-Eye Coordination.

Wouldn't it be nice to think that's what happened. That I killed off my dread-raisin with booze.

Of course, I don't believe it. Now that I've identified the bastard, I can pick it out, I can see it lurking in the shadows. It may be down. But it's not out.

Meanwhile, it would seem today's the day to get a few things done.

First stop, the library. When I don't find what I'm looking for in a back issue of *Re:Strain* (idiotic name for a journal, by the way, Joanne, did you come up with that name? Did you find it was *up your alley?*), I head to the university catalogues, yank out the 1973–74 edition from Ralston. The page is still marked at *Department of English* from when I pulled out this same book to find an address to send Schofield his cheque.

Hoisting the catalogue under my arm, I head to the stair-well where the pay phones are and chat with the operator a while. I give her the number in Ontario and make sure any long-distance charges go to my number at home.

In the electronic interim between the click of being trans-ferred, the distant whirr of wires, I reflect upon how unre-flective I was during my chat with the operator. That is to say, I didn't feel awkward or stupid, or worried about the way I was phrasing my request; I didn't wonder what she was thinking of me. It is a glorious thing, this lack of dread. How do I kill it off for good? How do I shrivel it into a staggering raisin, cause it to keel over once and for all? There have to be means besides rum.

Ring, ring, Department of English, Professor Schofield please, just one moment, ring, ring some more, and by God he picks up.

The raisin trembles. Plumpening?

"Why hello, Larry!" He sounds more pleased than surprised, even.

"Hello!" I shout back. My voice booms monstrously throughout the stairwell.

"Holy God, Larry, where are you calling from? It sounds like . . . an indoor swimming pool or something."

"Sorry," I say, lowering my voice. "I'm in a stairwell in the library."

"Ah." Weird pause. It's my turn to talk, and so I don't. "And how are things at Westcock?" queries Schofield at last.

"Great!" I say.

"Glad to hear it. And you got my letter with the cheque, yes? Everything's okay?"

"Yes," I say, and, after another weird pause, decide I might as well get right down to it. "I was just wondering if you got those poems I sent you."

"Oh, that's right—you sent in some poems, didn't you?"

"I did!"

"I'm sorry, Larry, I should have let you know when I wrote back. I suppose I must have just passed them along and forgot about them."

In the distance, wires whirr. I can picture them stretched taut along the highway to Wethering, vibrating in the wind.

"Sorry?" I say. "You . . . passed them along?"

"To the editors."

"Ah," I say. "Um, oh. I guess I thought you were the editor."

"Officially," says Schofield, "I'm the 'editorial advisor.' The review itself is actually student-run."

Student-run? So Joanne? Is a student? I can't yet tell if this makes things better or worse.

"Anyway!" sings Schofield, as if cleansing the conversation of detritus. "What can I do for you, Larry?"

"Oh," I say again. "Well, that's basically what I was calling about. My poems."

"To see if we got them? I'm sorry about that, Larry, but it's still pretty early in the process. I should have warned you it usually takes forever for the editors to respond. It has to go through first readers, then the board itself has to have their kick at the can—a lot of duelling egos involved there, I can tell you—then . . ."

"Sorry?" I interrupt. "First readers?"

"Mm. Undergrads in the department."

The wires hum like descending locusts.

"Larry?" says Schofield.

"Actually," I say at about the same time, "I did get a response."

"Oh," says Schofield. "Already?"

"Yeah. That's what I was calling about."

"Hm," says Schofield.

"Yeah," I say. "The thing is, I thought that you—"

"You know, Larry," Schofield speaks over me, "these are the perils of student journals. Young writers often have very particular ideas of what poetry should be. Hell, it's not an attitude restricted to undergrads. And so this sometimes means good work can get overlooked."

"It's just that," I push on, "I thought you would be the one looking at my poems. That's what I had hoped."

"O-oh!" says Schofield, for what feels like a long time. "I'm so sorry, Larry. I guess you would have no way of knowing otherwise."

"I don't—I just didn't understand."

I am not used to people like Schofield—people so readily apologetic, so willing to take the blame.

"Send them to me," Schofield decrees without warning.

"No, no, no," I start yelling—the word echoing in the stairwell around me—even though this was precisely what I had been hoping Schofield would say. "You're busy, I just should have known—"

"Send them to me, Larry. Really. I'd love to see them."

But I know that I won't. I can barely stand to think about those poems anymore. B-poems. Not Up My Alley. *A confection, ultimately.*

"Maybe I could send you . . . something else?"

"Send me anything you want. But Larry, honestly—you can't let this discourage you. If you let one rejection throw you off, it's going to be all the harder to park yourself down in front of the typewriter again, do you know what I mean?"

I know exactly what he means. But how do you stop it? How do you kill that particular raisin?

Dermot Schofield is the only person I've ever met who seems more comfortable talking on the telephone than in person. As we continue to converse—easily, amiably—I keep trying to reconcile my memory of him writhing in his chair at the Crowfeather, blushing and stammering through the preamble of his reading. The guy on the phone I can picture with feet up on his desk, arm dangling over the back of his chair, jacket removed, tie loosened—perhaps even set aside. Schofield sounds like he'd be happy to talk to me all day.

The result being that it doesn't take as much courage as I had expected to ask if he would mind advising me on a personal matter.

His office door is open a crack, the way he always likes to keep it—Jim doesn't leave it gaping like Dekker or some of the other profs. It's sort of a begrudging crack: *Enter if You Must.* I push the door open farther, gently, moving it aside like a curtain. I don't think about it, I just do it.

Toc-toc-toc, I knock. Deliberately unthinking, deliberately unreflecting. Dermot's words have got me operating on pure impulse. Jim glances up with only his eyes. His head stays bowed.

Arsenault is a genius, nobody's denying that. I suppose the problem is he knows it. I'm not saying he's an egomaniac, I'm saying when a man with that much talent knows he has that much talent, it's got to be difficult to reconcile the—the mundane obligations of day-to-day life. The fact that people of equal or even less ability are—you know—frolicking on Greek islands, drinking red wine on Patmos. That so many are being exalted for so much less. And there he is, sitting in an office, marking essays . . .

He's got the place dark, the blinds closed. Only his desk lamp is on, pointed at a low, harsh angle. The light pools over a pile of papers stacked so haphazardly, it's as if they've been shoved together into the centre of the desk in preparation for a mini bonfire. There's also a smaller pile of Kleenex in one corner. Jim is sniffling. Fighting off another cold.

But you're just as talented as Jim, and you don't . . .

Okay, Larry. Listen. What's wonderful about Arsenault— what's difficult about Arsenault . . . he's a dreamer. That's the quality of his poetry that makes it so gorgeous, so compelling. That's the quality of his personality as well. I'm . . . I guess I'm a congenital pragmatist. I've never been told I was special. I've never felt I had any sort of destiny to fulfill. If I've managed to achieve the kind of life where, every once in a while, I get to write a poem . . . you know . . . I'm happy. That's enough for me. But Jim—

"Larry."

"Hi, Jim."

He reaches for what looks like a random wad of tissue, unwads it slightly in order to enfold his nose. There's a brief, musical honk. I've never seen his hair so carefully combed, the ruts still in it, shining wetly.

The used tissue gets replaced in its pile. Jim sniffs long and wet, as if blowing his nose has made things worse in there, opened the floodgates all the more. He blinks up at me through the rheum. "So how you doing, kiddo?"

"I'm good," I tell him, nodding hard.

He makes a limp attempt to straighten the haystack of papers in front of him before shoving them to the opposite side of his desk from the balls of Kleenex. He knocks a coffee cup to the floor in the process. We both look at it.

"Well," he says. "Shit."

Nothing's spilled. Jim leans back and sighs without bothering to retrieve the mug. "You wanna sit down?"

I perch on the frame of the toilet-chair.

"How are you, Jim?"

He nods and doesn't look at me, rifling through a drawer. "Sick. Sick, again. This time of year always kills me."

"Me too," I say. It doesn't feel like the time to tell him what a good, dread-free day I've been having. Besides, the jury's still out. I may already have pushed my luck too far. It feels as if the raisin could recover its rosy plumpness and come bouncing back to life at any minute.

Jim pulls a folder out of his desk, glances up at me again with eyes dark and teary as a bloodhound's.

"I suppose you're here to talk about your grade."

He glances away again, opens the folder, and all at once I know what I'm supposed to say.

The thing to remember about Arsenault, when he's mad, is that he doesn't want to stay mad. He wants to get mad, yes. And he wants to be mad. And he wants to be able to get mad whenever he wants, and he wants you to put up with it. But he doesn't want to stay mad. It's your job to help him not be mad anymore. He slams the door, and he wants you to be the one to come knocking afterward. He can't open it up again himself.

———

"I'm here," I say, "To see how you're doing, Jim. I'm just here to say hello and get caught up."

Jim looks up again—it's an awful glance, like a kicked dog expecting more of the same. I can't believe he'd look at me like that. He exhales a breath and sinks a little in his chair.

"Oh well, you know how it can be after the holidays around here. A bit—a bit deathly."

"Stark," I say. "I always find this time of year so stark."

Jim runs his hands along the edge of his desk—away from each other, and then together again. It is a shy sort of gesture, which startles me.

"Stark," he whispers to the desk. "Jesus, you got that right, kiddo."

My next question is a gamble—but better to get it over with than let the topic fester in the air between us.

"How *was* your holiday, by the way, Jim?"

He's in the middle of running his hands along the desk's edge some more. Halfway through, when his hands are as far apart as they can get without falling off the ends, his eyes slide up to meet mine.

"Not bad, Larry. Thanks for asking. Not too-too bad."

"Did you and Moira go anywhere, or—?"

"No, no," says Jim. "Stayed put. Neither of us is all that close with our families. Moira's youngest brother stopped in." Jim shakes his head. "Drunk. Made a fool of himself as usual."

Another quick glance from Jim. Did I say shy? Perhaps I meant sly. He smiles. I smile bigger.

"You know my cousin?" I say, seizing on the topic of family. "You know how I told you my cousin was pregnant and my family was freaking out?"

Jim frowns. "I believe you mentioned that, yes."

I hesitate, remembering that when I mentioned this, it was of course the night of Dekker's party, walking home from the bootleggers'. I remember I introduced the topic as a way of changing the subject—a last-ditch means of distracting Jim from all the betrayals, all the lies, all the rocks to be pushed up all the hills.

It's possible, because of how drunk he was, that Jim has no memory of any of this and doesn't know what I'm talking about—that he is pretending to. Either way, I launch into the story of Janet. I do my jowl-quivering impression of Grandma Lydia for him. I talk movingly of Uncle Stan shaking his head back and forth. Then Janet in Little Billy's, confessing to me all her stunning lies, her Machiavellian manoeuvres. I wave my hands until Jim's leaning forward, smiling. I don't stop until the two of us are laughing, until Jim is shaking his own head in amazement and disbelief. Until I'm certain he has shaken off his mistrust and reserve. Until I find myself feeling tired, maybe even a little resentful of the effort, trying to remember what it is I did wrong, what exactly I'm trying to atone for.

Not five minutes after leaving Jim's office, the magic sheen of my day is forcibly, physically explained to me by a wave of nausea that descends like a black bird. There's a moment where I can almost see it approaching in the distance. The potato chips I grabbed for lunch rumble emptily in my gut. Acid gurgles up around them and saliva spurts beneath my tongue. I remember as a kid in springtime, walking down the path from Grandma Lydia's to the beach, being cawed at by nesting crows. The whole way there, I'd be terrified as they swooped directly at my head, veering off only at the last possible minute. That's what it's like, this thing coming at me, this thing I know has no intention of veering off at the last minute. This thing is my hangover, delayed. I've been having such a good day because I've been residually drunk all morning.

I bolt into a washroom and retch nothing but bile and chips. A couple of guys at the urinals laugh and provide uninspired commentary—"Whoa! Rough night, buddy?"—until they get bored and maybe start to feel guilty.

I close my eyes and hold some tissue to my nose to act as a smell-filter. I try to think about this morning's snowflakes, clean and white. I think of Dermot Schofield's reedy poet's voice, so comfortable and far away across the whirring wires.

But what I see is Jim's face—transformed and animated thanks to me, all my painstaking effort. Him opening his blinds, stretching with sudden, startling vigour as the winter sun poured in. I thought he might perform a couple of jumping jacks for a minute there. Instead, he turned to me with a startled look.

By God, Larry, I don't think we even had a chance to discuss your portfolio, now, have we?

The phlegm had gone completely from his voice.

Well—I realized what I was supposed to do. I was supposed to wave my hand, act unconcerned, and so I did.

No, no, no, I've been meaning to talk to you about some of the pieces. Great work, kid. Really.

And going over to one of his shelves, and rifling through his stack of copies.

When we were both in Toronto, said Schofield, *we spent a lot of time together. I can't tell you how much I admired him. The confidence he had even then, in his talent. It was inspiring to me.*

And throwing himself back into his chair, tossing his long legs up onto the desk, sending the balls of Kleenex flying on the updraft.

The sequence, he said, flipping pages. *The short poems with*

*the similar titles. Some really smart stuff here. "Showdogs"—
that was a great one, Larry.*

I mentioned "The Ass of the Head." I said I understood
why he hadn't cared for that one as much.

*No, no, it wasn't that, Larry, I just didn't feel it had the pre-
cision and coherence of the others. It kind of stuck out. Plus, to
be honest, it was the more suitable piece for discussing in class.
More meat on it. But I liked it, I really did.* He raised his head,
cocked it at me. I knew that cock. I knew that look. Throw
the ball, it said. I'm waiting.

Why would you think I didn't like it, Larry?

We'd go out, said Schofield, *and he could be so crazy. He
could—it never occurred to him he should have to hold himself
back, and at first that was wonderful, in a way. Exhilarating to
behold when you're a young man. It's precisely the way you think
a genius should be.*

Well, I said, and I knew what I was supposed to say. *My grade.*

Blank look. *But you got an A.*

Then I was supposed to act a little shy and shamefaced. I
was supposed to shrug apologetically. I was supposed to
explain to Jim I hadn't, in fact, gotten an A.

At that point, Jim was supposed to look appalled, yank
open a drawer, and withdraw the folder he kept his marks in.
Flip it open. Run his finger down the page. And finally smile
with relief—shooting me a mock-scolding look: Naughty-
naughty. Playing games are we?

It's an A, Larry. Broad grin. *Right here in black and
white, kid.*

I ad libbed at this point. I argued a bit with Jim. I insisted
my mark had been a B—it was written on my portfolio.

It was? Were there any other comments?

No, there hadn't been any other comments.

It was a mistake, kiddo. I mistook your portfolio for someone else's. Sorry about that—it's a crazy time of year with all the marking. Must have given you a scare, though!

Yes, it had given me a scare.

It's a good thing you came in. I bet some poor kid thinks he got your A. I should double-check with everyone. I watched Jim scribble himself a note and stick it in the folder before shoving the whole thing back into his top drawer.

What I wasn't supposed to do was jump to my feet and yell, *What the hell is going on?* I wasn't supposed to kick the toilet-chair over to one side, or reach over and topple Jim's haystack of papers. I wasn't supposed to grab him by the shirt, or shout in his face, or yank the top drawer from his desk to see my original grade for myself. Of course, I wasn't supposed to do any of those things. And of course, I didn't.

I was feeling a little queasy at that point anyway; there was a heaviness settling itself inside my head. All the toppled raisins were ballooning to full strength at once.

After a while, said Dermot Schofield. *After a while, though—I don't know. I was tired. Just take care of yourself, Larry, okay? It's as important as anything else.*

I stood and smiled, went to shake Jim's hand, but got pulled into his musty chest for a moment instead. He bashed a hand between my shoulder blades a few times then set me loose with a light, companionable shove toward the door. The raisins swelled and strained—a million frog's eggs popping open deep in the marsh's awakening depths. In the distance, a black-winged shadow getting ready to dive.

4

we seethe and writhe

28

JIM SHOWS UP in class every week, comb ruts dug across his scalp. He introduces us to a new form called the ghazal, which is basically a series of unrhyming couplets, and shows us some very old Persian translations as well as a couple of modern examples by a poet named Jim Harrison, who is wonderful. I try to keep from getting too excited. It's one of the loveliest forms I've seen. It's muscular and vague all at once—*Potent yet airy,* says Jim. I like it so much I want it to be just mine. I don't ever want to write anything else. I have this childish urge to stand up in the middle of the class and insist that no one else be allowed to experiment with this form. Where does it come from, I wonder, that mean human desire to keep all the most beautiful things to yourself?

My immediate urge following Jim's class is to run to Carl's, order one of their bottomless pots of tea, and work on ghazals for the rest of the day—an urge I mercilessly squelch, forcing my feet in the direction of the library. It's frustrating that Jim would hit me with this now, considering my new resolution to back off from poetry for the time being and turn my attention to something I'm actually good at: school. The new plan is to stay in on weekends in order to save money, study, and—*only* on weekends—work on my poems. Nothing but schoolwork during the week. But it's as if Jim has intuited my new resolve and is trying to tempt me back into the fold, like someone waving a drink in front of a reformed alcoholic.

This has all come out of my most recent meeting with Sparrow, whom I went to see not long after my makeup session with Jim. I asked him to tell me more about what I would need to get into Oxford. Sparrow's eyebrows had performed an exultant swoop or two before settling into a no-nonsense furrow.

"Of course, it's no small matter, you understand, Lawrence. It has to be nothing but the canon from here on in, yes? Nothing but serious scholarship. If you want to apply somewhere like *Oxford*"—and only here did Sparrow allow his eyebrows another upward spurt, uttering the sacred name like any other man would utter *titties*—"your . . . other interests may have to take a back seat for a while."

I nodded. Sparrow watched me nod, a clinical look to his eyes. It was as if he had injected me with something—some kind of drug, or poison—and was tracking its effects.

Everybody else is organizing everything—it feels almost as if they've intuited my new regime and have helpfully, wordlessly picked up the slack. Dekker has been helping Jim with our second poetry reading of the year, which has suddenly become a big deal because the guest poet, Abelard Creighton, has of late been awarded some sort of poetry prize by the city of Toronto. In class, Jim pointed out the irony of this—the fact that Creighton winning a Toronto award was national news but if someone from out here won a Charlottetown award or a Fredericton award it would be considered irrelevant to the country as a whole. Still, you could tell Jim was pleased. Dekker confided to me that Creighton was an old mentor of Jim's. His award made Jim look good in the eyes of the department, because Jim had fought to get Creighton invited.

"He insisted," Dekker recalled. "He told us when he was hired that there was a handful of writers in this country whose work was absolutely crucial, and he said in a few years they would be so prominent as to be beyond our reach. He said if the English Department genuinely cared about the literary innovations of today it would make a concerted effort to get people like Schofield and Creighton out here."

Dekker told me this at the Stein, where the student poetry reading—organized entirely by Sherrie—was being held. He sat looking dreamy, telling me about the days after Jim had been hired, the promise perfuming the air. I was glad to hear him speaking of Jim with as much affection as ever. They had both forgotten Christmas—at least it looked as if they had. Just like it probably looked as if I had, too.

"I'm thinking this gets Jim back some of his credibility," Dekker confided. "I hope it will have reminded the department why they hired him in the first place."

"What's Creighton like?"

"Older guy," said Dekker, "A staunch nationalist from what I understand—he's published essays dealing with culture and national identity."

A sigh interrupted us. We looked over and were surprised by the person of Ruth. She'd been talking to Sherrie, but Sherrie must have gone off to get another drink, and so Ruth had sidled noiselessly across the bench to join us. She was on my side of the table, her ass only inches away from mine. I could scarcely believe I had been sitting that close to a warm, breathing presence and not realized it.

Ruth's sigh was not like Moira's. Moira sighed as punctuation to something she had already said. Ruth sighed in statements, declarations. She sighed to announce herself.

"Pardon, love?" said Dekker, inclining his bristly chin.

"Nationalism," said Ruth. "The ultimate colonial giveaway."

"Ah, Ruth," said Dekker, actually turning his head 90 degrees away from her. And so Ruth looked my way.

"Should a country wish to announce itself as a backwater," she said, gazing at me the way you might a blank wall, a void surface, "should a country wish to flaunt its insecurities—indulge in nationalism."

———

Up until about then, I had been feeling well-disposed toward Ruth because Ruth was one of the only people present at our reading who wasn't a student. Sparrow didn't come, although I left a message with him through Marjorie—casually adding that Marjorie herself was more than welcome, should she be free. Of course I didn't expect the blowsy Marjorie with her brood of children waiting at home to take me up on the invitation. But I had thought Sparrow might show. I'd thought Jim might, too. I had even, in all my deluded idiocy, imagined my reading might somehow bring the two together in their swelling pride and appreciation of a shared protégé. I would stand motionless, reciting under a spotlight, and they would stand rapt on opposite sides of the dead-silent room, lost in the power of my words. Through this transcendent experience, they would gradually come to realize how similar they both were, how much they had in common, how ultimately they both wanted the same thing—my success and well-being. I imagined one striding up to the other—probably Sparrow, the first move would be his—hand extended. *Professor . . . Jim. You should be proud.* And Jim grasps the smaller man's hand with firm, resolute dignity. *The pride is ours to share, Sir.* Their eyes blaze into one another's—dark into light. Afire with emotion, understanding, and mutual respect. Hostilities melt into nothing, swords are turned into ploughshares, and—it's spring. A million flowers burst from the dead earth.

But neither of them came, and so I was left shouting about showdogs and pinpricks over a bunch of girls who I later found out had been sitting there drinking in celebration of someone's birthday since four in the afternoon. I was the first to read, since we went in alphabetical order, and the microphone wasn't working. I recited two poems through the indignity of ongoing girl-shrieks and giggles—one of them growing so bold as to yell, "Show us your thing!"—before sitting down in disgust.

Claude sauntered to the stage afterward, pausing to speak to the bartender, who made some vaguely technical motions with his hands. Claude fiddled with the mic, tapped it, blew, and finally wiggled the cord. The cord-wiggling was what did it, and unbelievably, all his fiddling around up there had managed to attract the interest of the whole room. By the time Claude was ready to read, everyone present was ready to listen. Even the sounds of the birthday girls had descended to intrigued murmurs.

"He's got *presence*," Ruth Dekker leaned over to say to Sherrie.

"I think we should have gotten an MC," I announced to no one. "We should get an MC next time, to introduce people."

"I'm sorry, Lawrence," whispered Sherrie, because apparently Claude's *presence* and the power of his work demanded hush, working microphone or no. "Do you want to go up again?"

I glanced around to see if anyone was looking at me, if anyone was showing a particular lively interest in what my response would be. My gaze collided with the smiling eyes of Todd. I turned back to the stage and forced a yawn.

"I'm fine."

"I don't say this to be disparaging," continued Ruth. "We are from a colony as well, after all."

I glanced over at Dekker to gauge his willingness to re-enter the conversation. But Dekker's neck was actually straining—I could see the tendons bulge beneath his stubble—so vigorously had he turned his face from Ruth.

"I don't think we really see ourselves as colonists anymore," I remarked. "I mean, my grandmother will talk about 'the empire' from time to time . . ."

"You can never underestimate the deep-seatedness of the colonial mindset," Ruth interrupted.

I craned my own neck around the bar, perhaps not as casually as courtesy would dictate.

Blessedly, Ruth excused herself to lumber off toward the ladies' room, man-hands swinging like dual pendulums. Heads turned to follow her height and shining blondeness— male and female heads alike. Ruth too had presence.

"Lawrence," Dekker called, causing me to look up. I realized as I did that I had been sitting there feeling somewhat gut-punched.

"Ruth didn't mean to be insulting. She's homesick."

I nodded again. Was I insulted? Todd would be insulted—he'd be apoplectic. Not so much at the suggestion that Canada is a backwater, but at the insinuation that there's anything wrong with that. But I wasn't Todd. Hadn't I shaken off such provincialism, placed myself above it? Wasn't I going to Oxford?

"This is the *greatest* country," he told me, leaning in. "Call it boring!" Dekker suddenly challenged me. "Call it boring if you will! Peace *is* boring. Sanity *is* boring."

"I didn't call it boring," I objected, feeling defensive. I didn't, did I? Thinking and saying are not the same thing— not the same kind of betrayal.

Dekker stared at me for a strangely blank moment before sitting back. His eyes darted toward the ladies'-room door.

"I know you didn't, Lawrence. I'm sorry."

I looked up, suddenly curious. "So then—where did you end up going to school? Did you go to school in Canada?"

He sat blinking a bit longer than I would have expected for such a basic question.

"Well I—I did an undergraduate degree in Cape Town, of course."

"But then where? What got you out of there? Did you go to Oxford?"

He smiled, releasing a breath of laughter. "Oxford? No. No, Larry, I went to school in America. They wouldn't have let someone like me within a mile of Oxford."

Now it was my turn to blink. Each blink served to shape a growing certainty behind my eyes. Each blink was an echo of the words *someone like me.* I didn't want to ask, because I was afraid I knew the answer already. I didn't want to hear it, but I echoed, I asked.

"Someone like you?"

More self-deprecating smiles from Dekker—I was starting to think it was the only kind of smile he knew.

He scratched the scruff of his neck, still smiling. "How did I hear you put it one night? The way you described Rimbaud?"

I thought for a moment, and then it swam to the surface of my brain. "*Rimbaud was just some hick from a farm,*" I restated. With, I imagine, not quite as much aplomb as the original.

Dekker nodded at me, tapping himself in the chest.

Like me. Like us.

After which there is not much to do but get drunk under the pretence of "celebrating" the dismal poetry reading, which is what I proceed to do. So. Let's see where we stand here. Poetry? Nope, draw a line through that. How many cosmic hints do you need, after all, how many bolts to the head? How many alleys to be scuttled in and out of before you see you're not wanted up any of them?

Oxford? That's another line. Forgot where you came from for a minute there, didn't you, big shot? Hullo, stranger. Welcome to the Highwayman Motor Hotel and Mini-Putt (adjusts crotch, removes sprig of hay from teeth). My name is Mungo, and I'll be changing your sheets and replacing your toilet paper for the rest of my natural life.

I finish my beer and gaze for a while at the bottom of my mug. When no one is looking, I hork into the mug, drawing it out. Making it last. I have christened the bottom of my mug Joanne.

Time passes and people ignore me, as is only fit. Slaughter shows up once he can be good and sure the poetry is over—not, as you might expect, on his own inclination, but because it turns out Sherrie asked him to stay away out of an attack of shyness. It's ten o'clock and Slaughter is already well beyond three sheets to the wind, slapping my back so hard in greeting my vision of Joanne vibrates briefly. When Sherrie, still high from the success of her event, babbles to him how great Claude's reading in particular was, how people applauded for him, and how some of the birthday girls even hollered—*Woo-woo!*—Slaughter suddenly whirls, grinning, and seizes Claude by the head.

"*Guck,*" says Claude in the ensuing silence.

We all watch. Slaughter has grabbed people like me and Todd and flung us cheerfully back and forth like Raggedy-Andys on countless occasions. But it's not the sort of thing you do to Claude. Nobody is smiling except Slaughter, who looks glazed and far away as he buries his knuckles into Claude's scalp, rubbing furiously.

"Good for you, there, Frenchie!" he enthuses. I can hear bone grind against bone.

"*Charles,*" says Sherrie. And Slaughter lets Claude go.

"What? It's a congratulatory noogie!" Then he follows it up with what I suppose has to be a congratulatory shove. Claude staggers, but straightens up quickly. He smooths his dishevelled hair and looks at his watch. Todd starts to laugh, and I'd like to punch him.

"I'm going to get a beer," says Claude, looking off toward the bar since he can only look at his watch for so long.

"Okay," says Sherrie, seeming to gasp for breath. "But, um."

Slaughter drowns her out by yelling for a pitcher, and I'm the only one who sees when Claude walks past the bar and out the door.

Chuck keeps bellowing, "Let's do the Mariner, you assholes, whaddya say?" every five minutes, and jumps up, ready to herd us into the street.

"The Mariner makes you too crazy," Sherrie vetoes whenever he does this—but Sherrie would probably veto Slaughter if he suggested going out and making snow angels, after what happened with Claude. "You get weird about the Mariner."

"*You* get weird about the Mariner!" Chuck hollers back, cheerfully incoherent. "You and Rory, it's all you can talk about half the time, kicking his fuckin' head in. You're obsessed."

"Yes, that's right, Charles."

"I'm getting damn sick of it, if you want to know the truth. What did that asshole Rory ever do to you?"

"Nothing, Charles."

"Nothing! Poor old Rory anyway, everybody wanting to kick his head in. Rory's had a tough life. Rory never hurt anyone."

"I thought he was some kind of gangster," Todd interrupts.

"That's just town gossip," says Sherrie.

"He *is* a gangster!" Slaughter insists. "He fuckin' bootlegs. Sells drugs. Whores. It's like the Old West down there."

Sherrie closes her eyes like a clubbed baby seal after *whores*. "He does not."

"Campbell's a wildman," yells Slaughter, suddenly grabbing me around the shoulders. This causes the entire room to shift as if we are in a ship's hull. "Me and him, we musta snorted coke off every whore on Rory's payroll."

"All right," says Sherrie, looking around the room as if for Claude. It's been hours since he left.

"I'm telling you he's got whores on the go! I got a different kinda sore on my dick from every last one of them!"

The clubbed-seal look again from Sherrie and then a hearty round of *hawg, hawg, hawg.* Todd tries to join in, opening his mouth, but then shuts it abruptly. It's a look I've drunk with him enough to recognize. He weaves hastily to the men's room and I know it's the last we'll see of him all night. Todd gets shy when he gets sick, slinking off like a hurt animal to tough it out on his own.

Twenty minutes later, the waitress yells last call. Slaughter stands, then falls like a wounded moose, then heaves himself up again, using Sherrie and me for balance, laughing.

With some people, the cold air makes them sober. But Slaughter, I realized after seeing him sink to the floor, was beyond being sobered. The cold air is like a slap. Like a punch. It makes him crazy. He runs ahead of us toward Scarsdale Holdings, ready to poach another flag and singing "I Am Woman" by Helen Reddy at the top of his lungs.

Sherrie and I look at each other. "I hate that song," she tells me. "He knows it."

Even half-cut I can feel the trouble coming.

I hear a whoop out of Chuck, peer down the street, and there it sits, parked—huge and yellow—just a few feet past Scarsdale's. The driver is probably off drinking himself somewhere.

Slaughter forgets all about the flag—he runs right past—

it even flutters in the breeze he creates. "Oh my God," Chuck howls. "The keys are in it, man! The fuckin' keys are in it!"

"Chuck," I call, breaking into a wobbly run.

"Let's go dig up the graveyard!"

He vaults into the seat before we can even catch up with him. He starts up the thing before we can say a word.

The noise is like a backhoe belching itself to life in a small town in the dead of a winter's night. Slaughter keeps gesturing like a train conductor for us to climb aboard, and we keep hopping up and down shaking our heads back and forth, yelling "No," and "Stop," and not hearing ourselves.

After a minute or so of this, he turns from us in disgust and yanks one of the levers in front of him. The backhoe belches and lurches like a goosed dinosaur. He shoots us a prideful grin as if to say, *See how well I'm doing?* and pushes the lever forward. The thing gives a roar and begins to move.

It is happening so stupidly fast, I decide this must be one of my nutso dreams. We'll follow him to the graveyard and Lydia will pop up from behind a tombstone waving her Milton, exhorting us to rein in desires lest we get fat like Janet, warning us off temptation.

And then Slaughter will lower the shovel, pierce earth, and—snakes. Serpents everywhere.

29.

CHUCK WAVES ONE HAND in the air like a cowboy riding a bull as he trundles off down Livingston Street. Sherrie and I run about a block in the opposite direction, panicked and sobered by the sudden criminality saturating the air—desperate to get away from it. We've always been so good.

I hear myself yelling, when I can hear my own voice again. I'm yelling that Slaughter is crazy.

This is how we end up bushwhacking our way through the paths that encircle the marsh. People come here in summer to picnic and make out because it is private, surrounded by shrubs and the occasional stately willow. This allows them to imagine it to be a romantic lagoon-type place, as opposed to the swamp that it is. But Sherrie and I have plunged into the paths to hide, jazzed on the fear that someone has noticed Slaughter's hijack—and who wouldn't notice a backhoe roaring to life at two in the morning?— and called the cops.

Reeds poke up from the snow, frozen cattails. I've never been in here at night, or in winter. We push our way through the brush like adventurers, a full moon piercing down. I am freaked out and babbling, demanding to know what the fuck is wrong with Slaughter, and what the fuck Slaughter thought he was doing, and does Slaughter want to get us all the fuck arrested and expelled.

"He drinks too much," Sherrie whispers. "And does God knows what else. And then he gets crazy."

"Well that's—" I stammer, aware of the liquor and adrenalin battling it out for supremacy in my brain. "That's— that's pretty much obvious now isn't it? But he can't pull that kind of shit."

Sherrie is walking ahead of me and whispering so that I can hardly hear her over the noise of our feet punching through the snow, the bone-rattle of frozen branches as we move them aside.

"What?"

"There is something wrong with Charles." She keeps whispering, but turns her head to say it this time.

"Once again, stating the obvious."

Sherrie stops walking and I bash into her.

"Oh, look," she says. Through a break in the trees, we can see the whole marsh, the ghostly brightness of the moon, the glowing snow. Jutting reeds and branches, leafless, sagging. It feels like another graveyard, but a natural, incidental sort of graveyard—which means peaceful, and deathful, but without all that human fear.

What *is* wrong with Slaughter, anyway? Why would he want to disturb such peace? So immediately? So instinctively?

Now that we've stopped walking, nothing but winter silence. No birds, no bugs. No distant noise of some marauding backhoe. We stand in it—the cold silence—very much alone together.

And I swear I didn't even know it was coming. It's my still-racing heart, my booze-heated blood. The words sneak out before my brain can catch up. It's like I'm dreaming awake again.

"Is there," I hear myself saying, "a thing with Jim?"

Sherrie turns to face me. Her big eyes seem to lose their colour in the dark, seem black inside—all pupil.

"A thing with Jim."

"Um," I say.

"What do you mean? A thing with Jim and Charles?"

"No," I say, "I'm not talking about Slaughter anymore."

Sherrie goes back to gazing at the marsh.

"It's just that," I say, "there's been a couple of times when you seemed sad. About Jim."

"Well we're all sad about Jim." She waves a hand.

"Yes," I agree.

"About what's happened to him," Sherrie adds.

"Yes," I say. "But—I don't know. There's just been a couple of moments where. Um. You seemed. Particularly sad."

Sherrie sucks a lungful of frozen air into herself as I speak, raising her shoulders to her ears and then letting them drop as she exhales.

"I'm your friend," I add. I put my hand on one of the shoulders because somehow it seems like the thing to do. "And so. I thought I should ask."

"I know you're my friend," Sherrie whispers, looking down. I am actually kind of surprised by this.

"You're probably my best friend at Westcock, Lawrence."

I'm *really* surprised by that. My hand is still on her shoulder, and I knead it a little, moving closer as I do. This also seems like the thing to do. That's how it works in dreams, after all. Things just happen. It's not like you have any say. I put my other hand on Sherrie's other shoulder and turn her to face me. She keeps her eyes on the ground.

"But I can't talk to you about it right now," she says. "I want to, and I probably will, but right now I have to wait."

She won't look at me. I feel like she's resisting the dream, struggling to wake us both up. What's supposed to happen, I feel very strongly, is that she is supposed to look at me. And then I look at her and we *see* each other and she folds herself into my chest and the smell of her hair wafts up my nose and things start to warm up around here.

"Wait for what?" I whisper, squeezing her shoulders with creeping impatience. My fingers are already starting to tingle with the cold and I want to shove them back in my pockets. I can feel a very un-friend-like desire taking hold of me. "Prurient interest," I think it's called. I heard the expression in a bootlegged Lenny Bruce recording one time. It means wanting to know what you know you shouldn't know. It means wanting the dirty details.

"I have to wait," say Sherrie, glancing up at me, "for the time to be right."

"To be ripe?"

"To be *right*."

I wiggle my toes around in my boots to keep them from going numb, to get my curiosity under control, the overwhelming need to wheedle. With that—the cold and the curiosity prickling away at me—the stupid dream dissipates. I awake to find myself a drunken, runny-nosed fuckwit in the middle of a frozen swamp.

"So let's not talk about it right now, okay?" she says, glancing up at me in a kind of plea. "We will. But not now."

I let my hands drop, turning away to look up at the moon. There *is* a thing with Jim. Fuckwit. There is.

"Slaughter," I say. "Speaking as a friend? It might be best not to get too attached to him. He just wants to get into your pants."

Sherrie sputters laughter, which is not the effect I was angling for.

"Okay, Lawrence. Thanks for the tip."

"Yeah," I say, shifting my weight and shoving my hands in my pockets. "Can we go?"

"No," says Sherrie, putting her hand on my chest because I've started to move away. "We have to stay for a couple more minutes."

I turn back to her, sighing, and the next thing I know I am sighing into Sherrie's mouth. I freeze. I stop breathing entirely. Then I put my hands on her shoulders again and try to resume, inhaling surreptitiously through my nose. The smell of her hair fills my head.

And just when things are starting to warm up the way I dreamed, she isn't there anymore. I open my eyes, groping for her.

"I want us to stay friends," she tells me, stepping back. "Just friends. Okay, Lawrence?"

I'm hopeful for a moment. "So we can we keep doing that? Every once in a while?"

"No," she says. "That was just to get it out of the way."

"I am having a terrible semester," I fret to Sherrie. "Nothing is working out for me."

So Sherrie gives in and lets it happen one more time.

30.

THE MAIN EXHIBITS of the Hollywood Horrors used to give me nightmares as a kid, just like everybody else I grew up with. And then we all got a little older, got used to them, and started laughing at our younger, chickenshit selves, scared of a cartoon character like Vincent Price with his pencil moustache. In the summer, we would go into the Hollywood as a joke, run our hands up one of Tippi Hedren's cold thighs if the caretaker's head was turned, take turns positioning our necks beneath Dracula's dripping fangs. The real test of fear was approaching the dummies, extending your hands to them, making contact. Dracula's leering rictus didn't scare us at this point. The monsters weren't the problem. It was the physical reality of the dummies themselves—and the small, gruesome details of the regular-people dummies, the ones under attack.

Eventually, though, we got used to that too. We forced ourselves to get used to it because that's what growing up is all about.

But right around that time we were deemed old enough to ascend to new levels of psychic discomfort. At sixteen, you were allowed to view the legendary "hidden" exhibit. The older kids had always terrified the younger ones with stories of what lay beyond a thick set of curtains in the back of the museum—curtains so black that light got lost in them, and if you didn't know they were there, you never would until the day someone drew them apart with a malignant flourish and bade you witness the abominations that lay beyond.

Spikes through heads, the older kids avowed. Brains, dripping. Women pinned spread-eagled on tables, naked. Working guillotines. Expelled eyeballs, dangling from heads. By the time we hit thirteen, no self-respecting kid claimed to believe in the hidden exhibit. The older ones who kept insisting upon its existence were a pack of boys crying wolf as far as we were concerned. We stopped up our ears, wore sneers the moment the subject came up. How stupid did they think we were? Tell us the one about Santa Claus next. Tell us about the guy with the hook where his hand should be.

But you know what? It was there. I got to see it before anyone else in my grade because that was the year Cousin Wayne got hired, when I was fifteen. Wayne made an age exception for me. It was his first job. It was the only job Wayne had ever wanted in his life. He was eager to show off his realm.

Wayne didn't really have the imagination to build it up to me, however—to try and weave an air of suspense around the hidden exhibit's unveiling. It wasn't even his idea to let me see. When I found out he'd been hired, I sought him out and asked him point-blank whether or not it existed.

"You mean the Torture Chamber?" he said. "Yeah, come by this week and I'll show you when nobody's around. It's really gross."

I remember being disappointed. I had been planning on rounding up a few guys and taking them with me to witness this greatest of our childhood mysteries revealed. But Wayne's offhand affirmation—sure, the hidden exhibit existed; yes, it was gross—stripped the thing of its allure. It sounded like nothing; it was probably boring. The hidden exhibit was just another story the island told itself about the world beyond its shores—a world of spooky shadows, plastic bogeymen. I decided it was no big deal, that I could just as well see it alone.

That's what I was dreaming about last night. The day Wayne showed me.

Jim arrives not quite ten minutes into class, rosy with rush. He favours us all with a grin and an apologetic wave, dumping a pile of handouts onto his desk and raking a hand through his windswept, unrutted hair. It's the first time I've seen him without the comb ruts all of this new year. He looks like Claude after his congratulatory noogie. Jim hums to himself—the long, quavering notes of Hank Snow—taking a few moments to organize the handouts into piles, and pausing between hummed verses to glance up at us all and mutter various benedictions—good to see everyone, hope we've all been writing, everyone ready for the Creighton reading, and so forth. A few people up front, including me, answer him. It's impossible not to—he meets our eyes in expectation and his demeanour draws it out of us. The atmosphere Jim has brought with him—and, I realize only today, Jim always brings an atmosphere—is light, intangibly festive. It reminds me of how he was at the beginning of the year, and, now that I'm reminded, the exhilaration of that time comes burbling back, like a stream unleashed, water bursting through ice.

The Jim-thrill—there it is again—straightening my spine, singing through my veins. I am surprised to realize how long it's been, but already I'm forgetting what the lack of it was like. I lean forward. Jim winks as he places a batch of copied poems on my desk for me to pass back. He goes to tousle my hair with one hand but enjoys the feel of my head so much, he brings his other hand into it and massages my head like I'm a dog, growling with affection.

The class laughs. Jim laughs. I laugh. And—it's spring.

―――

In real life I was alone—ushered by Wayne—but in the dream Janet was with me, although sometimes it seemed as if Janet, like Wayne, was an employee of the museum and had known about the exhibit all along. In real life it was Wayne who drew back the curtain, but in the dream, sometimes, it was Jim. In real life the first thing I looked for was the naked lady on the table, and that's what I looked for in the dream as well. In real life she wasn't really naked, but naked under a sheet, and you could see the dent of her groin, the muscular triangle of her legs, spread open, tied apart. You could see her nipples, eternally erect. The look on her face was stunned and the requisite leering madman hovered a couple of feet away, hands clasped against his chest as if to say, Goody!

In the dream the lady was naked. It was as if I had come upon her too late. The sheet had been torn aside, the stunned look had been wiped from her face. She was no longer tied up because there wasn't any reason. She had been alive just moments before but now she was dead, and the madman was nowhere in sight—perhaps hiding.

She was Brenda L. She had been Brenda L.

"That asshole," said Wayne in my dream, annoyed in a janitorial kind of way. "Shit." And he went and placed the sheet back over Brenda L.'s torso and tied her hands and feet again, which I thought was ridiculous.

"You're not fooling anyone," I complained to Wayne, who was Jim, and told me to shut up.

"I *won't* shut up," I declared, feeling nervously audacious and wandering off toward the next exhibit. Janet had gone off on her own ahead of me but every once in a while would cast an amused look over her chubby shoulder.

———

It was true. In real life most of it was true. There were spikes through heads. There were dangling eyeballs. There was a guillotine—even though a guillotine has nothing to do with torture, per se, a guillotine is simply death—and I doubt if it actually worked, as people had said. The guillotine cradled a freshly decapitated victim—you could see the severed spinal cord in his neck, surrounded by a red murk of muscle and tissue. Placed before the guillotine was a basket, of course, and in the basket, a baffled head.

In real life Wayne remarked, "I mean, that's sick. They really did that, apparently, back in the old days, the goddamn frogs. What in hell is wrong with people, eh?"

"I hear it's actually pretty humane," I said for something to say. "As far as executions go."

We stood side by side gazing into the basket.

"Yeah, it looks really goddamn humane," Wayne replied. He killed living things for sport, my cousin Wayne. It struck me for the first time that this bestowed its own kind of wisdom on a person.

Next, Jim lets us know about everything we can expect from Abelard Creighton's visit to Westcock this week, making it sound like a kind of intellectual Mardi Gras. Creighton will be giving a lecture in the Social Sciences department as well as an unprecedented two readings—one in the daytime for students and faculty only, and one in the evening for who-ever wants to come. Jim encourages us to attend both events and ask questions, particularly at the student reading. To that end, he hands out five of Creighton's poems. I flip through the pages. All mercifully short.

After the Thursday-night reading, he adds, a reception will take place in the lobby of Grayson Hall, to which we are all of course invited.

"The reading's at Grayson Hall?" I ask, not bothering to raise my hand because it isn't that kind of day.

Jim nods, "Yes, Larry—thanks. I should have made that clear to begin with. Grayson Hall, everybody. Eight o'clock. Write it down, please."

A murmur sounds among us, for we are impressed as a group. Grayson Hall is where convocations are held. Jim must be expecting a huge turnout.

In the dream there was no guillotine, but there was a head— a tiny one like the kind you see in movies about cannibals, who carry them around on sticks. The head had been shrunk, and looked like a shrivelled orange gone brown and hard, forgotten in the fridge—an oversized raisin with a pinched, angry face. A wild dog sat chewing and pawing at the head compulsively. Panda. Panda with rabies.

"Everybody," says Jim, placing himself in his favoured peda-gogical position—in front of his desk, buttocks lightly poised against its edge. "One more thing before we begin today. I don't think I've told you all how much I've appreci-ated your support this year, let alone what a great group of students you've been. We're coming up toward the end of the year and, yes, it's been a bumpy one. You've all been patient, loyal, and somehow not one of you has managed to lose sight of the most important thing going on here—the thing that really matters. The work. You've all continued to grow and develop and explore, and I want you to know I really admire you for that."

There is something going on here. Jim's words are generous and wonderful. I can feel the people around me loosening at the sound of them—hardened layers of tension, built up like plaque on teeth over the past few months, now crumbling away. Behind me, I hear actual sighs wafting toward the ceiling.

But I'm not loosening. I'm tightening. My shoulders seem to be inching themselves up toward my ears.

Jim shakes his head, smiles whitely. For a guy who's never placed that high a premium on personal hygiene, his teeth have always dazzled.

"Anyway, we're coming into the home stretch here folks, and I just thought you should know how well you've all done in your own way. You're one of the finest groups I've ever taught, and I thank you. I just really thank you."

This sounds like the end, but Jim continues to ramble a bit longer and I know why. He has to say more, because he's not really saying what he's saying. He's saying something else. I know it, and so does one other person in the room.

"Anyway, I'm rambling," apologizes Jim. "I just wanted to say thanks to all you folks. And let you know that you've done great, and—all is well. All is well."

Somehow I know the code. I know the message. The message is *forgiveness,* and it isn't meant for me.

31.

THE DREAM SETS OFF this mini-cascade—it's as if a dammed-up part of my brain has broken through. I write sixteen ghazals in the course of one marathon afternoon at Carl's. Six are about the hidden exhibit, its various displays. Four are about the Hollywood Horrors itself, and going there with my friends as kids—forcing ourselves to get used to all the awful human dummies in their monstrous predicaments. Tippi Hedren squinting through her spider-lashes at the descending flock of crows. The violent mess of black in the air above her.

dangling, mid-attack, I describe the crows,
from dusted wires

Another one is about staring into the guillotine basket alongside Cousin Wayne. I describe the anticlimax of finally seeing the hidden exhibit, and the way Wayne's dull, familiar presence de-toothed it in my mind. But then the last few couplets evoke how Wayne surprised me with his compassion for the head—how he saw the guillotine as not just a cool, gross gimmick the way thugs like him were supposed to, but a mark of something real and upsetting about people.

his humanity, I end the couplet,
throwing heat into mine.

I sit back after that one, liking it. I'm not sure about the word *humanity,* it might be too straightforward, but I like the last line, the idea of shared heat. I can go back and work on *humanity* later. This is wonderful. This hasn't happened to me in ages.

I wonder if there is a word for developing an immediate fascination for something, or someone, you immediately despise. For fixating on it, and being able to speak and think of nothing else, precisely as if you were in love. I read somewhere that hate isn't the opposite of love—indifference is. So if hate isn't anti-love, it can only be a sort of insulted version of it.

I should say first and foremost that the five poems Jim gave out by Abelard Creighton were not bad. They read a bit like jokes, some of them—or cocktail party anecdotes—starting with an image or a scenario, usually well evoked, and then ending with a wry kind of punchline observation which tied the thing together, made you sort of go, *huh!* They were clever. They were too short and sharp to really blow my mind, but they made me interested enough to want to read more. As Jim might say, they held promise.

The poems Creighton reads today are not short. In fact, he is about five minutes into the first one before I even understand that it's a poem. He announced he was about to read a poem. He said the poem had to do with an experience he'd had in Paris with "the tourist trade," and smiled around the room for a moment. Then he gathered up the sheaf of papers resting on the lectern before him, glanced down at them through a pair of bifocals and started to talk.

"There I was in the city of Proust," said Creighton. "City of poets. In Hemingway's cafés I lingered, light-footed in the city of lights. Ah, but those bastard sons of the great white hunter and gun, there came the American dreamers . . ."

This went on for a bit, Creighton telling us about Paris, what the women were like ("smokey-slim"), and how young he was ("green as grapes"), how entranced by the city's romantic past, when a bunch of Americans showed up and ruined everything by being vulgar and boorish. Eventually I leaned against Sherrie.

"I wish he'd get on with it," I whispered.

She lowered her head to hiss back. "You don't like it?"

"I just wanna hear the poetry."

Sherrie turned her head to listen. I thought for a second she was just pausing to pretend she was listening, the way she did in Dekker's Shakespeare, but after a few more stories of cobblestones and cafés she ducked her head toward me again.

"I think this is it, Lawrence."

I sat up and searched Sherrie's face for seriousness. She nodded. I turned and paid very close attention after that. Todd was leaning so far forward, his ass was practically hovering over the seat of his chair.

So Creighton reads for forty-five minutes. Every single poem he reads is about Americans or America. Every single poem begins with the words *I was,* or *There I was,* or *Here I am,* or *I am.* Every single poem talks about Creighton being somewhere and meeting Americans, and the Americans being some combination of stupid and greedy and vulgar and cruel. Actually, that's not true. Some of the poems talk about Creighton being somewhere and talking to a Canadian who doesn't think Americans are all that bad. Then the poem goes on to reveal the combination of stupidity, greed, and vulgarity in the featured Canadian.

Forty-five minutes of this. I keep waiting for Jim, sitting up front, to throw up his hands in an uncontainable show of mirth and yell April Fool's or something. I keep looking around expecting someone to leap to his or her feet in outrage, denounce the proceedings as a sham, a joke. At the very least, I expect to meet the indignant eye of someone like me, someone desperately looking around for someone like them.

Finally, Creighton stops talking and smiles. He's been pausing between lines of poetry to smile deliberately around at us throughout the recitation. The smiles always arrive on the heels of what Creighton obviously believes to be his wittiest, most cutting lines, as if to help us along in our understanding of his drollery: *Clever, no?* It's a taut, closed-mouth, crinkle-eyed smile, and insufferable.

In the hallway, after the reading, Sherrie keeps begging me to keep my voice down, and I'll look around before hunching toward her and reiterating my objections in an urgent series of mutters. I think I'm doing a pretty good job, but a few minutes later Sherrie hushes me again, and I realize that I was practically shouting and people on their way down the hall had to duck to avoid my flying arms.

"You get so *angry,* Lawrence," Sherrie hisses.

"I'm not angry," I hiss back. "I'm perplexed. I don't understand."

"Shh!"

I pull my arms in and glance around. Jim is herding Creighton out into the hall, hand resting on one of the poet's shoulders. Todd trails in their wake like a flower girl after a bride and groom. Claude is also nearby, leaning against a wall with his arms folded, close enough to hear what I'm saying but bodily placing himself outside the conversation.

"I feel like I must be missing something," I hiss.

Sherrie puts on a patient, teacherly face.

"It's just a different kind of poetry, Lawrence. It's kind of Bukowski, I thought. In the narrative sense I mean. You don't have to like it."

This infuriates me.

"No! That's bullshit!"

"Shh!"

I look around again. Jim is now standing between Creighton and Todd, as if mediating their conversation. He looks over at me and grins.

"He heard you," Sherrie accuses.

"I agree," says Claude.

"What do you mean, you agree?" says Sherrie. Meanwhile, I'm agape because, looking at Claude, I already know.

Claude hoists one shoulder as if he can't even be bothered producing a full-on shrug. "I mean I agree with Lawrence. It's jingoistic claptrap."

My gape widens into an open-mouthed, all-embracing smile. "Yes! Yes! See?" I pinch Sherrie's shoulder by way of emphasis. She gives me a look before rounding on Claude again.

"I'm surprised at you. You're usually so tolerant of different kinds of work."

"I am, if it's good," admits Claude. "But this—" He gestures down the hall toward Creighton. "—is no good. The only difference between me and Lawrence is that I don't see the point in getting worked up about it."

"It's *jingoistic claptrap*," I exclaim. "It's just one big polemic."

Claude's nodding. "Polemics and poetry don't work."

"No," I agree. "They don't." I have to suppress an urge to slap Claude on the back, or start pumping his hand or something.

Sherrie seems to have taken a micro-step away from us both. "Well," she says, "Jim seems to like it."

We all glance toward Jim and note that he's approaching. He ambles smilingly down the corridor, taking his time, trailing his still-sunny atmosphere along with him, warming the hallway. Our faces turn to him like flowers.

"Folks," he greets, arm landing soft across my shoulders, like a blanket. No crazy heat burning from his armpit these days, but there's a smell. The unlaundered Jim-smell of outdoors and woodsmoke and dog. I haven't noticed it since before Christmas.

"So howdja like that?" Jim asks of us all.

"I enjoyed it very much," says Sherrie after a moment.

"What about you, Claude?" asks Jim, grinning as if he's just set some sort of ingenious trap. It occurs to me that I have never seen Jim speak to Sherrie directly, except when he answers her points in the seminar. But even then he's responding in a general, classroom-oriented way.

Claude smiles and shrugs. Jim points an endless index finger at him.

"That," he says, seeming pleased, "is exactly what I was expecting."

He laughs, and turns his laughing face to me. For some reason, I'm the guy appointed to laugh with him.

I don't let Jim down on this front. I don't see how I can. Claude just keeps smiling, arms folded tightly as if to lock himself into a permanent shrug. Sherrie, after a moment or two, turns away—either to look for Todd or else just to look at something else—and I feel, for some reason, queasy. Lately a pair of words keeps popping into my mind unbidden, always accompanied by the feeling I associate with Janet and her bedroom—an eight-year-old's bowel-level shame.

occasionally struggles

Once we've finished laughing, Jim gives me another little pat and wipes his eyes. "Now, I just wanted you folks to know," he says, "you're all invited over to my place Friday night after the second reading."

Sherrie turns back, and I'm not sure I can describe the expression on her face except to say that I feel for her the way you do when a good friend's fly is open—I want to take her aside, to usher her out of view until she's properly zipped up.

Charles Slaughter is sitting at his desk with a pile of mushrooms and medicinal capsules in front of him, methodically bashing the mushrooms into dust with a hammer. A few guys were gathered meekly around his open door when I arrived, pleading with him to stop because they were trying to study, and Slaughter, not looking up from his work, was yelling at them to go stick their heads up their asses if they were looking for quiet, and not to be such fucking useless pussies while they were at it, because he was *busy.*

It turns out Chuck is preparing for the weekend. He had the capsules from an old prescription lying around, he tells me, and had discovered that once he cracked them and dumped out the medicine, he could bash about twenty mushrooms up into a fine powder and cram all the powder into a single capsule. I sit on his bed watching him for a while, wincing every time the hammer lands. Chuck is turning the surface of his desk into a pitted moonscape.

"See?" he says, holding up a completed capsule. "This way, you can do, like, twenty mushrooms in one pop."

I lean forward to squint my appreciation. "But," I say, "*should* a person do twenty mushrooms in one pop?"

"Of course, a person should," says Charles, and swallows it.

"Please stop the noise," a timid freshman calls from the doorway.

"I will come over there," replies Slaughter, "and I will impale you on my fist."

Slaughter may seem like an odd sort of friend for a poet to have—I certainly thought so when I learned of his friendship with Jim. But now that I've gotten to know him, it seems to me that Chuck is a kind of poet himself. That is to say, there is a poetry about his weirdness, and his bigness, and his violence. His good cheer and his loyalty. I don't really know how to explain it, but I heard someone describe poetry once as something you experience not intellectually, but with your nerves and instincts—and this is how I've always experienced Slaughter. Nothing is laid out or explicit with him, but evoked. You never know quite what the deal is, but you get feelings—feelings of unease, or warmth, or tension—and they circle. They never seem to land but just keep circling, blurring into one another.

"What ever happened with the backhoe?" I ask once we're sitting across from one another at Quackers.

"What backhoe?" says Slaughter, gazing over my shoulder, out the window and onto the street.

"On the weekend? You stole a backhoe."

Slaughter's mouth opens. "I did, didn't I? Fuck, that explains it."

"Explains what?"

"Why Mittens has been so pissy all week."

I don't mention Claude, or Slaughter seizing him by the neck, which seems to me a more obvious, if less flamboyant, motive for Sherrie's pissiness. Instead I ask, "What is the deal with you and Sherrie, anyway?" stretching my arms to illustrate how relaxed I am. "Are you two going out or what?"

"Well, she's mad at me now," grunts Slaughter. "So, no. I don't fucking know."

"She's mad about the backhoe?"

"Oh, who knows what she's mad about." Slaughter keeps staring past me out the window. He doesn't seem much for conversation today. "I'm too big an asshole when I get drunk or something."

"So are you going to the Creighton reading?" I ask, since a conversation-change is clearly what's required here.

Slaughter frowns. "Who is this Creighton fuckwad, anyway?"

I lean forward. "He's *awful*. He's the worst poet I've ever heard."

"Let's kill him," says Charles, cheering up.

"I'd like to. I hate him. Like—the moment I saw him."

"I love that," says Slaughter, nodding approval. "I love hating people like that."

I point across the table. "I thought of you, actually. When I was sitting there hating him. It was just like you and Rory Scarsdale."

Something happens then in Slaughter's face and, it seems, throughout the bar. The lights are lowered in acknowledgment of evening, voices grow subdued, the jukebox music shrieks and grates. Night falls all at once.

It takes me a moment to realize what's happening.

Slaughter just sits there, letting silence fill up his turn to talk. His mouth hangs open and his eyes have wandered off—he grows a crease between his eyebrows. It's like he's listening to a distant, unfamiliar voice.

"What's the thing with Scarsdale, anyway?" I say. "Is it because he threw you out the one time?"

Slaughter grips the edge of the table, causing our beer mugs to shudder.

And then Slaughter starts talking like this:

"It's because there are all these fucking men, all right? And they're saying stuff and showing you . . . like . . . all this neat stuff. And you don't know, you just go along, right? Because you figure they know what they're doing. And everybody's supposed to be fucking friends. You're sitting around and it's like, Okay! This is how it is, I get it, and it must be true because they say so, we're looking out for each other, you know? And then one day the fucker hands you a shovel. And he's like, dig. And you're like, why? And he's like, because I fuckin' told you to dig. And you're like, well that's not a good enough reason, that's not, it's not *reasonable,* and everything you told me before, it's all—like all of your reasons are based on . . . on *reasonability,* right?"

"Charles," I say, looking around.

"And it's like they hate you all of a sudden! And then you're thinking that maybe they hated you all along! And maybe this was all a big fucking ploy! And maybe the whole deal was to just get you *here,* in the middle of a *yard,* with this goddamn *shovel* in your hand, as if everything's been your fault all along and they've just been waiting to *punish* you and make you *suffer* for it!"

"Charles," I say, "people are . . ."

"I didn't do anything, Campbell!"

He's yelling at me.

"I know, Chuck," I tell him.

We stare at each other. The bar has gone quiet and noisy all at once. That is, it's so quiet, tiny noises like coughing and pouring and muttering seem amplified.

"I gotta—" says Slaughter, looking slowly around. "Fuckin.'"

"Chuck?" I say. "How you doing?"

"I gotta call Mitts. I'll be right back."

And then, instead of pushing himself away from the table, Chuck pushes the table away from himself and beer flops itself from the mugs, onto me and everywhere else.

When I look up, Slaughter's gone. I flag the waitress for help and she comes with a rag and tells me that I, and my university compatriots in general, are slobs and idiots to a man.

"Little Lord Fauntleroys," the waitress keeps repeating, never raising her head to look at me as she sops the spilled beer. "Every one of you kids. Townload of Little Lord Fauntleroys flouncing around. Doing whatever the hell you please."

I sit at the bar for the next half hour or so, not self-conscious about it because there is such a fuss of activity all around me that the fact of my being here alone isn't pathetically apparent. Besides, it feels kind of cool to be sitting at the bar by my lonesome. The poet, alone with his musings, needing drink but not company. It strikes me as a pose I might find Claude in.

After a while, though, I'm feeling bold and bored enough to let my eye wander around the bar, see if anyone is taking note of my poetic isolation. Just as I turn on my stool, Cousin Janet, whom I haven't seen since Little Billy's, walks in. She is with a gaggle of girls and looking thinner since Christmas.

"Hey, Larry!" Janet's eyes are glassy and wobbly as puddles. I'm fogged by a dual waft of patchouli and vodka fumes.

"Janet," I say. "You're half-cut."

"I'm fully cut," says Janet. "I'm fully cut, *mon cuz.* You have to meet all my friends!" And the next twenty minutes or so are lost in a disorienting deluge of hails and sloppy, hollered introductions. The other girls are as fully cut as Janet, shine-eyed, rose-cheeked, and they all seem delighted to meet me. One of them yells that they have been having a party. Another yells that Janet is the best friend she's ever had. Janet bellows like a cow and hugs this person before leaning into me and explaining the party was for her. A going away party. A congratulations party.

Whooo! The girls suddenly exclaim in unison and raise their drinks. I'm starting to feel a bit overwhelmed.

"For Columbia?" I holler to Janet.

"Yes," she says. "For Columbia!"

"Are you excited?" I yell.

"I don't know," Janet yells back, staring at me through the puddles of her eyes.

"You don't know?" I repeat.

"I don't know," she says. "I'm drunk. I'm just drunk. That's all I know for now." Janet grins at me, face shining and slick.

"What about your folks?" I say, not sure what I'm asking, but speaking intuitively.

Janet shakes her head. "They don't care what I do anymore. Nobody cares. Who cares?"

Janet yells the "Who cares?" around at her friends and they all raise a bizarre hybrid racket of mournful celebration. One of them throws her arms around Janet.

"We care," she keens. "We love you!"

"I love you guys too!" Janet yells, turning from me—just getting lost in her friends for a while.

Another half hour later I'm back at the bar about to place an order of margaritas for Janet's gang when in the mirror I notice Charles Slaughter lumbering up behind me wearing the same open-mouthed, distant-eyed expression he had when he shoved the table away.

"Chuck," I say, turning.

"Fuckwit," he acknowledges. On the stool beside me is a girl's purse, and on the stool beside the purse, a girl. "Anyone sitting here?" Chuck asks the girl, lurching toward her as if the floor has suddenly shifted beneath his feet.

The girl looks way up at Slaughter, having to lean back slightly. I can see a decision being made. "My—" she stammers, gesturing at her purse. "My bag is."

Slaughter looks down at the bag, swoops it up in one of his paws and places it in the girl's lap as he sits down.

"Well, now *my* bag is," he tells her.

The girl is hardly charmed. The girl, who is pretty but not intimidatingly so, whom I was thinking I might talk to at some point, gets up and leaves.

"Gallant," I say to Chuck.

Slaughter just ahems and places his hands in front of him, staring at himself in the mirror behind the bar.

"Did you talk to Sherrie?" I ask.

Slaughter's arms are such that just resting them on the bar means he can almost reach over and grasp the inside of it. He leans forward a little, and does exactly that. The position reminds me of a guy on a police show—a plainclothes cop having leapt on the hood of the getaway car, braced for a long and dangerous ride.

"I dunno," says Slaughter. "Yeah. Mittens is mad at me."

"Still?"

"She's mad at me," says Slaughter.

I watch him for a moment or two. Slaughter hasn't taken his eyes from his reflected eyes in the mirror since he sat down.

"Charles," I begin.

"Lawrence," says Charles, stopping the words in my mouth, because Slaughter has never addressed me by name since I've known him. "I think you should get away from me. I think I'm going crazy."

32.

SOMETHING HAPPENS. The evening goes mad. It's not just Chuck, soon it's me too, and everybody. I only remember drinking one margarita, but it felt like I drank it for an awfully long time. Green, sweet, and numbing.

I find a pay phone and call Sherrie. Ring, ring. She's there. Something Slaughter. Something crazy. He thinks you're mad at him, he's losing it, Sherrie. You have to come.

Yeah, I am, I am mad at him. There's no talking to him, Lawrence, he thinks he can get himself all fucked up and then come over and have a serious conversation with me, it's ridiculous.

But he's really messed up right now, I don't know what to say to him.

I know he's messed up. I almost called campus security to get rid of him. I told him I'm not going to deal with him when he's like that.

Come, I say, and my voice feels like it's happening above my head. Please come. Like someone else is doing the talking.

Sherrie's voice goes wah-wah in my ear for a while, like the grown-ups in a Charlie Brown cartoon. One of Janet's friends comes over carrying a blue cocktail and yells and laughs holding it up to my face until I agree to have some.

It's good! I say.

It's not good, says Sherrie, whom I can suddenly understand again. It's not good, Lawrence.

What's not good?

This thing with Charles. It's not good.

I can feel myself drifting again, eyes bouncing lazily, balloonlike, around the bar. They alight on Janet, on her friends as they dance and swoon together, football players, the angry waitress. I want to drop the phone but a lone remaining tadpole of coherence thrashes its way to the surface of my brain, pokes its head out, demanding to be heard.

But why? asks the tadpole. Why are you so mad at Chuck anyway?

Scarsdale, says Sherrie, and now I've lapsed back to catching Charlie Brown snippets as the crowd seems to swell then subside like the middle of the ocean. Wah-wah *whores,* says Sherrie in the distance. Wah-wah *sores.* He wasn't kidding about that, Lawrence. He wasn't kidding about any of that stuff.

One of Janet's friends tells me her name is Susan, and I seize upon this. Susan, I say. Susan, can I tell you something, Susan?

Susan is laughing at me. Janet is nearby. Susan tells Janet I'm hilarious.

But, Susan, I say. Listen to me will you Susan?

He is so fucked up, says Susan.

Not he, Susan. Not he. Me. Come on Susan I'm right here.

Okay, I'm sorry I'm sorry but it's funny.

Okay.

So, says Susan. What is it Lawrence? What would you like to say?

Here's what it is. Here it is Susan. *Poetry.*

Susan looks at Janet, is about to say something, but then remembers—*not he.* So looks back at me.

What? says Susan.

He really likes poetry, explains Janet.

Not he! I yell. Me!

He's getting upset, says Susan.

And so I am. I get up, and they call for me not to go.

I go. I don't know where I go.

It's dark and warm and soft, the place I happen to be.

Sherrie, I say. Oh, Brenda L.

Her laughter is dark and warm and soft.

The sun glares in at me through gauzy white curtains; curtains which actually seem to embrace the light instead of keeping it out. The curtains pull the sun into the room, fling it around. I'm on a couch, and not in the mood to leave it any time soon, more in the mood to turn over and lose my face in its cavernous dust-smelling crevasse, which is what I do.

A no-thought period ensues for a while, here in the dark of the couch, which I enjoy. I shove my fingers into its depths and feel around. Crumbs, and cool metal springs. I feel blindly for a while, groping like a baby, for no purpose but sensation.

Then the brain starts up. Suddenly, horribly. The raisin of dread leaps to attention, shockingly none the worse for wear after last night. Nourished, it would seem, on margaritas. Enlivened.

There are only two I can think of. Lord Byron and Edgar Allan Poe.

It seems typical of a Little Lord Fauntleroy like Byron, totally in keeping with his entitled, nothing-off-limits approach toward the world. I don't like that Byron is one. I'm not supposed to have anything in common with Byron.

All I really know about Edgar Allan Poe is that, coincidentally enough, he was a huge fan of Byron. So points off Poe right there. And, since Poe got famous as a writer of horror stories, I assume I can safely dismiss his poetry. I always envisioned Poe as being like the pencil-moustachioed Vincent Price in the Hollywood Horrors—a kind of cartoon creep. The thing with his cousin confirmed that image.

With Byron, it was his half-sister Augusta Leigh. It was a huge scandal and he had to leave London. That's the limit, society told him. It's been very flamboyant and Dionysian and all, but that's about as much as we can take from you, Byron.

Poe's cousin's name was Virginia. She was thirteen when he married her, and he loved her faithfully until she died.

I turn over again, masochistically allowing the sunlight to rake my eyes, not just because I know I deserve to suffer, but because I've realized all at once how very important it is for me to get up and leave right now. I'm fully clothed, thank God, and suddenly hot. One of Grandma Lydia's knitted afghans has been thrown on top of me at some point. I fling it away, and months of settled dust takes wing, riding the sunbeams. I feel suffocated. I sneeze. The sneeze is bad, it shakes things loose, wakes things up I'd rather keep dormant.

Temporarily unable to leap to my feet and bolt out the door, therefore, I let myself lie back to gather strength and do some thinking. I think to myself that there are only a few months left of school. I avoided her most of last semester, certainly I can avoid her for most of this one. If I am very careful, I might well be able to avoid her until September, when she'll be safely across the border, Big Apple bound, out of sight and memory.

And now it is imperative I try and sit up again.

———

It's a perfect day for hating, the hangover shaping itself into a thundercloud behind my eyes, and I take my seat in the back rows, primed for hatred, ready to seethe and writhe. Seethe and writhe—this reminds me of how I used to mishear the national anthem when I was a kid. Only a geek who read dictionaries for fun would misinterpret such a simple construction as "we see thee rise" as "we seethe and writhe," but the *thee* threw me off, and that's what I thought it was for years. *With glowing hearts, we seethe and writhe, our true north strong and free.*

Creighton's wearing his signature white shirt and a skinny Texas-oilman tie, but today, perhaps since he's in his academic's hat, we're favoured with the requisite tweed sports jacket. Once the bifocals get positioned just above the pinkish bulb of his nose, the professorial picture is complete.

So where's the hate? By all rights it should be rising like bile at this point, but I can't seem to really get it going today. My mood is black, no question, but the rest of my being is otherwise exhausted from the surreal excesses of the night before. Maybe my raisin of hatred has been toppled for the time being. Maybe that's how it works. Maybe different brands of booze knock out different cerebral raisins.

More likely is that I am finding Creighton less obnoxious out of his poet's hat. He's talking about Canada today, and how wonderful a place it is. It's sort of soothing to listen to. Our nation glimmers, he tells us, with potential and cultural distinctiveness. By some, it has been called a "frontier"—and these people mean the word to have less than flattering connotations. But it is indeed a frontier, affirms Creighton. A new frontier, an intellectual frontier, still being shaped by the precious raw materials that we are fortunate enough to claim as our birthright.

Around me, on occasion, I hear sighs. Sighs of boredom, sighs of impatience—the standard thing at lectures. Still, some of the sighs sound more pertinent than others, more deliberate—closer to actual comments. At one point, as Creighton scoldingly asks the students present how many of us plan to do graduate work outside of the country, one sigh comes at me with particular vehemence, and because I feel goosed by the question, I turn around to glare.

White-blue eyes meet mine, smiling, inviting collusion. I glance into the brown ones beside them, and the smile they send me is one of apology. Sitting even farther back than I am. They must have come in late. But why in God's name would he bring *her* to *this?*

Even more surprising, I note another latecomer, lingering in the back doorway, as extreme latecomers often do. Latecomers, but also people with a message to get across. A slouch to the shoulders, a loose, dismissive fold to the arms.

Before I can jerk my face forward again, he catches my eye. Another conspirator's smile. Another invitation—one I can't very well turn down.

The first thing I see, after emerging into the hallway after the lecture, is the mind-mussing triad of Jim, Creighton, and Robert A. Sparrow, department head. All of Jim's poet friends are gigantic like himself. He and Creighton loom over the dainty Sparrow. As I gape, Jim makes introductions, gesturing from one to the other. Sparrow extends a delicate scholar's hand to the crinkle-eyed Creighton.

The presence of Sparrow is the one force in the universe capable of prying Todd from the orbit of Jim and Creighton. He skulks a few feet away, pinning himself against a wall— seemingly trying to flatten and wriggle himself in behind a bulletin board.

I arrive at Todd before approaching the mirage farther down.

"They shook hands," Todd whispers. "Just a second ago. Sparrow, like, *hailed* him. And walked over there. And they shook hands."

"Well—that's good," I say.

Todd shakes his head. "I don't like it."

"They're smiling," I observe. But are they? Their mouths are smiling—corners turned up. Although Creighton has one of those odd, droll smiles where the corners turn down. But his is not either of the smiles Todd and I are interested in.

"They *look* like they're smiling," I amend.

"They're putting it on for each other." Todd sounds like he's begging. "You can tell they can't stand each other."

At the same moment as I take a step forward, Sparrow makes gestures of self-extraction from the triad. He bows toward Creighton, shakes his hand a second time. A quick farewell remark to Jim, who nods—smiling? Smirking? Either way, Sparrow is now fully extracted and hoofing his small-boned way toward Todd and me. Todd pulls his head in like a turtle, turns, and faces the bulletin board. He mutters to himself as if reading, as if it were possible to read documents when they're shoved practically up your nose.

I do nothing to adjust my naked gape, however. So, unlike Todd, Sparrow takes me into account.

"Hello, Lawrence," he nods, he slows, but slightly.

"Hi, Sir."

"You haven't been to see me of late."

"No," I say.

"Make an appointment with Marjorie," he calls over his shoulder. "We must get caught up."

Instead, I follow him down the hall. Todd is long gone in the opposite direction.

"Do you have a minute now, Sir?"

"I have a minute. I'm on my way to a meeting—you can walk with me, can you?"

"Sure," I say. We walk. Down the stairwell—flinging loud, echoing footfalls into the air around us—and out the door. Into the quad, where the freakish warmth of an early thaw hits us.

"This is lovely," says Sparrow, inhaling rot. "This warm spell we're having."

I look around at the bare trees, the yellow grass. "It'll be depressing," I remark, "when the cold hits again."

"Never," avows Sparrow. "I can't believe that winter ever was."

"One of the worst blizzards I ever saw," I tell him, "was in late April, after everything had melted. Birds were back, crocuses were coming up. Knocked out the phones and electricity for weeks."

Sparrow laughs at me. "Do stop, Lawrence," he entreats. "You'll have me heading straight for the English stairwell."

That's the Westcock euphemism for suicide.

I walk Sparrow across the quad to the Administration building without managing to make any further conversation.

"Well—here we are," he prompts. He turns to me in front of the building's Gothic double doors.

"How did you like the talk, Sir?" I ask, voice girlish with a strained attempt at casualness.

Sparrow's eyes flutter behind his glasses. Often when we speak I've noticed I find myself wishing he'd take off his glasses. Sometimes I twitch to simply lean forward and bat them off his face.

"The talk?" repeats Sparrow.

"The lecture," I say.

"Oh, just now, you mean! Well, I found it very interesting, Lawrence."

Sparrow's eyes are a dark, muddy blue, if that's possible.

Blue murk, like the marsh from a distance on the clearest of days. And he's shorter than me, too. I've never noticed that before.

"Did you," I say. "Do you think it's accurate? What Creighton said?"

"Mister Creighton? Oh yes, I suppose he did make some good points."

Sparrow glances at his right wrist, which is bare. He frowns slightly, then raises his left, which sports a watch. Sparrow beams down at it like you would a newborn babe.

"Ah, I'm late," he coos. "I must be off, Lawrence."

All of a sudden, I'm Slaughter. I'm my cousin Wayne. That is to say, a dumb bloodlust descends and I want nothing more than to grab that bird-boned wrist of his. Sparrow is a shrimp! I could take him. I could yank his wrist behind his back, and up, up, up, until he squealed. Then might be the time to inquire why he's been waving his Oxford bullshit under my nose these past few months—simultaneously shooing me off poetry like a fly from a pie.

"But," I say, wringing my hands to keep them from flying out at him. "I mean . . . do you think that's something I should be thinking about? What Creighton said, about not doing graduate work in Canada?"

Sparrow hauls on one of the double doors, grunting slightly with the effort. He looks like a child in a fairy tale— Jack sneaking into the giant's castle.

"Indeed, indeed," he tells me, nodding with vehemence. "He's absolutely right. There's no point doing graduate work in Canada. None at all, just as the man said. But do come see me before exams, Lawrence."

His voice is echoing now, throughout the lobby of Administration. "We'll talk about your course load for next year."

The door heaves itself shut between us.

———

I don't know what it is, but I go directly home after this conversation. I sit down at the typewriter without taking off my jacket or boots, type up a bunch of my new ghazals, and put them in an envelope addressed to Dermot Schofield at Ralston University. I walk to the post office and, on impulse, fork over some extra coin to send the letter express. Not just to expedite things, but because I know it will make the missive look like something official—something far too important to pass on to the lowly likes of Joanne or one of her fellow editorial barracudas.

Now it's Friday night and I still feel hungover from Wednesday. It's the oddest hangover so far. I haven't felt sick. What I feel is *decelerated,* like a movie in slo-mo. Minutes drag. Walking home from campus, I noticed how the wind seemed to crawl up my body like a big, sun-stupefied lizard. I forget about my kettle, it takes so long to boil. Big Blue refuses to steep.

In particular, my thought process. I dwell. I linger. I'm not able to yank my thoughts up and away from a particular notion in my usual yo-yo-like fashion. It's a handy skill of self-preservation, the ability to bounce one's thoughts away from unsavoury truths like a flea escaping a looming thumb. That's what I've been doing a lot of lately. Not much dwelling. Very little lingering. And now that the hangover has forced the condition on me—made measured thought compulsory—I understand why.

Because there's this bland checklist in my head. I always make checklists when I'm studying—it's the final step of my overall regimen, which begins with the taking of detailed notes in class that I write out over and over again in my notebooks, gradually trimming the information of any superfluous detail, so that eventually all I have left on the page are a series of points. A list. Gleaming gems of information, polished into the perfection of a mere handful of words. Concepts, dense with meaning. Study-poems.

Because apparently my subconscious has been honing all the experiences of the past few months down into a similar kind of list, just waiting for the right moment to present it— neatly typed, in point form, unassailable—to my conscious mind.

Because it's like this:

- The head of my department, upon whose good graces my potential academic career hangs, is either malicious or dense—one or the other.
- I had some sort of sexual congress with my first cousin on Wednesday night.
- This is something hillbillies do.
- I think the poetry of Abelard Creighton is a joke.
- Jim Arsenault doesn't think the poetry of Abelard Creighton is a joke.
- I think Jim Arsenault is a genius.
- I want to be a good poet. I want to be a genius.
- I have no idea what good poetry is.
- *I know what I like.* This is the cry of the dilettante.
- Dilettante: *n:* A dabbler in the arts, or field of knowledge. See *amateur.*

Furthermore:

- *If* Jim Arsenault is a genius, *then* I need Jim Arsenault to take me seriously as a poet.
- I need Jim Arsenault to love me.
- Because that will mean I have worth. That will mean there is a point. That will mean I am not a PEI hillbilly going *hyuck-hyuck,* chawing on a

sprig of hay (or in my case maybe a hunk of raw potato), and poking around with his first cousin.

- It will mean, instead, that I am a free spirit, an iconoclast, a brilliant, unfettered Dionysian soul from admittedly humble means—which makes my literary ascendancy all the more astonishing.
- The Real Thing.
- The truth I am not.

Finally:

- Jim Arsenault has been messing around with my grades. With my head. With my poetry.
- There is no possible universe wherein the above could be interpreted as gestures of esteem.

33.

AT CREIGHTON'S RECEPTION, Todd and I stand on either side of a table eating steadily from a plate heaped with cheese cubes, as though we are in competition. I use a toothpick to spear them one by one, but Todd just stands gobbling the cheese by the handful. If it *were* a competition, he'd be winning.

"Corpse of milk," I say after a moment or two. Watching Todd has subdued my interest in the cheese somewhat.

"Whaf?" says Todd behind his hand.

"Cheese," I say. "Joyce."

Todd chews and swallows before replying. "Joyce," he sneers.

"He's an Irishman," I say. "Catholic boy like yourself. Doesn't he win any points there?"

"The Irish don't even like him," Todd says. "Most of them don't even know who he is."

His teeth are bright orange. I look away, around.

Creighton's final reading was an embarrassment for all concerned, though no one has acknowledged it, and Jim and the visiting poet himself seem genuinely oblivious. Grayson Hall was cavernous in its extreme lack of audience. It's been renovated to seat a hundred at least. There were about seventeen of us in attendance—the only locals being a smattering of granny types. Old ladies in their hats and gloves, desperate for diversion, something to nibble at their intelligences besides doilies and church. Mrs. Dacey not among them.

By the entrance, Sherrie is quietly tearing a strip off Charles Slaughter, who stands with his arms folded, staring grimly ahead like one of the Queen's guards at Buckingham Palace. The reading was a particular embarrassment to Sherrie, because Slaughter lumbered in about halfway through and started belching her name. Her other name.

"Mittens. Mitts! Mitts, Mitts! Mittens!" The belching tone, I could only assume, was Slaughter's attempt at a whisper.

Creighton had stopped reading and given a baleful crinkle. A fart in church—that's exactly what it was like. *Well, that went over like a fart in church,* my mother used to say in moments of social indecorum.

"It would seem someone's mittens are lost," the poet remarked. Tart, puckered lips. Another expression of my parents' drifted to mind—my father this time: *Mouth on him like a hen's hole.*

I hadn't been expecting it, Dad's voice, Dad's words, so clear and wry—which made things worse for Sherrie when I burst out laughing. Her hands went red and she scrambled down the aisle, hunkering down, practically crawling on all fours.

Todd notices me watching the pair of them and turns to look for himself, grinning when he takes into account the pissed-off hunch to Sherrie's shoulders. Whatever she's been saying has finally penetrated Slaughter's demeanour—he glares around the room like a bouncer seeking provocation. Waiting for someone to slip up, be bad.

Todd smirks around his cheese, blowing crumbs. "Never thought I'd see a guy that big so whipped."

"Claude didn't even bother to come," I note after a while.

"Claude," says Todd, the same way he said *Joyce*. Which makes me a little jealous of Claude.

Dink-dink-dink! A sound reaches us. *Dink-dink-dink!* Jim stands shoulder to shoulder with Creighton alongside the table where Creighton has been swapping books for cash. Every granny now has a signed copy tucked into her bag.

Dink-dink-dink! Jim is tapping on a wine glass with a knife, so hard it makes me cringe.

"Shh!" scolds a granny, and everyone does.

"Everybody!" says Jim. "Well, now. I just wanna thank you all for coming tonight to this very special event, and I'd like you to join me in thanking Abe Creighton for a wonderful week—for having enlightened and entertained us. This guy, I think you'll agree, this guy talks a lot about cultural resources. Well, he's one of the richest founts we have."

Everyone smiles and heh-hehs and then, at Jim's instigation, we clap. It was a clumsy remark, delivered like a joke, cueing laughter as opposed to eliciting it. But Jim's mood, Jim's smile, is not to be denied. It's grown a bit goofy in the last half hour or so. There is something in the air, tickling everyone's expectations like a communal sneeze.

"Jim's looped," Todd mutters with approval.

"Thank you," Creighton calls around to us, raising hands like the pope. He turns to Jim in the wake of applause and gives his shoulder a squeeze, speaking into his ear. Jim nods and signals for quiet.

"All right," says Jim. "To hell with it. It's a bit early to be making this announcement, but I look around and I see I'm among friends. Good friends—some of the best I've ever had. It's been a rough few months for me, as most of you are aware. But even such trying times as these—you know—it makes you realize there's a reason for everything. You learn, under this kind of pressure, and you learn fast. I learned who my friends were, and that's been invaluable and heartening—very heartening I'd like to say. That's what got me through this very difficult year: your friendship."

The grannies, who have no idea what he's talking about, are nonetheless transfixed. When we break into applause, it's a granny who's initiated it.

Smiles all around. Jim's teeth, Creighton's teeth (yellowed, like his hair), and, a few feet away, Dekker's teeth. Dekker knows what's coming, I can tell. There's not a hint of expectancy on his face, which is more relaxed than I think I've ever seen it in Jim's presence.

Ruth Dekker hasn't bothered to put in an appearance either. Ruth and Claude. They're the only two people who can make themselves more present in their absences.

"Listen, I'm lousy at giving speeches, so I'll get to the meat of this thing," Jim continues once the cheers have died. It's fortunate the lobby of Grayson Hall is more cloistered that the auditorium—the cheers possess power, conviction. I don't like to think how mewling they would have sounded within. Creighton's applause had come across like splatters of paint hitting the ground.

"First, I'd like you all to know," says Jim, eyes dancing around the room, "that in response to everyone's efforts and support, the administration has agreed to reconsider my application for tenure. Second, I'd like everyone present to come to my home and drink themselves silly tonight in celebration."

———

Squeaks, gasps. And then a huge communal roar and it's nothing but clapped backs, pumped hands, even a hug or two. One of the hugs, authored by Todd, is received by me. He practically leaps across the tray of cheese the moment the announcement is made. Doubly stunned, I do nothing in return. Todd draws back so fast I'm not sure it happened for a moment. It's like in Superman comics, when Superman saves you with super speed. One moment you're in the path of an oncoming bus, you blink, and you're on the sidewalk.

I stare at him with a cube of de-toothpicked cheese crushed to putty in my right hand. Todd smiles and shakes his head in a gesture of disbelieving glee.

"All right!" he exclaims. "Far out! Can you believe it, man?"

And in his need to make a celebratory gesture, in his struggle to negate the uncool display of a second ago, Todd instigates a ritual I would never have expected from him. He extends his hand palm up for me to slap.

I place my cheese in it and wander away.

It's funny. I should be dancing. I should have smacked Todd's grubby white palm with gusto. I should have hugged him back, at least, bashed him between the shoulder blades the way guys do. Instead, I'm moving through the crowd as if inside a sturdily shimmering bubble. Maybe the news just hasn't registered yet. This is good news, yes? This is *great* news. Jim Arsenault is at Westcock to stay.

I float into the presence of Slaughter and Sherrie.

Sherrie is saying, "I'm not your mother, you know—I'm not available to you around the clock—whenever you just decide you want to hang out."

"I know you're not my fucking mother," answers Chuck. He's got a vague, angry look on his face as though annoyed to be not exactly sure where he is.

"I know—I'm sorry, I didn't mean that," Sherrie says quickly. "Anyway, this is Jim's night. Lawrence!" She catches sight of me in my bubble and I get another hug—a visceral reminder—warmth in the middle of the frozen marsh.

"It's so great about Jim! Oh my God, what a relief!"

She pulls away, revealing Slaughter's face to me from behind her nimbus of hair. His face has changed a little now that I'm here. His eyes have focused in—narrowed, even—whatever that means. It's something I've always read in books—depictions of people's eyes narrowing, but I could never picture what it meant. Now I have a picture. Slaughter's muddy brown ones turning sharp, honing in.

"Chuck," I say. "Are you all right?"

"He's on something—he won't tell me what it is." Sherrie twists her mouth.

"I'm all right," Slaughter barks. Very much at me. I decide it would be prudent to resume my drift through the crowd at this point.

Next I arrive at Bryant Dekker, in his own little bubble, standing against a wall a few feet away from where Creighton and Jim are holding court over a congratulatory clutch of departing grannies. They congratulate Jim, whom they don't know but whom they assure they are very happy for, and thank Creighton for his enlightening performance.

"You know, I usually don't even *care* for poetry," I hear one of the women confide in a marvelling tone.

"Lawrence," greets Dekker, pumping my hand. "What do you say?"

"Great news," is what I say.

"I thought *you'd* be pleased," he grins. "It's all paid off—everyone's faith and hard work. Gives a person renewed hope in the entire system."

Together we watch Creighton and Jim smile and press frail hands.

"Is the system that hopeless?" I ask after a moment or two.

Dekker turns to look at me. "You mean the university? Well. I shouldn't be cynical. I was a bit idealistic about the whole thing when I started, I suppose. Those old illusions die hard."

I nod. We watch Jim and Creighton some more. Jim catches my eye. The famous wink.

"Not that there's anything wrong with idealism," amends Dekker, sipping from a plastic glass of wine. "That's what gets you there in the first place."

"If," I say, "it's where you truly want to be."

Dekker nods and scratches a bristled cheek. This seems like the last thing we should be talking about, with people celebrating all around us.

"Did you always want to be a professor?" I ask.

"Oh God." Dekker smiles and drains his wine convulsively. "I don't know if anyone starts out wanting to be a *professor*. I wanted education, and everything that represented. I wanted to read great works and sit at the feet of masters and just—soak everything up. You have to understand my background. Maybe certain temperaments just fixate on having the one thing they're told over and over again is impossible for them. Maybe if people had told me over and over again I could never be a farmer, I'd be in South Africa right now, turning soil."

Dekker smiles some more. He's reminding me of someone right now. The self-conscious wriggling around, the confessional, apologetic demeanour. Dermot Schofield discussing the love of his life.

Over by the book table, Jim beckons to me, saying something in Creighton's ear. Creighton glances over with interest, peppered eyebrows at full mast. Jim gestures again, waving a copy of *True North,* Creighton's prizewinning claptrap. I smile, hold up a finger, and turn back to Dekker.

"I was told all my life I *could* have it," I tell him. "That it was a really rare and special thing, but I could have it because I was rare and special too."

"Then you were very fortunate, Lawrence," says Dekker, drawing himself in a bit.

I think about it. My parents giving up their stately Georgian inn for the hicky Highwayman. Just to get me somewhere like Westcock.

"So you didn't know what you wanted to do?" I ask Dekker. "You just went into it—education—as an end in itself?"

"Well, I was probably a bit more single-minded than most." He bows his head meditatively. "It would never have happened," he tells me, "if it weren't for the bank. None of it—I wouldn't be here. Our farm was doing poorly and the bank kept sending my father these official letters. Written in English, which nobody in my family could read. So I got sent to school to learn to read and write English because I was the youngest. Well, from the first day I realized that the moment everything was worked out with the bank was the moment I'd be pulled out of school and put back to work. I was told as much."

I didn't think it was possible for Dekker to come from what was clearly a bigger pile of sticks than where I'm from. Imagine a place where even sending a kid to school is seen as big-feeling—as putting on airs.

"So what did you do?" I ask, striving to sound less fascinated than I am.

"I started writing the bank, in secret," he tells me. "I wrote them every month—sometimes more—under my father's name, which happened to be the same as mine. I asked them inane questions—whatever I could think up. Pretty soon I struck up a correspondence with the head teller—he became a kind of pen pal. His letters would arrive on bank stationery and I'd tell my father it was just details about his loan, financial gobbledegook, nothing too worrisome, but a *little bit* worrisome, or so I would hint because I didn't want my father getting too comfortable. Really, my teller friend would be responding to my last letter, telling me about his day, what his wife cooked him for dinner, and so forth."

"How long?" I demand in amazement. "How long did you have to write this guy?"

"I wrote him every month, right up until the month I graduated from high school," shrugs Dekker, a coolness coming through in his tone. "And then I got out of there. I never wrote to him again."

He looks at me and smiles, blinking like a baby who's just woken up.

"So your dad is named Bryant too?" I ask.

The smile disappears but not the vagueness. He seems to have no idea what I'm talking about.

"My father? Oh!" Dekker laughs. "No. My father's name was Obed. Bryant was—is—the name I chose for myself."

He looks away, embarrassment descending again.

"That's interesting," I say. I don't ask him why he changed his name from his father's because I can guess that one. "Why did you call yourself Bryant?"

Dekker sighs and rolls his eyes at himself. "Oh—I suppose I thought it sounded sophisticated. I was—Well, I'll be honest with you, Lawrence." He seems to make a decision and hunches toward me.

"I couldn't bring myself to change my name to Byron," he tells me, voice low—smile small and wry. "Which is what I really wanted to do. I thought Bryant sounded close to Byron."

I blink at him. "You liked Byron?"

"Liked?" repeats Dekker, cringing at the memory of his

young self—himself at more or less my age, it occurs to me now. "Worshipped is more like it. Byron—" Dekker shakes his head. "Ah, well, say what you will about Byron. With his skull, and his turban. But he's what got me out of there. I told myself: Byron existed, so that way of being had to exist as well—which meant there must be lots of ways of being. That's what I needed to believe. My father used to say to me, You really think it's any different anywhere else? You really think you can go somewhere and be any different, be any better than you are here?"

Dekker pauses to smirk at the memory and I realize our faces are just inches from one another. Over the noise of the crowd I've drawn closer and closer to hear him. I can see the follicles like an angry rash across his jawline, red and brutalized from hasty shaving.

"Byron was my proof," he tells me. "He was the most flamboyant refutation of my father that I knew of." Dekker glances at me, not quite able to keep his distancing smirk in place. We meet eyes and it feels for a moment like I've been grabbed by the shoulders.

And then: I *am* grabbed. I'm in a headlock.

34.

JIM, CORRALLING EVERYBODY for the next phase of celebration, which will take place at his house out at Rock Point. But first he finds it necessary to drag me by the head over to Abelard Creighton for proper introductions.

"Whaddya think yer doin'?" Jim demands on the way, sporting his full-on backwoods twang. "Can't even be bothered to tell a fella congratulations?"

"Congratulations," I call up from beneath his arm, laughing and choking.

"That's better."

And I'm released before Creighton, who stands in his white shirt and Texas tie, looking for all the world like Colonel Sanders.

"Here he is," announces Jim. Creighton extends a big warm hand.

"It's nice to meet you, son. Jim tells me you're his star protégé."

"Really?" I ask, grinning like a fool.

My bubble's been punctured and now I can feel the craziness in the air. Jim leans against me and I keep having to shift around on my feet in order to bear his weight. All around us, people seem to be shrieking laughter.

"Yes, indeed," Creighton affirms.

"I told him," Jim yells in my ear, "I said, this is your man right here, Abe—this is what you've been talking about all along. If anyone is gonna save Canadian poetry, it's Larry Campbell."

All I can do is laugh breathlessly at this.

A wine bottle gets knocked off the table and clunks noisily, emptily onto the polished floor. Jim is yelling around at everyone to get their coats.

It's hard not to watch the way Ruth watches Moira. She sits on the couch beside Dekker, draped in a shawl the colour of dried blood over a burgundy velvet dress. She looks like mulled wine. She is the best-dressed person in the room.

"Can I help you with anything?" she said to Moira upon our arrival.

Moira, in a pair of floppy-assed jeans, seemed physically unable to look upon Ruth. Her eyes kept darting toward and then bouncing away from her.

"I don't plan on doing a goddamn thing," she huffed. "Beer's in the fridge, food and wine's on the table. If anyone needs anything else they can talk to that one there." And jabbed her cigarette at Jim, crouched by his record player. "I been cutting fuckin' vegetables all afternoon." She held up her hands to show us where she had nicked herself in the process.

"Well, it's very nice to meet you," said Ruth after a glance at Dekker.

The comment met with Moira's back.

"Don't tease that dog," she was yelling, hustling her ass-less way across the room.

"She's so *thin*," murmured Ruth.

After a while, Panda gets shoved into the kitchen and guests are instructed to enter cautiously when they have to pass through to use the washroom or get a beer. By no means should they look Panda in the eye, or respond in any way to his ball-nudgings. So every time I go into the kitchen, I'm reminded of my dream. Panda crouched in the corner, gnawing, mad-eyed.

At some point, Jim has passed me my very own copy of *True North*. He bought it for me and got Creighton to inscribe it as a way of saying thanks, he told me. For all I've done throughout the year, all my friendship and support. I smiled up at him, thinking how much I would have preferred a signed copy of *Blinding White* since pages were starting to fall out of mine. Anyway, I smiled, thanked, and Jim hugged me for what felt like a good minute. He's been going around hugging everyone all night long, leaving sweetish wafts of rum-smell in his wake.

"Ah, kiddo," I heard him say. I could hear him speaking through his shoulder, which my ear was pressed against. The words seemed to vibrate their way directly from his vocal cords into my brain. "It's all been worth it, kid. The hordes have retreated—for the time being, anyway."

It struck me as funny that Jim thought of stodgy, traditionalist Westcock as the rampaging horde, himself as the desolate fortress under attack. You'd think it would be the other way around—Jim, the barbarian at the gate. It's like with all the old French forts perched on their wind-blasted hills up and down the coast—signifying either victory or defeat, depending on how you look at it.

Sherrie and Todd and a few others from class are being smart and taking advantage of Creighton's presence among us. That is to say, they are gathered more or less at his feet as he rocks in Jim's rocker pronouncing on God knows what while Jim calls merrily to him from time to time, to consult on matters such as what records to play and what he would like next to drink.

Slaughter looms against a nearby wall, having resumed his bouncer's posture. Or maybe it's that of a bodyguard. Even as I'm talking to him, his eyes stay on Sherrie, flickering at the every flick of her hand.

"How you doing, Chuck?"

"I'm all right."

"You seem kind of out of it tonight."

"I'm a bit fucked up," Slaughter admits. "I took something."

"Not another one of those capsules?"

"Nah. Something. I just fuckin' got it from a guy down at the Mariner. Put me in a bad mood."

"That's too bad."

"Yeah, it's a real fuckin' bummer if you wanna know the truth, Campbell."

Slaughter speaks like he's reading off a cue card. We stand in a not particularly friendly silence.

"Mitts keeps hassling me about it," he mutters a moment later.

"About what?"

"About taking stuff all the time. Like," Chuck unfolds his arms suddenly and becomes animated, grimacing and gesturing, "she doesn't get that guys are different than chicks. She's this tiny little person and I'm this great big person. She can't drink a couple of beer without getting shitfaced. I can handle whatever I take, she doesn't get that. It's drugs though, mostly. She thinks dope is dangerous."

"Hm." I'm trying to sound noncommittal.

"I go to her, look at Campbell. He's half as big as me, and it didn't hurt Campbell."

I gaze at Creighton as he leans toward Sherrie to impart some particularly savoury morsel of insight.

"Chuck?" I say after a moment or two. "*What* didn't hurt me? When we did the mushrooms at the Mariner that time?"

"The other night," says Chuck, resuming his surveillance of Sherrie. He refolds his arms. "Whatever it was we had at Quackers. Might be the same thing I'm on now."

I stare some more at Creighton and his crowd, mouth open.

My father: every single thing he warned me about the summer before I went off to Westcock—regarded by me at the time as nothing so much as an island bumpkin's rantings against the "big city"—is being replayed in my head.

Now, don't you go touching that wacky tabaccy, because people will tell you it's fine but it's not. You lose control and you can find yourself jumping out a window, or out in front of a car or some such thing—you saw those goddamn armpit sniffers on the news, they didn't know where the hell they were rolling around in the mud up there at that show in New York.

Dad—it's New Brunswick. It's a ferry ride away.

They send the drug dealers into all the university towns— they come up from the States. Sometimes it's the goddamn draft- dodging professors who do the deals, the way I hear it.

Dad—Westcock professors aren't drug dealers.

Well, you don't know, now, do ya? You've never been there now, have ya? This is my point—you don't even know what it is you're walking into. You go in there thinking, oh yah, this is just great, everybody's my friend and all that, and then some bastard you think is your friend sticks a needle in your ass, or slips some- thing in your drink at a party and then what happens?

Dad—nobody is going to

I have to go to the kitchen and drink a beer. I have to sit on the floor and pet Panda for a while. To calm myself, work through my rage. I can't yet tell if I'm more angry about Slaughter dosing me or about the fact that my father's been proven right about something other than lawnmowers or dif- ferent kinds of paint. How dare Slaughter side with my father in this way. How dare he exemplify every boneheaded, fear-mongering stereotype about our generation. How dare he make us look so bad, so foolish. So naive—above every- thing else.

Although I probably look quite serene, sitting here. People keep coming in to get beer or go to the can, and they always pause at the sight of me and Panda huddled so companionably.

"Aw," they'll say for the most part.

In comes Jim. He sees me here, cuddled up with his dog, smiles, and takes down a bottle of rum from a high shelf in one of the cupboards. It looks to me like it is a secret bottle of rum, one that's been kept from prying eyes. Without a word, he clinks a couple of glasses together in one hand, picking them up, and comes to sit on the floor across from me. Panda whines and nudges him the ball.

"Shut up," says Jim, replacing it beneath Panda's muzzle. He reaches over and starts scratching the dog between ears. Panda resigns himself and goes back to his obsessive gnawing.

"Well, then," Jim says, pouring me a drink. "Here's to us, and tonight. This fine, long-awaited celebration. To friendship, eh?"

I put my beer down on the floor beside me so I can accept the glass.

"To friendship," I say, shoving Slaughter from my thoughts and taking a sip.

Jim looks at me, smacking his lips. His rum is gone.

"You have to down it."

"Oh," I say. I close my eyes and down it. "I usually have it with Coke," I explain, blinking at him.

"The only thing you should mix with rum is spit," pronounces Jim, glass in the air as if he's making another toast. "Now, what are you hiding in here for, anyway? If you were smart, you'd be out there shooting the shit with old Crotch. He runs a small press out of Toronto."

"Does he?"

"Publishes a lot of first-timers, too, always on the lookout. I been chatting you up."

A first book, a Toronto press, maybe before I even graduate. I peer at him through my rum-watered vision. "Jeez. Thanks, Jim."

Jim smiles and meets my gratitude square in the eye. He knows exactly what he's doing for me, exactly how much it means.

"But I can't do all the work, so you get out there at some point, all right?"

"I will," I promise.

Jim pours us two more shots, in silence. If it could be always like this, I think in a kind of mourning. Just two men quiet on the kitchen floor together.

"Why do you call him Crotch?" I ask, just as Moira comes in. She notices us and takes a few steps forward, hands on her nonexistent hips.

"Oh, what?" huffs Jim, looking away.

"You're an arsehole, is what," says Moira. "You're a stupid cocksucker, is what." And then she turns, as they say, on her heel, and leaves without doing whatever she came in here to do.

Jim grins at me. "I told her I wouldn't." He raises his glass meaningfully, and knocks it back.

"Is she mad?" I ask, hoping she isn't. Not for Jim's sake in particular, but because I'm starting to feel there's a surplus of madness curdling the air tonight.

And so I just want to stay here for a moment, I just want to dwell on the ensuing half hour or so, when Jim and I sit talking and drinking by ourselves in the kitchen, muted crowd sounds coming to us from the next room. I just want to stay here because everything turns to shit so rapidly afterward.

This is the sacred moment, after all, the scenario I've been pursuing for the past two years—this is what I've dreamed of. *Dreamed* is a good word for it too, because the whole set-up has been a lot like a dream—one of those endlessly aggravating dreams where you come within a hair's breadth of getting what you want only to have it shimmer into nothing, or turn to something like mercury and slither between your fingers at the moment of attainment. Jim, I realize, is the White Rabbit. Jim is my White Rabbit, and I've been like Alice, diving heedlessly into Wonderland after him.

But all I've wanted is this, which is not such a big deal

really—which is not so much to ask. Alice wouldn't have been able to tell you what she wanted, but I've known what I wanted from the beginning. I just wanted this. To get Jim alone. To sit and talk, quietly, with Jim.

The amazing thing is, we don't even discuss poetry. True, it's Jim who does most of the talking. He tells me about Creighton. Not my favourite subject, but at the very least he expounds upon his fondness for the guy—which I assume explains his willingness to overlook the fact that "Crotch" is an atrocious poet. I mean, Jim has to know this, and at some point he's going to shoot me a black-eyed wink, an impishly meaningful look, which will blast all doubt from my head in this regard.

Creighton was one of his profs at U of T, he tells me as I sit waiting for the look. Creighton published an early chapbook of Jim's, one I've never heard of, to my surprise, and one Jim says I never want to read. ("Juvenilia," he dismisses.) The important thing, says Jim, is that Creighton gave him hope, and encouragement when he needed it most. He made Jim believe poetry was important enough to give his life to.

"That was a *gift*," emphasizes Jim. "You see that, Larry? That was the greatest gift I ever got."

"That's what you've done for me," I say. I just let myself blurt it out. I don't let myself think about it—how it sounds, how it might make me look in Jim's eyes. I don't care, I just say it.

Jim was in the process of downing another shot when I did. Now he lowers his glass and his thrown-back head slowly. He smiles, also slowly, and draws in breath to speak. I swallow in preparation for the words, am leaning toward him. His black eyes nestle themselves into mine. For the first time ever, the first time since we've met, I genuinely have the feeling that Jim sees me. I'm *here* for him suddenly, in a way I haven't been before—real and breathing and alive. More than that—I can tell he knows what I need to hear, I can see from the placid comprehension dawning in his face. At long last. Oh, long-awaited day.

35.

"UM," SAYS SHERRIE, embarrassed to be interrupting us, "Charles is crying."

Jim and I continue to sit spellbound for a second or two as our moment disintegrates around us. We glance at each other, then Jim pulls himself to his feet, weaves his way past Sherrie, and exits into the next room without a word.

"Slaughter's *what?*" I say.

"He's just standing there crying," says Sherrie.

Guilt and a low-key kind of horror take me by the guts. Horror at the thought of it—giant-man Slaughter crying in the middle of a party, people standing around watching, taking note.

"God," I say. "When did this start?" I'm positive it has to be my fault—what I said to him.

"I don't know, I just noticed it when I went over to talk to him. He's just *standing* there, Lawrence, with his arms folded, with tears rolling down his face."

I stand as if full of purpose, taking my glass and the bottle of rum with me. I place them on the table, but that's about as far as I get. Sherrie and I look at each other. Neither of us want to deal with this, it would seem. Neither of us want to go out there.

"Did he say anything to you, Lawrence?" Sherrie wants to know.

"He was being kind of an asshole when I spoke to him," I tell her, and Sherrie seems to levitate slightly, chewing her nails.

"He's pissed off at you, Lawrence. I should have said something, I'm sorry."

"Slaughter's angry at *me?*"

"It was that thing you said about him just wanting to get in my pants. I made a joke about it a few days ago. I knew— I mean, I didn't take it seriously."

I remember myself in Slaughter's dorm two days ago. Sitting so companionably on his bed. Slaughter with the hammer, destroying his desktop.

"Holy shit, Sherrie." I shake my head and have to lean against the table, legs gone to juice. It's like I've been dangling on the edge of the Grand Canyon all week and have only just looked down. "You told him about the *marsh?*"

She shakes her head rapidly. "I only told him what you said. That one thing."

"Well, why in God's name would you tell him something like that?"

Sherrie stares up at me, her guilt-spark abruptly extinguished. Now it's a different kind of spark.

"I don't know, Lawrence," she snaps. "Maybe it was the same reason you'd say what you did to me."

And so the guilt-spark gets transferred. It was me all along. I'm the guy my dad warned me about. I'm the friend who can't be trusted.

"His mother died last year," Sherrie tells me.

I try to imagine it, and find that I can't.

"Oh, man," I say.

"He goes out, he gets as messed up as he possibly can, and then he calls and begs me to come over. And then he just cries all night, Lawrence."

"Jesus Christ," I say, controlling the urge to cover my ears. Why do I not want to hear this so much?

Then Jim returns with an entourage, as noisy as he was quiet when he left the kitchen a moment ago. Jim has an arm around Slaughter, babbling about how good and okay everything is going to be, and Creighton is walking ahead lecturing them both on the salutary effects of ice water. Todd trails behind as though tethered to the bunch of them.

Jim sits Slaughter down at the table, keeping up a steady stream of patter, and not taking his hands off Chuck, as if he fears that the moment he does, Slaughter will leap to his feet and do or say something irrevocable. So as Jim speaks, he punctuates and embellishes with soothing, miniature pats and the kneading of muscles.

"Yahhh, the big guy just needs a shot of coffee or some such thing, wha? Maybe something to eat, eh, Chuck? You try any of them cocktail wieners we got out there, I bought those just for you, now . . ."

Creighton, meanwhile, is bashing an ice tray against the counter, undertaking his own non-stop line of patter, with which he occasionally responds to Jim.

"Ice water is the thing, I always keep a tall glass of ice water at my side these days, keeps the senses sharp, the sufferings of the morning after at bay—oh good Lord, Jimmy, don't offer him those, surely you have real food to put before the young man . . ."

I remember this from being a kid. Bee stings, the ball in the face. This is what men do when boys cry. They talk and talk loud until it's over.

It's odd, because Slaughter's face hasn't changed. It hasn't crumpled, or otherwise contorted. It's exactly the same as when I spoke to him earlier. Closed, impenetrable, like a building boarded up. The only thing is the tears, the blood-shot eyes.

"It's just the drugs," I hear Slaughter say.

"Oh, for Christ's sake, Chuck, that's what you goddamn well deserve if you're gonna take that crap," complains Jim.

"What'd you take?" inquires Todd.

"I don't fucking know," says Slaughter.

"That's right responsible now, isn't it," says Jim.

"There now!" Creighton places a plastic tumbler of water, clunking and brimming with ice cubes, in front of Chuck. "Sip that slowly, young man. Bracing."

Slaughter scoops a chunk of ice from the cup and places it in his mouth. I watch him, wincing because Chuck is chewing the ice too slowly. I can feel my teeth start to ache from the roots.

All the while, Jim grinds tiny circles into Chuck's shoulders with his thumbs. Slaughter doesn't appear to notice, just keeps staring straight ahead.

"How's that?" Jim keeps asking. "How's that now? Ya want anything else?"

"I'm all right," says Chuck, chomping away. He scoops a couple more ice cubes from the cup. Creighton, I notice, is also watching the ice-chewing performance with some discomfort crinkling his face.

"Drink, boy," he commands. "Take a nice long sip of that, now."

"Where's Sherrie?" says Chuck, not looking around. "Mittens?"

"I'm right here, Charles," says Sherrie.

"Where's Claude?" says Slaughter.

Jim looks over at Sherrie and me, and Sherrie and I look at each other.

"I called him when we got here," Sherrie tells Chuck. "He wasn't around."

Slaughter closes his eyes, picks up the tumbler, and drinks the whole thing down—much to Creighton's crinkle-eyed delight.

"There you go now, son!" he exhorts as Slaughter's doorknob of an Adam's apple bobs away. "Refreshing, isn't it? Now you just keep that filled up for the rest of the night."

Jim's thumb-circles have meanwhile evolved into a full-on pummelling of the muscles beneath his hands. "That's it, you listen to Crotch, this old bastard's learned more than a few tricks over the years when it comes to drinking—taught me a few good ones back in the day, haven't ya, Abe?"

I feel impatient watching the two of them grin and wink across the kitchen at each other. I want to tell them this has nothing to do with getting drunk in Toronto ten years ago. It doesn't have anything to do with them. It doesn't even have anything to do with poetry, for a change. It's all just Slaughter and the world of his weirdness, which I'm starting to think none of us have a clue about.

Slaughter returns the emptied tumbler to the table—he places it precisely within the water ring it made when he picked it up.

"Ahhh," he says, and I can tell it's an insincere Ahh, an Ahh performed for our benefit.

"How 'bout a beer?" Slaughter requests with an abashed smirk, and the two poets clap hands and clap shoulders in a display of muted jubilance, like their team has scored a point.

That's when I have my epiphany. Concerning, of all people, Sparrow. I didn't realize Sparrow had been fluttering in the back of my mind this whole time, but the moment the epiphany descends, it's clear he has. The question of Sparrow. The mystery of Sparrow, his blank looks, his Oxford chimera—chewing away at my subconscious all evening long.

And here it is. That maybe Sparrow isn't malicious. Maybe Sparrow isn't dense. Maybe Sparrow hasn't been deliberately screwing with my hopes and dreams and expectations all this time after all.

Maybe people just live their lives hearing whatever they want to hear and thinking whatever they want to think. Maybe it's as simple and as stupid as that.

Sherrie has gone, so I decide to go find her.

—

And I'm drunk. The door separating the kitchen from the living room takes me from relatively sober to all-of-a-sudden drunk, like some kind of mystic portal. Like the rabbit hole to Wonderland. I stand on the other side of the door, surveying the party, trying to keep myself from weaving. Moira and Ruth are side by side on the couch. Moira is talking, twisting her knuckly hands around in front of her like she's making incantations. I intuit she's describing her brother's Dragon Blade again, demonstrating how perfectly balanced it is. Ruth nods and smiles from her crimson depths. The two of them make a striking pair—Moira's deep-socketed eyes, Ruth's harsh-angled jaw. The weird sisters minus one.

Sherrie is a few feet away from them, huddled over the telephone with a finger shoved into her free ear. I make my way over, balancing like a tightrope walker.

"You," Moira calls to me, interrupting her monologue. "Some help you are. Some goddamn help."

"What?" I say.

"You're supposed to be his friend," snipes Moira, jabbing at me with the heat-bright tip of her cigarette. "You're supposed to be so *decent*. You're just like the rest of those assholes."

"I am not," I assure her, "just like the rest of those assholes."

"The bunch of you," Moira complains, "just treat him like King Shit. I don't know what in hell is wrong with you. Your husband, too," Moira turns abruptly on Ruth, who doesn't even flinch, who actually smiles a little.

"For Christ's sake, that one could be—he could take a *crap* on your kitchen floor," Moira sputters, turning toward me again. "He could be hitting himself on the head with a hammer saying, how do you like that, now, boys? Whaddya think about that little trick? And what would you bastards say?"

At this point Moira actually pauses as if I'm going to answer her.

"I don't know," I tell her.

She folds her arms. They remind me of two tree roots woven together above the earth.

"You don't know," says Moira, turning to Ruth. "He doesn't *know*."

"Perhaps they would say," offers Ruth in her strange accent, "yes, King Shit. Very good, King Shit."

For the first time since I've met her, Moira laughs. She laughs worse than Ruth. She coughs as she laughs, a smoker's cough, harsh, wet, and red-sounding. Gravel scrapes her windpipe. It makes me want to shrivel up and die.

"*Very good, King Shit,*" caws Moira, smacking Ruth across a velvet thigh. Aren't they just getting along like a house on fire.

Ruth smiles some more, rubbing where Moira smacked.

"So what am I supposed to do?" I hear myself saying. It's like I'm suddenly in one of my dreams somehow. I have a lot of dreams where I'm being accused of something, and furiously defending myself. "What am I supposed to do?" I repeat. "I'm supposed to tell Jim not to drink?"

"Oh, heaven forbid," says Moira, rolling her eyes like a bad actor. "Heaven forbid you ever did that. World would end. Sky'd come falling down."

I continue my high-wire act across the room toward Sherrie, fuming somewhat. Moira has to be kidding. *Jim, your wife would really prefer it if you didn't drink. As some nineteen-year-old idiot, I feel it's my place to tell you this.* Besides, haven't I already told him? I told him at Christmas. And look what it got me. *A confection, ultimately.* Exile—from which I've only just managed to claw my way back.

"Everybody's here, though!" Sherrie is hollering into the phone, finger still jammed into her ear to block out the party noises. It's practically buried up to the second knuckle.

"Where have you been all night? *Why?* Really? But why?"

"Is that Claude?" I say.

"But come on! Everyone's having a really good time!"

"It's a crazy party!" I yell to be helpful.

"That's Lawrence!" says Sherrie. "He wants to talk to you!"

The phone is in my hand, against my head.

"No, I have to go, I don't want to talk to him," Claude is calling.

"Hi!" I say.

"Hey, Lawrence," says Claude.

"What's the matter, you studying or something?"

"Yeah, I'm studying," answers Claude in a strange, slurred voice.

"You don't sound like you're studying."

Claude sighs something in French.

"Pardon?" I say in French back at him. *"Donne moi le poulet."*

Claude snickers. "You're in a good mood."

"I'm just really drunk," I tell him. "You hear the good news?"

"I heard," says Claude. "Congratulate Jim for me."

"I think the idea is for you to come and do that yourself."

"I'm not feeling so good," says Claude.

I look up at Sherrie. "He says he's not feeling good."

She takes the phone back from me.

"Why aren't you feeling good?" Sherrie demands, turning away.

I just stand there while Sherrie harangues, watching her shoulder blades moving beneath her sweater. I can't quite muster the will to turn back to the party as yet, although I hear it, swelling, behind me. I hear Moira hack as though her previous laughing fit has shaken something loose, and Ruth's low, gleeful croak in reply. I can hear that Crotch is back out among us now, holding forth on the Black Mountain poetry movement and the TISH Group, and, if I'm hearing this correctly, trying to convince someone that the word TISH is *shit* spelled backward. Those are the voices that drift above the crowd—the high notes. Below them, it's just a garbled chorus.

And now my consciousness seems to be getting snagged on moments, like when I was in the kitchen with Jim. Time drops away and I'm drifting, dreaming awake in the eternity of right now with the party behind me, Sherrie's back in front of me, her shoulder blades jerking. Next month I will turn twenty, and more years will follow that, supposedly. I can't imagine them, just as I can't imagine Slaughter's mother dying—what it would be like. The future is theoretical, thank God. How will I be? I won't be—I can't imagine it. I just am. I'll always am. I'll stay in this moment forever, this hinge of time. Secrets need not be revealed, the trauma of knowledge and experience can be forgone. There won't be any more of those shattering, heartbreaking moments that hit you like a ball in the face and cause your personality to grow at warped and unexplored trajectories. Nothing left to learn, nothing from which to recover. I'll just stay here, drunk and out of sync. Turned away, and turned away from. En-bubbled in this moment.

"Well, something is very wrong there," says Sherrie, blue headlights shining in my eyes like a cop's flashlight.

"Your eyes are so beautiful," someone above me says.

Sherrie's face squeezes itself up with mirth and pain. "Oh God, Lawrence, snap out of it."

I do, but can't help resenting her for starting time up again.

"I'm hammered," I tell her quickly. "Sorry. I mean they *are,* you—you probably know that. I'm not hitting on you, honest to God."

"I know, Lawrence, stop babbling."

"I like fat girls," I babble.

This arrests Sherrie's attention completely. Everything about her stops except for the flap-flap of her eyelashes.

Both my hands have at some point jammed themselves against my mouth. I remove them to amend: "I mean, not fat, exactly. You know, bigger girls. Just girls with . . . more meat on their bones." That sounds disgusting—like I want to slap them on the barbecue.

Blink, blink, blink, goes Sherrie, like a tentative, big-eyed bird hopping toward somebody's picnic.

"Please don't tell anyone." Though my back's still turned to the party, I imagine every face burning into me like the tip of Moira's smoke. The talk has become more focused, scandalized, intent. Soon the voices will gather together as one to condemn and pronounce, like in a Greek tragedy.

And then my vision is washed in gold, my nose invaded with the unearthly smell of Head and Shoulders shampoo.

"I would never tell *anyone*," Sherrie promises, releasing me. "It's nothing to be ashamed of, Lawrence, I think it's *lovely.*"

"It's not *lovely,* Sherrie."

"Well it's *fine,* then."

"Okay," I tell her. "I just wanted—this whole conversation—I came over here wanting to tell you I'm sorry for what I said about Chuck—that's all. That night in the marsh."

Sherrie waves her hands to make me stop talking. She looks down at the floor.

"I was just being an asshole because—" I stop and glance around, not so drunk it doesn't occur to me to lower my voice. "The whole thing with Jim. I really wanted you to tell me what was going on, uh . . . with you guys. And you wouldn't. It was none of my business but—it pissed me off."

There was more to it, of course, but that seems to be the only aspect I'm able to articulate.

"Anyway," I say, exhausted all of a sudden, "we can change the subject now if you want to."

Sherrie looks up at me, finally. It turns out she doesn't want to.

36.

AND YOU KNOW, it's nothing really. It's nothing I couldn't have worked out on my own, just by putting two and two together. I see now I was too preoccupied with my own prurient imaginings—my lurid little worst-case scenarios. I can be forgiven for this, can't I? It's undeniable there's a quality about Sherrie that makes a guy assume the worst. And there's a similar quality about Jim, now that I consider it.

And at the very moment I'm considering it—this quality of Sherrie's coupled with this quality of Jim's—the universe rushes up to agree. The universe scrambles to provide an illustration of this principle in the person of Todd Smiley. Hovering, as he does. Looming silently, sullenly a few feet away, waiting to be taken into account. But we take him into account too late, Sherrie and I, deep in conversation as we are.

Sherrie had been saying: So it was all my fault. The whole thing with Sparrow, the whole thing with his tenure. I just knew it had to be my fault and I felt so *horrible.*

And I had been saying: Sherrie, there are lots of reasons Jim's tenure could have been pulled.

And Sherrie was saying: But it happened right after I made the complaint. Right after, Lawrence!

And then I heard myself saying: Lots of people could have complained about Jim. You're right—he misses classes, he doesn't keep office hours. He . . . he fucks people around.

That statement—monumental as it felt—was not the part Todd heard—at least I don't think it was. Imagine Todd bearing witness to such blasphemy. He'd bring the temple down on all our heads.

Sherrie looked at me with her wide-open face—eyes and mouth agape.

"He *does*," she squeaked. "He *does* fuck people around. He fucks people around, and I was *tired* of it. Are you saying he fucked *you* around too, Lawrence? Is that what you're saying?"

I nodded. I couldn't do more than that. The sense of betrayal had caught up with me, and my brain felt heavy and sluggish like a cloud full of rain.

And then something happened to Sherrie's face I'd never seen before. It went ugly.

"He never read my poems," she whispered. "I know he didn't. One or two short ones, maybe. I would ask him about them, and I could see him faking it. I mean, half the time he wouldn't even put any effort into it, Lawrence, he couldn't even be *bothered* faking it. Or he'd just change the subject—I came in to talk to him about my assignment one day, and Jim just launched into this lecture on Sexton, told me I should read her. I mean, Christ!"

I kept nodding. I gave her arm a squeeze, hoping to calm her down and relay empathy without uttering further mutinies. But also I was kind of struck dumb. Sherrie's pink face was practically pulsing. Her enormous blue eyes were squeezed into Schofield-esque pinpricks. Her teeth were even bared. This might seems strange to say, but all at once Sherrie made sense to me. Sherrie the poet, that is. In her anger.

Here's what Todd would have seen and heard as he approached: Sherrie gone ugly, gesturing in jerks and swiping at her eyes, talking fast and squeaky. A tantalizing word or phrase might have reached him—*I know he didn't . . . faking it . . . effort into . . . he'd just . . . him . . . Jim . . . Christ!* Me standing close, nodding urgently.

"I had such respect for him," Sherrie was saying. "I mean,

I still do, Lawrence. Jim's brilliant. I love him." She stopped talking abruptly and seemed to suck for a moment on the inside of her mouth as though getting ready to spit. "That's why it was so infuriating. I loved Jim so much and he just fucked me around. He didn't even care."

That's what Todd comes in on. Those last two sentences. At least, that's when we finally take him into account. Having just arrived, perhaps, but already veering away.

At a party like this, the problem is, you lose track. You don't keep your attention focused where you should. It switches around, seemingly on its own accord—like when someone else is controlling the radio dial. Sherrie and I, for example, should have stayed focused on Todd—and what the universe was trying to impress upon us—instead of watching him veer, dreamy-seeming, off into the crowd. We should have called him to us, pulled him into our circle instead of letting him drift away like an unmoored ship with a cargo of gunpowder.

Things began to speed up, then, blink on and off. I lost time, found myself in the kitchen listening to vomiting, castigations, and barks coming from outside (which a peek out the window informed me were Jim, Moira, and Panda respectively), lost more time, sat beside Ruth for a while insisting that Moira was the *real* poet of the household (Moira was an oral storyteller, I maintained, embroidering outlandish dreamscapes—or something like that), until I noticed Dekker standing a few feet a way listening and grinning a little too broadly, so got up and went outside to take a piss and clear my head. Jim was still there, breathing fire, or so it seemed. It was snowing and going to snow, the temperature had dropped, the air was winter-cold, and so his breath came out like smoke. Or no—he was smoking. It *was* smoke.

He sat on the chopping block, smoking and going to

smoke, with Moira no longer in sight, but Panda spent at his feet. There Jim was.

And here I am, back in now.

I pee discreetly before preparing to say hello, but don't have time to say hello because this is where Charles Slaughter comes in. Comes out, that is. I see him and think through my haze that there is something I should have been keeping on top of tonight. What was it again? I meant to be paying attention to something. Todd. He should be here. We haven't talked since I walked away from his proffered palm. I have a feeling I shouldn't keep walking away from Todd like that. And Slaughter—what about him? He keeps lurching out of place. The universe and I, we pin him neatly down under headings like "friend," and "sane"—he rips himself off the page and blunders off, headingless, till we can pin him down again.

Then Todd does appear, almost as if I have invoked his stubby presence, which materializes in the doorway just as Slaughter is approaching the chopping block. Jim turns, chucking his cigarette into the night, and sees me standing behind him apparently playing with my groin as I tuck myself in. He sets his lips for a bemused comment, but is interrupted when Charles shoves him off the stump.

"Hey, man," Smiley calls to Slaughter.

"Well—" says Jim from the ground, as if collecting his thoughts.

Slaughter kicks Jim.

You weren't supposed to hear that, man, Todd is in the middle of saying—this drowns out any further sound Jim might have made.

Jim rolls away fast, like a tumbleweed. Slaughter takes a step forward and, get this: Todd—Todd hurls himself onto Slaughter's back.

And Panda's gone. Panda's lost it. Panda all but turns himself inside out. He shrieks and capers.

Todd goes flying and rolls away in awkward imitation of Jim. Slaughter takes another step forward and I am yelling *Charles, Charles Slaughter, Chuck you stop right fucking now* as Panda yells a crazed-dog version of the same thing. Jim has gotten to his feet and now hunkers on the other side of the yard, monkey arms a-dangle at his sides. He's not bothering to protest or demand an explanation. He's putting everything he has into being ready.

"*Ugfh,*" says Todd from the ground as Slaughter takes another step away from him, toward Jim. Jim moves slightly to the side. Soon they will be circling each other like gladiators.

"*Slaughter, Slaughter, look at me,*" I'm yelling. Slaughter takes another step forward. "*Look at me you—you goddamn ape!*"

Slaughter takes another step forward, so I yell louder. I yell and yell—variations of the above. I force the words into higher decibels with every step he takes. My voice scrapes away at my throat like a harrow, but I keep yelling, I keep screaming. What else can I do?

Until finally Slaughter turns his head. He turns to me, the universe slows, and the five of us seem to hang in time, like planets across the void. Even Panda goes quiet, haunches trembling.

37.

RING, RING.
    Ring, ring.
    Ring, ring, ring, ring, ring, ring, ring, ring, ring, ring, ring, ring, ring, ring.

Oh, why.

Ring, ring, ring, ring, ring, ring, ring, ring, ring, ring—

"Hello!"

"Larry?"

"Yes!"

"I'm sorry. Were you . . . just getting up?"

I look up at my kitchen clock. It's one in the afternoon. I am just getting up.

"No, no, no, no. No. I was doing something in the bathroom."

"Ah."

"Having a shower!"

"I see."

And then I recognize the voice. My body unclenches and drops onto the couch.

"Oh my gosh. Hi, Dermot."

"Hi," he laughs—slightly. "You know, I can call back."

"No!"

"No?"

"I mean—I'm sorry. I am just getting up, actually, I lied."

"I can call back," says Schofield again.

"No, it's great to talk to you. Sorry, I'm just all fogged up."

I scratch. I'm cold—the temperature has dropped to a ridiculous degree over the weekend. It's going to snow again—you can taste the crystal in the air. I'm naked. I reach behind me and pull at the afghan draped across the back of my couch. It's an identical pattern to the one in Janet's apartment, only composed of man-colours like black and green. Crocheted by my grandmother's own two grudging hands.

"I just found your letter in my mailbox this morning, Larry, and I had some time, thought I might as well give you a call," says Dermot. "The poems were great, by the way."

I'm warm.

"The poems?"

"The ghazals? A bit unorthodox in terms of some of the content, strictly speaking. But some compelling stuff. There's an energy there."

"I wrote them all in one afternoon," I tell him.

"Is that right?"

"I wrote sixteen of them! I can send you the rest if you—"

"Well, I'd encourage you to send them into *Re:Strain,* eventually, yes. And, my goodness, if you have sixteen of them, don't hesitate to shop them around, Larry, you won't hurt my feelings. We'd like to publish one or two from this batch if that's all right with you. As long as the editorial board okays it."

"Don't let Joanne read them."

Dermot laughs. "I have some sway with Joanne, Larry, I wouldn't worry."

"Which ones," I ask. "Which ones do you want to publish?"

"Well, I very much like the ones about the wax museum."

"The Hollywood Horrors?"

"Yes. Don't tell me that's a real place."

"It is! In Summerside! You never went when you were there?"

"I must have missed that," Dermot confesses.

I lay back on the couch. "What did you like about them?" I can't stop myself from asking.

Dermot chuckles, hearing the loopy joy in my voice. "Well, they have a certain vividness, I think. They really evoke the notion of childhood as a kind of Gothic landscape. This wax museum, it's a great metaphor. The intermingling of glamour with the grotesque. Hollywood Horrors."

"I didn't even send you all the poems I wrote about it."

"I can see it carrying a whole book," says Dermot. "You should think about that."

I don't answer him. I'm thinking about that.

LYNN COADY

"Surely," ventures Schofield after a while, "Jim has told you something similar? You mentioned Jim's been overseeing the work?"

"Jim," I repeat, and have to pause because it's the first time I've spoken *Jim* today, and the word still brings on pain.

Another Friday. We all sit staring into the void of the blackboard. There was no notice on the door. Dekker hasn't yet come bustling in to substitute.

Fifteen minutes, we're still sitting. Everyone's pre-class conversations have long since died to silence.

"You know," someone announces in back, "to hell with this." He scrapes his chair, and walks out. A couple of people follow after a moment.

Another few minutes, and the class has nearly emptied itself except for the four of us.

Sherrie says, "We should call. We should call and see how he is. Has anyone spoken to him since Friday night?"

I stayed overnight but don't feel like telling anybody this. I don't feel like describing the Arsenault household in the scarred morning light.

"I thought you said he was okay," says Claude, turning around. His lips are still pretty swollen. He kind of looks like Mick Jagger.

"He was—he wasn't hurt at all," Todd hurries to assure him. "Chuck only shoved him a couple of times."

Todd's voice is loud. It echoes in the almost empty classroom. He looks over at me like a dog desperate for a pat.

"Because of Lawrence," he adds. "Campbell got everybody out there, on top of him, so fast."

"What *about* Slaughter, anyway?" I say, pointedly not to Todd. "What happened to Slaughter, has anyone seen him?"

"He went to the Mariner, afterward," says Sherrie, leaning her face on her hands. At this moment she looks to me like one of those remote, round-faced women you see in Renaissance paintings—women whose very blankness meant the height of desirability. "Dekker took him home, but he went out again. I heard he went and tried to pick a fight with Scarsdale."

"Have you talked to him?" I ask.

Sherrie keeps herself blank. "Nobody's talked to him. Nobody's seen him."

"Jesus Christ!" says Todd. "Isn't Scarsdale some kind of gangster?"

Above the blackboard, the minute hand moves. We all hear it click into place.

"It's a nice day," Claude remarks. We've ended up walking down Bridge Street together. I'm on autopilot for Carl's—tea and studying. Sherrie's drifted back to her dorm. Todd didn't even have it in him to hover very long.

"Cold though," I gripe. "It's going to snow again."

"Maybe not," says Claude.

We trudge away, the sun in our eyes. The ranks of students downtown have noticeably thinned. Midterms. They're all in their hovels, panicked over books.

We stand together at the intersection.

"You going to Carl's?" I inquire. Claude has never struck me as the tea and french fries type.

"There's a coffee place a few doors down," he says. "I thought I'd get some to go and walk around for a while. I'm kind of glad about Jim, actually."

I jerk like I've been bitten or pinched.

"What do you mean, you're glad about Jim?"

The light changes—the only traffic light in town. Claude glances at me, and we make our way to the other corner.

"I just mean I'm glad there was no class. I know it's bad news—it's really bad for Jim. Someone's bound to complain. I just meant—I'm glad there's no class, just for today. I feel like getting some air, going for a walk."

We trudge. We're almost at Carl's.

"I feel like going for a walk too," I say.

We take our coffees down to the marsh, to the paths tucked away behind the flesh-toned church, where I last went with Sherrie.

"The sunshine is good," says Claude, strangely chipper for a guy in a black turtleneck. The dead vegetation crunches beneath our shoes.

"You know," I say after a while. After pondering how to bring the subject up. "My grandmother punched me in the face once."

Claude frowns and sips between his puffed lips, bathing his own face in steam.

"In the mouth? God. How old was your grandmother?"

"Oh, who knows, she's always been around a hundred. She's ageless, like Satan." I also take a sip. Coffee is horrible, I learn. It tastes the way it looks—blackness.

"No, not in the mouth," I continue, swallowing with effort. "And actually she didn't really punch me. But she might as well have. My nose had just been broken and she, like, flicked it really hard."

"Jesus Christ," says Claude.

"Yeah. I was only twelve or something. I'd gotten in fights before," I say. "That is, I got beaten up, by guys my own age. But this was the most violent thing I'd ever experienced. It was—" I look for a word that won't make me sound too ridiculous—too much like I'm groping for the right word. "It was shattering."

"Because of the betrayal," says Claude.

I nod and sip, wincing again at the taste. We crunch our way through the skeleton cattails.

"Well," says Claude after a while. He slurps his coffee the same noisy way I slurp my tea. "I can't say it felt like that with Slaughter. It's not like we were friends. He just put up with me because of Sherrie—he made that pretty clear."

"So you didn't feel betrayed?" I ask—wondering if that would really make it any better.

"No," says Claude with a bored exhale. Although I'm starting to realize that what I always assumed was boredom with Claude is something else altogether. Something closer to fatigue.

"You know, there's an upside to betrayal," he tells me. "If you get to expect it all the time. Eventually it just becomes— experience."

"Yes," I acknowledge after a while. "That's cheering."

We walk for a bit until we come to the same spot I stopped with Sherrie, the place where the trees part and you can see all the way across to the other side of the marsh. The water is blue like the tropics today—you could convince yourself it's summer if it weren't for the grasping, naked trees and yellow reeds.

"Why do you think he did it, really?" I ask after a while. "I mean, come on, man, it must have been kind of *surprising* at least."

Because we eventually pried the information out of Claude that Slaughter came right to his door that Friday. Slaughter made his way to Claude's residence in the middle of a sunny, warmer afternoon than this, climbed the stairs, ambled down the hall, knocked on the door, greeted, "Hi, faggot," punching Claude in the mouth. *Lightly, actually,* said Claude. Meaning not as hard as Slaughter could have, but hard enough.

———

My parents call. Lydia has broken her hip, as grandparents will, and now she thinks she's dying.

"She's never been sick a day in her life," my mother tells me. "She was always so careful. I don't even remember her ever hurting herself. That's why she was always so impatient with me and Stannie, whenever we got scrapes, or caught a bug. It was our own fault. We weren't being careful enough."

"She said *fuck*," exclaims my Dad before I can comment.

"No, she didn't," negates Mom in an instant.

"Your mother blocked it out. It's the damnedest thing. She heard it just as well as I did."

"Oh, Dad, I did not."

"Your mother'd probably go blind if she saw the old thing naked."

"I would not," maintains my mother.

"Gramma said *fuck?*"

"No," says Mom. "Your father's crazy."

"We're having dinner over at Stan and Maud's. She's heading to that downstairs bathroom—you know how she is, she wobbles around like she's riding a goddamn unicycle, but oh no, she never needs any help—"

"I think her knee gave way—"

"We all heard it, plain as day, you just ask your uncle Stan when you're here, son."

"Your father *laughed.*"

"You laughed, Dad?"

"Well, I couldn't believe my own goddamn ears!"

"An old lady falls and breaks her hip—"

"Well, I didn't know she broke her hip. Wayne laughed too, a little."

"Oh, he did not."

"Your uncle Stan just turned white."

"Because she fell! Because he knew she'd hurt herself, he heard the crack!"

"There wasn't any crack—"

"There was so a crack, that's what you heard."

"I did not hear any crack, I know what I damn well heard, Larry."

"Don't you listen to him, Larry."

"Anyway, now she thinks she's dying. The old thing's in the hospital, probably cursing out the nurses. Talking about her will, gathering her loved ones to her."

"Midterms are starting soon," I say, because I know what's coming.

"Well, you can come home for a weekend, can't you?" my mother demands.

"I have a break in February," I stammer, because it's not usually my mother who does the barking down the phone. "And one on Easter . . ."

"Hear that, Mom?" chortles Dad. "He'll be there to see her rise on the third day."

There's some silence, and then: "You *Catholics*," she hisses down the wires at my convert father—shocking us both.

Then the heavy, plastic noise of the phone going down.

"Mom?" I say after a second or two.

"Ah, Christ," mutters my father. "Made her mad, Larry."

"No kidding."

"It's not funny, I s'pose. Brick shithouse like Lydia. It's thrown your mum pretty good. Her and Stan both."

"I *guess* it has," I agree, still rippling with the shock of it. My mother has never hung up on me.

"Like watching your house burn down or something, I suppose. House you grew up in—never thought it wouldn't be there."

Dad with his fires.

"Well, your cousin is over, anyhow. She's been a good help. Saw her at the hospital."

My cousin.

"Janet?" I say. "Janet's there?"

"Came back when she heard about Lydia," Dad tells me. "Came right over. Stan and Maud picked her up."

Dad relays this last piece of information with a slight emphasis. What he's emphasizing is the fact that Stan and Maud didn't let her take the bus, like they usually do when she comes over alone. Not this time, though, not even with the excuse of Lydia being in the hospital. This time Janet was worth the trip.

This is interesting to me—I can tell it's interesting to Dad for the same reason. That slight, thoughtful emphasis he gives. I hear him rolling it around in his mind.

Now that she has hurt them back. Now that she has made the break. Now she's welcome home.

38.

HERE IS THE STORY of the red morning at Jim's. Memory delayed doesn't make memory better. Memories strengthen like cheese, when put aside. That has been my experience this year. That is the biggest of all my discoveries. The longer you wait to open the container, the more the smell will knock you out when you do. Corpse of milk—the smell of the corpse. So here is the story of the red morning at Jim's.

I woke up early and had the place to myself for a while, which would have been nice except that I was freezing. I tried to remember the proper way to light a wood stove, casting my mind back to afternoons in the Humphrieses' cottage. It seemed to me I couldn't go wrong with kindling and newspaper, which happened to be in a box by my feet, so that was what I used, dumping a couple of logs in on top of it, and finally a match. Then I just dragged a chair over and huddled up beside it like a baby chick against its mother for warmth. I had a quilt Jim had tossed at me from the night before around my shoulders, and had pulled on my jacket, gloves, and boots the moment I woke up.

There was nothing to do for the next little while but sit and wait to get warm. So this is how Jim lives, I thought. I imagined having a bath—immersing myself in a tub of hot water—but remembered there was no bathtub. Jim was a professor at Westcock University, the most respected undergraduate college east of Ontario. He had a full-time job, an expectation of tenure. Why did he live like a goddamn pioneer?

Tea, I thought after a while, on early-morning instinct, and then recoiled. The word—the night—the Lions Club mug on its side in the corner. We hadn't bothered to pick it up and put it away, afterward. Even more remarkably, the thing was still intact. It hadn't even been chipped.

I was there because Jim said, *Don't go. Don't go. I need my friends around me tonight. I need to know who my friends are. Stay the night, Larry. Don't go.*

"Always," Moira was reduced to repeating, once she had barked herself out. The sight of him like that at the kitchen table seemed to infuriate her. The defeated slouch. The refusal to go to bed, to let anyone else, to put the booze away.

"Always-always you get like this. You know you're going to get like this and I tell you you're going to get like this, and then you just go and you get like this. I watch you do it."

"I'm off to bed," sang Creighton, his tone an attempt to radiate light. "Now, Jimmy. You mustn't let yourself get so morose."

Jim stared at the table. "Stay up with me, please, Abe."

"No, no. Early start tomorrow, you know that, Jimmy."

I'd noticed Creighton couldn't get away from him fast enough once Jim had settled into his funk. Slaughter had long been rousted, calmed to a degree, and stuffed into Dekker's car before he could wind himself up again. But instead of shrugging and putting the whole thing down to drunken stupidity, as everyone else was more than ready to do, Jim took the incident as some sort of divine negative portent, like a black mark on the sun. He'd stationed himself away from the party, at the kitchen table with his no-longer-secret bottle of rum, for the rest of the night. Any remaining levity had pretty much fizzled from the party after Slaughter. People trickled from the house.

But to be fair, it wasn't Slaughter who was responsible for this. A lot of people found the fight kind of exciting, as well they might. The party was shot through with adrenalin at first—I could hardly hear my thoughts or Sherrie's laments over the keyed-up babble on all sides of us. Slaughter's attack was the sort of thing you stayed up all night animatedly discussing, marvelling over, dissecting from every angle. So the fight wasn't the problem—the fight, if anything, should have given the night longevity.

The drain was Jim. It was Jim who stopped the party cold. Jim sat down at the kitchen table and made himself a vortex.

Creighton drew himself up and looked around with evident impatience. His light tone and easy gestures couldn't penetrate the metastasizing gloom, and you could see him feeling his powerlessness—a feeling Creighton clearly didn't like.

"James, now. Come on. A kid got drunk and took a swing at you. So what?"

"A kid I trusted. A kid I asked into my home, and counted as a friend."

"Always," intoned Moira, hoarse by this point. "Always, always." With that she left the kitchen huffing and puffing like a long-distance runner.

Soon Creighton gave up. Defeat and disgust throbbed briefly on his face as he looked over at me. "I really must be off to bed," he insisted to neither Jim nor me in particular. "Train in the morning. You have young Larry here. He'll keep you company, won't you, son?"

And so it was left to me. Me and Jim—the dog and dying stove.

"There he goes, Larry. One of my oldest and dearest friends. Mentor and confidant. Off he waltzes to his beddy-bye. Can't haul ass back to Toronto fast enough."

I gazed down the hall as if still watching Creighton—who had already disappeared up the stairs—retreat. "Well, he's got an early day tomorrow."

"Early day," agreed Jim, shoving himself abruptly from the table. This was the first move he'd made in well over an hour. His chair shrieked, and Panda, who had been dozing on his blanket, leapt to his feet as though goosed. He barked once, pathetically, looking around for reassurance.

"Shut up," answered Jim, hauling open the fridge. He was looking for more beer.

"What about some tea, Jim?" I suggested.

"You like some tea, Larry?"

"Be a nice way to end the evening."

"Ah, but the night's still young." Jim placed a Ten-Penny in front of me and, before I could protest, cracked it with an opener he seemed to have produced from mid-air. I looked at the beer with mixed feelings. I'd drunk so much beer, it kind of made me want to vomit. On the other hand, I'd drunk so much beer, it seemed I might as well drink more. It wasn't logical, but it was nonetheless the case. I took a swig.

"But I'll getcha some tea if you want some tea," Jim said, whirling lopsidedly toward the cupboard. "Tea and beer don't go too badly together. And by the time it's steeped you'll be done anyway."

"Have a cup with me, Jim."

"You know, Larry," said Jim in the forced and fakey tone he'd been using since Creighton had creaked his way upstairs. "There's nothing more embarrassing than one man trying to trick another out of his booze. It's something a woman would do. Like in that song there. 'Don't hide my liquor, try to serve me tea.' You know that song?"

I flushed. "Yeah."

Jim folded his arms and leaned against the stove. He stared at me for a moment, then nodded a sharp, upward nod like an animal sniffing the wind.

"You think I'm a drunk, Larry?"

Fatigue dropped over me like a net. I was responding viscerally to the turn of Jim's mood, feeling the suddenness of it in my guts like when a car hits a patch of ice and starts to spin.

I rubbed my face.

"Because if you think I'm a drunk, you should just come out and tell me. You know, like a man would do."

I slapped my hands onto the table and sighed. "I just think it makes you miserable, all right? I don't like to see you miserable."

Jim kind of hooted under his breath. He held his beer up in front of him like a guy in a TV commercial. "This? You think this is the cause of my misery? If anything, this is what makes it bearable."

"I think that's an excuse, Jim."

He gazed at me with sudden, fearsome lucidity. This happened at Christmas, I remembered—Jim sharpening up, vitalized by hostility.

"Oh, you do, eh, Larry? An excuse for what, exactly?"

This was a good question. I'd said what I said without thinking, it had just arrived on my lips. An excuse for what?

"An excuse . . ." I said, "an excuse for . . ."

"A-an excuse, an excuse-fer," Jim repeated like a retarded parrot.

I looked up at him, speechless, in high school, bashed against lockers, tackled from behind.

"A-an excuse, an excuse-fer," slobbered Jim. "Wonderful point, Larry. Brilliantly executed! By God, you'll go far in this world."

I blinked down at my beer.

"The red face on him," Jim remarked after a moment, as if to a cadre of like-minded thugs.

"That's so," I said, trying to keep my breathing even. "That's so *childish.*"

"I'm the one who's childish," declared Jim, gesturing with a ceramic Fredericton Lions Club mug he'd brought down from the cupboard at some point. "I merely ask you to clarify your point in such a way as I can understand it, and all you can do is sit there stuttering and stammering with your face all red."

And then Jim did it again, contorted his face, adjusted his voice. *"A-an excuse, an excuse-fer,"* he drawled. "An excuse for what, Larry? For what? You'll have to do better than that airy-fairy crap."

I looked up, and I think I was about to tell him. I think I really was for a minute. But then I noticed something. The way Jim's eyes were dancing, how he kept wetting his lips, swinging the Lions mug around, pushing his face at me. This was Jim making himself feel better. This was why Jim needed me around.

"You hear me, Larry? I have to say, now, you're losing some esteem in my eyes. You're usually so goddamn articulate. An excuse for what? For what? Come on. Pretend you're in the classroom. Pretend that A average of yours is at stake—that oughta snap ya to attention. An excuse for what?"

He wasn't fake-goading me, he really wanted to hear it, whatever it was. The worse, the better. He was hoping I would say something irrevocable. He wanted me to pull the house down on our heads.

He wanted it, because he wanted the *attention*.

"Let's have tea," I said, gripping my beer with both hands.

"Sure!" declared Jim, waving the mug with a sarcastic flourish, whirling away from me, toward the stove. He'd had his fingers curled loosely around the mug's handle, and maybe as a result of the sarcastic flourish, maybe the whirl, the Lions mug flew from his fingers, across the room, catching Panda—who had settled into his blanket again—on the head.

It made this sound.

Panda leapt again to his feet, assuming a weary, yet defiant sort of dog-stance, as if to announce he had finally had enough. He took a gurgling step forward, all business, and then his knees gave out.

I'd never seen a dog fall in quite this way. A kind of slow sinking.

"*Oh,*" gasped Jim. He wrapped his endless arms about his torso like a panicked child.

———

Gradually, I came to grasp how early it was. My skull and bones had a throbbing, hollow feeling, which I now had enough experience to recognize as the precursor to a pretty serious hangover. I hadn't woken naturally, I realized—I'd woken from the booze and assumed it must be time to get up. But it wasn't anywhere near time to get up. Nobody else would be up for hours. Maybe Creighton, although it seemed obvious he'd been exaggerating about his early-morning train—he'd just wanted to get some sleep, to get away.

Likely, there wouldn't be anyone stirring until noon at least considering the time we went to bed. Which would have been only about three hours ago. As I was comprehending this, the light coming into the kitchen went from grey to red—as if bombs had exploded outside. I could hear winter birds going crazy at the sudden, violent dawn. Red sky in the morning is a shepherd's warning. That's one of the first poems I ever learned.

But maybe Jim wouldn't be getting up at all today. I had a feeling. There was not just the exhaustion of the late night to take into account, but the hour of futile digging out by the chopping block. Hacking and stabbing at the frozen earth until finally we agreed to simply drag the thing into the woods and leave it there. The awful white gash of the moon overhead, Jim's white face luminescent and pleading.

Don't tell her. Don't leave me. Don't Larry let anyone leave me.

My own hands throbbed, and I pulled off my gloves for a moment to look at them. The pads below my fingers glowed as red as the room.

I left the gloves off long enough to lace my boots and zip my jacket up to my neck. I put two more logs on the fire even though there wasn't quite enough room for them in the stove, leaving the cast-iron burner balanced where the edge of the log poked slightly out. I figured the wood would burn down fast enough. They'd be all day waiting for the house to heat up otherwise.

I pulled my gloves on again and just stood there looking at Jim's squat black stove for a while, listening to the famished licking of the flames inside. Smoke billowed through the crack.

I stood there so long that the red of the kitchen had started to mellow and shift—give way to something more gingery—and finally sat back down in the chair, thinking I'd better wait for the logs to burn down at least enough so I could close the stove properly. It was bad enough to be leaving a fire unattended while people slept. I tried not to think of what my father would say.

i came here looking for you

39

I came here looking for you man
your wernet hereI hung around &ate
some peanut butter an& like allllll
yuor
     chips.

          Rueiwoqpowierj jeioseidrju
a;lskdfjsldkowseirun v

ilike your typerwriter.

%##%·&$+··#$Y·*******!%#$%·********!2
1%%#·&&&&&&&?
          Thts me fuckin cursing
man!!!
!!·##$12334454556667888090-0101010101
%#·!*$(%($*$·&%)!$(**%·#_(%·*&·#)^

     things are sooooooooo fucked
rightnow im deqad man. Ii hiding
fromit
howdo youmake tyhe quotatin marks
klike rory
     ???,.,'""ask 4 roryasswipe"!!!!

"I" am "drunk" write "now"

goooooo000000000000000ooooooooodbye

" "
.

    hry man look im writiig you a
pome

    this is a peom ffor
wheneveryou get
    home.

acknowledgments

Thanks be to:

Charles Barbour
Denise Bukowski
The Canada Council for the Arts
for faith, hope, and charity.

Peter Badenhorst and family, Patrick Toner, Joy James, Mark
and Sheila Balgrave,
for some invaluable incidentals.

James and Phyllis Coady
for advisories on roadside motels, and the proper firearms for
rousting crows and teenagers.

Especial thanks to my editor, Maya Mavjee.

about the author

LYNN COADY was nominated for the 1998 Governor General's Award for Fiction for her first novel, *Strange Heaven.* She received the Canadian Author's Association/Air Canada Award for the best writer under thirty and the Dartmouth Book and Writing Award for fiction. Her second book, *Play the Monster Blind,* was a national bestseller and a Best Book of 2000 for *The Globe and Mail; Saints of Big Harbour,* also a bestseller, was a *Globe and Mail* Best Book in 2002. Her articles and reviews have appeared in several publications including *Saturday Night, This* magazine, and *Chatelaine.* Lynn Coady lives in Edmonton.